COMMAND AND CONTROL

DAVID BRUNS

J.R. OLSON

SEVERN RIVER
PUBLISHING

COMMAND AND CONTROL

Severn River Publishing
www.SevernRiverBooks.com

This is a work of fiction. Names, characters, businesses, places, events and incidents are either the products of the author's imagination or used in a fictitious manner. Any resemblance to actual persons, living or dead, or actual events is purely coincidental.

ISBN: 978-1-64875-408-1 (Paperback)

ALSO BY BRUNS AND OLSON

The Command and Control Series

Command and Control

Counter Strike

Order of Battle

Threat Axis

Never miss a new release! Sign up to receive exclusive updates from authors Bruns and Olson.

severnriverbooks.com/series/command-and-control

This work is dedicated to:

Edward J. Wallin
Richard "Dick" Weathers

Lifelong readers
Early supporters of our writing
Favorite uncles

1

Pyongyang, North Korea

Ian Thomas despised North Korea.

In his thirty-eight years, he had lived in some dark places, but the Democratic People's Republic of Korea was hands down his least favorite country on Earth. A cult of personality masquerading as a nation-state—with nuclear weapons.

If the Minister were here, he would most assuredly endow Ian with some bit of ancient wisdom that boiled down to the simple fact that he wasn't in Pyongyang to pass judgment on their quality of governance. He was there to deliver a pointed message to the leader of this godforsaken country and get back to Vladivostok before his cover was blown.

Ian hadn't seen his mentor in person in years and wondered how the old man was doing. In fact, if he tried to picture the man's face now, the details washed away in his memory.

It had been that long.

But that was the life of a deep cover agent. He was an instrument of the State, the tip of the spear, the knife-edge of a scalpel, so sharp that the victim often failed to sense the first cut.

Enough daydreaming. He drew his fingers away from the missing chunk of flesh on his right earlobe, the reminder of a fight from his very first mission as an operative for the Minister. The first of many injuries in his work for the Minister, but certainly the most visible.

The defect manifested as a slight imbalance to his face, not enough to be off-putting, but it gave the viewer the sense that something was vaguely wrong with Ian's appearance.

When deep in thought or under stress, Ian had a habit of tugging that earlobe as if trying to lengthen it enough to hide the imperfection.

This task from the Minister was different in a way that was difficult to quantify. It was the simplicity of the task itself that bothered him. When was the last time the Minister used his premier deep cover operative as a messenger boy?

Outside the warm car, a cold spring rain streamed down the windows.

The drive from the Pyongyang airport was like a trip through time. From a distance, the city of Pyongyang appeared to be thriving, a model city. But cracks in the façade could be found anywhere you looked. The streets were scrupulously clean, but the maintenance was poor and the wide boulevards were empty of cars save official vehicles like the one Ian rode in now. Behind the bright storefronts, Ian spied empty shelves.

None of those externalities bothered him. The worth of a country was not in its economy; it was in the people.

The North Korean people were afraid, Ian decided. There was no other word for their actions. The way their eyes scanned his car, then immediately dropped to the wet pavement. Their shoulders hunched involuntarily, the way a dog that has been beaten too many times flinches at a sudden movement.

Ian shivered and snapped up the collar of his overcoat in sympathy to the sodden pedestrians. Only twenty-four hours ago, he had been poolside in his Singapore apartment, drenched in sun and far from this icy dampness.

The alert had arrived via an X-rated internet solicitation in his email spam folder. The email triggered him to log in to a secure server to retrieve the details of his next assignment from the Minister.

Proceed to Vladivostok. Pick up the contents of a dead drop and deliver them to the North Korean leader.

It was simple to arrange a visit to Vladivostok. His role as a risk assessment manager for Global Risk Ltd, a massive multinational shipping insurance firm, required Ian to inspect client ships all over the world.

Further instructions had awaited him at the Lotte Hotel in Vladivostok. Within fifteen minutes of checking in, Ian had met a limousine in the alley behind the building and was en route to the border crossing with North Korea.

On the back seat of the limo was a slim leather valise containing a new 5G mobile phone, a dated list of shipments assigned to various North Korean freighters beginning in two weeks and extending six months into the future, an oversized sealed envelope, typed instructions for Ian on a single sheet of flimsy paper, and a cheap plastic lighter.

He memorized the instructions, including the Dubai bank account number, and burned the sheet of paper.

The Minister had plans, he decided as the black limousine swept through the open wrought iron gates in front of the mansion of the Supreme Leader of the Democratic People's Republic of Korea. This errand was the beginning of something much, much bigger.

He took a deep breath, rehearsing the upcoming encounter in his head.

Be firm, be clear, be merciless. In the mind of the Supreme Leader of North Korea, the color gray was not in the decision-making palette.

The limo drew to a halt, and Ian waited for the driver to open the door. He stepped into the rain and accepted the proffered umbrella from the man. Carefully raked pea gravel crunched beneath the soles of his loafers as he made his way past the manicured shrubs and up the wide stone steps. The rain made a soft pop on the skin of the umbrella, and the air smelled of the coming spring growth.

The tall bronze double doors at the entrance of the palace were open, and a man waited to greet Ian. Chairman Kim's private secretary had thinning hair combed straight back from his broad forehead, hollow cheeks, and hooded eyes. He bowed, and Ian returned the honor. Park Yong-nam had first served as the Supreme Leader's tutor and then as his personal secretary for decades, which made him one of the most influential men in this troubled country. He was also, Ian suspected, on the Minister's payroll.

"The Chairman will see you immediately, sir," Park said in perfect English.

"The Chairman's sister should join us," Ian replied. He watched the man's face for a reaction. Park was unflappable, but no one in this country was that good. His right eyelid ticked.

Park cleared his throat. "Madame is not available—"

"The Chairman's sister will join us," Ian said firmly. "I insist."

Ian knew Kim's younger sibling was in the palace because the Minister's instructions had said so—and the Minister was never wrong. He had long seen the younger sister as a backstop to her unhealthy and often erratic brother. A sudden heart attack—or an assassination—of the Hermit Kingdom leader could prove catastrophic to global stability. That was not a risk the Minster was willing to take.

"As you wish, sir." The secretary bowed again. "I will see to it myself."

Park led Ian through the wide entrance hall and up richly carpeted stairs. Pausing outside a set of gold-inlaid double doors, he nodded at the uniformed guard to open the door.

"The Chairman will see you," he said, his brow creased in worry lines. "I will summon the mistress."

As the door opened, Ian saw Park hurry down the hall at a half run.

The interior of the Leader's office was richly styled in gold and mirrors, like a drawing room in the Palace of Versailles. An enormous self-portrait adorned the wall behind the great man's desk, flanked on either side by his father and grandfather. The desk itself was stacked with neat piles of official-looking documents, but the Leader's attention was on a Chinese-made iPhone knockoff. He was laughing when he looked up.

Ian entered at a brisk pace and paused before the desk to offer a half bow. "Your Excellency, thank you for seeing me on such short notice."

Ian caught a glance of the mobile phone screen. Internet cat videos.

The Supreme Leader of North Korea stood, his fleshy face wreathed in a smile. He led Ian to a sitting area, two gold-threaded sofas flanking a gold-lacquered coffee table. An enormous bowl of fresh fruit occupied the center of the table.

Ian set the attaché case on the floor and took a seat while the younger man collapsed into the opposite settee. He plucked a grape from the bowl of fruit and tossed it into his mouth, closing his eyes in rapture as he chewed.

"California grapes," he said without opening his eyes. "The best in the world. Have one."

"No, thank you," Ian replied.

The Chairman opened his eyes. "I said have one."

Ian stared at him with dead eyes. "And I said no, thank you. That's how a conversation works."

The Chairman struggled to sit up. His complexion darkened.

"You are in my home—"

"We are waiting for your sister to join us," Ian interrupted him. "Then we'll get started."

Ian was taking a calculated risk. Kim's lack of self-control was legendary, but Ian was betting that even the leader of the DPRK would not harm a messenger from the Minister.

Of course, Ian could be wrong, too. He mentally cataloged the number of armed guards he had passed since he'd entered the palace. The math was not in his favor. Of course, that was probably why the Minister had decided to send Ian in the first place.

A discreet knock at the door interrupted their staring contest.

Park stepped into the room and announced, "Your Excellency, your sister is here. Shall I show her in?"

Kim plucked another grape, then nodded.

The young woman who entered was the exact opposite of her brother. Trim, composed, professional. She bowed to her older brother first, then offered Ian a Western-style handshake. Whereas her brother sprawled in his seat, legs agape, his sister seated herself primly on the edge of the sofa cushions, her hands folded in her lap.

Ian admired Kim Yo-jong's reserved nature. Her outward demure pose disguised an understated personal charisma and a razor-sharp intellect.

Right bloodline, wrong gender. A pity.

Still, the Minister was not a man to waste time on lost causes. She was more than just a backup plan, Ian decided.

"You have something for me?" the Chairman snapped at Ian.

Ian opened the valise and extracted an oversized envelope that he knew the Chairman so admired.

The look on Kim's face changed from annoyance to a wide smile. "Is it from him?" he asked, the hope evident in his voice.

Ian nodded.

Kim snatched the letter from Ian's grip and raced back to his desk. He seized a gold-plated letter opener with an ivory handle and sliced the envelope open with one stroke. The envelope contained a single sheet of heavy parchment. His expression tightened as he scanned the page.

Ian did not know the exact contents of the letter, but he could make an educated guess. Someone had just told this man-child to behave.

Ian waited for the Chairman's next move. On an emotional level, the big man was just barely holding it together. The next sixty seconds would tell the full story. Ian was unarmed, save for the short stabbing blade that was hidden in his belt buckle. If things went sideways, he had no intention of being taken prisoner in this country.

The woman kept her gaze on the floor, watching from the corner of her eye as her brother stomped back to the sofa and crashed into a sitting position. He leaned across the table, stripped a handful of grapes from their stems, and crammed them into his mouth. He chewed noisily, his mouth flapping open.

"What do you want from me?" he said finally. "The letter said you had detailed instructions."

"You will rejoin the global community as a trusted ally," Ian said. He paused, waiting for a reaction from Kim.

The chewing slowed, eyes narrowed.

"Next month," Ian continued, "you will make a trip to the United Nations where you will make a speech—in English—proposing a peace deal with a multilateral group of nations. You will renounce all nuclear weapons development activities and say to the world that North Korea is pursuing a strategy of cooperation with the global community.

"Effective immediately, you will cease all testing of nuclear weapons or enrichment of nuclear fuel. You will cease all inflammatory rhetoric against South Korea, Japan, and the United States. You will reopen the border and welcome South Korean investment."

Kim's jaw hung open, mashed grapes on full display. His sister's frame had gone rigid during Ian's speech. She stared at a spot on the table as if her gaze might burn a hole through the lacquered surface. Ian wondered how many men she had seen her brother murder for lesser reasons.

"Do you have any questions?" Ian asked. "A week should be enough time to make the necessary arrangements, I think."

The Chairman's jaw snapped shut. His throat rippled as he swallowed the contents of his mouth. He smoothed a stray hair back into place and smiled at Ian, his teeth stained red by the grapes.

"Why would I do all those things?" he said. "It would destroy my family's legacy, put my country at grave risk to invasion by the Americans."

"You do not need to know why," Ian said coldly. "You just need to follow the instructions I have given you."

The Chairman's face flushed dark. His jowls trembled.

Ian allowed his gaze to rest on the man's younger sister. It was only a glance, but it was enough to remind the Chairman that even he was expendable. Ian paused to make sure the point landed, then he smiled.

"Also, there will be compensation," Ian said.

He withdrew the list of shipments from the valise and slid it across the table. The North Korean leader's eyebrows ticked up when he unfolded the paper.

Ian's smile broadened. Lead with the stick, finish with the carrot.

"These shipments require experienced captains who are able to evade the prying Americans," Ian said. He drew his new mobile phone from his breast pocket. "Payment terms are half now, half on delivery. I'm ready to transfer funds now."

Millions of dollars moved in the blink of an eye, but still the Supreme Leader was not satisfied. "Tell me what's going on," he said.

Ian shrugged and told him the truth. "I am just a lowly messenger. I know nothing."

The other man nodded his head slowly, as if considering his options—of which he had none. "And when this is all over, I can go back to the work of the Kim dynasty? The Democratic People's Republic of Korea will be a nuclear power. I have promised it shall be done."

Ian stood. He walked to the great man's desk and plucked the letter from the leather blotter. He spooled the paper and lit it using the plastic lighter. Flames flared. The paper was impregnated with a compound to make it burn fast and clean—the Minister was a man who left no detail to chance.

When the letter had burned down to the last few centimeters, Ian dropped the remnants onto the bowl of fruit. As he bowed at the Supreme Leader, Ian shot a glance at the sister. She nodded at him ever so slightly.

"Of course, Mr. Chairman."

2

Emerging Threats Group
Tysons Corner, Virginia

Don Riley, Director of the CIA's Emerging Threats Group, leaned his back against the wall of the conference room and watched the magic happen.

Like most of the people in the room, he'd been up all night. His body had moved beyond exhaustion to the stage where his senses felt strangely keyed up and sharp. That wouldn't last long, he knew, but he wanted to enjoy these final few moments with his team.

Lieutenant Janet Everett moved through the room with the confident stride of a young professional at the top of her game. The large conference room had been configured as a command center for Operation Clear Sky with workstations for two dozen analysts and cyber operations experts. Most had departed with the rising sun, their part in Janet's final evolution at ETG complete. She moved among the remaining analysts, answering a question here, patting a shoulder for encouragement there, sharing a laugh.

Don felt himself welling up. Jesus Christ, he was going to miss that kid.

Kid, Don chided. Listen to yourself. You're pathetic. Next thing you'll be wearing socks with sandals and shouting "get off my lawn."

Over the last three years, Don Riley built up the Emerging Threats Group from an idea into an operational unit of case officers, cyber warriors, analysts, and special operators. Emerging Threats, or ET, as they were derisively called by the other CIA divisions who resented their work, had one mission: find the next threat to the United States and deal with it before it became a bigger threat.

He had identified Janet Everett, along with Andrea "Dre" Ramirez and Michael Goodwin, while the three were still midshipmen at the US Naval Academy and Don was a guest lecturer. The three midshipmen helped Don stop a North Korean cyberattack that could have led to World War Three.

From those successes, Don had been given a charter to form the Emerging Threats Group. Janet, Dre, and Michael were his first recruits.

It had not been easy to get Janet back into the CIA, he reflected. After her time at the Academy, she earned her place as a submarine officer in the Fleet. For her shore tour, Don had convinced her to come back to Washington, DC and help him start ETG.

Although Don had hoped she would stay permanently, his wish was a fool's errand. Janet had made her intentions to return to the Fleet perfectly clear. Today was her last day at ETG.

She was leaving, and nothing Don said could convince her to give up her slot as Weapons Officer aboard the USS *Idaho* out of Pearl Harbor.

Don blinked, trying to convince himself that the only reason he was so emotional was because he was over-tired. He smiled as he watched Janet move through her remaining analysts. Even in the midst of personal pain, he felt a swell of pride.

Janet Everett knew how to go out on top.

Operation Clear Sky was her last hurrah with ETG. Over a year ago, Janet was the analyst who had discovered the Iranian hacker group, and she'd come up with the plan to trap them.

Normally, newly discovered hacking collectives were assigned an in-house name according to their threat category and then numbered sequentially. For example, APT65 stood for Advanced Persistent Threat number sixty-five.

The Iranian hackers they were taking down today were anything but ordinary, and Janet got permission to break the normal numbering system.

These guys were known as APT666, the Devil's Hackers. They were fast, clean, and surgical in their work. A friendly argument had circulated on the office internal messaging system about whether APT666 had Russian backing.

Janet hatched the idea for Operation Clear Sky when a National Security Agency bulletin came across her desk about a major vulnerability in a widely used commercial VPN software package.

Thousands of US companies used virtual private networks to allow their remote employees to establish a secure connection with their company's internal network.

The NSA had discovered a vulnerability in the VPN software itself, a fatal flaw that opened up any user as a potential access point to secure company servers. As was protocol, the NSA had a plan to notify the virtual private network companies so they could issue an emergency software patch.

With millions of users spread across thousands of companies, there would be a period of time between when the public was notified and everyone updated their software. Based on her experience with APT666, Janet was willing to bet the Iranian hackers would use that window of opportunity to their advantage.

She chose fifty multinational companies—automobile manufacturers, credit rating agencies, banks, social media conglomerates, electric utilities —and set up a sting. Her team set up shop inside the company networks and waited for APT666 to come calling.

It had worked like a charm. In the twenty-four hours since the announcement by the NSA, APT666 had hacked into thirty of the fifty companies on her list.

And the hackers were good. APT666 breached the company networks using the vulnerability, then moved laterally within the system to make an assessment for future hacks.

They were also highly disciplined. The APT666 hackers used custom-designed secure shell tunneling software to set up back doors into the compromised systems. They carefully tested their new means of secure entry, then moved on to their next target.

Back doors like these were a ticking time bomb on a network. They could remain dormant for years, almost impossible to find, until required for some future hack. Ransomware, data manipulation, data destruction, or some kind of computer attack that hadn't even been invented yet.

Michael Goodwin stood up from his workstation and stretched. He strolled to the front of the room and struck a name off the whiteboard list with a flourish. He winked at Janet.

"That's three for me, boss lady," he said. "Can I go home now?"

Janet eyed him with mock sternness. "Have you compiled your IOCs?"

Apart from ridding the company systems of the Iranian hack, the whole point of Operation Clear Sky was to develop Indicators of Compromise so that antivirus companies could incorporate the latest threats into their next release—hopefully later today.

"Already emailed them to you," Michael replied.

"To Mark, you mean," Janet replied.

Michael's expression shifted. His eyes cut to where Mark Westlund, Janet's replacement, bent over Dre's workstation.

"Yeah, right. I'll email them to him, too." He started to say something else, but Janet cut him off.

"I'll come say goodbye before I shove off," she said.

Michael laughed at the use of naval slang, a remnant of their time together at the Naval Academy. He left the room whistling "Anchors Aweigh," the Navy fight song.

Don shifted his attention to Captain Mark Westlund, US Air Force. Like all members of ETG, the young man had ditched his military uniform for a coat and tie. But like many of the military officers, he wore his civilian clothes like a uniform, right down to the tuck in his dress shirt.

Mark had stayed on the op center floor all night, shadowing Janet. He had taken his suit jacket off, rolled up his shirt sleeves, and loosened his tie, but he moved between workstations with a quick step. Even after being awake for more than twenty-four hours, he still looked fresh and alert.

The analysts had thinned to three. Dre Ramirez and two others. As Don watched, one of the two signed out of her terminal, hugged Janet goodbye, and left.

Mark was looking over Dre's shoulder at something on her screen. The young woman's eyes were red. Her hair was pulled back into a ragged bun and speared through with a government-issue ballpoint pen. She chewed on a fingernail, shaking her head as Mark spoke. Don knew from the set of her shoulders that Dre was getting irritated.

"Mark," Don called. "Janet."

The two young officers headed to Don's post at the back of the room.

"Ramirez is pretty intense," Mark muttered as he reached Don.

Janet shot a look at Don.

"Dre's got some history with the Iranians," Janet said. "It's personal."

To his credit, Mark didn't ask the obvious follow-up question.

"It's a good team," he said to Janet. "It must be tough to leave."

"They're the best," Janet agreed. "Dre'll come around. She's just tired."

"I can hear you," Dre called over her shoulder.

Janet grinned. "By the way, she has excellent hearing, too."

Don watched the easy exchange with deepening nostalgia. This was likely the last time he would work with this remarkable young woman.

Janet seemed to sense it as well. Don felt a gulf of uncomfortable silence open up between them.

"I'm going to wrap up the last few details," Mark said, "then I say we call it a day."

"Good plan," Janet replied. "Leave Dre to finish on her own time, though."

Together, Don and Janet watched Mark walk away.

"He'll be fine, Don," Janet said. "Dre and Michael will get him sorted. He's smart. In a week, you won't even know I'm gone."

Don nodded. He tried to swallow the lump in his throat.

"It's just something I have to do, Don," Janet continued. "If I don't go back to subs now, I'll never get back. I know you understand that."

When Janet embraced him, Don thought he might actually lose it.

"Thanks for everything, Don," she whispered.

"Take that, you Iranian assholes!" Dre Ramirez shouted. She slapped her keyboard, then jumped to her feet, both fists in the air. "You messed with the wrong lady this time." She performed a victory dance all the way to the whiteboard and crossed off three company names. Mark watched her with a raised eyebrow.

The tension between Don and Janet evaporated in a shared laugh. Janet punched him on the arm.

"You see, boss. You won't even know I'm gone."

3

Khasab, Sultanate of Oman

The only sound in the empty room was the occasional slap of a bare foot on the tile floor and the smooth sigh of a man's measured breathing. With floor-to-ceiling windows overlooking the Strait of Hormuz, it was a room meant to impress premier guests of the luxurious Atana Hotel and Resort.

Dominik Koskinen had cleared the room by moving all the furniture flat against the wall and rolling up the rich area rug to reveal the tile floor. He had instructed the maid to leave the room in this condition. She had complied, of course. As a member of the housekeeping staff at a luxury resort frequented by jet-setters from around the globe, she was used to all sorts of odd demands. She didn't complain. The more outlandish or questionable the request, the bigger her tip.

Outside, the sun had not yet risen. On the Strait, the navigation lights of merchant vessels, oil tankers, tiny fishing boats, and military ships dotted the dark waters like fireflies. They were concentrated into the two-mile-wide shipping lanes curving around the point of Oman that jutted into the waters at the entrance of the Persian Gulf.

Ships transiting the Strait had to make a ninety-degree turn in one of the busiest shipping lanes in the world. From a satellite picture, it looked like organized chaos, but in the predawn darkness, the lights appeared as beautiful jewels.

Dominik's fingertips grazed the tile floor as he moved into the next position of his routine. He had learned the forms as a child and still practiced them every morning—if conditions allowed for it.

The men who had taught him these movements had given him everything in this life. Food, a place for an unwanted child to lay his head, and a mental discipline that grounded his existence. They were moral men and had done their best to fill Dominik's eager young mind with their code of ethics.

But over time, the young man saw fit to expand his definition of morality. His awakening had begun in grade school, when he had been selected by the Minister himself for further specialized training.

Language schools followed. The boy was a quick study and soon spoke American and British English in numerous dialects as well as conversational Spanish and German. By the time he was sixteen, the Minister had placed him in a sort of espionage finishing school and began to build his legend.

The young man attended undergraduate at Stanford University in the United States and landed a job with Global Risk Ltd in Singapore.

He blew out a long breath as he twisted his body, feeling the rippling muscles in his midsection relax. He stabbed his fingers at the window as he drew up his right knee and launched a fluid kick that lifted his body off the ground. He landed lightly on the ball of his foot, his frame flowing into the next form as naturally as water spilling over a dam.

A thin sheen of sweat covered his naked body. He loved morning moments like this when he felt at one with the universe. Muscles loosening, breath steady, skin warm with a light film of perspiration that told him he was alive. His right toe traced a wide arc as he prepared for another kick—

A *ping* sounded from the open door of the adjoining bedroom.

He drew in another measured breath and ignored the sound. He raised his left knee, snapped out a flipper kick, then followed through with his right leg sweeping a long arc across the floor.

Ping! This time the interruption was followed by the hollow sound of someone tapping on the keypad of a mobile phone.

He stretched both arms out in front of him, parallel to the floor, and bent slightly at the knees, ready to launch—

Ping!

He closed his eyes, stood straight, and bowed his head at the rising sun. Then he strode into the bedroom to confront the young woman who was busily tapping away on her phone with both thumbs.

"Out."

He picked up her dress from the floor where she'd left it the evening before. It was flimsy black material shot through with gold thread that made it glitter in the light. A short fringe adorned the hem. Dominik recalled how the fringe undulated against her thighs as she moved on the dance floor.

Had she said she was a professional dancer? She had a dancer's lean body, but he might be misremembering that detail.

"Out," he said again.

The woman sat up in bed, letting the phone drop onto the crisp white sheets over her lap. Her breasts stood firm in the morning light, her bare flesh prickling in the chill of the frigid air conditioning. A frown creased the space between her perfectly shaped eyebrows.

"Dom," she said. "You're throwing me out?"

Her eyes traveled up and down his naked body, taking in the chiseled pectoral muscles. The ripple of his abdomen. The sculpted thighs and calves.

Dominik sighed. The nightclub and the woman had been a welcome distraction, a way to keep his skills of personal manipulation sharp.

And now, he reflected, possibly a mistake. He'd been trained by some of the premier espionage experts in the world to manipulate other human beings. A young woman partying in a nightclub was hardly a challenge.

Dominik fingered his right earlobe.

His feelings about women were basic. They satisfied a need for him. When the need was fulfilled, they needed to go.

She licked her lips. "I don't have to be anywhere for a few hours..." She let her voice trail off.

Ping!

Dominik hooked a finger through her black lace bra draped over the back of a chair and tossed it to her. It landed on top of her phone.

"Out," he said. "I won't ask again."

The young woman dressed quickly and departed, making sure to slam the door on her way out.

Dominik stepped into the bathroom and turned on the cold water in the shower. He stepped into the spray, barely flinching as the icy water sluiced over his skin. Like his morning exercise routine, this was a practice he had learned as a boy. After decades of repetition, his body registered the chilled water as normal, just another brick in the wall of self-discipline that formed his life.

Even with the sun barely over the horizon, stepping outside was like walking into a steam bath. Dominik felt his polo shirt stick to the small of his back.

Dressed casually, with a pair of aviator sunglasses and a three-day stubble, he looked the part of a tourist. Carrying only a small duffel and an aluminum attaché case, he stepped across the portico of the Atana Hotel to the waiting Land Rover with the name of a local touring company painted on the door.

A young man, dressed in the company uniform with a matching *mazzar* on his head, greeted Dominik as he took his bags.

"Good morning, Mr. Koskinen," the young man said in English. "My name is Aaron. I'll be your guide for the overnight backcountry tour, sir." He opened the liftgate to reveal two large black Pelican cases and a small generator.

"All the equipment you requested is here, sir," the young man said. He lowered his voice. "The other guest is in the back seat."

Dominik smiled. "Let's get started, shall we?"

He felt refreshed, ready to meet the day. Too often on field ops, he had to rough it or rely on cash-only accommodations to stay off the grid. But today, as a rich Kazakh tourist, he was required to leave a very liberal paper trail of his visit.

Dominik slid into the back seat next to a heavyset man with swarthy features and close-set dark eyes. His eyes were rimmed with red, and his clothes were rumpled.

"Any issues with the shipment?" Dominik asked as the driver pulled away from the hotel.

The heavyset man shook his head and answered in heavily accented English. "The ship was more rust than metal, but the North Korean captain was there on time—with his hand out for payment, of course." He closed his eyes. "I'm going to get some sleep."

Dominik studied his companion in profile. Another choice by the Minister, he reflected. This part of the world was not familiar to him and he required a fluent Arabic speaker for the job, so he'd gone along with it.

Aaron noticed Dominik's attention and misinterpreted the meaning. "We met the ship in Salalah yesterday and drove straight here, sir."

The port of Salalah in southern Oman was a fifteen-hour drive and required them to transit through the United Arab Emirates to get to the northern tip of Oman overlooking the Strait of Hormuz. The pair had been up all night.

Dominik nodded and looked out his window.

The scenery in this part of the world was starkly beautiful. Crumbling brown mountains thrust up from the blue turquoise of the sea. The contrasting colors of ocean and land reminded Dominik of southern California. But the humidity here—often over eighty percent—cloaked the starkness in a gauzy softness lacking on the American coastline.

As they left the village of Khasab, the trappings of civilization fell away quickly. The paved road turned to gravel, then dirt, then just ruts in the soil. Dominik gripped the handle over his head and held on as the driver navigated the terrain. Finally, he pulled into the shady lee of a boulder and turned off the engine.

"We walk from here," Aaron said. "I scouted a location about a hundred meters further. Just over that ridge." He pointed up a steep, narrow goat path.

Dominik picked up the attaché case. "Good. Bring the rest of the gear."

The short climb up the path left Dominik soaked with sweat. Between the brutal heat and the humidity, he might as well have been in a sauna.

But the climb was worth it.

From the top of the ridge, the land fell steeply toward the sea a few hundred meters below. A small depression, easily covered by camouflage netting, offered a commanding view of the Strait of Hormuz.

Nearly a fifth of the world's oil, over twenty million barrels, passed through this chokepoint every day. From his perch he counted five oil tankers in transit between the Persian Gulf and the Arabian Sea.

Dominik squinted at the smudged landmass on the horizon. This was the narrowest part of the Strait, with the Islamic Republic of Iran only twenty-one miles away. Since international waters extended twelve miles from a country's borders, the Strait was completely within the shared territorial waters of Iran and Oman.

The great powers of Europe and the United States, of course, made exceptions to the law of the sea for their oil habit. They carved out two-mile-wide shipping lanes in and out of the Gulf as a safe right-of-way through the territorial waters of Iran and Oman.

Two miles seemed like a lot of room until one considered an oil tanker was 250 meters long and had a turning diameter of two kilometers.

The Strait of Hormuz had a long history of international incidents, mostly between Iran and Western nations. In recent years, as economic sanctions over Iran's nuclear program had been renewed, the Islamic Republic routinely threatened to close the Strait.

As Dominik had expected, the recent peaceful overtures by the North Koreans had delighted the international community. The Supreme Leader's speech at the UN denouncing his nuclear program had only increased pressure on Iran to come back to the negotiating table and give up their nuclear ambitions.

"We could have world peace in our time," the head of the United Nations claimed in an interview. "If only Iran would join the international community…"

Maybe not, Dominik thought.

He heard his two companions traversing the path behind him, dragging the Pelican cases and the generator behind them.

Dominik assisted the two men in staking a sand-colored camouflage net over the grotto in the mountainside and setting up a rudimentary camp. He opened the first Pelican case and unpacked a Russian-made satellite receiver and ruggedized laptop and connected them to the humming generator. He established a satellite internet connection and logged in to a site that showed maritime traffic.

Dominik centered the screen on the Strait of Hormuz. Ships in transit showed up as colored arrows. When he clicked on an icon, it gave him the vessel name and registration as well as its destination, speed, and heading, all updated every few minutes by satellite.

In the section of the Strait before them, the shipping lane made a ninety-degree turn and dozens of arrows congregated in the area of the bend. At the top of the screen, the Iranian port of Bandar Abbas showed a cluster of brightly colored arrows and dots. Mixed among the cluster was a sizable contingent of Iranian Navy combatants.

"Open the other case," he said to Aaron. "Get the transmitter powered up."

Dominik stepped out of the tent to survey the scene with field glasses. He focused to the east, visually matching a fully laden merchant vessel entering the shipping lane with the icon on the screen.

The *Minotaur* was a bulk carrier en route to Mesaieed, Qatar, with a full load of grain, moving at ten knots into the shipping lane.

She was perfect.

"Ready, sir," Aaron called.

Dominik opened his attaché case and extracted a cord, which he connected to the transmitter. The bulky transmitter unit was Russian military surplus, with peeling labels in Cyrillic notation.

Aaron watched him with interest.

"You see those ships out there?" Dominik asked the young operative. "Every single one of them uses GPS to navigate. Most of them are on autopilot all the time."

"What are you going to do?" Aaron asked.

Dominik booted up the meaconing device in the case and waited as it synchronized with the Global Navigation Satellite System. He typed in the offset he wanted to introduce into the GNSS signal when he rebroadcast it from his transmitter.

Dominik jerked his chin at the distant landmass of Iran across the water. His fingers stroked the squared-off tip of his right earlobe.

"I'm going to send everyone five kilometers that way."

On the Russian unit, Dominik flipped the switch to TRANSMIT. Then he scooped up his field glasses and stepped outside to watch the show.

4

USS *Delbert D. Black* (DDG-119)
Eastern approaches to the Strait of Hormuz

Lieutenant Commander Ryan Wilkins raised the binoculars to his eyes and stared sightlessly through the bridge windows at the far horizon.

I think we should see other people.

Even six hours after reading the email from his fiancée back in Mayport, the words still crowded every other thought from his mind.

See other people? They'd been together for five years. They were engaged. Well, technically, he'd only given her a promise ring, but still, they were committed.

You didn't just throw away five years of commitment to "see other people." This wasn't high school. This was a life commitment they had made to each other.

The sun's glare from the calm ocean around them radiated into the bridge. Wilkins found the space directly underneath an air conditioning vent and pulled off his ship's ball cap. The icy blast stung his wet scalp.

This place is like being inside a brightly lit teakettle, he thought. But I might as well make the best of it. For the next sixty-three days, this is home.

The way Navy deployments were getting lengthened, he'd give even money the *Black* would be extended for another thirty days or so.

Wilkins raised his gaze to the words painted above the bridge windows: *Haze gray and underway*. That had been his motto since the day he got his commission as an officer in the US Navy. He was good at what he did, the best. This was where he belonged, right here on the bridge of a United States Navy warship en route to protect national interests in the Persian Gulf.

"Mr. Wilkins, sir?" The voice belonged to a young third-class petty officer, an electronics technician.

The sleeves of his underway uniform were rolled up to his elbows. The uniform was smudged with dirt and too big for his slight frame. His haircut was shaggy, and the kid hadn't shaved.

Normally, Wilkins would have dressed the kid down about his sloppy appearance, but today he couldn't manage it.

"What is it, Jensen?" he snapped.

"Sir, we still haven't done the Navstar maintenance yet. If I don't get it done before the end of watch, the chief'll have my ass." Jensen hailed from somewhere well south of the Mason-Dixon line, and he swallowed his vowels. The word *ass* came out in two syllables: *ay-us*.

Wilkins eyed the sailor. The maintenance had been authorized in the Captain's Standing Orders for the day, but it should've been done hours ago. A fact he had overlooked while he was wallowing in self-pity over his failed love life. Wilkins mentally kicked himself. He should've made sure it was done.

Wilkins raised his voice. "Quartermaster, how much time before we hit the shipping lanes in the Strait?"

"About forty minutes, sir." The young woman at the nav station looked like she was barely out of high school. Hell, he realized, they all looked young to him these days.

"Very well, quartermaster." He snatched the tablet from Jensen's hand. "What are we doing?"

Jensen shrugged. "Just a clean and inspect, sir. Simple diagnostics. It's ten minutes, maybe fifteen. Easy-peasy stuff. I'll be done before you know it."

Wilkins hesitated. The maintenance had been authorized for this watch, but he knew full well the captain had expected it to be completed long before they were anywhere near the Strait. He *should* call the CO to get approval.

Wilkins authorized the maintenance and handed the tablet back to the petty officer. "Get it done quickly. If it's not completed in the next fifteen minutes. I want you to button it up and return the Navstar to service, understood?"

The Navstar system was the military global positioning system. The *Black* used a Position, Navigation, and Timing, or PNT, system that drew inputs from both military and civilian satellites for the most accurate and up-to-date location data.

The young sailor drew himself up to what he probably thought was attention. "Aye-aye, sir."

On another day, Lieutenant Commander Wilkins would've called the kid back and chewed him out. But today was not that day.

I think we should see other people. The words still stung every time they careened into his thoughts.

Wilkins laughed at himself, tasting the bitterness of rejection on his tongue. Anne was leaving him no choice. The only way was forward. See other people? Hell, he'd see so many other people when the *Black* got back to Mayport that his phone would explode from all the Tinder action.

Wilkins dragged his forearm across his eyes. He checked his watch. Another hour until his relief showed up. He'd get some chow, hit the rack, and dream of all the other women he'd see to forget about Anne.

The VHF radio squawked. The *Black*, like all US Navy ships, left the unit tuned to the international distress frequency. Listening to VHF radio was like listening to somebody shout underwater, but his practiced ear was used to it. The male voice spoke in heavily accented English, and he was yelling, rushed, clearly under stress.

"Any ship in the Persian Gulf, this is merchant vessel *Minotaur*. We are a Maltese-flagged merchant ship under attack by the Iranian Navy. They are attempting to board us. We are in international waters. Request immediate assistance."

Wilkins's mind snapped to the present moment, his pulse hammering, all thoughts of his personal distractions gone.

Iranian aggression, right in the Strait. This was the reason why the *Black* was here. He snatched the IMC handset out of its cradle.

"Captain to the bridge," he said in a crisp tone.

Less than twenty seconds later, Captain Gino LaVecchia charged through the doorway at the rear of the bridge.

Wilkins, stationed at the nav plot, started talking as soon as the captain was within earshot.

"Captain, we received a distress call from a Maltese merchant vessel." Wilkins pointed at the plot showing their position and the *Minotaur*. "Approximately fifteen miles bearing zero-four-seven. They say they're under attack from the Iranian Navy. Recommend we go to general quarters, sir."

Gino LaVecchia was a pro, probably the best skipper Wilkins had ever sailed with. In addition, his four prior Gulf deployments lent him a level of experience with the Iranian threat possessed by few in the Navy. If there was ever an officer to serve as a role model for Wilkins, it was this man.

With a full head of wavy gray hair and sharp eyes with creases at the corners from squinting into the sun, LaVecchia even looked like a ship's captain. Wilkins remembered at that moment that his commanding officer was also a confirmed bachelor. Maybe they had more in common than he'd first realized.

LaVecchia studied the screen for a full three seconds. "Very well. Mr. Wilkins. I have the conn." His voice was mild but carried through the open bridge.

"Captain has the conn, aye, sir," Wilkins replied in a loud voice. "Mr. Wilkins has the deck."

The captain was responsible for maneuvering and fighting the ship; Wilkins was responsible for everything else.

"Helm, steer course zero-four-seven," the captain said. "All ahead flank. Sound general quarters, Mr. Wilkins. Prepare to launch the Fire Scout."

With the announcement of general quarters, the *Black* came to life. The GQ alarm pulsed a steady rhythm in the air like a beating heart, the heavy sound reverberating in Wilkins's chest. Sailors pounded through passageways to their action stations, watertight hatches slammed shut. The bridge filled up with new watchstanders. Someone handed Wilkins a flash hood. He discarded his ball cap and pulled the tight stocking cap over his head, smearing sweat across his face.

The bow of the *Black* rode up in the water, and brilliant white foam curled away from the knife-edged bow slicing through the flat ocean. The wind, which had been no more than a whisper, roared at the open doors leading to the bridge wings.

Wilkins felt energized as adrenaline coursed through his body. This was why he joined the Navy. This feeling, this moment.

"Ready to launch the Fire Scout, sir," Wilkins reported to the captain, who nodded.

"You have permission to launch, Mr. Wilkins."

The MQ-8 Fire Scout was an autonomous mini-helicopter that could race ahead of the *Black* and relay back video and over-the-horizon targeting information before the ship arrived on scene.

The unmanned vehicle was controlled from the *Black*'s Combat Information Center, or CIC. Wilkins gave the order to launch the Fire Scout, then watched from the video screen as the UAV took off vertically from the fantail of the *Black*, peeled away, and sped ahead of the ship.

It took the Fire Scout four minutes to begin transmitting images back to the *Black*.

Wilkins stood at LaVecchia's side as the captain studied the screen. The freighter had gone dead in the water. From the high-definition color video being relayed by the Fire Scout, Wilkins could make out rust stains spilling down the side of the hull, men running back and forth on the bridge. Wilkins could see her crew had rigged fire hoses, ready to use high-pressure streams of water to repel Iranian boarders. At least a dozen small patrol craft, looking more like gray-painted cigarette boats than military vessels, circled the larger vessel like a motorcycle gang in a B movie.

"Captain, looks like a swarm, sir," the XO said over the intercom from CIC. "Iranian Boghammers."

On the *Black*, Captain LaVecchia preferred to fight the ship from the bridge, leaving the XO and Combat Systems Officer to run the Combat Information Center.

"Agreed, XO," LaVecchia replied, over the same comms circuit.

One of the Iranian vessels raked the side of the *Minotaur* with .50-caliber fire, rust fragments exploding as the bullets stitched across the hull. The crew on deck manning the fire hoses dropped out of sight. Two of the patrol craft slowed and came alongside the larger merchant vessel.

"Looks like they're going to board her, sir," the XO warned.

"Ready the five-inch gun," the captain replied.

"Mark 45 is ready in all respects, sir," came the immediate reply. "We have solid targeting data from the Scout, Captain."

"Very well, Combat," LaVecchia said. "I want a warning shot. Let's put it a hundred yards to the stern of the *Minotaur*."

The helmet-like housing of the Mark 45 gun on the bow of the *Black* swiveled, and the barrel of the big gun raised up a fraction.

"One shot, one hundred yards to the stern, aye, sir." The XO's voice was tense with excitement. "Ready, Captain."

"Fire."

The Mark 45 banged out a sharp report. A shell ejected onto the deck. A few seconds later, Wilkins saw a geyser of water erupt to the stern of the *Minotaur*.

The effect on the Iranian patrol craft was immediate. All of them moved to the lee side of the merchant ship, putting the larger ship between them and the *Black*.

The *Minotaur* was visible on the horizon, and the captain studied her through his binoculars. "Nice shot, XO. That'll give them something to think about until we can get closer—"

A new report interrupted the captain: "Bridge, Combat. New surface contact on an intercept course for the *Minotaur*, moving at high speed." The XO's tone took on an edge of adrenaline. "Based on radar signature and ESM, new contact is classified as Iranian frigate *Sabalan*. She carries anti-ship missiles and is an active threat, sir."

The frown on LaVecchia's face deepened as he absorbed the new information.

"Looks like our friends are planning on making this a party," he said.

"We have a firing solution, Captain," the XO said.

"Understood, XO," the captain said. "Mr. Wilkins, send a flash message to Fifth Fleet. Tell them we are responding to an emergency call from a merchant vessel in international waters. The ship is under attack by Iranian naval forces."

Before Wilkins could acknowledge the order, the VHF bridge-to-bridge radio squawked to life. In heavily accented English, a deep male voice said: "United States warship, this is Iranian frigate *Sabalan*. You are in Iranian territorial waters. Your hostile actions are an act of war. Withdraw immediately, or we will be forced to fire on you. This is your only warning."

LaVecchia snatched the radio handset off the hook and smashed down the press-to-talk button. "*Sabalan*, this is USS *Delbert D. Black*. We are responding to a distress call of a ship in international waters. If you fire on us, we will respond in kind. Repeat. We are responding to a distress call in international waters." LaVecchia released the transmit button. His gaze searched out Wilkins.

"Verify ship's position, Mr. Wilkins."

Wilkins was already at the quartermaster's table where the ship's position was laid out on the flat computer screen. The shipping lanes through the Strait of Hormuz were clearly delineated, and both the *Black* and the *Minotaur* were inside the boundary.

"Ship's position verified, Captain," Wilkins called out. "We are in international waters."

"Bridge, Combat." The XO sounded like he was about to crawl through the intercom. "We have two new air contacts, possible Iranian fighter jets. They are on an intercept course, sir. Fire control radars are not active."

LaVecchia's posture was rigid, his lips pressed together. "Someone wants to up the ante on this thing, XO. Stand by for anything. If they're looking for a fight, we'll give it to them."

The *Minotaur* was only a few thousand yards off now, with the *Black* closing rapidly. Through the binoculars, Wilkins could make out the faces of the men on the bridge. They were waving at the *Black*, cheering. He felt a rush of pride.

On the distant horizon beyond the *Minotaur*, Wilkins saw a fiery eruption spike into the sky. He opened his mouth, but the XO beat him to it.

"Bridge, Combat, the *Sabalan* is firing. We have one...two...three missiles in the air, sir."

LaVecchia crowded up to the computer screen, where the missiles showed as arrows crawling toward the center of the screen.

"Time to intercept, one minute, Captain."

"Combat, launch interceptors."

From the grid of vertical launch tubes located forward of the bridge came a *whoosh* as four Sea Sparrow missiles were launched in rapid succession. A burst of fire and smoke erupted in front of the bridge windows.

"Combat, target the *Sabalan* with the five-inch gun and fire at will," LaVecchia said, his tone ice-cold.

The five-inch gun turret snapped to the starboard side and began hammering out 127mm rounds in a steady rhythm. Wilkins felt each shot reverberate against the flesh of his belly.

"Stand by to deploy countermeasures, Mr. Wilkins," the captain said. "Stand by for evasive maneuvers." He had his glasses up to his eyes, scanning for the incoming missiles.

Wilkins saw an aerial explosion, then another.

"Two missiles taken out," CIC reported.

The captain did not lower his glasses. "Launch chaff."

Wilkins activated the chaff countermeasures. He heard a series of loud pops, then looked aft to see a massive fountain of metallic confetti tower over the ship. Hopefully, enough to confuse the incoming missile.

"Left full rudder," the captain called.

The *Black* heeled over at a steep angle as the ship took the turn at speed. The captain watched the cloud of chaff.

"Steady as she goes," he called.

Seconds ticked by. To Wilkins everything seemed to be unfolding in slow motion.

"What's the status of the last missile, Combat?" LaVecchia called out.

Instead of an answer, the Phalanx close-in weapons system sprang to life with a deafening *bzzzt* as the unit poured bullets at the incoming missile at a rate of 4,500 rounds per minute. The missile disintegrated in midair at the same moment as the five-inch gun stopped firing.

"Missile down and multiple direct hits on the *Sabalan*, sir," the XO reported from CIC.

"What about the fighters?" the captain asked.

"Bugged out, sir," came the reply.

"Well done, everyone." The captain looked like he needed to sit down. "But this is not over yet. Let's get this merchant vessel on her way safely." He hoisted himself into his leather captain's chair. "Mr. Wilkins, give me a course to put us in the middle of the shipping lane."

"Aye, sir."

For Wilkins, it was impossible to capture what he was feeling right now. Euphoria, fear, adrenaline all mixed together into some heady mess in his body. Never in his life had he experienced this sort of feeling before—awful and wonderful and out of control all at the same time.

He gripped the edge of the nav plot to hide his shaking hands.

"What's my best course, quartermaster?" he said.

The sailor stared at the plot.

"I...I...it just updated, sir," she began. "I don't know..."

Wilkins's gaze fell to the screen. The *Black* and the *Minotaur* were not in the shipping lanes. They were at least two thousand yards into Iranian waters.

"Sir, I...," the quartermaster began.

The Navstar maintenance. The thought clicked in Wilkins's brain. The military GPS was turned off, and they had been spoofed. The whole attack was a setup.

"Captain?" Wilkins called out. "Sir—"

He looked up just in time to see a pair of Iranian patrol boats burst from the smoke and bits of silvery chaff that hung in the air like a fog bank. The lead boat headed straight at the *Black*, bow riding high, a rooster tail of water spouting behind it. Even without his binoculars, Wilkins could make out the bearded driver, his teeth bared, his face set in a grimace.

Wilkins heard the Phalanx system start up again. The first boat took a direct hit from the incoming stream of bullets.

The blare of the Phalanx close-in weapons system ceased. A strange silence settled on the bridge.

The second craft swerved around the shattered hull of the first Iranian attacker. The driver spun the wheel and cut his speed, flaring the small craft broadside to the *Black*, giving his gunner a clear shot. The man braced his legs and shouted as he aimed the weapon at the *Black*. The wide-bore muzzle spit bits of smoke and flame in rapid fire.

"Incoming!" the bridge lookout screamed. He had binoculars glued to his face and his arm outstretched, index finger pointing.

As Wilkins watched, a series of projectiles flashed through the open bridge door of the *Black* and ricocheted around the space. He hit the deck, the steel floor cold against his cheek.

Then the bridge exploded in white-hot fire.

5

When Don Riley saw the door to the Situation Room snap open, he rose to his feet automatically. Don—along with every other person in the packed briefing room—studied the untested commander in chief to see if he could discern how the leader of the free world was going to handle the stress of his office.

On paper, President Ricardo "Rick" Serrano was having an epically bad day.

The forty-eighth president of the United States had been sworn in scarcely three months ago. Although he had run on a muscular foreign policy and reasserting the role of America in the world, the last thing anyone wanted was another military entanglement in the Middle East. The unprovoked attack on the USS *Delbert D. Black* in the Strait of Hormuz was the new president's first major international crisis. He would be judged on its outcome by anyone with an opinion and a social media account, not to mention by the historians.

Serrano sported a full mane of dark, tousled Hollywood hair. Streaks of silver glinted at his temples, lending an air of gravitas to his rugged features. He was a compact man who walked with a bounce in his step that telegraphed he was eager to tackle this next challenge in his life.

That had been Serrano's campaign slogan—*No challenge too great for America*—and he had lived the kind of rags-to-riches story that could only happen in the land of the free and the home of the brave.

Born to teenage Mexican immigrants, Rick Serrano grew up dirt poor in a Texas border town. His hardscrabble life story pushed all the right buttons for a solid electoral majority in any state: military service, self-made fortune, name recognition, and a gifted communicator to boot. His political rise was nothing short of meteoric as he hopscotched his way through the Texas state legislature before jumping to Washington, DC, and the presidency.

As the first Latino president of the United States, Serrano wore his heritage like a badge of honor. One of his major campaign pledges was to increase ties between the United States and their southern neighbors, and he had already issued a blizzard of executive orders on reducing narco-trafficking, boosting economic ties with South America, and calling out the rogue Venezuelan government.

Serrano took his seat and motioned for the room to do the same. He opened up a leather folio to a blank sheet of paper and picked up his pen as if ready to take notes. Over his right shoulder, not seated at the main table, a grandfatherly-looking gentleman settled into his chair.

Chief of Staff Irving Wilkerson was derisively known as Serrano's Obi-Wan. Behind the carefully groomed gray hair and kind smile was one of the most competent political infighters Washington, DC, had ever seen. Wherever Serrano went, so too went Wilkerson.

"Defense," Serrano said in a pleasant baritone. "What's the status of the *Delbert Black*?"

Secretary of Defense Kathleen Howard sported a middle-aged mom vibe, which she used to devastating effect on colleagues who underestimated her keen intellect and political savvy. Her tone was all business.

"The ship was escorted to Bahrain, sir," she said. "In total, eighteen dead and at least another couple dozen casualties."

Serrano nodded and blinked heavily. "I've been on the phone all morning with the families of the ship's crew," he said. "I can imagine what you're going through, Kathy. Let's make sure we take care of those sailors." He paused. "Where are we on the investigation?"

"No new information," Howard said. "We're reconstructing the entire event using data from all available sources, but so far, it looks like the Iranians decided to attack a defenseless merchant vessel. Wouldn't be the first time."

"Keep us posted." Serrano's gaze swung to the Chairman of the Joint Chiefs. "Mr. Chairman, talk about our military response options."

Marine General Adonis "Adam" Nikolaides rarely smiled. Tall and lean with a gray crew cut that caught the light, he turned his somber face to his commander in chief.

"Sir, our most effective and quickest military response is by air. USS *Abraham Lincoln* is in the Indian Ocean, and I recommend we move her north into the Arabian Sea immediately. Furthermore, the *Ford*, currently on station in the eastern Med, should transit down through the Suez Canal and join the *Lincoln*. Within the next seventy-two hours we should be able to conduct nonstop air operations against the Islamic Republic of Iran from the sea. We can quickly add to that combat power if we send Air Force assets forward as well."

Although he was offering suggestions to the president, his tone sounded like he was giving orders and everyone in the room knew it, including Serrano. The skin around the new president's eyes hardened a bit, but he let the chairman say his piece.

"The USS *George H. W. Bush* is in Norfolk completing final preps for a scheduled deployment later this year," the chairman continued. "She's scheduled to replace the *Ford* in the Med. We can speed up that timetable."

As the general spoke, one of his aides began to update the world map on the wall screen at the end of the table, highlighting the three aircraft carriers already mentioned.

"We have two Marine amphibious ready groups currently on deployment, one in the Med and the other in Perth, Australia. We recommend these groups be positioned in the Arabian Sea in the event they are needed to protect CENTCOM forward assets in Bahrain or Qatar. If we choose to invade Iran, the Marines can also take some of the Iranian coastal islands as jumping-off points for a land attack, if ordered."

Don watched the screen zoom into the region of the Persian Gulf and highlight the affected US Navy assets in the Gulf. His mind worked overtime as he studied the map. Iran was a huge country—as big as Iraq and Afghanistan combined. Had the chairman really just talked about putting Marines ashore on Iran?

Serrano nodded as he absorbed the information. He sat back in his chair and steepled his fingers while the room waited to see what the new president was going to do.

"For the moment," he said, "I want to use air power against the Iranians. The goal here is to kill two birds with one stone."

He leaned forward in his chair and placed his palms flat on the table. "I'd like to turn this tragedy into an opportunity. I'm giving the military free rein to decide specific bombing targets, but focus on Iran's ballistic missile capability and any suspected nuclear facilities. You are authorized to use bunker busting weapons, if necessary, to wipe out that program." He stared hard at the chairman. "Avoid civilian casualties, General. Our issue is with the Iranian military, not the Iranian people."

The president's quick gaze sought out the Secretary of State next. Henry Hahn was a statesman straight out of central casting. Aristocratic in bearing, dressed only in the finest bespoke suits, and speaking with a touch of Oxford in his tone, the Washington joke was that Henry Hahn had monogrammed underwear.

"State," Serrano continued. "Once we start to see effects from the air attacks, I want you to back-channel to the Iranian government that I wish to reset our relationship. If they're serious about talking, we're ready."

Hahn nodded gravely, his expression blank. Don knew he'd served on the State Department team that had negotiated the original Iranian nuclear deal in 2015 and that he would love nothing more than to revitalize that accord.

"If I may, sir?" General Nikolaides said.

Serrano nodded.

"We have assets in South Korea," the general said. "If we believe the North Koreans are serious about peace, we could redeploy those forces."

Chief of Staff Wilkerson leaned forward and whispered in the president's ear.

"Let's table that for now, General," Serrano said. "What I really want to know is: what is the Iranians' next move? They started this party, after all. I'm concerned about their proxies."

The Director of the CIA spoke up. "Mr. President, I have Don Riley here from Emerging Threats. He has the most experience of anyone here with Hezbollah."

Don stood and felt Serrano's eyes lock on to him. There was encouragement in the commander in chief's magnetic gaze. Don felt his nervousness dissolve.

Serrano smiled. "It's Don, right? I know we haven't met, but I read about some of the things you've been involved in. Impressive work."

Don felt himself blushing. "Thank you, sir." He fumbled with the buttons on his suit jacket. "Mr. President, there's a sizable number of Hezbollah operatives in the tri-border region in South America."

"That's the area where Brazil, Argentina, and Paraguay meet, right?" Serrano said, his eyes never leaving Don's.

Don nodded vigorously. "Yes, sir. That's the one. It's sort of a no-man's-land. The governments involved usually take a hands-off approach to the region, but they're ready for anything. Argentina has put troops on the border and preemptively shut down any of the Jewish-related facilities. They don't want another community center bombing like the one in 1994. We know that Mossad has sent a squad of operatives into that area to have people on the ground in case something crops up."

"Do we expect them to come north, Don?" the president asked.

Don shook his head. "At present, we don't see any sign of increased activity at the border. I think the Department of Homeland Security can back us up on that. But, it's early days."

The Secretary of Homeland Security nodded his head. "I concur with that assessment, Mr. President."

Serrano chewed his lip and nodded for Don to sit back down. He looked back over his shoulder at his chief of staff, then traded glances with his National Security Advisor.

"And that brings me to the next point of discussion for this meeting," Serrano said.

Don saw glances ricochet around the table. The purpose of this meeting was to lay out a strategy for dealing with Iran, and that business was concluded.

"I want to begin planning an armed response to deal with the failed state of Venezuela."

The chairman's gray eyebrows bunched together, and the general started to speak. Serrano held up his hand, and the Marine's jaw snapped shut.

"I know what you're going to say, General, and I understand why you're going to say it," Serrano said. "But I want to make one thing clear right now: I ran on a platform of restoring order to this hemisphere, most especially in South America. Mr. Riley just briefed us about Hezbollah operatives in the tri-border area that have been ignored by countless administrations before mine. Those kinds of problems do not get better with time. They fester and they spread."

He smiled grimly. "I have always maintained there is no challenge too great for America—and I believe that in my heart. Venezuela is a humanitarian crisis on our doorstep, one that we have let continue for too long. That ends now. The next election in Venezuela will be free and fair."

He got to his feet, and the room rose as one.

"And you can consider that an order."

6

Moscow, Russia

The Russian president surveyed his guests over the rim of a glass of vodka.

"To your health," he said to the two men occupying the armchairs on the other side of his desk.

Defense Minister Viktor Yakov got to his feet to refill all three glasses. He was a stump of a man with thick gray hair that looked as if someone had glued a scrub brush to his scalp. Yakov was the opposite of a politician. He could no sooner hide his emotions than he could stop breathing. As a military man, he was a fearless soldier and an inspiration to his beloved troops, but for Luchnik's purposes, he had one quality that superseded all others: he was loyal to his president.

Another toast. This time to victory. Luchnik felt the vodka warm his belly. He savored the feeling. He rarely drank anymore, but tonight was a special occasion.

Luchnik took few meetings in his personal residence. As an intelligence officer for most of his career, he had worn many faces, lived many lives. What little personal life remained he took pains to preserve in this house, away from the prying eyes of the rest of the world.

Minister of Foreign Affairs Sergey Irimov got to his feet to make the next toast. Tall, with a patrician bearing, carefully combed hair, and rimless glasses, he looked the part of the Russian Federation's most senior diplomat. He was also a gifted liar and had spent the entire afternoon denying Russia had provided any military assistance to the Islamic Republic of Iran.

Irimov was the opposite of Yakov in every way, save one: he, too, was fiercely loyal to Luchnik.

The foreign minister swayed slightly as he told a meandering story ending with another toast. The tall man collapsed back into the leather armchair.

Neither guest noticed when Luchnik discarded his drink in the wastebasket under his desk. He rose to fill their glasses again.

"The Iranians claim they shot down an American F-35 this afternoon," Yakov said with a grin. He had spots of color high on his cheeks. Despite his bulky physique, Yakov was a lightweight when it came to alcohol. "So much for the Americans' stealth fighter." He made air quotes around the word *stealth* and laughed at his own joke.

Luchnik smiled in agreement, raised his glass, and discarded another drink under the desk.

"How many of the new missiles do the Iranians have left?" Luchnik asked.

"Two," Yakov replied. "They want another shipment as soon as possible."

Luchnik stood, feeling the buzz of the vodka and the warmth of the room. He sat on the edge of the desk.

"Shall we send them more, Sergey?" Luchnik asked Irimov.

The foreign minister was a mournful drunk. He scrunched up his face as he considered the question, then slowly shook his head.

"We got lucky. Our advanced weapons were in the right place at the right time," he said. "The Americans are in it up to their necks. Let the situation develop."

Yakov slapped the arm of his chair, sloshing vodka on the leg of his dark green uniform.

"Screw the Americans and their airpower," he shouted. "Let the Iranians have all the missiles they want."

"And who is going to pay for them?" Luchnik asked.

He smiled when Yakov sputtered. Money was a perpetual problem in the Russian Federation, and the Iranians could not pay in the currency of choice: American dollars. How ironic that he only accepted American dollars for weapons to shoot down American planes, Luchnik thought. Poetic, in a way.

Suddenly restless, Luchnik strode to the world map that covered the entire east wall of his office. The Russian Federation was at the center of the map, painted a glorious red.

In his solitary evenings, he often studied this map, memorizing every detail of the borders of his country, evaluating how he might strengthen or expand each millimeter of the solid red line.

His eyes settled on Crimea, and he allowed a smile. He had personally hand-drawn the new border on the map after annexing that bit of Ukraine. It would not be the last, he swore to himself. The Russian Federation deserved more, and he would deliver it.

Irimov and Yakov, glasses in hand, joined him at the map. Luchnik turned to the foreign minister.

"What did you mean when you said we got lucky?" he asked. The phrase had bothered him somehow, but he could not define the discomfort.

Irimov gave an exaggerated shrug. "The Iranian Navy made a mistake. Taking on a US Navy warship is a death wish."

"The American ship was damaged," Yakov offered.

"The American ship sailed away under its own power," Irimov snapped back. "The Iranian ship was sunk." Irimov shrugged again. "Like I said, we got lucky."

If there was one thing the president did not believe in, it was luck. Everything happened as a result of an action. The question was whose action had started this chain of events?

He knew of no covert operation in Iran but made a mental note to question his intelligence service head in the morning.

Meanwhile, although Luchnik did not believe in luck, he did believe in exploiting an opportunity.

"You can send them eight more advanced missiles," he said to Yakov. "After that, our terms are cash in advance."

Yakov's wide grin made his reddened face look like a pumpkin.

"Yes, sir," he said and tottered off to refill his glass.

Luchnik studied his map again. In the west, Belarus would fall in the next few years, but the rest of that border was proving resistant to his normal tactics. Ukraine was still standing, and Estonia was getting stronger as time went on. In the south, he had neutralized the conflicts in Chechnya and Georgia, but the resistance had not gone away.

His eyes drifted north. Now there was opportunity for the Russian people. For all the hand-wringing over climate change, it was opening up the Great Northern Sea Route to Russian control.

Soon, he promised himself. Very soon the world would again recognize the greatness of Russia.

"You are thinking of Ukraine, Mr. President?" Irimov's question was a reminder of work yet to be done.

Yakov rejoined them. He gestured at the map with his glass, his eyes gleaming with alcoholic bravado.

"This is our chance to reclaim Ukraine. The Americans have their own problems. Europe is weak. We must strike now."

Luchnik could tell Irimov wanted to speak but held back. Always the shrewd diplomat. Even drunk, he wanted to know what his boss thought before he spoke.

Luchnik slowly shook his head. This was not the time, he thought. Not yet, but if they could extend the American military even further...

"I think not, Viktor." He slapped the defense minister's shoulder to soften the rejection, although the man was likely too drunk to care. It was like slapping a side of beef.

"The world needs to forget about Ukraine." He eyed Irimov in his periphery. "I think perhaps we need to accelerate the process."

Luchnik stepped to the map and tapped his finger.

"Bosnia," he announced. "Send some advisers, money, weapons. Let's see what happens."

Silence settled in the room when his guests departed.

Luchnik retrieved a fresh glass from the sideboard. He filled it and his own glass, then settled into his chair and put his feet up on the desk.

A hidden door in the wall opposite the map clicked open, and a man entered.

Vitaly Luchnik had truly loved only three things in his life: his country, his bank account, and his sister.

Natasha Luchnik had died at thirty years old, leaving a six-year-old son, Nikolay, and a worthless drunk of a husband. As her older brother and only living relative, Luchnik had taken the boy into his home and systematically destroyed the husband.

Nikolay Sokolov, now forty-two years old, was Commander of the Pacific Fleet and the youngest admiral by far in the Russian Navy. His rise in the ranks had been equal parts Luchnik's prodding and Nikolay's considerable talents. There was talk that young Sokolov might even be the successor of his uncle and adopted father.

Luchnik waved to his nephew to take a chair.

"Sit down, Nikolay," he said. "Tell me what you heard."

His nephew smiled—he even smiled like his mother—and picked up his drink.

"I heard three old men getting shit-faced," he said. "Mr. President," he added.

Luchnik laughed. No one else in the entire country of Russia would dare to speak to him like that. It felt freeing in a strange way.

For the next few minutes, Nikolay recounted the meeting in detail along with his observations. Luchnik nodded his approval.

"What did you think of Yakov's suggestion about Ukraine?" he asked.

Nikolay snorted. "I think Yakov is a fool, Uncle."

"Yakov is loyal," he replied.

"Loyalty is overrated, Uncle. If you want to rebuild Russia, you need leaders who can think for themselves."

Luchnik sighed. "Men are tools, Nikolay. A loyal man is a reliable tool. Yakov will do anything I tell him to do. That is his value."

Instead of answering, Nikolay retrieved the bottle and filled their glasses.

"I think you are right about Ukraine, Uncle. The Americans are temporarily distracted in the Gulf, but they are still formidable. This is not the right time." He raised his glass. "Yet."

Luchnik drank, eyeing the younger man. There was clearly more that Nikolay wanted to say.

"And?" Luchnik prompted.

"Irimov is an old woman, Uncle. I know he's been loyal to you, but he fears the Americans too much."

"He knows what they are capable of," Luchnik replied. He could feel the effect of the vodka now. "Irimov can adapt to international reaction like he changes his underwear. He has a gift."

Nikolay toyed with his glass, not listening to Luchnik.

"What is it, Kolya?"

Nikolay looked up at the use of his late mother's pet name for him. It was one of the few things he remembered about his mother.

Nikolay downed another drink before he answered.

"I wish to come back to Moscow, Uncle," he said quickly. "I hate Vladivostok. This is where the action is. Close to you."

Luchnik sighed. He would love nothing better than to pass on the mantle of leadership to his nephew, but there were life lessons this young man had to learn first.

"You must be patient, Nikolay," he said. "Right now, the best place for you is far away from Moscow. There are men who are jealous of you, of your skills, of your connections. We must use distance to ease their minds. Prove your worth in Vladivostok, far from my influence, and I will welcome you home with open arms."

Nikolay's smile was so much like his mother's that it took Luchnik's breath away.

"There is nowhere in the Russian Federation that is far from your influence, Uncle."

7

Emerging Threats Group
Tysons Corner, Virginia

In a less stressful situation, Don Riley would have enjoyed watching Dre Ramirez trying to school Air Force Captain Mark Westlund on the inner workings of US combat ships.

But these were trying times, and the topic was deadly serious.

Dre had a schematic of an *Arleigh Burke*–class destroyer on the wall screen and was pointing to a white protrusion high on the ship's superstructure.

"This is a CIWS," she said, pronouncing it *see-whiz*.

"What's that?" Mark asked. "Another radar?"

She leveled a look of disdain at him. "Close-in weapons system, Mark. It's a twenty-millimeter Gatling gun used to shoot down close-aboard threats."

"Weapon of last resort," Michael Goodwin chimed in.

Don could sympathize with the Air Force officer. The Navy way was to cram an entire city inside a steel hull with systems designed for everything from shooting missiles out of the sky to making enough water to take a decent shower.

And that was just the platform. The threats were another can of worms. The ships could be attacked from the air, the sea, or underwater by missiles, guns, torpedoes...or just some random sailor firing an automatic grenade launcher from a patrol boat one-tenth the size of the ship.

For all the firepower and sensors on the USS *Delbert D. Black*, that last threat had turned out to be the chink in the warship's formidable armor.

Don's attention drifted. The muted TV monitors on either side of Dre's tutorial screen were tuned to different news channels. The pictures they displayed were worth far more than a thousand words.

In the days after the attack on the *Black*, it seemed like every channel on the planet showed a repeating loop of the damaged US Navy destroyer, dark smoke still billowing from the forward part of her superstructure. Remarkably, the ship was still under her own power, and the pair of warships accompanying her away from the Strait of Hormuz were only there as escorts. When the news channels wanted to mix it up, they showed a clip of Iranian sailors abandoning their own ship, which was on fire and listing to one side.

Occasionally, they interspersed an interview with the captain of the merchant vessel saved by the crew of the *Black*. His ship had survived the attack with no more than a few bullet holes. The man had nothing but praise for the Americans and anger for the Iranians.

Then the US aircraft carriers arrived in the Arabian Sea and commenced a nonstop bombing campaign on Iranian military targets—all carried live on television, of course.

After a few days of continuous coverage, even the images of US Navy jets catapulting off aircraft carriers became old hat. The same pundits used the same cartoonish maps to show where the US was conducting bombing runs. Don had seen the same loop of "life in Tehran" at least a hundred times.

The crimson banners proclaiming "Conflict in the Gulf" still flared across the screen every quarter hour, but no one seemed to care. War was boring.

The Foreign Affairs Minister of Iran, a short, bespectacled man with a trim goatee and a placid demeanor, continued to assert—to anyone who would listen—that both the merchant ship and the USS *Delbert D. Black* were in Iranian territorial waters at the time of the attack. Investigative reporters had delved into the publicly available automatic identification system (AIS) data and disproven the Iranian claims, but the foreign affairs minister continued to insist he was correct. The final blow for the Iranians' credibility came when the Supreme Leader of North Korea denounced the Iranian attack on the US Navy.

The chyrons at the bottom on the screen scrolled: *United Nations Security Council in emergency session.*

Don shook his head. Behind the scenes, the situation was a mess. In the National Security Council briefings, Don learned that the US was running out of military targets to bomb in Iran. The presidential requirement to avoid civilian casualties and civilian infrastructure left the US forces with the same few targets that they bombed over and over again.

That said, the missions were still incredibly dangerous. The Iranians seemed to possess an unlimited supply of Russian-made S-400 surface-to-air missiles, which were deadly accurate at ranges of up to 250 miles. The US forces had lost three aircraft to enemy fire already, and they were not even a week into the fighting.

Don sighed. The attack on the *Black* had killed the bridge crew instantly, but that was only the beginning of the ship's problems. The incendiary devices had started a fire on board that melted decks, collapsing in on the *Black's* Combat Information Center. Seawater used to fight the fire had further damaged the space. According to Dre, who followed the Navy investigation closely, recovery of usable data from the *Black* was a total loss.

"Don," Dre said, "I'm showing the video now."

This video was why he had stopped by Dre's office in the first place. Although she wasn't part of the investigative team, Dre had used her connections to gain access to a new Navy incident investigation system called Amalgam. According to Dre, Amalgam was able to take data sources like video from the Fire Scout drone, commercial maritime traffic reports, satellite images, and clips of bridge-to-bridge communications and knit them together into an interactive, narrative timeline.

Don watched, transfixed. Over the course of twenty-two minutes and thirty-seven seconds, events unfolded from the distress call from the merchant vessel *Minotaur* to when the grenades detonated on her bridge. In that time, the USS *Black* fought off a swarm of patrol boats trying to board the merchant vessel, sunk an Iranian frigate, evaded three incoming missiles, and deterred two jet fighters before she was successfully attacked by a patrol boat.

Most of the action had all happened in the last six minutes, all of it recorded by the Fire Scout.

The last thirty seconds of video was especially hard to watch.

The silent video showed the *Black* a mere two hundred yards from the merchant vessel. The air was thick with smoke from her missile launches, and bits of metallic chaff clouded the space between the two ships.

Two Iranian patrol craft rounded the stern of the *Minotaur*, racing toward the *Black*. The Phalanx CIWS engaged the first target, a steady stream of bullets rippling across the calm water like a living thing. The first small boat erupted in a fiery blast, bits of the hull traveling forward from the target's momentum.

The CIWS six-barrel muzzle shifted to the next target.

Then it ran out of ammunition.

Don knew the CIWS fired 20mm rounds at 4,500 rounds per minute, putting up a wall of metal to shred an incoming missile. But the last-ditch weapon had a limited magazine. It could only fire at that rate for less than a minute.

The resolution on the video was good enough that Don watched the spinning gun barrel slow and stop. He winced, knowing what was coming next.

The second boat careened through the wreckage of its partner, closing on the *Black* at high speed. Mark could make out the features of a bearded man behind a grenade launcher mounted to the deck of the speeding boat. He braced his legs against the bulkhead and sighted down the barrel. His mouth moved; he was yelling.

The driver spun the wheel, putting the patrol boat broadside to the *Black*. The Iranian boat appeared tiny next to the gray hull of the *Black*. Pips of white fire spewed out of the muzzle of the grenade launcher, lancing up at the bigger ship.

For a second, nothing happened.

Then the bridge windows of the *Black* blew out in a massive explosion.

Blast after blast erupted on the superstructure of the *Black* as the grenades exploded one after another. A narration on the video reported the Iranian weapon was a Nasir 40mm automatic grenade launcher. The belt-fed device had managed to get off almost thirty shots before it sped away. The shots were a deadly mix of conventional grenades and white phosphorus rounds.

Don felt his rib cage contract in sympathy. He closed his eyes, trying to imagine what it must have been like on the bridge of the *Black*. With the ship at general quarters, there would have been at least a dozen crewmembers up there when the first grenade detonated.

Don cleared his throat. He'd seen enough. What had happened to the *Black* was tragic, but it was also a fluke, a lucky shot by a lone gunman. The Iranian Navy had picked a fight with the wrong opponent, and now they were paying the price. Case closed. It was not the job of Emerging Threats Group to investigate it.

"Dre—" Don began.

"There's more," Dre interrupted. Her dark eyes shone with frenetic energy. "Five minutes, boss. Then I'll shut up, I promise."

Reluctantly, Don nodded.

"During the attack on the *Black*," Dre began, "we did not have any recon satellites over the region, but I was able to find one partial image." Dre pointed at the screen. "This is from a low-angle bird at the time of the attack. It was discarded by the investigation because it has incomplete coverage and they have excellent orthogonal shots starting about thirty minutes after the attack."

"Dre," Don said. "The investigative team is going to assess all the data that they have—"

"The *Black* moved," Dre said with an edge in her voice. "After the attack, I mean. She still had power. She escorted the merchant ship away from the scene of the attack."

Don paused, wondering where she was going with this.

"No one thought anything of it," Dre said, "because the next satellite pass fixed her location precisely."

Don did not like the look in her eyes. Wild, unsettled. Worried.

"Continue," he said.

Dre took a deep breath. "When you apply geometrical rectification to this crappy oblique-angle satellite pass from the time of the attack, it shows that the *Black* was not in international waters."

Don listened with growing concern as she ran through her calculations using a process called space oblique Mercator projection theory to turn a low-angle image into a top-down picture.

"It's a crappy image," Dre said. "Very low angle and partially obscured by the mountain ranges along the coast, but there's enough there to catch the stern of the *Black* and the Iranian destroyer in this one frame. Maybe they just missed it when they did a data sweep. Or maybe I was just looking harder for clues."

Dre pointed at the screen. Using the new location data, the USS *Delbert D. Black* and the merchant vessel were both at least a thousand meters outside of the shipping lane.

Don felt sick to his stomach. If Dre was right, then the United States had gone to war on false pretenses.

On the adjacent TV screen, yet another Navy jet was rocketing off the USS *Abraham Lincoln*, en route to drop more bombs on the Islamic Republic of Iran.

"How certain are you of your calculations?" Don thought his voice sounded loud in the quiet room.

Dre's face clouded. "I did the math myself, but I have a call in to a friend over at..." Her voice trailed off. "No, Don, I'm right. I know it."

Don stared at the screen. The lines delineating the boundaries of the shipping lane were bright yellow. On the scale of the screen, the outline of the US Navy destroyer was an inch away from that magic yellow border.

"Don't call anyone or do anything else," Don said. "This information does not leave this room. Do you understand?"

8

Visakhapatnam, Andhra Pradesh, India

When the battered taxi Roger Tan was riding in stopped at an intersection, a horde of beggar children swarmed the vehicle, hands out, their voices a chorus of wails and pleas.

Despite the thirty-three-degree Celsius heat and the barely functioning air-conditioning unit in the car, Roger rolled up his window. The car smelled of baked dust and old curry. A kid pressed both hands flat on Roger's window and peered inside.

Roger looked away. He touched the missing chunk of his right earlobe, then quickly dropped his hand back into his lap.

He hated India. The noise, the chaos, the unrelenting poverty...It was all too much. Places like this dredged up memories that he'd rather leave buried.

The driver laid on the horn and inched the car forward to clear away the tide of small brown bodies around them. He caught Roger's eye in the rearview mirror.

"You here for the beaches, sir?" he said in lilting English. "I know the best beaches. Lots of pretty women."

"No," Roger said. "Just take me to the port."

A shrug. "As you wish. The port."

The Minister had selected Visakhapatnam carefully. The port, on the eastern coast of India, was large enough for the North Korean freighter to go unnoticed among the other shipping traffic but small enough to ensure the security was less than state-of-the-art. The city was also a tourist destination, which meant a large transient population.

The Minister's choice did not disappoint. Security consisted of an open gate and a uniformed guard dozing in a booth. The taxi driver motored past without waking the guard and parked outside the offices of Garduba Trading Company.

"Wait here," Roger said to the driver.

The interior of the Garduba Trading Company was only slightly cooler than outside. A ceiling fan moved the thick air, stirring up a musty smell. Roger pulled his sweaty shirt away from the small of his back.

The man behind the desk did not look up when Roger entered, keeping his gaze fixed on his computer screen. He was gray-haired and pear-shaped, seated behind a desk heaped with stacks of paper. Bulky headphones were clamped over his ears. The whiteboard hanging on the wall behind him should have been a shipping schedule, but a quick glance showed the information to be years out of date.

Roger advanced to the desk and leaned over. The man was streaming a movie. The woman on the screen was dressed like an Indian princess with a jewel fixed to her forehead, her dark hair flowing over her shoulders. Her sequined red dress showed a generous amount of cleavage.

"Excuse me," Roger said.

The man grimaced and touched his keyboard to stop the movie. He slid one side of the headphones away from his ear.

"What do you want?" His voice was drowsy.

"Has the *Hoe Ryong* docked yet?" Roger asked.

The man sighed and minimized the movie on his screen. He tapped at the keyboard. "North Korean?"

"Yes, that's the one," Roger replied.

The man shook his head and cursed. "Idiots," he muttered.

"Problem?" Roger said.

"They dock at eight o'clock," the man said, "but Customs goes home at five. They'll sit there until morning."

"I see," Roger said. "Will I be able to contact them tonight? Maybe a night security guard can get them a message for me? I can pay, of course."

The man snorted. "Security? Here? They just shut the gate and go home." He restarted his movie, settled the headphones back on his ears, and slumped in his chair. "Come back in the morning."

The Indian princess had tears in her eyes, her henna-tattooed hand clutched at her heaving breast.

Roger's phone buzzed with an incoming text. A name and address.

"You've been very helpful," Roger said.

The Percolator Coffee House on Dr. NTR Beach Road was in the trendy part of Vizag, as the city of Visakhapatnam was known locally. The modern interior was blond wood, black stone, and gleaming chrome. The clientele was split between mid-twenties with laptops and groups of two or three young women, gossiping and laughing. Everyone was young and beautiful and smiling with brilliant white teeth, uncaring of the fact that hungry children begged on a filthy street a mere two blocks away.

The coffee house was an island of sterile modernity in a chaotic city. According to the text message, it was also owned by an operative in the employ of the Minister. Here, Roger could download a secure message from his mentor.

Roger smiled at the pretty young barista as he ordered a hot tea.

"Is Krish available?" he asked her.

"Of course, sir," she said. "I'll get him for you."

He found a corner booth and opened his laptop. A few moments later, a man in his mid-thirties, dressed business casual in khakis and a blue polo shirt, delivered Roger's tea.

"I am Krish," the man said. "How may I help you, sir?"

"I'm here to study the migration of the snow cranes," Roger responded.

The man paused, glanced around the room, then offered the correct coded response.

Bonafides established, Roger turned his laptop toward the man. "The Wi-Fi password, please."

The man logged Roger in to the secure router and left. It took a full minute for Roger's computer to navigate the security protocols and display the latest communique from the Minister.

He scanned the message and felt his pulse quicken. His next assignment would not require a cover identity.

Ian Thomas was taking a work trip to Panama.

To Roger's eye, the *Hoe Ryong* looked like it had more rust than metal left in her hull. At barely a hundred meters in length, she was small compared to most of the ships he'd seen along the pier that afternoon.

Roger approached the man standing watch on the ship's brow. His dirty face could have belonged to someone eighteen or thirty-eight years old. He was thin and dressed in ragged dungarees and a stained T-shirt. He wore battered sandals, and the thick, curving toenails looked like claws in the dim light. He eyed Roger with a narrowed gaze.

"Get captain," Roger said in his rudimentary Korean.

The man pointed at the pier as an indication for Roger to stay put.

The night air was hot and heavy with the smell of rotting fish and water fouled with sewage. There was no breeze. Besides the *Hoe Ryong*, there was only one other ship on the pier, and it looked deserted.

The silhouette of a man made his way down the brow to the pier. The captain of the *Hoe Ryong* was dressed similarly to the sailor, but his T-shirt was stretched tight across a generous belly and he wore red suspenders to hold up his trousers. Roger could smell the alcohol on his breath, and the man swayed slightly when he came to a stop before Roger.

"My cargo is ready to offload?" Roger asked.

"You have my money?" the captain replied.

"You've been paid already," Roger said.

"That was before I knew I was transporting weapons," the captain said. His grin loomed in the dark. "I'm not a soldier, but I can recognize an AK-47, an RPG, and C-4 explosives when I see them."

Roger pulled his mobile out of his pocket and opened the WhatsApp account set up by the Minister. "I'll bring the trucks around," he replied.

The captain, thinking Roger was toying with him, stepped closer. The sour smell of rice wine on his breath filled the air between them.

"I need to be paid before any of the cargo is moved off my ship," the captain said.

Without dropping his gaze, Roger reached into his hip pocket and drew out a fat envelope. He split a stack of US dollars with his finger and handed half to the captain. The man's eyes widened with greed. Roger let his fingertip riffle the remaining bills.

"Half now," Roger said. "Half when the job is done."

The captain snatched the bills away and turned on his heel. He shouted in Korean, and the deck sprang to life. Two men unlimbered a deck-mounted hoist as two more threw open a deck hatch.

At the end of the pier, headlights turned the corner, stabbing the darkness. The lights were higher off the ground than a passenger car, indicating they belonged to a heavy truck. Four more trucks followed.

The first vehicle pulled to a stop next to the *Hoe Ryong*. Like most of the trucks in India, it was painted in bright colors with elaborate tasseled hangings inside the cab. As was typical, the trucks had no side mirrors. Roger noted the figurines of Hindu deities normally found on the dashboards of these types of vehicles were missing. These drivers were Muslim.

The cab door of the lead vehicle opened, and a man swung down to the ground. He was huge, nearly two meters tall, with broad shoulders and a thick neck corded with muscle. His unruly dark hair hung to his shoulders, and he wore a thick beard.

Roger studied the Al-Badr leader as he approached. The man walked with a swagger that to Roger suggested the self-righteousness so often found in these kinds of militant groups. When they clothed their violence in the trappings of faith for long enough, they started to believe their own preachings. In their minds, they became gods.

He was perfect; the Minister had chosen well. With that religious confidence came a sense of invincibility. Properly armed, a man like this could cause much chaos in the world, which is exactly what Roger assumed the Minister had in mind.

The Al-Badr was an Islamic militant group operating in the Jammu and Kashmir region bordering India, Pakistan, and China. Originally funded by the Pakistani ISI, Al-Badr had gone independent in recent years and become a major contributor to friction with India. Now, that friction was about to burst into flames. Armed with Roger's weapons, Al-Badr had pledged to take a terror campaign into the heart of India.

"The money is ready," the militant leader said. "All I need is your account number."

Roger sent him the numbered bank account information via Whats-App. Although it went against his instincts, the Minister had been very clear that Roger was to use the phone and the social media account to conduct his business with these terrorists.

Roger trusted the Minister. If he wished to leave a digital trail of this transaction, he surely had a reason.

The offloading went swiftly. The Korean captain, drunk on both *soju* and Roger's cash, supervised his men in removing crates from the hold and lowering them into the waiting trucks. The crates contained enough firepower to start a small war.

Or even a big war, Roger mused.

When the last truck was being loaded, Roger led the militant leader to the deck of the *Hoe Ryong*. The captain watched them board, his dark eyes following Roger's every move, a greedy leer on his lips. He checked off something on his clipboard with an exaggerated gesture.

"Fifty crates of machine parts delivered, sir," he said to Roger, handing him the clipboard. "Please sign here."

"Where is your first mate?" Roger asked.

The captain whistled at the man operating the winch. The mate was younger than the captain by about a decade and wore a clean T-shirt tucked into his dungarees.

"How long have you sailed with the captain?" Roger asked in his basic Korean.

"Seven years," the mate replied in the same language.

"Congratulations," Roger said.

Roger took the pencil tucked into the clipboard and stabbed the captain in the neck. The man made a wet retching sound, and his eyes snapped open wide. Blood spurted out of his neck and ran down his chest, staining his dirty T-shirt. He reached for Roger, who stepped out of his path. The captain dropped to his knees and toppled over.

All movement on the deck of the *Hoe Ryong* and on the dock froze. In the stillness, Roger heard the gentle slap of water on the hull of the ship, the rumbling murmur of idling diesel engines from the trucks.

Roger inspected his clothes for any blood spatter and found none. He handed the clipboard to the first mate.

"You are the captain now. Put his body in the freezer and dump him when you get out to sea. The cash in his pocket is yours."

9

Emerging Threats Group
Tysons Corner, Virginia

On the flat-screen TV mounted to the wall opposite his desk, Don watched the Supreme Leader of the Democratic People's Republic of Korea stride up to the lectern to address the General Assembly of the United Nations. His carefully groomed hair was gelled in place, and round, black-rimmed glasses were pressed firmly against his fleshy cheekbones. His tunic fitted slickly over his tubular body, and he looked like he was in excellent health, defying news reports to the contrary.

For Don, the unprecedented event was a strange juxtaposition of peace amid an otherwise conflict-ridden world.

Until a few weeks ago, the news had been wall-to-wall coverage of the US airstrikes on Iran—even when there was nothing to report. Then a sudden, violent uprising in Kashmir managed to knock that story off the front page.

Now, in another abrupt twist, North Korea was taking center stage with a completely unexpected peace proposal. The offer delighted the United Nations and worried the United States. The American team wondered what was behind the sudden change of heart.

Don felt much older than his almost fifty years. Was it his imagination, or was the pace of change in the world just happening that much faster?

A knock at the door interrupted his reflections. Don muted the TV and turned to greet Mark Westlund. Mark wore a dress shirt with a loosened tie and rolled-up sleeves.

"You wanted to see me, Don?" Mark asked.

Don gestured at the open seat in front of his desk. "Come in, Mark. Close the door behind you, please."

Mark's look turned wary, but he followed Don's instructions. He perched on the edge of his chair and eyed Don with caution.

"What's up, boss?" He had a generous mouth and a ready smile, but Don could tell it was forced. His eyes fell to Don's uncluttered desk.

Don was a manager who preferred paper reports to reading off a screen. Normally his desk was piled with stacks of reports interleaved with multi-colored sticky notes, but this morning he had taken twenty minutes to clean up his office in anticipation of his talk with Mark. He rested his elbows on the newly uncovered work surface and smiled at the newest member of the Emerging Threats Group.

"I wanted to chat with you," Don said.

Mark's smile faltered, but he managed to keep it in place.

Don had recruited Mark to replace Janet Everett for many reasons. He was a second-generation American of Chinese ancestry. Don had seen him interact with a visiting Chinese PLA Navy admiral and had admired the way the young man moved fluidly between the expectations of both cultures. His language skills were another plus, and he had a strong background in intelligence gathering.

Based on his service jacket, Captain Mark Westlund was a man who was going places in the United States intelligence community. But something happened during his prior tour at the NSA.

Somewhere, somehow, Mark had stepped on the wrong toes or colored outside the lines with the wrong manager. When he came up on Don Riley's recruitment radar, he was anxious for a move away from the NSA. In truth, that air of mystery was part of what had made Don consider him as Janet's replacement. Don's experience was that mavericks tended to fit in well at ETG—or that's what he told himself.

Now Don was wondering if he'd made a mistake in recruiting Mark. And it was time to figure that out.

"Coffee?" Don asked, indicating the thermos he kept on a sideboard. Mark nodded, and Don covered the awkward silence by pouring them both cups of coffee. He offered cream, which Mark refused.

Don gave an inward sigh. Waiting wasn't going to make this any easier.

"You've been here...what?" he began. "Two months? How are you fitting in?"

Mark shrugged. "Michael and I get along fine," he said. "Dre? Well, she's another matter. We get along okay, but I get the feeling I'm not measuring up somehow."

Don laughed. "Ms. Ramirez is special."

"She has a thing about Iran," Mark said. "I can tell you that."

If you only knew, Don thought. In a prior operation, Dre Ramirez and another US operative had spent weeks locked inside of an Iranian prison, certain they were going to die at the hands of their captors. To say that Dre had a thing for Iran was like saying Winston Churchill had a thing for Hitler.

The silence returned. Don tried another angle of attack.

"Emerging Threats is a special place. We're not like other directorates. We're the guys who shine lights in the dark corners and find the ugly things that don't make sense. Then we deal with that ugliness before the rest of world even knows it exists. We challenge the status quo of our peers, and that can make some people uncomfortable." Don took a deep breath. "But that's also why I hired you, Mark."

The younger man studied Don's face. "But?" Mark said. "I'm not measuring up? Is that what you're getting at?"

"That's not how I'd put it."

"Then how would you put it?" Mark had a challenging edge to his tone.

As Don held the other man's gaze, he had a sudden disquieting thought. *What if the problem had nothing to do with Mark Westlund at all?*

For years, Don had prided himself on his ability to nurture talent like Janet, Michael, and Dre. In truth, his own career success was due in no small part to their efforts under his direction. But as he faced this obviously talented young officer, Don was forced to look at that success in a less flattering light. If he was such a great talent manager, how come Mark was struggling to fit in?

"This is my fault, Mark," Don said.

Mark cocked his head. Clearly, this was not the response he expected to get. "How so?"

"Our job is to find the signal in the noise," Don said, searching for the words as he spoke. "The world is a loud, dirty, cluttered place. Every day, we dig into that mess and we try to make sense of it. We try to predict the next problem before it's even born."

He gestured at the muted TV, where the Supreme Leader of North Korea was still giving his speech.

"Who could have predicted that?" Don said. "A few months ago, that man was persona non grata at the UN. He was leading a nuclear terrorist state, and now he's making a speech at that same institution. India is marching into the Kashmir. Iran is a mess. And North Korea is a leading voice for peace in the world."

Don leaned across the desk. "Our job is to figure these things out *before* they happen. Did we see North Korea suing for peace? No. Did we see the Iran conflict coming? No. The truth is we didn't see any of it, and that means we failed."

Mark leaned back in his chair. "What can I do?"

"I want you to do some analysis on something that's not in your portfolio," Don said. "Something outside of your experience. Try to analyze it with fresh eyes. Peek into the dark corners."

"I'm up for that, Don," Mark replied. "What did you have in mind?"

That was an excellent question, Don realized. Right now, everyone was focused on Iran. He needed to give Mark a chance to step back and start with a new subject.

Don's gaze slid back to the TV. It looked like the leader of North Korea was finishing up. The lights of the assembly hall gleamed against the man's sleek hair. He recalled a report on 5G software vulnerabilities he had seen as he cleaned off his desk.

"I want you to look at the 5G installation going on in North Korea," Don said. "Look at the hardware, analyze users on the system. Tell me something I don't know. See if you can find any links between this technology rollout and that." Don pointed at the TV.

The Supreme Leader had finished speaking. The hall was filled with diplomats, applauding in a standing ovation. The speaker's face squinted with pleasure as he smiled broadly.

Mark stood. "I'll get right on it, boss." He walked to the door, put his hand on the knob. "Open or closed?"

"Closed, please."

The door clicked shut, and Mark was gone. Don found the remote, and he switched channels on the TV.

The BBC was showing a report from Kashmir. A young reporter stood on an empty city street. Behind him, a plume of thick black smoke rose into the sky.

10

USS *Enterprise* (CVN-80)
50 miles west of Kaohsiung, Taiwan

Through the thick windows of the flag bridge on the USS *Enterprise*, Rear Admiral Chip Sharratt watched the sun rise as he paced on a treadmill. In a ship filled with thousands of sailors, this tiny overlook reserved for flag rank officers was the one place where he could be truly alone.

"Beautiful," he said aloud to the empty room. "Just freaking beautiful."

The flight deck below was as wide as an eight-lane highway and three football fields in length. Four and a half acres of the good old United States of America ready to go anywhere in the world accessible by sea.

The flight deck was quiet but poised for action. Somewhere in the skies above them, two F-35 Lightnings flew combat air patrol. The air plan he had reviewed called for a layered defense to any People's Liberation Army Navy response to their transit of the Strait of Taiwan.

An MH-60 helicopter was on deck in search-and-rescue standby, and a pair of F-35 Lightnings were staged on the catapults in alert-five status. Additional air resources stood by in lower states of readiness just in case the situation got complicated.

Sharratt stopped the treadmill and walked the perimeter of the narrow flag bridge to check on the other ships in his carrier strike group. The USS *Shiloh*, a *Ticonderoga*-class guided missile cruiser, rode a scant half mile off the port quarter of the carrier. A pair of *Arleigh Burke*–class destroyers, the USS *Benfold* and the USS *Mustin*, also rode to the port side of the carrier. The *Constellation*-class guided missile frigate, USS *Chesapeake*, ran point three thousand yards ahead of the battle group.

Combined with the USS *Topeka*, a *Los Angeles*–class fast attack submarine that was part of the *Enterprise* strike group, the four surface escorts were capable of providing defense against air, surface, or subsurface threats.

Over the last six weeks, the *Enterprise* and her escorts had traveled from the Seventh Fleet home port of Yokosuka, Japan, through the South China Sea to Singapore. As the new commander of the carrier strike group, Sharratt had driven his team hard. Drills simulating air and undersea attacks, carrier flight ops in all manner of weather, time of day, and EMCON conditions, as well as ship-wide drills for fire, flooding, and whatever other acts of mayhem his drill monitors could dream up.

Still, he groused to himself, it all felt like play-acting. In the Arabian Sea, United States pilots were in harm's way, flying real combat missions over Iran. Meanwhile, he was sailing his ship between mainland China and the "rogue province" of Taiwan just to score some diplomatic points.

The brilliant morning sun shafted through the windows, forcing Sharratt to put on his dark sunglasses. He gripped the heavy metal railing under the windows, chuckled to himself, then looked around the empty room with a guilty smile.

He could not help himself. He was happy. Beyond happy, actually.

If he could go back in time and tell nine-year-old Chip Sharratt how his life would turn out, the kid would never believe his future self. This seafaring life in the far Pacific waters was as far from rural Minnesota as the surface of the moon.

At fifty-three years old, Sharratt was a WestPac sailor through and through, having spent most of his naval career based out of Japan. It had been love at first sight for Sharratt when he arrived in Japan as a young lieutenant junior-grade, newly qualified as a weapon systems officer, or Wiz-O, in EF-18 Growlers. Suki, a Japanese woman he met while on his shore tour as part of the Seventh Fleet staff, cemented his love affair with the region.

They married when he was a twenty-eight-year-old lieutenant, and Sharratt had promised his new bride he would do everything possible to remain in Japan—even if it meant career sacrifices. He and Suki now had two daughters in high school. Apart from the occasional long-term temporary duty stateside, Sharratt had managed to keep his promise.

And this tour was going to be his last, the pinnacle of his career. He had sailed and flown the Western Pacific oceans for more than a quarter century. He knew the region and the regional issues in a personal way, better than most analysts or admirals. He belonged to the Pacific. Although he would prefer to be flying over the water, riding in the United States Navy's newest *Ford*-class aircraft carrier was not a bad way to travel.

The heavy phone mounted under the railing buzzed.

"Sharratt," Chip answered.

"Admiral," came the rough voice of his chief of staff, "we are officially in the Strait of Taiwan, sir. The Chinese started broadcasting their protestations immediately, and we're following the script in response."

"Very well, Tom," he said. "Steady as she goes, right down the line. At ten knots, we'll be on the other side by dinnertime. What's the status of our Russian tailgaters?"

On the other end of the line, Captain Tom Zachary snorted in derision. The Russian spy ship *Admiral Krilov* and her escorting corvette, the *Gromkiy*, had been trailing the *Enterprise* since they'd left Singapore. Always keeping a few miles astern, always watching, always sucking up valuable intelligence.

"Still there, sir. Looks like they intend to follow us through the Strait."

"What about the PLA welcoming committee?" Sharratt asked.

"Looks like their older carrier, the *Liaoning*, and two destroyers are heading our way from the north," Zachary replied. "If they maintain course and speed, we'll see them shortly after lunch. I'll have all the details in Battle Watch for your review."

"Very well, Tom." Sharratt hung up.

Freedom of navigation operation, or FONOPS in Navy-speak, was one of his least favorite duties. Unfortunately, in WestPac it was becoming all the more frequent.

He squinted through the windows. Fifty or so miles off the port beam was the coast of the People's Republic of China. Fifty or so miles to starboard was the Republic of China, better known as Taiwan. Since the end of World War Two, both entities had claimed the Strait of Taiwan, the name for the waters between their shores.

In 1955, the United States had drawn a line down the middle of the Strait, the median line, and pressured both parties to stay on their own side. That tacit agreement had held until nearly the year 2000. Now it was violated on a regular basis by the PLA Air Force.

The USS *Enterprise* carrier strike group, with orders to sail down the median line of the Strait, was about to engage in one of the oldest customs of the United States Navy.

Harassing the competition.

In this part of the world, far from the US mainland, China was executing a strategy, while the US had tactics. In the long run, Sharratt knew, strategy won every time.

Chief among the US tactics was FONOPS. In 1982, the United Nations Convention on the Law of the Sea established "freedom of navigation" as a right for all states on the high seas. Simply put, the Chinese claimed territorial waters where they had no right, and the US vowed to sail through those waters to demonstrate the freedom of the seas.

The net result was usually a diplomatic hissy fit. Both sides made their point, then everyone went home and nothing changed.

A hell of a way to run a Navy, thought Sharratt. Instead of lending their considerable air power to the fight over Iran, the *Enterprise* was poking the Chinese Navy.

But these operations were not without risk. When two heavily armed naval forces came into close proximity, someone might make a mistake.

That's how wars started.

It was also a good way to shorten a long, satisfying naval career, which was why Rear Admiral Chip Sharratt was on high alert this morning.

Zachary's prediction that they would meet the Chinese welcoming party by lunchtime had proved premature. The PLA Navy vessels had increased speed to twenty knots and were closing fast.

When Sharratt strode into Battle Watch, he could feel the tension in the air, like the smell of ozone during a storm.

Battle Watch, located beneath the flight deck and seven levels below the lofty perch of the flag bridge, was the area of the ship set aside for the admiral to oversee the actions of the *Enterprise* strike force.

The room was dominated by the BattleSpace table. Measuring twenty feet square, the holographic display was the centerpiece of Battle Watch. Into this three-dimensional display, every bit of data from every sensor across the *Enterprise* strike group as well as external platforms, such as satellites, was merged into a comprehensive tactical picture of the surrounding ocean.

Chief of Staff Tom Zachary met him at the entrance to Battle Watch.

"We've got eyes on the Chinese, sir," Zachary said as he guided Sharratt to a flat-screen monitor showing a live-feed image of the incoming PLA Navy vessels.

The *Liaoning*, a Chinese Type 001 aircraft carrier, was a butt-ugly ship, Sharratt decided. The ship had begun life in 1985 in the shipyards of Crimea as a Soviet *Kuznetsov*-class aircraft cruiser, a unique Russian designation designed to avoid Black Sea treaty restrictions. Following the fall of the Soviet Union in 1991, the Ukrainians sold the stripped hulk to the Chinese. With its bulky stacked superstructure and ski-jump style flight deck, the one-thousand-foot-long ship retained a distinctly old-school Soviet look.

In contrast, the escorting PLA Navy destroyers appeared more modern in design, especially the *Chengdu*, a Chinese guided missile destroyer, commonly referred to as the Chinese Aegis. The newer ship, sporting flat-panel radar and vertical launch missile blocks, was advertised as the PLAN's first multirole destroyer.

To Sharratt's eye, the design showed clear US Navy influences in armament and sensors. Decades of industrial espionage by Chinese intelligence agencies had closed the gap between the US and Chinese militaries. He turned his attention to the BattleSpace display.

"Tighten up the range, Lieutenant," Sharratt said to the BattleSpace operator.

"Aye, sir," said the young officer wearing VR goggles and manipulator gloves. He pinched two fingers on his gloved hand, and the scene shrank. "That's ten miles square, sir."

Sharratt grunted a reply and rubbed his jaw as he considered the plot.

The periodic warning from the Chinese came over the VHF: "United States Navy vessels, you are in Chinese territorial waters. You are directed to leave immediately. The People's Republic of China will be lodging a formal complaint with your government."

The *Enterprise* and her escorts were riding the median line down the center of the Strait. The PLAN force, now only five miles ahead, was hugging tightly to their side of the line.

The Chinese apparently wanted to play chicken.

Two can play that game, Sharratt decided.

"Watch Officer, order the *Chesapeake* to alter course to starboard," he said. "Take the Chinese ships down their port side. Do not get closer than two thousand yards."

The frigate was running point for the strike group. He'd move the smaller ship to one side, but he'd be damned if he would alter the course of a United States aircraft carrier for any Chinese vessel.

"Order the other escorts to close to within one thousand yards of *Enterprise*. Maintain course and speed."

Sharratt waited until the order had been repeated, then said: "Get me the captain on the horn."

Three seconds later, the commanding officer of the *Enterprise* said, "Yes, Admiral."

"I think these pricks want to play, Sam," Sharratt said into the phone. "I moved the escorts closer. Advise the Chinese captain that we intend to maintain course and speed."

"Aye-aye, sir. I'll make the call myself."

"Admiral." Commander Jerry Sorenson, his N2 intel officer, approached the BattleSpace display. His normal watch station was in SUPPLOT, a top-secret space adjoining Battle Watch. "We have the P-8 out of Kadena on approach for a fly-over. Do you want to have them hold off, sir?"

Sharratt motioned for the BattleSpace operator to expand the range on the display until he saw the incoming aircraft. Based on a Boeing 737 hull, the P-8 Poseidon maritime patrol platform was packed with surveillance equipment. With the Chinese carrier, her escorts, and the trailing Russian ships, this run would be an intelligence goldmine.

"Permission granted," Sharratt replied. "The more the merrier." He checked the display again. The first Chinese destroyer was passing the *Chesapeake*. The PLA Navy ships had not altered course yet.

"Admiral, we've got air activity from the Chinese coast," the Battle Watch Officer said. The BattleSpace operator expanded the display range. "Two fighters out of Fuzhou on an intercept course for this location."

Sharratt smiled as a thought came to him. What a perfect teachable moment for his carrier strike group.

"Battle Watch Officer, direct the strike group to go to general quarters. Weapons tight. Make sure you repeat that order—weapons tight. Do not fire unless directly threatened by PLA forces."

"Aye-aye, sir!"

Sharratt turned to his chief of staff. "That'll get their attention, Tom."

"That it will, Admiral," replied Zachary.

The US Navy P-8, flying at five thousand feet, arrived on station and continued its flight path south.

The PLA fighters, cruising at twenty-five thousand feet, vectored south as well, flying parallel to the median line of the Strait. Suddenly, they broke to the east.

"Sir!" came a shouted report. "The Chinese have crossed into Taiwanese air space! The Taiwanese are launching IDFs out of Penghu Island."

Sharratt gritted his teeth. He'd hoped the Chinese would back down, but they seemed willing to raise the stake even more. He hoped that P-8 was collecting a whole lot of intel.

The intercom crackled. "Now launch the alert fighters!"

On the BattleSpace display, the pair of F-35 strike fighters of the *Enterprise* combat air patrol vectored toward Penghu Island and the invading Chinese fighters. The two newly launched fighters appeared on the holographic display, their data tags spooling as they climbed to their ordered altitude.

Sharratt chewed his lip. This was escalating fast. Too fast. On both sides of the Strait of Taiwan, hard-charging young pilots were flying high-performance aircraft. In this kind of pressure situation, anything could happen. The last thing either side needed was more aircraft in the mix.

"Battle Watch Officer," Sharratt snapped. "Advise CAG to keep our aircraft at a safe distance. Let the Taiwanese handle this."

Illegal Chinese incursions into Taiwanese air space were a regular occurrence these days, and the Penghu Island–based squadron was on the front line. Sharratt had seen the Ching-kuo Indigenous Defense Fighters up close and visited with the "Heavenly Colt" fighter squadron on Penghu. The Taiwanese could handle this on their own.

"CAG acknowledges to keep our distance, Admiral," came the report.

A petty officer handed him a handset.

"Sharratt," he said into the receiver.

"Admiral," the *Enterprise* CO's voice was tight, "these assholes are going to put us in extremis."

Sharratt shot a glance at the BattleSpace display. The carrier and one of the Chinese destroyers had slightly altered course to starboard. They would clear the US strike group easily.

But the trailing Chinese ship had not altered course. It was headed right toward the *Enterprise*.

"I think he plans to drive right between us and the escorts," Sharratt said into the phone.

The other man cursed. "Admiral, I recommend we—"

"Maintain course and speed, Captain," Sharratt roared back. "That's an order." He hung up the phone.

The next ninety seconds passed in one painful time increment after another.

Sharratt was doing the right thing—he knew that—but the risks were immense. If that Chinese destroyer so much as scratched the paint job on any of the US ships, it would be an international incident and his head would be on the chopping block.

Still, he felt strangely at peace with the decision. It was time for his country to stop getting pushed around by the big kid on the block in this part of the world. And if that meant he was the guy to draw the line in the sand, then so be it.

He stared at the BattleSpace display for a full ten seconds, then turned on his heel and climbed to the flight deck. A stiff breeze pushed against his body as he jogged to the railing.

Below him, the Chinese destroyer flashed by. The ship was a toy compared to the massive carrier, not even a tenth the size, and it was close enough that Sharratt could make out people on the deck.

On the bridge wing of the Chinese ship stood an officer in uniform. He held binoculars to his eyes, and he was scanning up at the carrier island.

The captain of the Chinese destroyer raised his hand. Without thinking, Sharratt did the same.

Then the PLAN ship was gone, leaving only a white wake behind.

11

White House Situation Room
Washington, DC

Don arrived early for the eight a.m. meeting and settled into a seat against the wall, directly behind the CIA director's chair at the table.

He could tell from the muttered conversations of the principals at the main table that if any of them knew the reason why the planned meeting of the National Security Council had been moved up from one p.m. to eight a.m., no one was talking. Don had been notified by text at five that morning. Brief conversations with staffers to his left and right indicated they had received the same amount of notice.

In addition to the typical players seated around the main table with the president—State, Defense, CIA, DNI, the vice president, and the National Security Advisor—there were two guests today. Chief of Naval Operations Holt Teale was a veteran submarine captain who took the adage "silent service" to heart. The spare, bald man with the long face and wintry blue eyes was famously dismissive of small talk. Even now, he spent his time before the commander in chief arrived studying a tablet, reading glasses balanced on his prominent nose.

Seated to his right, General Douglas A. Baden, known as Dabber to friends and enemies alike, was the CNO's polar opposite. Baden was a compact man in his mid-fifties with an outgoing personality, a ready smile, and borderline regulation-length hair that was almost fabulous enough to give the president a run for his money. The Commander of US Southern Command wore a green Army Service Uniform. The impressive rack of medals on his chest shook as he laughed at something the chairman had said.

At precisely 0800 the door to the Situation Room snapped open, and everyone sprang to their feet. President Serrano entered with his customary brisk pace, motioning for the room to take seats as he pulled out his own chair. Chief of Staff Wilkerson followed his boss like a gray ghost and took his seat behind the president's right elbow.

Serrano's normal sunny smile was absent this morning, and he wasted no time on pleasantries. His eyes sought out Secretary of Defense Kathleen Howard.

"Let's have the news, Kathy."

Howard's careworn face looked washed out by her choice of a mustard-colored pantsuit. Her brown-gray hair was barely contained in a stubby ponytail.

"Sir, we have found what appears to be a covert meaconing site on the Omani side of the Strait of Hormuz," she said, her voice glum. "This raises the possibility that the USS *Black* was in Iranian territorial waters at the time of the incident with the Iranian Navy."

The president's eyes immediately looked to his National Security Advisor for clarification. Valentina Flores squinted at the Secretary of Defense as if trying to figure out if the woman was trying to undermine her in front of her boss.

Flores addressed the president. "A meaconing attack is when navigation signals are hijacked to make a ship think it's in a different position." Her husky voice retained a tinge of her native Cuba. "It's possible that the suspect evidence uncovered by the Emerging Threats Group was accurate."

Don perked up at the mention of his team.

Since Dre Ramirez had found the partially obscured satellite recon photo and determined the *Black* had not been in international waters, her analysis had come under heavy scrutiny—hence, Flores's use of the term *suspect evidence.* Don had stayed out of the fray. His team had uncovered information and passed it along to the investigative team. His job was analysis, not policy, and he wanted to keep it that way.

"Once we realized," Howard said, her voice level, "that the USS *Black* was possibly not in international waters during the incident with the Iranian Navy, I asked to have this meeting moved up so we could address it as a team."

Despite Don's annoyance, he understood the stakes of Howard's admission: the United States had commenced hostile actions against a sovereign nation on the basis of false information.

Serrano's eyes narrowed as he studied Howard. He shifted his gaze to the CNO.

"Is it possible?" Serrano asked Admiral Teale. "Is it possible that a US Navy warship could be spoofed by a meaconing attack?"

The CNO pursed his lips. "Normally, I would say no, sir," he said. "US Navy ships have multiple inputs for satellite navigation, both military and commercial signals are used. I find it hard to believe that any Iranian operation could override a secure military GPS signal. If there was a major difference between commercial and military nav signals, the ship would take a manual bearing and verify their position."

The admiral paused. "That said, the circumstantial evidence is compelling that the *Black* was in Iranian territorial waters. The only way we could know for sure is if we were able to verify the ship's position using her onboard systems. Due to the damage on the *Black*, we can't do that.

"Bottom line, sir. We have sufficient reason to believe that we were in the wrong on this one."

Serrano had a habit of catching his upper lip with his teeth when in deep thought. It looked to Don as if he were about to work a hole into his lip.

"I see," was all the president said.

The National Security Advisor spoke: "Do we know who was behind the attack?"

Howard caught the eye of an aide who put an image on the wall screen, an aerial view of the side of a barren hill with a spectacular view overlooking the Strait of Hormuz. Using a laser pointer, she indicated a lighter patch of ground on the austere brown landscape. If she hadn't pointed out the discoloration, Don would not have given it a second glance.

"This is the meaconing site," Howard said.

The next image showed a picture underneath camouflage netting. In the dappled light, Don could make out black Pelican cases, a small generator, and a bulky instrument covered with heavy-duty switches and dials.

"The hardware is all Russian," the Secretary of Defense said. "Nothing special. Everything there is easy enough to acquire secondhand from multiple sources."

"Should we read anything into the fact that it's taking place on the Omani side of the Strait?" said the CIA director.

Howard shrugged. "If the Iranians wanted to confuse us, that makes sense. Launching an attack from their side of the Strait would confirm their guilt."

"On the other hand," said the Director of National Intelligence. "If someone besides the Iranians were responsible for this, then the Omani side of the Strait is much more accessible."

"Mr. Riley," said the president, causing Don to startle at the sound of his name. "What is the status of Hezbollah activity?"

Don jumped to his feet, feeling the stares of the entire room on him and wondering about the sudden change in conversation.

"Mr. President, we've seen Hezbollah activity in Buenos Aires and Rio, both of which we were able to hand over to the local authorities for action."

Don felt lighter, confident. The team's work on the Hezbollah threat had gone well. It felt like ETG was finally back in the swing of things after their intel prediction misses in the Persian Gulf and India. The Hezbollah threat indicators showed up in the expected channels, and his team ran them down like professionals.

"Two other Hezbollah teams were wrapped up in Panama," Don continued. "They were planning to attack the USS *Chaffee* as she transited from Third Fleet in San Diego to Mayport. Finally, we saw some activity in Lebanon, but that was handled by a joint Israeli-Jordanian special ops team."

"Did you encounter any indication that Iran had made advance plans with Hezbollah to take advantage of the situation, Mr. Riley?" the president pressed.

Don considered the question carefully. "No, sir. My assessment is that all of the Hezbollah activity was reactive in nature. We saw no indication of advance planning."

Serrano chewed on his lip, brooding, as Don took his seat.

"Until we have evidence to the contrary," the president said, "the attack on the *Black* was a trap instigated by the Iranians, designed to draw us in and to create an international incident. We will continue the bombing campaign against the Iranians."

Serrano's eyes snapped over to the Secretary of State, who was just about to take a drink of his coffee. Hahn sensed the coming question and carefully lowered the white china cup back into the saucer.

"Do we have any indications that the Iranians are willing to talk yet?" Serrano asked.

Hahn shook his gray head slowly. "No, sir. All my back-channel communications have gone unanswered to this point."

Serrano grimaced at the blank sheet of paper on his leather portfolio. The room was silent.

Finally, the president nodded. "Moving on. General Baden, you have the floor."

Dabber Baden got to his feet and moved to the lectern at the far end of the room. The screen changed to show block letters: DELIVER LIBERTY.

"Mr. President, you asked for a plan to liberate the people of Venezuela from their current government. For baseline expectations, the plan assumes catastrophic levels of starvation, no functioning food supply system, and a collapse of the medical system. Further, we assume that the Venezuelan military chooses to remain aligned with the current dictator. In other words, we would be entering hostile territory."

Baden paused as Serrano had a heated sidebar exchange with his chief of staff.

"Continue, General," the president said with a curt nod.

The screen showed a map of Venezuela and the Caribbean. Using a laser pointer, Baden highlighted the ABC Islands, to the north of the Venezuelan coast.

"The Secretary of State has gotten clearance from the Netherlands Antilles to stage from Aruba, Bonaire, and Curaçao at their international airports. We can airlift advance combat elements from the 82nd Airborne and the 101st Airborne to all three locations as forward staging bases. From those three locations, we can launch attacks against the cities of Maracaibo, Coro, and Caracas on the Venezuelan mainland.

"Mr. President, with these resources, we'll seize control of key government facilities and infrastructure such as power stations, major roads, and the ports to clear the way for the arrival of aid supplies. We've established contact with expat Venezuelan organizations ready to return to their native lands and with multiple NGOs to assist in the long-term aid effort."

As Baden spoke, the map on the screen highlighted each city and listed the assets that would be used to take the geography.

"What kind of resistance do you expect from the Venezuelan military?" Serrano asked.

"Light, Mr. President," the general replied. "The Venezuelan military is underfunded and in poor condition. Putting down civilian protests is about all they can muster these days. The Russians have provided them some assistance, but nothing we can't handle. The 18th Airborne Corps is the best in the business, sir."

The president addressed his Secretary of State.

"How confident are we that we will have real support in the region? This is not a modern-day version of gunboat diplomacy. This is a liberation, and the people in our hemisphere need to see and understand it as just that."

Hahn cleared his throat. "Mr. President, we have international support, assuming the contingency red lines are reached. The Global Engagement Center at the State Department will flood the cybersphere with the truth about the operation, but we can expect the Russians and Chinese will launch disinformation campaigns as soon as we begin any sort of troop movements."

"What's the date to begin the operation?" the president asked.

General Baden's jaw dropped. His gaze cut to the Chairman of the Joint Chiefs.

"Mr. President," the chairman said. "You asked for a contingency plan, sir. In the event that the situation in Venezuela worsened—"

The commander in chief cut him off.

"The situation in Venezuela is as bad as it's going to get on my watch, Mr. Chairman." He drove his extended index finger into the tabletop. "Operation Deliver Liberty is going to do just that—deliver liberty to the people of Venezuela.

"Cinco de Julio is Independence Day in Venezuela. This year the Fifth of July will mean something new. I want to start staging forces in the ABC Islands immediately with full operational capability by July first. Is that clear?"

"Yes, sir," the chairman said.

Serrano wasn't finished yet. "Ladies and gentlemen, I made a campaign promise that will define my tenure in office. It's time to foster democracy once again, aggressively, and we'll start by rooting out the tyrants in our own backyard. Is that understood?"

As the chorus of *yes-sirs* echoed around the table, Don's eye strayed to the screen at the front of the room. Sometime during the president's speech, General Baden had shifted the screen back to the default world map.

The current hotspots of India and Iran were shaded in red.

The United States was about to add more color to the map.

12

Panama City, Panama

With the setting sun, the gentle breeze flowing off the Pacific Ocean had faded away. The evening air was sultry, dense with moisture and hot as breath.

The humid mixture reminded Ian Thomas of Singapore. In his dozen years working in deep cover for the Minister, he had grown fond of his adopted home. Initially, the year-round equatorial weather, so different from his real home in the north, had bothered him, but Ian Thomas was nothing if not adaptable.

From his perch in the rooftop bar of the Villa Palma Hotel, Ian watched ships entering and exiting the shipping lanes for the Panama Canal. Red and green navigational buoys marking the wide channel winked in the velvety darkness.

To his left, the bright skyline of the business district glowed incandescent. To his right, the soaring structure of the Puente de las Américas spanned the width of the Canal. Beneath him, the neighborhood of San Felipe bustled with the electric energy of a Friday night. It was only nine in the evening, but crowds of young people filled the narrow streets. Somewhere in the distance, Ian heard a pulsing beat of dance music rise and fall as someone opened a door and shut it again.

He had twenty-four hours to kill before he met the ship that was scheduled to transit the Canal tomorrow evening. Ian Thomas did not need a cover for this assignment. He was to conduct an inspection of the North Korean break-bulk freighter in order to renew their insurance policy.

He gently swirled the ice in his glass and drained the last of his second vodka tonic. He motioned to his server for a refill.

Ian's cover identity had been built up through two decades of careful planning. The Minister had personally selected Ian's schooling, his choice of career, even his social circle—all with an eye toward establishing a bulletproof legend for his most valuable asset. The Minister intervened as little as possible, allowing Ian's legend to grow organically.

Ian was used sparingly, for only the most critical assignments and always reporting directly to the Minister. If he was burned, decades of planning would be wasted.

But now, Ian sensed something had changed. In the last few months, the pace and nature of his assignments from the Minister had changed dramatically.

In his mind, the visit to North Korea had been an unnecessary risk. He'd acted as a mere messenger. True, he'd needed to be firm with the Supreme Leader, but surely the Minister had other operatives with that skill set.

Same thing for the Strait of Hormuz meaconing operation. The job had taken place in Oman, not exactly a risky environment, and could have easily been covered by a less valuable asset.

And then there was India. Rarely in his career had Ian been able to draw a direct line between his covert actions and a real-world effect. The arms delivery had sparked not only the uprising in Kashmir but also a series of brutal terrorist attacks across the populous country. In his mind's eye, Ian could picture the Al-Badr leader with his thick dark hair and beard silhouetted in the headlights of the trucks. Using the weapons delivered by Ian, hundreds, maybe thousands, of people had died at the hands of that man and his followers.

He accepted a fresh drink from the server and dropped a US twenty-dollar bill on her tray. He ignored her smile and turned back to the dark ocean. The bartender had a generous pour, and he savored the bite of alcohol on his tongue.

The next two missions from the Minister had the potential to be even more destructive than India.

The Minister knew what he was doing, Ian told himself. The Minister had a plan, and Ian was part of that plan. If he began to doubt the Minister now...

He took another long sip. Down that path lay madness.

His gaze slid to the right, watching a massive Korean car carrier pass under the arch of the bridge and into the Panama Canal. From this distance, the two-hundred-meter-long freighter looked like a toy.

He sighed and drained his drink.

What he needed tonight was a vacation from his thoughts. Ian slipped his phone from his pocket and typed *nightclubs* into the search bar. He planned his evening as he scrolled.

Dinner at the Italian place a few blocks away that he liked, then troll for dessert in the local hotspots. That was the recipe to clear his mind for the tasks ahead. By tomorrow night, he'd be ready for anything the Minister could throw at him.

He looked up just as a woman topped the steps to the rooftop bar.

She was medium height and slim. Ian judged her to be mid-thirties. Her hair was pulled up, revealing a long neck, and tendrils of black hair framed her oval face. She paused on the top step, her dark eyes scanning the room, passing right over Ian. She walked to the bar, her steps sure, her body poised.

Intrigued, Ian continued to watch her. She was dressed for a night out in a silvery cocktail dress that flattered her trim figure.

She placed a matching clutch on the bar and took a deep breath as if trying to calm herself. Oddly, she radiated a feeling of strength and agitation at the same time, as if she had just successfully undergone some kind of stressful ordeal.

She spoke to the bartender, an older man dressed in a white shirt and black satin vest. He nodded, then placed a shot glass on the bar and filled it with vodka. Grey Goose, Ian's favorite.

Ian clicked off his phone.

The woman drank the shot. The bartender raised his eyebrows, asking if she wanted another. She shook her head.

On impulse, Ian signaled his server and whispered into the young woman's ear. She hurried back to the bar, where she delivered Ian's order to the bartender.

Two minutes later, the bartender placed a dark drink in a lowball glass at the woman's place. When she asked, he pointed in Ian's direction. Ian raised his empty vodka tonic in salute.

The woman stared at Ian for a full three seconds, her expression blank. He was surprised when she picked up the drink and walked across the bar to his table.

"I don't accept drinks from men I don't know," she said, placing the glass in front of Ian. Her voice was low and husky, but not angry. Up close, her dark eyes sparked with intensity.

He stood and held out his hand. "I'm Ian. Now you know me."

His hand hung in space as she stared at him. He felt like this woman was measuring him somehow. Ian resisted the urge to break eye contact.

Finally, she shook his hand with a strong, dry grip.

"Isabel Montez," she said. "But I'm not drinking that until you tell me what it is."

"Black Russian," Ian replied. "Coffee liqueur and vodka. You look like you've had quite a night. The sugar will steady your nerves."

Isabel sipped the drink and sat down.

Up close, Ian could see she had a delicacy to her features that suggested Chinese ancestry. She wore almost no makeup and minimal jewelry. Ian checked for a wedding ring. Her ring finger was naked.

Isabel Montez was attractive, but not stunning, Ian thought. Still, there was a quality about her that was different. A mixture of vulnerability and poise that captivated his attention.

"Do you want to talk about it?" he asked.

She smiled and shook her head.

"Being a single woman in my business has downsides."

"Do tell."

"Let's just say the 'Me Too' movement hasn't moved this far south yet."

Ian felt oddly protective of this woman he had just met.

"What line of business are you in?" he asked.

She sipped, letting her lips linger on the rim of the glass. "Finance. At Barker-Collins, we help people hide their money."

"From whom?"

"Everyone." A ghost of a smile graced her lips. "Tonight, I had a client who wanted to celebrate his deal in ways that I did not feel comfortable with."

"What did you do?"

Isabel's dark eyes locked with Ian's.

"I broke his nose."

"Good." Ian chuckled.

"Bad," Isabel replied. "My client is not someone who accepts no for an answer."

"I have an idea," Ian said.

"Do tell." She smiled playfully as she repeated his own phrase.

"Let me protect you." Her eyes were extraordinary, Ian thought.

Isabel drained her glass. "Why don't we start with another drink?"

Isabel insisted they walk the six blocks back to the Villa Palma Hotel. She seemed relaxed now and at ease with him, which filled Ian with anticipation for the next few hours.

His head buzzed with the effects of the alcohol he had consumed over the course of the evening. After drinks at the hotel, Ian had ordered wine pairings with each course of their meal and *fernet* as a digestif. The Italian liqueur, popular in Argentina, had a rough taste, but Isabel had said she liked it.

He was glad his identity for this mission was his normal cover. That meant he could see Isabel again.

That idea both disturbed and excited him. He had never—ever— desired a second date with a woman. Women were interchangeable to him. They were fun to catch, even more fun to bed, but after that the magic disappeared.

Ian felt this change come over him when she asked about his background. He stuck strictly to his cover identity. She nodded and watched him with a thoughtful gaze as he spoke. To Ian, it seemed as if she was making her mind up about him.

Then she told him about herself.

Isabel Montez was adopted by a wealthy South Florida lawyer and his wife. She described a happy childhood filled with private schools and the best of everything. She could not remember anything of her birth mother, but she spoke of the woman with a sense of loss that touched Ian. The person who lived deep inside the shell of Ian Thomas understood that pain of disconnection all too well.

That man is gone, Ian told himself. That man no longer exists.

Somehow, in the space of only a few hours, this remarkable woman had pierced the many layers of Ian Thomas to an armored core that he was surprised to find still existed.

These were the distracting thoughts that ran through Ian's head as they strolled along a deserted sidewalk. Far away, he could hear the muted thump of dance music and distant laughter like tinkling music on the wind. The breeze off the Pacific had freshened, and Isabel shivered. She took his arm, holding her body against his as they walked in step.

This section of San Felipe had a sleepy, residential feel. The bungalows lining the street had well-manicured lawns and showed no lighted windows at this hour. Every ten meters, a mature palm tree adorned the tiled sidewalk.

Isabel pulled him to a stop just short of a streetlamp. Her hand ran up his chest and snaked around the back of his neck, pulling him toward her. Her lips found his in the shadowy light, tentatively touching.

Ian wrapped both arms around her, crushing her body against his. A wave of heat flushed through him as her body responded to his touch.

Dimly, he was aware of car headlights turning down the street, then the roar of an engine as the vehicle accelerated. It was only when the car screeched to a stop next to the couple that Ian realized they were in trouble.

He reacted on instinct, pushing Isabel behind him.

The car door swung open, and the dark shape of a man started to get out. Ian kicked at the door, slamming the metal doorjamb against the man's head with driving force. He stepped forward, slipping his hand into the man's jacket and finding the expected weapon in a shoulder holster.

His hand closed on the grip of a Beretta 9mm. He could tell from the weight and resistance coming out of the holster that the sidearm had a suppressor attached.

The man seized Ian's gun hand. Ian hammered his nose with the butt of an open hand. The man's head snapped back, and his body went slack.

There was a second man in the back seat. His door was open, and he stood next to the car. Ian saw the dull gleam of another weapon sweeping across the roof of the vehicle.

He dropped to the ground and fired three shots underneath the car into the lower legs of his standing opponent.

"*Alto!*" The driver of the vehicle stood over Ian, weapon drawn. "Stop!"

Ian assessed his situation in a split second and did not like his odds. The driver was too far away from him for Ian to sweep his legs, and this close, the man could not miss.

On the other hand, the driver hadn't pulled the trigger yet, so they obviously wanted Ian alive.

Ian took his finger off the trigger and laid the weapon on the ground.

On the other side of the car, the man he had shot in the legs moaned and cursed in Spanish. Next to Ian, the thug he had knocked unconscious stirred. The driver's shooting stance was solid, and the muzzle of his weapon did not waver.

The Minister would not be pleased.

Out of the corner of his eye, Ian saw a blur of silver-gray move with fluid grace. Isabel's front kick connected with the butt of the driver's gun hand, knocking the muzzle skyward even as the weapon discharged.

Ian felt the bullet pass over his head and heard it shatter a tile in the sidewalk a meter past him.

The driver recovered quickly, bringing the weapon down again.

But that split second was all Ian needed. He snatched up the Beretta, leveled it, and pumped off three rounds.

The knock on the door of the suite echoed through the open space.

Ian surfaced from sleep slowly. He reached his hand across the bed, searching for Isabel's body, but found only cold sheets.

He blinked his eyes open, surprised to see sunlight streaming through the windows. He checked his watch.

Eight o'clock.

Isabel was gone. His own clothes still littered the floor and the furniture, dropped wherever he had stripped them from his body. Last night, her clothes had been tangled with his, but they were gone now.

The knock sounded again. Ian rose, snatched up a bathrobe, and stumbled to the door.

A young man with carefully combed dark hair and dressed in a hotel uniform stood in the hall, holding a tray.

"Room service," he said in a thick accent.

Ian opened the door.

"I didn't order this," he said. His head ached from all he had drunk the previous night.

"Ms. Montez ordered it for you," came the reply.

Ian smiled and threw the door wide.

His first sip of coffee was glorious. The acidic bite cut through the fog of sleep as he walked to the window. The sun rode high above the horizon, and the streets were alive with tourists.

He checked his watch again. He didn't have to meet the North Korean freighter until 10:00 p.m. tonight. He had a whole day to spend with Isabel...

Ian called the front desk and asked to be connected to Isabel's room.

"I'm sorry, Mr. Thomas, but Ms. Montez checked out an hour ago."

13

Captain Kang Sok-ju looked out the bridge windows of the North Korean merchant vessel *Chong Chon Gang* toward the still, moonlit waters of Miraflores Lake. The serenity of the scene did nothing to still his frantic thoughts.

Captain Kang had a good life. His position provided him with an excellent salary and plenty of disposable income. As part of the Supreme Leader's famed "ghost fleet," he had achieved a special status in North Korean society and a level of trust with the Kim dynasty that had endured the leadership change between father and son.

Although his job took him away from home for weeks at a time, he was still happily married to the same woman after twenty-five years. Their only child, a daughter, was in school in Pyongyang. He would find her a good match in the Party to ensure her continued welfare once he and his wife were gone. His job also allowed him to bring back Western goods into the country to use as bribes to maintain his status.

Yes, he had a good life. He wanted to *keep* that good life. But moments like this reminded him of the price he was paying for his silent cooperation.

Many times in his career he had been directed to perform certain duties for the State. Usually, the assignments were minor, used to avoid UN sanctions. The most common task was to transport North Korean coal to the Russian port of Nakhodka, where it was unloaded and reloaded onto Russian freighters for sale in Japan or South Korea.

Occasionally, he was told to bring a passenger or a piece of cargo into a foreign port. Once, he had even transported weapons to Havana.

But all that history paled in comparison to this mission.

The ship waited in the second and final Miraflores Lock of the Panama Canal, allowing water levels to equalize before the ship continued its journey north to the Atlantic Ocean.

Captain Kang's fingers fumbled with the zipper of his breast pocket for the letter.

When the *Chong Chon Gang* had been ordered to take on special cargo at the Russian port of Vladivostok prior to his voyage to Venezuela, he'd thought little of the orders. This kind of thing happened in his line of work, and he had made the run to Venezuela many times carrying all manner of cargo—both legal and illegal.

They had docked at a distant pier in Vladivostok, and he and his crew were restricted to the ship by a contingent of armed men on the dock.

A cohort of dock workers loaded his cargo without help from Kang's crew. They left on deck a pallet of six barrel-shaped objects, each about the diameter of a fifty-five-gallon oil drum but half again as long, and wrapped in opaque plastic. Another two dozen crates, labeled "machine parts," were placed in his cargo hold.

Kang had been around the water long enough to recognize the care with which these men loaded the cargo. The same kind of care that was taken when loading weapons on a naval ship.

His concern deepened the following afternoon when a team in matching coveralls came aboard and installed a new piece of equipment on the stern of the *Chong Chon Gang*.

When Kang protested to the crew leader, he was greeted with stony ignorance. The installation team departed four hours later, leaving a canvas-covered box on the starboard stern of his ship. He was informed at the last moment that two of the men from the installation team were to sail with his crew but had no duties other than to stand watch in the hold over the cargo.

Kang kept up the fiction with his crew about the last-minute cargo and the mysterious box on his stern, but secretly he worried. Just last year, a North Korean freighter attempting to transit the Panama Canal with a load of weapons for Cuba had been detained for months. One nosey inspector and Kang could find himself at the center of an international incident.

The Supreme Leader did not look kindly on ship captains who caused international incidents.

The paper crinkled as he withdrew it from his pocket.

Kang's concern had only deepened when the *Chong Chon Gang* sighted the Pacific side of the Panama Canal. The Bridge of the Americas at the port of Balboa was in sight when one of the men who guarded the special cargo had appeared on the bridge.

He'd told Captain Kang to expect a passenger at any moment.

The Airbus H135 helicopter had shown up only five minutes later. It circled the *Chong Chon Gang*, then hovered over the main deck. A man rappelled to the deck, and the helo departed.

The man had introduced himself as Ian Thomas, a risk assessment manager for Global Risk Ltd in Singapore. Kang was aware of the company name, but in all his years of service, he had never been subjected to an inspection.

Ian Thomas had the trappings of a business professional—stylish haircut, soft hands, good clothes—but his attitude was hard, and the way he moved suggested he knew how to take care of himself. The two men who had shipped with the *Chong Chon Gang* from Vladivostok treated him with extreme deference.

By way of introduction, Thomas had given Captain Kang the letter he now held under the small reading lamp next to the captain's chair on the bridge.

Kang read it for the thousandth time.

It was only a few lines, addressed to him personally and signed by the personal secretary to the Supreme Leader. The language was flowery, but the meaning clear.

Cooperate. Ask no questions. Say nothing.

The lock opened, and Kang ordered the ship to move forward. Just as the *Chong Chon Gang* cleared the lock, a low voice spoke in the captain's ear, startling him.

"My men will be working at the stern of the ship, Captain," Ian Thomas said. "I need you to keep the crew away from us. For safety reasons."

Kang's mouth was dry. This man unsettled him. It was the way he looked at people, Kang decided. As if they didn't exist.

He nodded.

"Maintain a slow speed and steady course," Thomas continued. "You may hear a splash. Pay no attention."

Kang found his voice. "I'll join you. So my men will not ask questions."

Thomas shrugged and glided away as silently as he had arrived.

When Kang arrived at the stern of his ship, the work lights were darkened and the men were using night-vision goggles. In the dimness, he saw that Thomas's men had uncovered the six barrel-shaped devices and lined them up next to the piece of equipment installed on the stern of his ship.

One of the men used a knife to strip off the plastic covering from the barrels. The second man removed the canvas covering from the table-shaped installation and threw a knife switch. A light on the junction box glowed green.

"Ready, sir," he said to Thomas.

"Stand by," Thomas replied, his attention focused on a tablet in his hands. The illumination cast a glow across his sharp features.

Kang stepped to one side so he could see the screen. It was a chart with the position of the *Chong Chon Gang* represented as a blue marble. The blue marble closed on a fixed red dot.

"Load," Thomas said.

The table tilted up until it was perpendicular to the deck of the ship. Mechanical arms extended and gripped the first barrel, then the table turned until it was parallel with the deck again. The arms retracted.

"Ready," the operator reported.

Kang saw the light on the tablet blink. "Release," Thomas said.

The table tilted up. The barrel rolled into Miraflores Lake. Kang heard a splash as the object hit the water. He peered over the fantail, but the barrel had already sunk out of sight.

For the next six hours, they repeated the process. Kang witnessed barrels going in the water at the Pedro Miguel locks, on either side of the Puente Centenario Bridge, and before Gamboa.

By the time the *Chong Chon Gang* reached the Chagres River south of Isla Barbacoa, it was just beginning to get light. When the men stripped the plastic covering off the final barrel before loading it on the table, Kang spied Cyrillic writing on the side of the device.

Captain Kang suddenly wanted no part of this operation. He wanted to hide in his cabin and pretend none of this had ever happened.

When the last barrel went in the water, Thomas snapped out an order to his men, and they went to work unbolting the launcher from the ship's deck. Together, the three of them pushed the entire loading device into the water.

Thomas turned to Captain Kang. In the predawn murk, Kang could see a sheen of sweat on the man's face.

"Congratulations, Captain," Thomas said. "You passed your inspection. When we clear the lock, steer a course for Caracas, Venezuela, at best possible speed."

Kang felt the skin on the back of his neck prickle as if someone had blown a cool breeze over his nape. Not trusting his voice, he nodded and turned away.

"Captain?"

Kang turned. He dragged his eyes up to meet Thomas's gaze.

Thomas put out his hand. "I'll need that letter back," he said.

As Kang watched, the other man slipped a lighter from his pocket and touched a flame to the letter. He toyed with the paper in the freshening morning breeze, then let it flutter over the side.

Thomas sucked in a breath and blew it out as if to say, "Job well done!"

Kang turned away again.

"Captain?"

He turned back slowly. Would this torture never end?

"What?" Kang said.

"You must be very proud of your daughter."

Kang swallowed. "Yes."

Thomas leveled a stare at him that made Kang want to sink to his knees and beg for mercy.

"That'll be all, Captain."

14

The Kremlin
Moscow, Russia

Vitaly Luchnik closed the cover on the intelligence report he was reading. Despite the surge of pleasure inside, he kept his face impassive. Without speaking, he stood and turned his back on the two men seated in leather armchairs opposite his wide desk.

Outside, in the closed courtyard, piles of dirty snow melted in the watery spring sunshine.

"You're certain this information is accurate?" he asked.

"Yes, Mr. President," answered Vladimir Federov, his Director of the Federal Security Service, or FSB.

It was a stupid question. Federov was nothing if not thorough.

Luchnik closed his eyes, basking in the warm glow of satisfaction at his enemies' misfortune. A mistake of this magnitude could sink an American administration—and give him room to maneuver on the world stage.

"Who do we have to thank for this gift?" Luchnik asked.

"The Americans discovered a hidden transmitter on the Omani side of the Strait of Hormuz, Mr. President," Federov said. He had an unnaturally high voice for a man of his size, and he spoke with distinct, clipped syllables. "Our informant says they believe the site was used to transmit false GPS data to ships in the Strait."

"Was it the Iranians?" Luchnik asked.

"All of the hardware recovered is readily available on the black market. Russian military surplus. Nothing can be traced directly back to us."

Luchnik pondered the phrasing of the comment, the way the FSB man had emphasized the word *directly*. He turned around to find Federov frowning.

"What is it?" he asked.

"There was a piece of equipment missing, sir," Federov continued. "There was no signal generator found. That would give us a clue about who was behind this attack."

Next to Federov, Foreign Minister Irimov squirmed in his chair.

"You have something to add, Sergey?" Luchnik asked.

"Mr. President, it doesn't matter who was behind the attack. The Iranians claim that the US ship was in their territorial waters. We should support the Iranian position. Place the Americans on the defensive."

Luchnik pinched his lip, still thinking about Federov's hesitation. "Could the Iranians have done this?"

Federov shrugged. "Possibly, with help."

"Did we help them?" Luchnik pressed.

"My inquiries have found no current operations."

Which was not the same as *nyet*, Luchnik thought. Federov was hedging his bets, but why? Had one of his many covert operatives in Iran taken some initiative?

Normally, the idea of unauthorized actions would merit swift rebuke, but in this instance Luchnik would allow it. An American president battling for his political skin in the first year of his term was a gift from heaven.

"Sergey," Luchnik said, "issue a strong statement of support for the Iranian claim, and hint that we will continue to supply them with weapons. Let's see how President Serrano deals with that."

Federov cleared his throat. "There is another matter we should discuss, Mr. President."

Luchnik, still enjoying the afterglow of his unexpected victory, nodded for Federov to continue.

"We have intelligence that the Americans are planning a military buildup in the Caribbean," Fedorov said. "It could be just saber-rattling with the Venezuelans, but it could also be preparation for military action."

Luchnik's mouth fell open in surprise. The Americans were staging to invade Venezuela? Serrano had campaigned on the issue, but would he actually be stupid enough to go through with it?

For the first time, Luchnik wished he had met the new American president in person to take the measure of the man. He swiveled his gaze to Irimov.

"What do you know about this, Sergey?"

The foreign minister shrugged his shoulders and brushed his lapel with a dismissive gesture.

"It is a show, Mr. President," he said confidently. "Serrano's poll numbers are terrible. He means to scare the Venezuelans so he can distract the public from his failures in the Middle East."

Luchnik reseated himself behind his desk. He tapped his fingers on the desktop.

"What's the status of our weapons sales to Venezuela?" he asked Federov.

The FSB chief shook his head. "They've stopped paying, so we've stopped shipping. The Venezuelan Army holds thousands of shoulder-fired missiles and small arms, but a full-scale American invasion—"

"There will not be an American invasion!" Irimov countered in a heated voice. "Every few years, the Americans resurrect the Venezuelan problem when it is convenient. I doubt President Serrano would be foolish enough to invade a sovereign country. This is a political move, plain and simple."

Luchnik watched the interplay between his two most senior advisers. Although he was inclined to agree with Irimov, the Russian Federation had invested years and millions of rubles into propping up the current Venezuelan dictator as a way to provoke the United States.

Too many rubles, he decided. The foreign minister was right. Bombing Iran was one thing, but Serrano would never have the stones to invade another country. His political enemies would eat him alive.

"No more weapons unless the Venezuelans can pay." Luchnik shot a glance at Federov. "And, Vladimir, make sure there are no unauthorized covert initiatives this time."

The FSB chief nodded curtly and got to his feet to leave.

Luchnik stood and shook hands with both men.

"The defense minister will be coming to you this week for permission to launch a cyber campaign in Bosnia," Federov informed him. "I told him I would mention it to you."

"Perfect." Luchnik smiled as he walked the men to the door. The smile remained as he strolled back to his desk, pausing at the wall map.

Idly, his finger traced the border between Ukraine and his country. He'd ordered the map maker to paint a thick area of cross-hatched red and white over the disputed Donbass region in the southeast.

Things were finally turning in his favor, Luchnik mused. The misfortunes of the new American president might be just the distraction he needed to execute the next stage in his plan to rebuild the Russian Federation to her former glory.

The weak sunlight coming through the window brightened suddenly, making the crimson shading of the Russian Federation glow.

15

Barking Sands Tactical Underwater Range (BARSTUR)
Kauai, Hawaiian Islands

The photonics mast of the USS *Idaho* broke the surface of the Pacific Ocean. The monitor showed a clear night and modest seas.

Lieutenant Janet Everett, stationed at the AN/BVS-1 control station, made a careful 360-degree sweep, first in low-power visual looking for lights of any nearby ships, then an infrared pass. Her eyes stayed glued to the monitor as she manipulated the optics.

"No close contacts, Captain," she reported.

"Very well, Officer of the Deck," the captain replied from his position in front of the auxiliary panel where he had been monitoring her actions.

At moments like this, Janet sometimes wanted to pinch herself just to make sure it was all real. The *Idaho*, the newest of the *Virginia*-class Block IV boats, handled like a dream. Everything in the control room was practically brand-new. Her last command before going back to work for Don Riley in Washington, DC, had been a *Los Angeles*–class boat with an older fire control system and old-style periscopes that penetrated the pressure hull and ran from the top of the submarine sail to the keel.

With the Integrated Modular Mast, "dancing with the gray lady"—the submariner term for moving around in circles with one eye glued to the periscope eyepiece—was a thing of the past. In fact, the new masts, which telescoped out of the sail like a retractable car antenna, allowed for all kinds of changes. The control room was now one level down from the sail, which left much more space to spread out the tactical stations. To her, the *Idaho* control room looked more like a set from a sci-fi movie than a submarine.

Janet maneuvered the camera to the north. The black bulk of Kauai loomed out of the ocean, blocking the stars. She could make out the glow of distant lights on the horizon. That would be Barking Sands Missile Test Range, she knew.

"Quartermaster, I hold a red navigation light on bearing zero-two-one," Janet said.

"Coincides with Makahu'ena Point Lighthouse, ma'am," Petty Officer Randler replied. She had a high-pitched, squeaky voice that contrasted with the mostly male voices in the control room, but nobody minded. Randler was the best quartermaster on the boat, hands down, and Janet was glad the young petty officer was assigned to her watch section.

The XO appeared at her side. "Any sign of our friends?" he asked.

Lieutenant Commander Ashton was a balding man in his mid-thirties who looked at least a decade older. He wore a walrus mustache and tended to pat his belly when he was thinking. Right now, his fingers beat a rapid tattoo on his midsection.

"We still have four minutes, sir," Janet pointed out. "Rendezvous is at 0500."

"I'm going to see if sonar has picked up the *Warner* yet," the XO said in a tense voice.

This was the final day of Operation CALYPSO, a SEAL insertion/extraction mission on the Barking Sands Tactical Underwater Range. Yesterday morning, the USS *John Warner*, also a *Virginia*-class sub, had completed the insertion part of the exercise by carrying the *Manta*, a prototype mini-submarine, into the op area and launching the unit for a shore-based SEAL exercise.

Unlike previous versions of a SEAL Delivery Vehicle, which required the passengers to be suited in SCUBA gear, the *Manta* was a dry submersible, capable of carrying a half-dozen combat-equipped SEALs. The craft was equipped with a lock-out chamber in the rear and a bulbous window in front for the pilot. According to the specs, which Janet had studied, it had a range of almost fifty miles and a top speed of ten knots. It even had a pair of retractable mechanical arms in the bow.

The exercise gave both the *Idaho* and the *Warner* the chance to conduct littoral ops and get familiar with a new tool in the Navy's arsenal, but there was more to it than that. They needed to complete the operation undetected by a submerged opponent. A very quiet submerged opponent.

Yesterday, the *Idaho* had hunted—and found—the *Warner*. Today, *Idaho* was the prey, and *Warner* was the hunter.

Commander Lannier, captain of the *Idaho*, had every intention of making sure the recovery of the SEAL mini-sub this morning went undetected by their opponent. Sub captains were a hyper-competitive lot. Janet would lay odds that her CO had a friendly bet riding on the outcome of the next few hours.

Which made her wonder why she was acting as OOD for this evolution.

Janet had been part of the *Idaho* crew for only a few months. She had completed her OOD requalification quickly, but there were certainly more experienced officers in the wardroom than her. In fact, most COs would take the conn themselves for a high-risk evolution like docking a submersible onto the back of their submarine.

But Lannier had kept the normal watch rotation in effect, and this was Janet's watch.

She tamped down a thrill. If Dre and Michael could see her now. They'd understand she'd made the right choice.

"What's my bearing to our contact, quartermaster?" Janet asked.

As usual, Randler was on the ball. "Contact should bear two-seven-niner, ma'am."

Janet spun the optics to the correct bearing and went to 10x magnitude.

"OOD," the captain said quietly. "Let's drop our speed. I don't want to throw up a rooster tail."

"Aye, sir," Janet replied. "Pilot, all ahead one-third. To Maneuvering, make turns for four knots."

She understood the captain's concern and chided herself for not thinking of it. To get detected by the *Warner* visually would be nothing short of embarrassing.

Both the *Virginia*-class subs were so quiet there were only a few ways either could be found. The op order called for the SEAL team to attempt to make contact with the sub by flashing light, but if that failed, they would resort to radio. If the *Warner* had their ESM mast up, they could detect the transmission and get a bearing on the *Idaho*.

The other way the *Idaho* could be detected was through a random sound. Known in the world of sonar as a "transient," a slammed hatch, a dropped wrench, or a sloppy docking by the pilot of the *Manta* was all it would take to give away the *Idaho*'s position. That's how they'd managed to find the *Warner* yesterday morning.

The optics rode higher out of the water.

"Mind your depth, pilot," Janet snapped.

"Aye, ma'am," the petty officer replied. "I'm a bit heavy in the front. Adjusting my trim."

Maintaining a level trim in a ship longer than a football field was as much art as science. Hundreds of tanks—wastewater, freshwater, fuel, trash, bilges—filled and emptied every hour of every day, creating a constantly changing equation. When the ship had some speed on, the control surfaces did most of the work in keeping the submarine level. But when the ship slowed, the bow planes and stern planes were less effective.

As the clock in the lower right corner of her monitor turned to 0500, Janet saw a pip of light on her viewscreen.

"I have contact, Captain," Janet called out.

"Very well, OOD," Lannier said. She could hear the relief in his voice. There would be no need for a radio transmission after all. "You have permission to reply in kind."

Janet brought up the screen that activated the LED light in the photonics mast. Using the touchpad, she tapped out M-A-R-C-O in Morse code.

The XO appeared at her elbow. "Jesus, Everett, did you learn Morse code just for this op?"

Janet smiled but kept her eyes on the screen. "Girl Scouts, XO, but I did have to practice to refresh my memory."

There was a pause on the other end, then the reply flashed out.

Janet read out the letters: "P-O-L-O. Quartermaster, verify that countersign."

"That checks out, ma'am," Randler said.

Janet went back to work on the Morse code keypad. "R-2-0-0-0-C-0-9-0-S-5-D-1-5-0." Range, two thousand yards, course 090, speed five knots, depth 150 feet. She'd just drawn a roadmap for the SEALs to find them. The docking part was up to the skill of their pilot.

The light in the darkness flashed an acknowledgment.

"Transmission acknowledged, Captain," Janet said. "Request permission to go deep, sir?"

"Go deep, OOD. Let's hope these guys know how to be quiet."

"Pilot, make your depth one-five-zero feet. To Maneuvering, make turns for five knots." The image from the photonics mast dipped underwater. "Lowering the mast."

Janet waited for the acknowledgments to her orders to flow in, then verified the ship's course, speed, and depth for herself.

The XO hovered behind the row of sonar consoles in the control room.

"No sign of the *Warner*, sir," the sonar supervisor reported, rolling his eyes at the XO's extra attention.

Janet studied the sonar waterfall display, a visual measure of broadband noise in the ocean around them. The ocean was a noisy place, and the constantly updating information flowed down the screen like watery static with whitish blips indicating possible contacts.

The XO sidled up to Janet, his hands in the pockets of his dark blue underway jumpsuit. "So how long do we have to wait for..."

Janet shot a look at her quartermaster.

"Rendezvous in sixteen minutes, ma'am," Randler said.

"Well done, Randler," Janet said.

The young woman beamed. "Thank you, ma'am."

The minutes dragged by. In her mind's eye, Janet envisioned the submersible driving through the dark water, lights blazing, the pilot squinting to catch a glimpse of the *Idaho*. You would think it would be difficult to miss an object the size of a nuclear submarine, but the Pacific was a great big ocean.

Just as with communications, the op order called the SEAL team to use visual means to locate and dock with the *Idaho*, but they carried a backup short-range sonar if they lost their way. Use of the sonar by the submersible could also give away their position if the *Warner* was close by.

Focus on the things you can control, Janet told herself.

"OOD, contact bearing two-six-five, range three hundred meters and closing," the sonar supe reported.

"Let's hope these guys don't mess up our paint job," the XO muttered.

The mini-sub would parallel the course and speed of the *Idaho*, then use their thrusters to maneuver sideways over the moving submarine until they had positioned their docking ring over the engine room hatch. A telescoping collar would magnetically seal their ship to the hull.

Watching the waterfall display, Janet saw a sharp white blip burst onto the screen.

"Conn, Sonar, the *Manta* is docked."

Janet sensed the extra drag on the ship, and she noted they had lost nearly two knots in speed.

The copilot said, "From the aft hatch, they have the all-clear signal from the submersible. Request permission to open the hatch."

The CO nodded at Janet.

"Open the after hatch and let our visitors on board," she said.

Janet saw the indicator for the after-hatch shift from green to red, indicating the hatch had been opened. She waited for the team to report the new status.

Instead, she heard the voice of the engineering officer of the watch over the 1MC. "Reactor scram."

For a second, Janet's brain stuck in neutral. With the reactor offline, they had no steam for propulsion. She clocked a glance at the XO. Was it possible he would run a drill during a submersible docking?

His face said he was just as shocked as her.

Already the ship had lost speed and the deck tilted upward as the weight of the mini-sub weighed down the aft end of the ship. The air conditioning that normally blasted into the space fell silent, and the temperature in control rose.

"Adjusting trim," the pilot said. Janet knew the automatic action would be to blow water from the tanks to restore buoyancy as quickly as possible. But that would be noisy.

"Pilot, override automatic trim control," she snapped out. "Pump from after trim."

"Recommend we blow tanks, ma'am," he replied. "It'll move more water."

"Negative, pilot," Janet ordered. "Pump."

"Pump from aft trim, aye, ma'am," he replied, but the tone of the chief petty officer's words told her that he disagreed with the order. "Three degree up bubble, down to two knots, one-eight-zero feet and sinking."

"XO," said the captain, "lay aft. Get that hatch shut, but do not detach the submersible unless I say so."

"Two hundred feet and dropping," the pilot called out. "Ten thousand out. Loss of steerageway. We're dead in the water, ma'am." His report was laced with accusation.

Captain Lannier stepped close to Janet. "What's your plan, Lieutenant?" he said in a low voice that would not be overheard by the rest of the control room.

"The submersible weighs forty K, sir, call it forty-two with a bunch of SEALs onboard," Janet said. "The specs say she's good to four hundred feet, so I'm gonna lighten up our tail and give the engine room some time to get the reactor back online."

"Two-three-zero feet," the diving officer said. "Four degree up bubble."

"Acknowledged, pilot," Janet said. "Keep pumping."

Lannier's gray eyes lanced into her. "Why don't you blow from aft trim? It's faster, and it's what your pilot recommends."

"Because it's noisy, sir," Janet replied. "If the *Warner*'s anywhere nearby, she'll hear us."

A muscle twitched in Lannier's jaw. "Carry on, OOD, but make sure you know your limits. Don't get us in extremis."

"Aye, sir," Janet replied.

"Two-eight-zero feet," the pilot said, his voice making it clear he thought Janet was making a mistake. "Five degree up bubble."

"Pump five K into forward trim, pilot," Janet said.

"You want to make us heavier, OOD?" The pilot turned in his chair. He shot a look at the captain, who ignored him.

"Five K to forward trim, aye, ma'am."

An excruciating minute passed. She wanted to call the engine room, but that would only distract the watch officer from getting the nuclear reactor restarted. Let the man do his job, she told herself, and you do yours.

Janet felt the deck tilt down slightly. Or maybe that was her imagination.

"Three-two-zero feet and dropping. Three degree up bubble."

"How much have you pumped out so far, pilot?" Janet asked.

"Thirty-eight K, ma'am," came the reply.

"Stop pumping at forty-two," she ordered. Janet knew if she overcompensated, they'd just float up like a cork, which was just as bad.

"Forty-two K out of after trim," the pilot said. "Three-four-zero feet. Rate of descent is slowing."

Janet had set 350 feet as her limit before she took more drastic action.

The submarine's depth gauge read 347 feet. It blinked. The deck tilted down to a normal angle.

"Steady at three-four-seven feet," the pilot announced. "Trim is good."

The intercom crackled. "Conn, Maneuvering. Ready to answer all bells."

Janet gripped the side of the console, her knees weak with relief.

"All ahead one-third," Janet said.

The deck under her feet thrummed with power. She blew out a long breath.

"Officer of the Deck, engine room answers one-third bell," the pilot announced.

Janet felt the ship begin to move forward.

"OOD, new submerged contact bearing one-seven-eight!" the sonar supervisor announced. "Designate contact Sierra one-six. It's the *Warner*, ma'am, and I don't think they know we're here."

Janet looked at her CO.

"Captain?" she asked. "We still have a few hours left in the operation."

Lannier smiled.

"Let's go hunting, Lieutenant."

16

Yokosuka, Japan

Rear Admiral Chip Sharratt snapped a perfect salute as he stepped onto the quarterdeck of the USS *Blue Ridge*. It was five minutes before nine o'clock in the morning, and already he could feel sweat popping on his brow. It promised to be another hot and humid Japanese day.

Sharratt entered the interior of the *Blue Ridge*, making his way swiftly through the busy ship. The lead vessel in a class of only two, the USS *Blue Ridge* was a Command, Control, Communications, Computer, and Intelligence—or C4I—platform. In 1960, she was conceived and commissioned as an amphibious command ship. Today, she was basically a floating computer.

At two-thirds the length of the *Enterprise*, *Blue Ridge* was among the largest ships in the Seventh Fleet. She carried no offensive weapons and possessed only minimal defensive capability. Instead, her deck bristled with satellite communication domes and antenna to support her primary mission as the nerve center of the United States naval presence in the eastern hemisphere.

LCC-19 was also the oldest operational ship in the US Navy. In her last major refit, *Blue Ridge* acquired the Consolidated Afloat Networks and Enterprise Services, CANES, which ensured the ship would remain viable for at least another decade, at which time she would be seventy years old.

Sharratt arrived at the office of Commander, Seventh Fleet, slightly out of breath and nervous as a plebe heading to a uniform inspection.

His summer whites were spotless, his belt buckle shined, the edges of his white shoes freshly dressed. He even sported a fresh haircut.

In a way, the idea that he was headed to an inspection was partly true. A lifetime ago, Vice Admiral Sal Mondelli, now Commander, Seventh Fleet, had conducted a daily inspection of Midshipman fourth-class Chip Sharratt.

In the rigid Academy hierarchy, first-years, or plebes, were trained by the class two years their senior, known as second-classmen. Every day, Mondelli grilled young Sharratt on topics ranging from his knowledge of weapons systems to uniform inspections, to memorization of trivia such as menus and schedules.

Mondelli had high standards, and Sharratt had worked hard to meet them. The two men had a respect for one another that had begun over a quarter century ago on the banks of the Severn River.

Sharratt was counting on that mutual respect for this visit. When he'd returned from the FONOP in the Strait of Taiwan, Mondelli had delivered a withering rebuke over the near-miss incident between the *Enterprise* and the Chinese destroyer.

Now he was back with an ask of his boss. A big ask.

He knocked, waited for Mondelli's normally gruff, "Come!" then entered.

The admiral's office on board the USS *Blue Ridge* was spacious. One corner of the room was designated as a sitting area with overstuffed armchairs surrounding a small coffee table. In the corner was a brick fireplace—the subject of more than a few jokes—but also a testament to the era of the ship's designers.

Besides the admiral's desk, which swam with reports and notes, there was a conference table with seating for eight and a flat-screen monitor fixed to the wall opposite the desk.

His boss was on the phone when Sharratt entered. Mondelli gripped the receiver and scowled as he listened.

"Yes, sir," Mondelli said. "I under—yessir. I do understand, and I will pass that along, sir. Goodbye."

Mondelli hung up and clenched his eyes shut as he pinched the bridge of his nose. Then he punched a button on his desk phone.

"Coffee for two, please," he said into the speakerphone. He got up from his desk and moved to the conference table, waving Sharratt to a seat as he walked. The admiral's fingers plucked at the nap of the dark blue tablecloth.

"I know why you're here, and the answer's no, Chip," he said.

Sharratt's carefully prepared argument was getting shot down out of the gate. He jumped in with both feet. "Sir, I believe you should ask to deploy the *Enterprise* to the Arabian Sea."

"No," Mondelli said.

"But sir, you haven't heard what I have to—"

"Goddammit, Chip, why can't you comprehend the shit storm you stirred up in the Strait?" The admiral pointed to his desk. "That phone call was the CNO, chewing me out again about your near miss in the middle of the fucking Strait of Taiwan! He's still getting harassed by State because the Chinese ambassador won't let it go. Now they want an apology for our reckless behavior and assurance that proper advance notice will be given for any future operations."

"We're not going to do any of that, right, sir?" Sharratt asked.

"Of course not!" Mondelli shouted.

The pinched features of Mondelli's narrow face were scarlet with anger. He was a slight man, and the wide, gold-covered admiral's shoulder boards on his uniform looked like wings on his slender frame. He rapped his fist on the table.

"You decided to play chicken with a thirteen-billion-dollar aircraft carrier in the Strait of Taiwan. That is not a smart career move, Rear Admiral Sharratt."

Sharratt kept his mouth shut. Mondelli was a good man in a bad position, a position that Sharratt had placed him in. Mondelli did not believe that shit rolled downhill. He believed that it was the job of a superior officer to answer for the actions of his command and deal with it professionally. The fact that he even mentioned the CNO's call indicated to Sharratt that the reprimand had been severe.

Besides, Sharratt suspected if his boss had been given the same set of circumstances, he might have taken the same action. Even if he couldn't say that out loud.

"Look," Mondelli said, "the drive-by was one thing. They're just as much at fault over that as we are, but did you have to arrange to have a P-8 intel platform do a flyover at that exact moment? All that did was up the ante. They violated Taiwanese air space just to show we hadn't gotten the best of them."

"Why are they making such a fuss about this op?" Sharratt asked. "I did drive-bys at Mischief Reef and Subi in the Spratlys. All we got was the normal 'get off my lawn' messages."

"I don't know, and I don't care," Mondelli said. "But I don't need you pushing the envelope out here. You're driving a brand-new aircraft carrier. If you so much as scratch the paint, Congress is going to have us both in jail."

Mondelli's color was back to normal. He took a deep breath and blew it out. "Okay, ass-chewing is over. Let's get back to the matter at hand."

Sharratt leaned forward, elbows on the table, and spoke in an urgent voice as he laid out all the reasons to deploy the *Enterprise* to the Gulf.

His boss steepled his fingers and let him talk. Sharratt had finished just as a culinary specialist entered the office carrying a tray with a pot of coffee and two cups.

"Leave the pot, Petty Officer Wagner," Mondelli said. He poured two cups of coffee and pushed one at Sharratt. Both men ignored the cream and sugar. Mondelli sipped his drink.

"Are you finished?" Mondelli asked.

Sharratt toyed with his cup. "Yes, sir."

"Good." Mondelli refilled his cup. "The answer is a hard no." He held up his hand at Sharratt's immediate reaction. "But not for the reasons you think."

The admiral went to his desk and fished around in a sea of paper for a message. He passed a page to Sharratt.

It was a diplomatic notification that the Chinese were moving the timing of the PLA annual joint military exercises. Normally, the exercises were timed to coincide with Taiwan's Han Kuang drills, the annual combat readiness exercises against a Chinese invasion, which occurred in the spring.

China was moving their combat readiness exercises up to January, only a few weeks before the Lunar New Year celebration and in the middle of winter.

"Damn peculiar," Mondelli said. "The Lunar New Year is the biggest event on the Chinese calendar. The whole frigging country shuts down for an entire week. Why run an exercise before a national holiday?"

"That's almost five months away, Admiral," Sharratt said. "We could be back from the Gulf by then."

"The *Enterprise* is not needed in the Gulf, Chip," the admiral said. "Two carriers is more than enough airpower to pound the shit out of the Iranians —and that's before you include the Air Force's contribution."

Mondelli shook his head. "Let's keep our powder dry, Chip. I think there's something else going on, something big. RUMINT says there's another operation being kicked around the joint staff but no one is talking about it."

RUMINT was the naval slang term for rumor intelligence. Mondelli's skills as an insider were considerable. Sharratt leaned forward.

"Another operation?" he asked. "Don't we have enough on our plate already?"

"You're goddamned right we do," Mondelli groused. "But ours is not to question why. Ours is just to do or die. And I plan to die following a nice long retirement, so let's refrain from driving our carriers straight at any more Chinese ships. How does that sound, Rear Admiral Sharratt?"

His tone was still testy, but he had a smile on his face.

Mondelli topped off their coffees and tapped the message about the Chinese exercises. "What does your gut tell you about this change in plans from our Chinese frenemies?"

Sharratt knew Mondelli respected his experience about this part of the world.

"It's probably another version of their power play against Taiwan. What the Chinese lack in originality, they make up for with hard work."

"But why winter?" Mondelli asked. "The weather's shit."

"Maybe they want to show the Taiwanese they can operate in any kind of weather," Sharratt said. "When I was a JO in the air wing here in Japan, we used to laugh our asses off at the Chinese. Their carrier program was just starting, and it was a disaster. The planes were terrible. The pilots were poorly trained. Every time they ran one of these exercises, they lost a few pilots in accidents."

Sharratt sipped his coffee. "But each year they got better. I think we still have them beat, but every year they get closer. It's just a matter of time, sir. The PLA Navy can project real sea power out into the First Island Chain now. Taiwan has every right to be worried."

Mondelli nodded glumly. "I hear you. Everybody knows the Chinese are getting better, but it's always the problem for tomorrow. Hell, if I had my way, we'd take one of those carriers in the Gulf and move it here to Japan."

Sharratt took the last comment as Mondelli's subtle way of letting him know the subject of the Gulf was closed. The last of his coffee went into a souring stomach.

"Well, sir, if I'm not taking the strike group to the Gulf, how do you want me to spend my time between now and January?" Sharratt asked.

"Well, I can tell you what you're not going to be doing, Chip," Mondelli said, the sharpness returning to his tone. "You were on my short list to go to the International Seapower Symposium at the Naval War College in Newport this year, but thanks to the stench caused by your recent activities in the Strait of Taiwan, no one wants you anywhere near a Chinese naval officer these days. In your place, I'd like you to recommend someone from your staff to accompany me."

Sharratt smiled. "You mean you want a commander to carry your bags, sir?"

"I can't be expected to carry my own bags, Chip," Mondelli shot back. "I'm not a heathen."

Sharratt laughed, genuinely this time, secretly glad. The last thing he wanted to do was go to Newport, Rhode Island, and hobnob with a bunch of admirals from around the world. He got to his feet.

"Thanks for hearing me out, sir."

Mondelli got to his feet and held out his hand.

"Sorry about Newport, Chip. It's just not in the cards for you this year."

Sharratt took his hand. "That's okay, sir."

That was the last time he saw Sal Mondelli alive.

17

Caracas, Venezuela

The port of Caracas was a dump. The sweltering air in the warehouse contained a miasma of heavy rotting smells that lay like a film on his skin and coated the inside of Ian Thomas's mouth.

Spilled oil, raw sewage, and decaying fish.

It was nearly midnight now and slightly cooler. He could only imagine what this place smelled like when the sun superheated the inside of the flimsy metal building.

Stacked neatly in the center of the cracked and stained concrete floor lay the cargo from the hold of the North Korean freighter *Chong Chon Gang*. Three black plastic suitcases and twenty wooden crates each about the size and shape of a coffin.

Ian drew another shallow breath of the putrid air and checked his watch. Ten minutes to midnight.

It had taken three days to make the trip from Panama to Caracas. Three days on the rolling open sea under a heavy sky the color of lead. He had taken the captain's cabin and avoided contact with the crew. During the day he stayed inside, but at night he walked the deck.

To his great frustration, Isabel Montez occupied his thoughts.

Why had she left without saying goodbye?

Ian felt like a fool. His entire life had consisted of slipping in and out of identities like he was changing clothes. Apart from the Minister, every other human interaction in his adult life was a transaction between interested parties. Trust, emotional entanglement, commitment. These were all words that had no home in his internal vocabulary.

And now, for the first time in his life, he found himself wanting to call a woman *after* he'd slept with her.

The irony of the situation clung to his thoughts like the foul atmosphere of this reeking warehouse clung to his skin.

It was a relief when the *Chong Chon Gang* turned inland toward the port of Caracas. The identity of Ian Thomas, risk assessment manager, was replaced by Dominik Koskinen, Eastern Bloc arms dealer.

Ian heard the sound of a car pulling up outside the warehouse, and he got to his feet. The door opened, and Venezuelan Army General Mauricio Hernandez entered.

For a moment, Ian was speechless. The general was dressed in his dark green uniform, complete with a chest full of medals and a high-peaked cap adorned with shiny gold braid. Through the open door, Ian glimpsed an official staff car.

What sort of moron came dressed in uniform to a clandestine meeting to buy illegal arms?

Hernandez was a big man with broad shoulders and a body that had succumbed to gravity. He walked with a ponderous rolling gait, as if each step was an effort. The dark hair above his craggy face was slicked back from his forehead. He had small dark eyes that flitted around the room, finally resting on the stacked crates.

Ian forced himself to smile. He was handing over state-of-the-art weapons to an idiot. But that was the job the Minister had assigned him.

"General." Ian extended his hand. "It is a pleasure to meet you."

"*Mucho gusto*," the military man replied, shaking Ian's hand but never taking his eyes off the crates. "Show me what you have."

Ian was more than happy to skip the small talk. He turned to the nearest crate and flipped up the lid with a dramatic flourish.

Inside, nestled in packing foam, was a shoulder-fired missile. The body

of the forest-green weapon consisted of a meter-long barrel, a boxy structure that both housed the electronics and served as the stock when the
weapon was fired, and a trigger mechanism.

Ian hefted the weapon out of the packing foam. It weighed about
twenty kilograms.

"Single-use weapon," he said. "The missile is preloaded and has a
warhead with one-point-five kilograms of high explosives. More than
enough to take down any fighter or helicopter."

Channeling his inner arms dealer, he slapped the square electronics
box. "Primary guidance system is a three-channel optical seeker. Ultravio-
let, near-infrared, and mid-infrared. This is a fire-and-forget missile. Once
you launch it, the missile will seek out an engine exhaust signature."

The general's lip curled in disgust. "I have thousands of these missiles
already. You waste my time, Mr. Koskinen."

"You are mistaken, General," Ian replied. "You may have missiles, but I
can assure you that you do not have any of *these* weapons. In fact, no one in
the world has this missile yet."

He handed the weapon to the general. "The Kinzhal 9K399 is a fifth-
generation man portable infrared surface-to-air missile. Nothing like it on
the open market today."

"It looks the same to me," the general said. "And the IR seeker you
mentioned is easily defeated by laser countermeasures."

Ian lifted one of the small black suitcases onto the crate and snapped it
open. "I said the primary guidance system was an optical seeker. The
Kinzhal is equipped with a secondary guidance system."

Inside the suitcase was a pair of sleek black VR goggles and a matching
black glove. "This is the secondary guidance system interface."

He had the general's attention now. The man ran his finger along the
rim of the goggles. "How does it work?"

"I asked you to bring a laptop with a DVD drive," Ian said. "Did you
bring it with you?"

The general raised his voice. "Colonel Maldonado, bring in the laptop."

A tall, rangy man with a full mustache and a thick black pompadour
entered carrying a laptop. Ian turned away quickly. The fewer people who
saw him, the better. When he turned back, the colonel was gone.

Careful to handle the DVD by the edges, Ian loaded the disc into the laptop and clicked PLAY.

The video showed a young soldier wearing the VR goggles and glove seated next to a parabolic dish. A few feet away, a second soldier had a MANPAD balanced on his shoulder as he sighted down the barrel.

The armed soldier shouted, then pulled the trigger. A huge gout of flame blew out the back of the MANPAD as the missile was expelled from the barrel. The missile booster ignited, and the weapon rocketed away, leaving a corkscrew of smoke in its wake.

"Watch, General," Ian said. "By default, these missiles use their heat-seeker technology to find their target, but they also come equipped with a brand-new targeting technology that cannot be defeated by any counter-measures. We call it beam rider."

The image on the screen split. On one side, the VR operator began to move his gloved hand. On the opposite screen, the image expanded, then zeroed in on a drone. The operator tagged the drone with a red target box. The parabolic dish next to the operator began to move as it tracked the target.

"Once the operator selects a target, the laser will continue to track it and guide the missile to its destination."

On the screen, the drone exploded in a ball of fire.

"It's like a video game," the general said, his eyes glittering.

"Exactly," Ian agreed.

"And this cannot be defeated by any laser countermeasures system? Even the ones used by the Americans?"

Ian shook his head. "It uses a different frequency laser. There are no countermeasures for this weapon because the Americans don't know that this weapon exists."

The general's heavy frame shook with anticipation. "I want these. All of them. How much?"

"That's the best part, General Hernandez," Ian said with a grin. "They're free."

"Free? I don't understand."

"My fee has been paid by a very generous benefactor who wishes to see the people of Venezuela defend themselves against the US invasion," Ian said.

"Invasion?" The general's eyes narrowed. "What are you talking about?"

Instead of answering, Ian opened a new video file on the laptop and played it.

A shaky video obviously taken from a handheld mobile phone showed US soldiers in combat gear filing off a military transport. Palm trees swayed gently in the distance. In the background, dozens of US Army helicopters were visible.

Ian let the images sink in before he spoke again. "This video was taken less than twenty-four hours ago at the Bonaire International Airport in the Netherlands Antilles, less than two hundred kilometers away from where we stand now," Ian said. "I regret to inform you, General, that the Americans intend to invade your country in a matter of weeks, if not days. I am here to make sure that does not happen."

The color drained from the military man's face.

"I have to take this information to the president immediately," the general said.

"Not yet." Ian patted the crates filled with the fifth-gen MANPADS. "You have a very powerful weapon, but you need to deploy it effectively."

"I'm listening."

Ian turned back to the laptop and pulled up a detailed topographical map of the area between the port of Caracas and the capital city.

"The invaders will come from this direction," Ian said. "You need to be prepared."

He indicated three red circles on the map. "Set up the beam rider stations here, here, and here. This will give you excellent coverage of the skies over the airport and the city itself. They'll never see it coming."

The general studied the map, his head nodding as Ian spoke.

"It's a good plan," he said after a long pause. "I will see that it is done."

"One last thing," Ian said. "It is important to maintain control of the demonstrators, especially around Independence Day. You must show strength and resolve by cracking down on these bad elements. Allowing them to roam your streets only gives the Americans an excuse to invade."

The general took out his phone and snapped a picture of the MANPAD.

"You said these are called *kinzhal*?" he asked. "What does that word mean?"

"Kinzhal is the Russian word for dagger," Ian replied. "Use it to stab into the heart of the American imperialists, General."

The general nodded, his gaze surveying the crates.

"Who are you?" the general asked. "Why are you doing this?"

Ian decided to answer truthfully. "I just do what I'm told, General."

18

Plaza Bolívar
Caracas, Venezuela

"The Americans are coming!"

The shout rang out from behind Gabriella Manos Eschevaria. She spun around to find her fourteen-year-old brother, Martin, holding his mobile phone in the air with a triumphant gesture. The late afternoon sun glinted on the cracked screen.

"I just saw it on Twitter," he shouted. "The Americans are coming!"

All around her, Gabriella could feel the rumor rippling through the crowd like someone had just thrown an enormous stone into a still pond.

She reached for her brother's arm and dragged him to her side. False hope would do no one any good. The watchword of this protest was peaceful discipline. That was the only way to win, the only way to help presidential candidate Valencia Corazón wrest power from Maduro and restore their country.

Discipline, not shouted rumors.

"What are you doing?" she hissed at Martin.

He squirmed in her grasp, then thrust the mobile phone screen in her face.

"I'm not making it up," he said. "The Americans are coming. Look!"

Gabriella took the phone. The tweet was from a Brazilian news agency that she recognized. She touched the screen to enlarge the image associated with the tweet.

It showed uniformed American soldiers dressed in camouflage with body armor, helmets, wraparound sunglasses, fierce-looking weapons, and heavy packs. At least a dozen helicopters crowded the sky behind the foot soldiers. Lethal-looking machines like angry wasps with rockets slung on either side.

The caption underneath read: *United States 18th Airborne Corps preps to invade Venezuela.*

She handed the phone back to her brother. "It's a stock photo, Martin. It's just a rumor."

"It's on CNN, too," someone called out. His voice was pitched with hope.

Could this possibly be true? Gabriella wondered. Years earlier, the US had supported Juan Guaidó but then withdrew their support when Maduro pushed back. She, like most of her countrymen, doubted the United States had the stomach for an invasion of a Latin American country, no matter how good the reason. But there was a new American president now, and he had promised to deal with Venezuela…Was it possible?

A story on a Brazilian news site was one thing, but CNN was an entirely different affair. Hating herself for giving into the impulse, Gabriella checked the CNN website on her smartphone.

The same story was there with the same picture. The article claimed the 18th Airborne Corps had deployed from Fort Bragg, North Carolina, two days ago to the ABC Islands, more correctly known as the Netherlands Antilles. She had never heard of that military unit before, but CNN said they were a force designed for "rapid deployment anywhere in the world." She clicked on a link and watched a video. They looked like real soldiers, the kind that could bring peace to the wreck that was Venezuela.

Gabriella felt tears start to well up in her eyes. Martin slipped his arm around her waist and laid his head on her shoulder. Her little brother was growing up. He was nearly as tall as her now.

"I think it's finally going to happen, Gabby," he said.

Gabriella kissed his forehead. He stank of sweat and smoke, and his skin was salty on her lips.

Unlike her younger brother, she could remember a time before Maduro, when Caracas was a thriving city. When they ate well every night and her parents had good jobs. That was before her brother was born. It made her furious that her brother had grown up thinking that this stinking pile of corruption that was Venezuela was normal.

If it was the last thing she did on this earth, she would give her brother a brighter future. That's why they were here in the Plaza Bolívar.

"Maybe," she said. "But that means it's even more important that we do our job. You know what that means, right?"

Martin sighed and rolled his eyes. "Discipline."

"Discipline," Gabriella repeated.

In her fragmented time in university, she had studied marketing and mass communications. Her skills came in handy when she joined the Liga de Estudiantes Reformadores, the student-led organization supporting Valencia Corazón for President.

With the election only a month away, the League authorized a peaceful takeover of Plaza Bolívar, the square in front of the Palacio Federal Legislativo, where the National Assembly convened. Their plan was to occupy the square until the election results were in and Corazón was declared the winner.

Discipline had been instilled into every aspect of this latest protest. Gabriella and her colleagues were committed to making sure this protest was going to be different.

Continuous, peaceful, orderly.

It was day seven of the protest. The previous Sunday afternoon, the students had flooded into Plaza Bolívar. They blocked all the streets with makeshift barricades and posted guards to monitor the traffic in and out of the square and to make sure supplies were routed to the correct destination. The League set up a soup kitchen, a first aid station, toilet facilities, and a police force to deal with any petty theft or fights. Protesters were assigned shifts so that they always had fresh people available.

The square was clean, peaceful, and organized. The League wanted to put on display the kind of discipline that would make the politicians and the rest of the country take notice.

This time was going to be different.

Although they were determined not to give the police any reason to disperse them, the League had contingency plans for that eventuality as well.

About two hundred young people had volunteered to act as a defensive force. They fashioned makeshift shields and staffs to repel the riot police. The League had a supply of gas masks, and everyone was encouraged to carry a bandanna and goggles when inside the plaza.

Gabriella bumped her brother with her hip.

"Go get some water," she said. "You need to stay hydrated."

As she watched him dart away through the crowd, she realized that was something her mother would've said. Her parents had passed away four years ago, penniless and starving, dying in squalor like their beloved city of Caracas.

Her father had begged Gabriella to take her brother and flee the country.

"Sell whatever we have," he said. "Go to Colombia. Make a new life with your brother, Angel."

Angel, the recollection of her father's pet name only deepened her sense of nostalgia.

Even on his deathbed, her father was out of touch with reality. They had few possessions of any value left, Gabriella knew. She had pawned her mother's jewelry and the family silver months earlier. Even if they managed to sell what little remained, the Venezuelan bolívar was a worthless currency.

With the passing of her parents, she and Martin existed on limited government handouts and the generosity of strangers. Gabriella did her best to continue her studies and keep Martin in school, if only to have a shell of normality in an otherwise chaotic life.

Every day was like the American movie *Groundhog Day*. She got up and went through the same motions, trying to find enough food and clean water for her and her brother to survive another day.

A group of students near her gathered in a circle debating the impact of the American invasion. She shook her head in disgust. Gabriella had long ago abandoned the fantasy that anyone was going to rescue Venezuela. If this problem was going to be solved, it was going to be solved by the Venezuelans themselves.

They had allowed a man like Maduro to come to power and build a military around him. They had to solve that problem for themselves.

Still, the rumor about the Americans lent new energy to the protest. Fresh students poured into the square, and the volume of chants increased. The heat of the afternoon sun turned the open plaza into a stew of human emotions.

As shadows lengthened, Gabriella felt the mood of the protest heighten. She saw the raw emotions in the faces of the protesters, heard them in their hoarse voices, smelled them on the sharp odor of sweaty bodies.

Anger was the dominant emotion, but there were others. Determination, resolve, even some fear. Hope, too. Hope was like a spice that flavored the crush of humanity. She let it flow around her, but she dared not let it sink in. Not yet.

Gabriella stood in line for a bowl of soup and a chunk of bread. The soup was mostly water with a few pale vegetables floating in the thin liquid. The bread was stale.

She looked around for Martin. He was supposed to check in with her every hour, but he was on fourteen-year-old time, and after the first day she didn't enforce the rule. Besides, he knew to stay in the square.

She ate in the shade of the statue of Simón Bolívar. The three-meter-high monument depicted a man seated on a rearing horse as he looked off into the distance. Gabriella's legs ached. She'd been up before the sun and on her feet all day. She set the plastic bowl on the ground and let her eyelids slide closed.

As she often did, Gabriella dreamed of happier times. Her mother and father still alive. Her brother young, just starting to walk and not yet talking.

The four of them were in a park. Her mother spread a blanket on the ground underneath a tree and was playing with Martin. Her father had brought a soccer ball, and he kicked it back and forth with Gabriella. She remembered the heat of the sun, the way her foot felt when she connected with the ball.

Martin toddled over and got in the path of the ball. Gabriella yelled at him, her little girl cries sharp, indignant. Her mother picked up the baby, and he kicked in her arms. His face melted into red frustration as he howled his indignation to the world...

"*Policía!*"

The shout snapped Gabriella awake. The plastic bowl rolled away as she used the side of the marble pedestal to push herself to her feet.

Police. The word made her stomach clench with fear. They had bet that if the League kept the protest violence-free, the police would leave them alone.

On the south side of the plaza, dusk shadowed the streets that bracketed the Palacio Federal Legislativo. The gold dome and white façade of the historic building filled the entire side of the square and seemed to glow in the gathering gloom. In the streets beyond the barricades, Gabriella saw the dark shapes of men assembling. She caught the glint of helmets and the angular outline of a high-wheeled military vehicle.

As if on cue, spotlights blasted away the darkness with a harsh white glare. Gabriella gasped. There were hundreds of black-clad policemen poised to enter the square.

The first row of policemen took a knee and raised their weapons to a forty-five-degree angle. Gabriella heard a distant pop, and she saw at least a dozen arcs of white smoke lofting over the barricades into the square. The canisters clanged to the pavement, spewing thick clouds of white smoke.

"Gas!" someone screamed. "Put on your gas masks!"

Where was Martin? Was he carrying a gas mask? She couldn't remember.

A girl, a friend of her brother's, ran by. Gabriella reached out and snagged her arm. The girl looked around wildly, tears streamed down her face, whether from the tear gas or fear, Gabriella couldn't say.

"Where is Martin?" she said to the girl. "Daniela, where is Martin?"

Daniela blinked at her. She opened her mouth to say something, then she went limp. Gabriella felt a warm spray across her face but ignored the sensation. She lowered the girl to the ground and rolled her onto her back.

Gabriella stared at the child, her mind refusing to process what she was seeing.

Half the girl's face was missing. A blackish pulp oozed onto the ground, like thick oil. Gabriella brushed her own face, and her hand came away wet and sticky.

She looked up at the tops of the buildings around the plaza to see flickers like fireflies in the dark.

The police were shooting at them. Not with rubber bullets, but live ammunition.

Gabriella stumbled to her feet, the smell of chemicals burning in her nostrils.

"Martin!" she screamed.

At the barricades, dozens of young men formed a ragged line. They carried metal garbage can lids, sheets of thick plexiglass. A pair of boys no older than Martin carried a closet door between them.

A young man, shirtless and with a wispy beard, shimmied up the lamppost on the corner. He waved a Venezuelan flag and shouted, "Shield wall!" His voice carried across the square.

Gabriella knew her brother would be in that line. She pulled on her gas mask and ran in that direction.

The military vehicles with the high wheels started to roll forward. They picked up speed at the end of the street and smashed through the barricades as if they were made of paper. To Gabriella's horror, they kept moving and plowed into the improvised shield wall.

Bodies flew in the air. More bodies disappeared under the tires of the vehicle. Scores of policemen, faces hidden by gas masks, followed at a trot into the breached line and fanned out across the square.

Gabriella waded through hip-deep tear gas, searching for her brother. Visored cops ghosted in and out of the mist. Young men and women staggered past her, coughing and retching. She finally saw Martin cowering in the lee of a tall oak tree as if trying to fade into the bark. He had a red bandanna tied across his face, but his eyes bled tears.

She gripped him by both shoulders.

"It's me," she screamed through the mask. "Where is your gas mask?"

Martin's thin shoulders trembled in her grasp. He cast his gaze around as if he were blind.

Gabriella did the only thing she could think of: she ripped her gas mask off and slid it over her brother's face.

Instantly, she felt the bite of the gas in her lungs, a burning sensation that made her ribs contract with pain.

She pulled Martin close to her chest and put her lips to his ear. "I'll never let anything happen to you."

It felt as if she were being pulled down. Her knees touched the ground, then her hip, then her shoulders...then everything turned to black.

19

Bonaire, Leeward Antilles Islands

The last time Lieutenant Colonel Kevin Merriman stood on the beach in Bonaire watching the sun set had been a decade ago under very different circumstances. The fresh sea air smelled clean, and it left a salty dew as it washed over his face.

For their tenth wedding anniversary, he had surprised his wife with a scuba-diving trip to Bonaire. His parents watched their four boys while he and Janie drank fruity rum drinks by night and slipped into the bathwater-warm Caribbean by day. Those two weeks felt like a world away right now.

Behind him, in and around the Bonaire International Airport, elements of the 2nd Infantry Brigade, 101st Airborne, were hard at work unloading C-17s and setting up logistics for over two thousand men and women of the United States Army, including the six hundred soldiers of his own unit, the "First Strike" 1st Battalion, 502nd Infantry.

It was a sight to behold. The single runway of the airport had seen more traffic in the last day than it had probably seen in the last three months. The logistics team from Echo Company, 526th Brigade Support Battalion, were earning every penny of their paychecks in the hot and humid tropical air of Bonaire.

Forklifts carrying pallets of supplies raced across the tarmac. A line of soldiers extended from the temporary mess hall. Rows of tents peeked over the fence around the airport.

An empty C-17 took off. Less than a minute later, a new one landed, carrying more supplies, soldiers, and warfighting equipment.

The higher he rose in the ranks of the military, the more the simple lessons of his four years at West Point became muscle memory.

Infantry wins battles, logistics wins wars.

Blackjack Pershing said that in World War One, and it was even more true today with the Army's reliance on technology. The amount of "stuff" it took to put a fighting company in the field was mind-boggling. And no one in the world was better at it than the United States military. He chuckled to himself. US Army logistics made Amazon look like a mom-and-pop delivery service.

"Sir, briefing in fifteen in the small hangar," said the voice of Major Sam Turner, his battalion exec. The thirty-two-year-old redhead's fair skin was already starting to burn after a few hours on the ground in the tropics.

Merriman blew out a breath and carefully put the memories of happier times with Janie back into the locked box in his mind. It was time to go to work.

The sand on the concrete apron made a scraping sound as he turned suddenly and started for the hangar.

"Round 'em up, Sam," he said. "I'll meet you there."

"Them" was the rest of his battalion staff. In addition to Turner, there was Major Lionel Partridge, a thirty-four-year-old Tennessee boy with a down-home accent that he used to tell stories of growing up back home "in the holler."

Sergeant Major Royal Jackson, who was the same age as Merriman, was a six-foot-three, lean Black man with a shaved head. Eight Ball, as he was called by the troops, had a placid demeanor, but he was one of the finest soldiers and fiercest warriors Merriman had ever met.

The squat figure of Sergeant Enrique Sanchez looked like a bear next to Jackson's spare frame. Merriman's radio operator was never more than a few steps away from his commanding officer. The kid had the shoulders of a linebacker and a ready smile.

The interior of the small hangar was like walking into a sauna. A team of enlisted support techs, sweat streaming down their faces and darkening the collars of their green T-shirts, were racing to set up the secure videoconference link. The large flat-screen monitor displayed a solid blue color. As usual, technical gremlins were making the support team's life hell.

Merriman let Turner deal with applying needless pressure to the already stressed technical team. He turned to a row of folding chairs that had been set up on the cracked concrete floor. On each chair was a thick binder emblazoned with top secret markings and the words *Operation DELIVER LIBERTY*, containing the material for the upcoming OPORD briefing. A pair of techs rolled in two large fans and set them up on either side of the assembled chairs. Emitting a dull drone, the blades began to move the stuffy humid air of the hangar.

Merriman turned his attention to the material in the binder.

In his two decades in the United States Army, Merriman had attended hundreds of briefings like this one. Military operation orders, or OPORDs, followed a standard five-section format: Situation, Mission, Execution, Sustainment, and Command and Control. The OPORD held all the details of the operation from the top-line mission and troop assignments down to the most mundane of details, such as the provision for religious services on Sunday.

The invaluable document had only one purpose: to preplan every possible detail in advance, knowing full well that all that careful planning would get blown to hell as soon as the shooting started. In words attributed to countless military leaders across time, no plan survives first contact with the enemy.

"I got them!" The young woman's red face was dripping sweat as she pumped her fist in the air. "Aruba is online."

The solid blue screen flashed to a crystal-clear image of a large conference room.

As Merriman's wristwatch ticked to mark the hour, a trim woman with the rank of a colonel affixed in Velcro to the center of her ACUs strode onto the screen. A Ranger qualification adorned the top of her left sleeve. Jump wings and an infantry badge showed above the US Army name tape on her left breast. Behind her a projection screen bore the name of the operation in block letters.

Colonel Anne Pratchett, the G3, or Operations Officer for the 18th Airborne Corps, was broadcasting from the headquarters tactical operations center, or TOC, which was based on the larger island of Aruba.

Partridge leaned close to Turner, whispering in his Tennessee drawl, "I heard the brass is staying in hotels on Aruba, while we're sleeping on the ground here."

Merriman cleared his throat. Partridge caught the hint and sat up in his chair.

Pratchett was an experienced briefer who understood the needs of her audience. Her clipped speech delivered the color they needed to understand their individual part in the larger context of the operation.

Deliver Liberty was a massive undertaking for the United States Army, and Pratchett did not sugarcoat the enormity of the task.

The USA was about to invade and resuscitate the failed state of Venezuela. The dictator in charge was being given one last chance to allow a free and fair election and a peaceful transition of power.

Based on the fact that four combat battalions of the 101st Airborne were now forward deployed less than a hundred miles from the coastline of Venezuela, Pratchett said the decision to invade was more a case of "when" than "if."

"What will trigger the decision to launch?" someone in the room at Aruba asked.

"The 'go' decision is solely in the hands of the president," Pratchett replied, "and could come at any time based on the evolving situation in Caracas." She turned back to the screen.

"Our highest priority is to secure the shipping ports, airports, and governmental facilities in the first twenty-four hours. That will allow us to secure our supply lines and bring in additional troops and much-needed aid. These people are starving."

Merriman studied the map of Venezuela as the colonel spoke. The other three combat battalions were assigned to take the ports of Maracaibo, Caracas, and Barcelona. Merriman's battalion was assigned to secure the government buildings in Caracas.

The detailed maps of Caracas showed their landing zone, the Parque Ezequiel Zamora, a green hilly park adjacent to the capitol district. From the park, his battalion would hold the high ground, be able to observe any and all Venezuelan troop movements, and provide supporting fire at will.

Next to him, his battalion exec and ops officer were comparing the paper maps with the versions loaded on their ruggedized tablets. All of his men would carry paper and electronic versions into battle with them. Paper never ran out of batteries. If you put a bullet through a paper map, it still worked.

He listened carefully as Pratchett described the logistics of the brigade level assault. First Battalion, his people, would be airlifted from Bonaire by Eagle Assault from the 101st Aviation Regiment. They would ride in CH-47 Chinooks, the massive two-rotor helicopters that carried fifty fully loaded combat troops. He and his staff would split up among several smaller UH-60 helos to guard against a loss of command in the eventuality of an in-air accident. In a few days' time, they'd also have close air support from a carrier strike group that was preparing to get underway from Norfolk.

Merriman's time in the Middle East had given him an appreciation for the scope of the task they were about to undertake. Regime change was not a short-term problem. He had no opinion on the politics of the decision—that was not his job—but he had very strong opinions about whether or not his team was playing to win.

He liked what he was seeing so far. If the US was willing to commit the full capabilities of the United States military to this problem, then they would be successful. If not, then in ten years, some politician would be yammering on about "forever wars" and other nonsense.

The only way to win was to make this fight as unfair as possible. Overwhelming force was called for.

Pratchett began the part of the presentation about expected opposition.

"The Venezuelan armed forces are a shell of their former capability. Today, they are used primarily as an internal police force and a way to intimidate their own people. That said, there could still be some fight left in this pup.

"The Venezuelan Army, correctly called the National Army of the Bolivarian Republic of Venezuela, is reported to be six divisions, but mostly conscripts. Morale is poor, and we do not expect much of a fight, except perhaps in the capital region.

"There, we expect some of their better-trained, more disciplined troops, who will likely be extremely loyal to the government and well armed. First Battalion should be prepared for resistance."

"Well, ain't that just dandy," Partridge muttered.

Pratchett continued, "Their air force has twenty-three Russian-made Sukhoi fighters, but our best intelligence states only three or four are flyable. Our air cover should have no trouble clearing the skies for the heliborne assault.

"In the past, Venezuela has been a good customer to the Russians, and they have a stockpile of Russian weaponry, including thousands of shoulder-fired missiles, or MANPADS. Again, these are old, mostly Igla SA-16s with dual-band IR guidance systems. All of our helos are equipped with ATIRCM." She said the last like *a-ter-com*, which stood for advanced threat infrared countermeasures. Merriman knew the laser-based system was extremely effective at countering older IR-seeking warheads.

"The best intel we have says the last shipment of Russian arms was over two years ago," Pratchett continued. "And we believe the Russians were just offloading old crap."

They reached the two-hour point when Colonel Pratchett concluded the briefing and asked for any further questions. Merriman's ass was numb from the hard metal chair, and his stomach rumbled with hunger. Pratchett had done a thorough job, and there were few questions.

"We're coming up on July fifth," Pratchett said in closing, "which is Venezuelan Independence Day, traditionally a major holiday in the country. It is possible there will be a civil disturbance large enough to trigger an authorization of Deliver Liberty.

"All units are now in an operational hold. No passes, no beach time. Get your units fully primed. A 'go' order could come down at any time." She paused. "Good luck, everyone. Let's get it done."

Finally, the briefing ended, and the screen went blank. Merriman stood and stretched. He felt the vertebrae in his back pop, and he groaned with relief.

Partridge spoke up. "I guess now we just stand the fuck by," he said with a chuckle.

"Don't think so, sir," replied Sergeant Major Jackson. His ebony pate gleamed in the florescent lights. He pointed at the TV set that was set up off to the side.

The set was tuned to CNN Brazil. Jackson found the remote and unmuted the TV. Although the announcer was speaking in Spanish, a translation was not needed—all of the men were able to understand the scene unfolding on the screen.

A statue of a soldier sitting astride a horse in Plaza Bolívar in Caracas. The words *EN VIVO* showed in the lower left corner of the screen.

LIVE.

Armed policemen wearing gas masks and body armor waded through swirling clouds of white fog. A burly cop wielding a baton coldcocked a skinny young man. The kid didn't look old enough to shave. When the young man's body hit the ground, he didn't move.

"Snipers," Turner said. He pointed to the upper area of the screen where winks of lights were visible. Another young man took a round in the chest and collapsed.

Merriman's breath caught in his throat. Those were not rubber bullets.

"Jay-sus H. Christ," Partridge said. "You think this is it, sir?" he asked of Merriman.

The battalion commander did not look away from the screen.

"Get some sleep, people," he said. "I think we have a busy day ahead of us tomorrow."

20

Caracas, Venezuela

Gabriella woke up to sunlight streaming through a window. When she touched the skin near her eyes, it felt raw and grainy with dried tears. A clear plastic mask covered her face. She tried to sit up and immediately began coughing again. The burning feeling deep in her lungs was still there.

There were four other people in the room. Like her, they were in their teens and twenties and dressed in street clothes. A young man on her left had a bandage on his head, and his face was bloated and purple.

A doctor in a white lab coat passed the doorway, and she waved at him frantically until he noticed her.

He looked to be in his mid-thirties with a trimmed beard and an automatic smile. His complexion was ashen, and he had dark circles under a set of piercing brown eyes. In another time she would have thought he was cute.

Gabriella pulled the mask away from her mouth. It was hard to draw a full breath, and her voice sounded hoarse and wispy.

"My brother," she said. "Martin Eschevaria. Where is my brother?"

The professional smile stayed in place. "You need to limit how much you speak. Your throat and lungs were damaged by the gas."

"My. Brother," she gasped.

"I'll send a nurse in," the doctor said, "but we have hundreds of patients here. All the rooms look like this one. Just because we don't have his name doesn't mean he didn't make it."

Didn't make it?

A wave of panic made her struggle upright. The doctor put both hands on her shoulders.

"Listen to me," he said. His voice was kind but firm. "You've been out for almost eighteen hours. There's mass confusion around here, and you need to give us time to sort it out. Please. If your brother is here, he's being taken care of."

Gabriella let him push her back onto the bed. She was so weak, she doubted she could have stood on her own anyway.

"What. Happened." Her voice sounded like something from a horror movie.

"You're lucky to be alive," the doctor said. His jaw tightened, and anger flashed across his face. "The police didn't use normal tear gas. They used something called CR gas, more commonly known as fire gas. It's what military doctors call an incapacitating agent."

Gabriella nodded like she was understanding him, but her head felt like it was stuffed with cotton.

Eighteen hours. Where was Martin?

The doctor seemed to sense she was about to try to sit up again. He put the mask back on her face.

"If you try to get up again, I'll have to sedate you," he said. "Do you understand?"

Gabriella felt fresh tears start to sting. He put his hand on hers.

"It's okay," he said. "I'll ask a nurse to track down your brother."

She nodded, then another thought surfaced. She pulled at the mask.

"How many...killed?"

The doctor's face pinched. "Many...we don't have a complete count yet. I'm glad the Americans are here. Maybe they can end this nightmare."

The Americans? The rumor was real?

The doctor saw the question in her eyes and nodded. "The news says it's the 18th Airborne Corps. They landed this morning at Caracas airport, and in Maracaibo and in Barcelona." He took a TV remote from a holder on the wall and turned on the ancient TV hanging from the ceiling. He left the sound muted.

"Try to get some sleep," he said.

She flipped channels until she found CNN-Americas en Español. Gabrielle tried to read the closed captions, but her brain refused to cooperate. She settled for watching the pictures.

An attractive woman with long, dark hair spilling over her shoulders was talking into a microphone. She wore a camouflage flak jacket over her long-sleeved shirt and a thick helmet with the chin strap buckled.

Behind her, the afternoon sun blazed down on a vast tarmac field. A pair of green-painted airplanes occupied the strip. Their rear ramps were down, disgorging a double file of soldiers. A row of armored vehicles idled in the heat. Gabriella had never seen an airplane that big in her life.

The newswoman twisted and pointed into the sky.

The Atlantic Ocean glinted in the heat-hazed distance. A row of dots floated above the horizon. As they drew closer, Gabriella could make out at least twenty helicopters flying in multiple V formations.

The bodies of the war machines were lean and narrow, and the undersides of the helicopters were laden with guns and rockets. She knew nothing about helicopters or soldiers, but they looked lethal to her. Another group of fat helos with dual rotors followed in their wake.

The camera followed the aircraft as they swept overhead, flying toward downtown Caracas.

The sight of the American military made her want to cry with relief. The Venezuelan Army was no match for this kind of force. The United States would crush Maduro's people. Maduro would be thrown out of office. Venezuela would be saved.

Gabriella closed her eyes. She was so sleepy.

When she opened them again, the world had changed.

On the television screen, a spike of white shot up from the ground. It touched one of the lead helicopters, and the aircraft exploded. Four more fingers of white speared into the air. Another helicopter erupted in fire.

The rest of the aircraft scattered like angry hornets, swooping and dipping. Three of them launched rockets at the ground. The sky was filled with smoke trails and fire and falling debris.

Gabriella blinked her eyes. One of the fat double-rotor helicopters exploded.

The camera view swung wildly, and she saw the airport again. The newswoman was on the ground, screaming into her microphone.

In the distance, Gabriella heard a thudding noise, as if someone was pounding on a door at the end of the hall. *Boom, boom, boom.*

Her mind registered the sound as explosions...

But she was so tired, and it hurt to breathe.

Gabriella's eyes slid closed.

21

Bonaire, Leeward Antilles Islands

Merriman's battalion didn't load up for Venezuela until nearly noon local time. That was how long it took for the 5th Assault Battalion of the Combat Aviation Brigade to make three round trips to the Venezuelan coast and back.

The troops whiled away the morning baking in the tropical sunshine and waiting. Merriman spent the time at his temporary command post inside the hangar sweating the details of their assigned mission to secure the capitol district of Caracas.

The primary landing zone was Parque Ezequiel Zamora, a teardrop-shaped, hilly patch of green in downtown Caracas, conveniently located adjacent to the capitol district of the city. Thanks to both high-resolution classified imagery and unclassified Google Earth, they even had pictures of the area. Street View on Google Earth was a godsend for ground-pounders like Merriman and his planning team. The lightly treed green space was dotted with elaborate fountains, gazebos, and grand stone staircases that looked more like something he might see in Rome.

There were tradeoffs to this location, which had been tagged the EZ. The only area suitable for landing the massive CH-47 Chinooks in the EZ was an open field on the eastern tail of the irregularly shaped park. They could land three Chinooks at a time, so there would be a holding pattern in the air over the city as the first three troop carriers touched down and unloaded before clearing the way for the next three to land. The smaller UH-60 Black Hawks would land in open areas deeper in the park. After troops disembarked, each company had a rally point and instructions to "flood the zone" around the capitol district and secure the seat of government.

The secondary LZ was a much larger green space with walking trails and open fields. While much easier to land a large number of troops, it was nearly three kilometers away from the capitol district. In a potentially hostile urban setting, a three-kilometer trek could be a dangerous and time-consuming distance to cover.

As expected, the Venezuelan military was all bark and no bite.

The three prior air assaults had encountered no resistance in the air. The Venezuelan Air Force was nowhere to be found, which, for Merriman, was a heartening thought. Resistance once on the ground was lighter than expected as well, another good sign. At each landing zone, the prior battalions had encountered small arms fire and a handful of shoulder-fired missiles. In each case, the ATIRCM laser countermeasures on the helicopters had "dazzled" the IR seeker head, causing the enemy missile to veer off course and crash harmlessly into the ground.

The 101st had lost one UH-60 helo to a maintenance issue and zero aircraft to enemy fire.

"Sir," radioman Sergeant Sanchez said, "the birds are thirty minutes out from our location."

Merriman stood. After reviewing the details of the operation so many times, the hours of waiting had devolved into a series of side conversations and restless chitchat. The news of the pending arrival of the 5th Assault Battalion was a much-needed jolt of adrenaline.

"Saddle up, people," he called out. "Our ride is on the way."

He took care with his own preparations.

In addition to his helmet, Merriman wore a tactical vest over a ballistic combat shirt. He checked his SIG Sauer 9mm sidearm and his rifle, the

Next-Gen Squad Weapon. He hoisted his pack containing extra magazines for both weapons, food, water, and a basic first aid kit.

When Merriman strode into the noonday sun a few moments later, the airfield was abuzz with activity as six hundred soldiers checked and double-checked their gear and fell into formation.

The aircraft of the 5th Assault Battalion appeared on the southern horizon as dots, then grew rapidly as the fleet of helos closed their position at 150 mph. In his time in Iraq and Afghanistan, Merriman had been part of dozens of air assaults, but always much smaller—normally a platoon-sized movement or at most a company movement of two hundred.

This was something else entirely. They were transporting six hundred fighting troops all at the same time.

The nine CH-47 Chinooks landed first. While the aircraft fuselage was fifty feet long, the massive tandem rotors extended the effective length to over one hundred feet. As soon as the heavy troop transports touched the ground, the maintenance crews started "hot pumping" the aircraft with more fuel for the trip back to Caracas. Since they hadn't encountered any fighting, the mini-guns on the Chinooks didn't need more ammunition.

Merriman's platoon sergeants began moving soldiers into position to race up the lowered rear ramp in double file once given the sign from the helo crew chiefs.

An even dozen UH-60 Black Hawks landed on the far end of the runway, their tapered fuselage looking sleek and slim next to the much heavier Chinooks. Merriman headed for his assigned helo with Sergeant Major Jackson and Sanchez in tow.

A UH-60 cabin could hold eleven combat soldiers, but it was a tight squeeze. In the rear of the two-meter-wide cabin, two rows of four seats faced each other. As his security team piled into the eight seats in back, Merriman, Jackson, and Sanchez took the three seats that faced forward. The Black Hawk had a crew of three: pilot, copilot, and crew chief.

The crew chief passed Merriman a set of headphones.

"Good afternoon, Colonel," the pilot said over the circuit. "Welcome to Venezuela Air, your preferred carrier for every South American invasion."

"Thanks, Captain," Merriman replied. "What's it like over there?"

"Nobody's laid a glove on us so far, sir," came the reply.

Merriman grinned. The man had a thick Boston accent that seemed out of place in the circumstances.

"We've seen a few missiles and the occasional pot shot or two, but it's been smooth as a baby's ass so far. Knock on wood." The pilot rapped on the side of his helmet.

"Well, let's hope it stays that way," Merriman said. "We're ready to go when you are."

"Please fasten your seat belts and place your tray tables in their upright and locked position, Colonel."

The pilot switched his radio circuit and spoke rapidly, then manipulated the collective by his side.

Merriman felt the deck under his feet tremble as the power to the rotors increased. The aircraft lifted up, then tilted forward as the pilot pushed the helo toward the south.

The flight from Bonaire to the coast of Venezuela took just under an hour. It also reminded Merriman how much he hated flying, especially in helos.

As a career infantry officer, he preferred the freedom to move and react to his surroundings. Packed inside of a UH-60 cabin was the opposite of freedom to him.

"Welcome to Venezuela, Colonel," the pilot said. His thick accent ended the word *Venezuela* with an R sound. Venezuel-ER.

They passed to the north of the Caracas airport. In the hazy heat, Merriman was able to make out a C-17 heavy transport plane lining up for a landing.

"The big guys're flying in already," the pilot said. "That's a good sign."

Merriman nodded without answering, watching the green coast draw closer.

"Sergeant Holden," the pilot said, his jovial manner gone. "We are approaching feet dry."

The crew chief took position behind one of the M240 machine guns. He checked his ammo feed and racked the bolt to the rear position.

"Request test fire, sir," he said over the circuit.

"You have permission to clear your throat, sergeant," said the pilot.

Holden shifted the weapon to the "fire" position and sighted down the barrel. He squeezed the trigger, releasing a short burst of gunfire.

"Test fire sat, sir," he reported.

Merriman cast a glance over his shoulder. The line of helos streamed behind in a loose formation of three aircraft across. A Chinook in the center with a Black Hawk flanking on either side.

The assault wave passed over a beach, a strip of green, then they were over a dense city.

"Feet dry," the pilot reported. His tone was flat and tense.

Merriman felt his heart rate tick up as they moved further inland. Caracas had a population of two million people. How many weapons were hiding down there?

"Approaching the LZ, sir," the pilot reported.

Merriman leaned forward to see out the front windscreen. Parque Ezequiel Zamora looked more worse for wear than what he'd seen from the internet pictures, but the topographical features were the same.

The assault team began to split up as the individual helos angled toward their assigned landing areas. A big-bellied Chinook thundered by and began a descent.

Merriman spotted a finger of white smoke lance up from the ground.

The descending CH-47 exploded.

Merriman stared in complete shock as the massive aircraft heeled to one side and dove at the ground.

Suddenly, incoming surface-to-air missiles laced the air with crazy corkscrew smoke trails. Another Chinook took a direct hit and broke apart in the air.

Merriman's helo banked and dove. He felt the fuselage shudder as heavy-caliber rounds hit them.

"We are taking heavy fire." The pilot's voice was even but taut with tension. "I repeat, heavy fire. Holden, what do you see?"

"Top of the park, sir," the crew chief shouted back. "Next to that fountain."

"Roger that," the pilot snapped back. "I'm making a run at it."

Merriman's mind raced. Why weren't the automatic laser countermeasures working?

The helo dropped to rooftop level and poured on the speed. Through the front windscreen, the green of the park came at them fast. At the last second, the pilot rose, skimming the tops of the tall trees. He unleashed with the GAU-19 Gatling gun in the nose of the aircraft. The helo banked hard, throwing Merriman against the bulk of Sergeant Sanchez.

"I see them!" Holden shouted.

The crew chief's face screwed into a grimace as he fired the M240 on full auto. Brass shells cascaded into the cabin.

Merriman caught a glance as they flashed by. A sandbag bunker, protected by a pair of .50-caliber machine guns. Three teams of soldiers were handling MANPADS, and a separate team was operating what looked like a satellite comms dish.

The heavy machine gun on the ground swung toward them and unloaded on Merriman's incoming helo. The aircraft shuddered. Merriman felt them lose power.

"We're hit, we're hit," the pilot called out. "I'm going to have to put us down."

Merriman shifted to the command circuit. "All units, Vanguard Six. Divert to secondary LZ."

"Can you get us to the secondary LZ, Captain?" Merriman asked the pilot over the circuit.

He could see both men in the front struggling with the controls. The touchscreens on the digital control panels flashed red, and the craft swayed from side to side.

"No can do, sir," the pilot replied. "I'm down to one engine, and it's failing. We're putting down as soon as I can find a clear space."

The helicopter took a sickening lurch forward. Both pilots fought to raise the nose of the craft. They lost altitude rapidly. The undercarriage of the Black Hawk brushed the treetops on the edge of the park, and the pilot banked hard to line up the nose of the chopper with a broad street.

The crew chief threw open both doors. Outside, Merriman saw the shadow of their rotors etched on the fast-rising pavement.

"Brace for impact!"

The pilot flared the helo at the last second before they slammed to the ground. Merriman's head snapped down. The helo bounced and lurched forward, then slammed down again. They ground to a stop.

Sergeant Major Jackson was out the door immediately, making a beeline for a nearby alley between a pair of three-story stone buildings. Merriman and Sanchez were only a step behind. The eight soldiers in the back seats of the UH-60 piled out from both sides of the craft and spread out along the street.

The street fronting the park must have once been a much sought-after address. The stone-fronted buildings reminded Merriman of brownstones he'd seen in the tonier neighborhoods of Brooklyn.

But that was in their past. The windows of the houses were broken, and the alley was a putrid, garbage-strewn mess. Jackson detailed four soldiers to move to the back end of the alley and secure their six. Merriman knelt next to an overflowing dumpster and spread the map on his knee.

The air assault fleet had moved past the primary LZ, but they could still hear the .50-caliber machine guns firing from behind the screen of trees. A UH-60 rose over the treetops and dove toward the hilltop bunker. Another SAM arced into the sky.

Jackson returned from checking their perimeter. "The area's deserted, sir. We're secure for the moment." He looked up the hill to where the machine gun was still firing. "What's the plan, sir?"

Merriman pointed to the park.

"We deal with that first."

22

Emerging Threats Group
Tysons Corner, Virginia

Don looked up from the daily intel briefing on his computer screen to the world map on his wall. If he plotted all the conflicts America was involved in on that map, it would look like the world was on fire.

Since the Iranian attack on the USS *Delbert D. Black*, the wheels had most definitely come off the global bus.

At this point, the war with Iran was an unlikely bright spot in an otherwise gloomy outlook for global stability. The US had committed three carrier strike groups, three Air Force wings, as well as strategic bombers to the Iranian mess. Central Command in Tampa, Florida, headed by a pugnacious Marine Corps veteran of the first Iraq War, was executing the Iranian problem with the kind of skill that can only come from experience.

In his daily press briefings, General Hillerman reported the Iranian military was degraded but not defeated. He emphasized the US strikes were surgical in nature, designed to minimize civilian casualties.

Don took some scant consolation that at least his country had learned one lesson from the three decades of conflict and crisis management in the Middle East. Completely removing the Iranian military and destroying the civilian infrastructure would only create a power vacuum. No one could predict what would fill that emptiness, but you could bet it would not bode well for regional stability or future American interests.

The fact that the USS *Black* had been in Iranian territorial waters when the attack took place had remained a secret—at least for the time being.

The highly classified report on the meaconing operation fingered the Iranians as the responsible party, concluding that it was "highly likely" that the Russians had only provided the hardware to the Iranians.

Case closed.

Don fumed about that for a solid day. The Iranian military had never been shy about claiming credit for their dirty deeds before. Why would they start now? In his view, a Russian connection made more sense when considered alongside the unfolding global chaos that had ensued since the *Black* incident.

The Indian subcontinent was a dumpster fire. Following five simultaneous attacks on major Indian cites by the Al-Badr Islamic militant group, the entire country had erupted in violence.

The Al-Badr forces selected soft targets, like hotels and resorts, reminiscent of the 2008 terrorist attacks on the Taj Mahal Palace Hotel in Mumbai. The terrorists were well armed and ruthless. Initial reports indicated casualties in the thousands, including dozens of vacationers and businesspeople from Europe and the United States. The TV coverage of the India attacks was horrific, replete with live news coverage and heartbreaking phone messages from loved ones trapped in the crossfire.

In response, Indian forces swarmed into the Kashmir region. Even as the United Nations urged restraint, unconfirmed reports of war crimes were finding their way into the global news networks. Hindu-on-Muslim violence was rampant, fueled by the nationalism of the Indian political party in power. All manner of reprisal attacks for both real and perceived crimes resulted in bloodshed not seen in decades all across India.

The US was involved there too, dispatching Marine Corps advisers to train the Indian Army in counterinsurgency tactics. US Special Operations Command had military and counterterrorism units on the ground in Kashmir.

And then there was Venezuela.

It was still hard to fathom what had happened there only two short days ago. What was intended as a public relations coup for the sitting president had turned into a meatgrinder.

The four battalions of the 101st Airborne forward-deployed to the ABC islands in the Netherlands Antilles had been intended as a warning to the Venezuelan government.

We're sitting on your front stoop. Don't do anything stupid. Time to step down.

That was the intended message.

Following the massacre in Plaza Bolívar, the president ordered the 18th Airborne Corps into Venezuela, and one of the most capable fighting forces on the planet had taken heavy losses, inflicted by the far inferior Venezuelan Army. Initial reports were that nearly one hundred soldiers from the 101st Airborne Division had been killed as their helicopters, a mix of UH-60 Black Hawks and H-47 Chinooks, were shot down by surface-to-air missiles.

It defied common sense. The Venezuelan military had SA-16 surface-to-air missiles in their arsenal, a fact that had been verified by military intelligence only a few weeks ago. The US helicopter fleet all carried laser countermeasures and flares that could easily defeat that older missile type.

The ambush over Caracas was not a lucky shot by some Venezuelan unit lying in wait for the US invasion. It was a turkey shoot.

Don clenched his eyes so tightly, he saw swirls of color in his vision.

Something was very, very rotten here. The Emerging Threats Group —*his* Emerging Threats Group—had not seen a single one of these global emergencies coming.

His stomach roiled. He felt embarrassment, to be sure, but it was more than that. This lack of ability to offer a vision of the future threats left America exposed. That vision was the purpose of his team. His purpose.

And he was failing. Big time.

In a few hours, the president would address the nation about the massacre in Caracas. The president was not backing down in Venezuela; he was doubling down.

The United States Army had no intention of being caught flat-footed a second time. This peace-keeping mission was now a grudge match. The president had already mobilized the Second Marine Expeditionary Force to effect an amphibious landing in Venezuela. Advance forces would land at Puerto la Cruz within forty-eight hours. After securing the port, oil refinery, and airport, the MEF would push into the interior of the country.

The last time an entire MEF had deployed was 2003 during the invasion of Iraq.

The United Nations General Assembly looked more like the trading floor at the New York Stock Exchange than a staid diplomatic body. They had already issued so many security council resolutions urging restraint that the White House had stopped responding to them individually. The press secretary just changed the header at the top of the press release and sent it out again.

Don jerked open his desk drawer and pulled out a plastic container of antacids. The pills made a hollow sound as he shook out a handful and slipped them into his mouth. He crunched the chalky pellets without thought, staring at the map of the world.

His computer chimed as his calendar flashed a meeting notice. Staff meeting in five minutes.

Don stood. His body ached from lack of sleep and too many hours hunched in front of a computer.

All for what? He was watching a pandemic of violence consume the planet, and he seemed powerless to do anything to help his country.

That ended now, he decided. Emerging Threats had to do better. *He* had to do better.

All ten of his senior staff were seated when he arrived at the large conference room. Normally, there would be banter flying and verbal jabs shooting across the table.

Today, there was silence. Ten tired faces watched Don take his seat at the head of the table. A large screen, used for viewing presentations, occupied the wall opposite Don. Someone had already powered up the projector and left the keyboard at Don's place, as if expecting him to have a presentation ready.

Mark Westlund sat in the chair to Don's right. Michael Goodwin and Dre Ramirez occupied the next two seats. On Don's left sat Harrison Kohl, a twenty-year CIA veteran.

Harrison was mid-forties and reserved, with short gray hair and chiseled good looks. He was a regular at the gym, as evidenced by his trim physique and flat stomach. Don had been surprised to find that his hobby was community musical theater. It seemed out of place for this unassuming man, but it also reinforced the adage that one should never judge a book by its cover.

Don pushed the keyboard away. He folded his hands on the table.

He had no notes and no clear picture of how he wanted to frame his thoughts.

"Good morning," he began.

Murmured responses.

Don winced at the sound of his own voice. Pitiful. People were dying out there, and he was mouthing platitudes.

"I take that back," Don said. "It's not a good morning. In fact, it's a shitty morning. Thousands of people are dead this morning. There's so many Americans around the world either dead or in danger, we can't even get an accurate count."

Somber faces studied him.

"We need to do better. We are *Emerging* Threats, and we predicted *zero* of the threats that have come to pass over the last few months. This will not stand. I won't let it happen."

The silence in the room was so complete that the only sound Don could hear was his own ragged breathing. He closed his eyes and opened them again.

"I'll be honest. I don't know what to do. I don't even know where to start. It's as if someone is running around the world lighting forest fires and we're just chasing them with a garden hose. We need to look at this with fresh eyes—I need you to help me see this with fresh eyes—because what we've done in the past isn't working."

"Maybe all these attacks are linked," Mark Westlund said. Although he spoke softly, his voice sounded loud in the quiet room.

"Explain," Don said.

"What if there is one organization behind it?" Mark said.

"You mean like a new Islamic State?" Don asked. He'd considered that avenue himself and discarded it. "We don't have even a whiff of evidence to support that idea. The rise of any organized group of this magnitude would leave a digital trail *somewhere*. We would find *something*."

"I know." Mark shook his head. "But this many outbreaks in so short a time. It's...It's too convenient."

"Convenient for whom?" Michael Goodwin asked. "Who benefits from uprisings in Iran, India, and Venezuela?"

"Don," Harrison said, "if I may. I think you've already answered your own question."

Harrison's voice was calm. Of all the people in this room, Harrison was the closest peer for Don. They were about the same age and level of experience, except that Don was a deputy director and Harrison was currently serving as a senior analyst.

Don had seen the redactions in Harrison's CIA career file and suspected that was probably the reason why he had not moved up the career ladder. He also knew that Harrison seemed perfectly content with his level of career advancement.

"My first desk job after coming out of the field was on the Latin America desk over at NSA," Harrison began. "Things have changed, I know, but not that much. What happened in Venezuela does not make any sense." He leaned on his elbows toward Don.

"First of all, where did those MANPADs come from? They made mincemeat of the United States Army." He pronounced *united* as *YOU-nited*. The only outward sign of Harrison's nervousness was how a slight Southern drawl emerged in his voice.

"But that's not all. Internet traffic and satellite imagery both show the Venezuelan Army is dispersing, not gathering to take the fight to the Americans. They're afraid. They're running away."

"You're suggesting someone else is in charge?" Don asked. "A splinter group?"

Harrison shook his head. "I'm not suggesting anything. I'm saying our normal tactics of cyber first aren't cutting it here. We need to go old-school for this problem. Boots on the ground."

Don rubbed his chin, the stubble from his unshaven beard grating against the skin of his knuckles.

"A field operation," Don said. "Can't we use whatever we get from military intel?"

"Military intelligence is going to be all over this, Don," Harrison replied, "but they're out for payback—not that I blame them. For now, all they care about is making sure they don't have a repeat of their last performance. We want to know who was behind it."

"You're volunteering for a field assignment, Harrison?" Don said.

Harrison met his gaze. "I am, sir. I'm fluent in Spanish, and I know my way around that part of the world."

Don wondered again about the redacted parts of Harrison's file.

"I'll go with him," Dre said suddenly.

Don looked at her sharply, as did Mark and Michael, but before he could say anything, Harrison jumped in.

"*Tu hablas español?*" Harrison said.

Dre leveled a cold stare at the older man. "You think just because my last name is Ramirez that I speak Spanish? Is that what you're saying?"

"No, I—I was just—"

"Don't sweat it, Harrison." Dre grinned at him. "*Hablo español muy bueno*. I'm just messing with you."

Harrison returned her smile slowly. "Okay, you're in. Wheels up in the a.m., partner."

As the meeting broke up, Don took Dre aside. Her face looked gaunt and drawn; her dark hair was dull. Like everyone else in the building, she looked tired.

"You're sure about this, Dre?" Don asked.

When she met his eye, her gaze was fierce. Don knew that look.

"I'm sure," she said.

23

Caracas, Venezuela

Once upon a time, the capital city of Venezuela must have been an amazing place. But what Dre Ramirez observed from the passenger seat of the black SUV was just a shell of a once-great city.

And now an occupied city, Dre thought as they weaved through their third US Army checkpoint since leaving the airport only a few miles away.

Harrison Kohl drove. He wore wraparound dark sunglasses, blue jeans, and a black T-shirt. Dre noted how his gaze scanned back and forth across the upcoming roadway, alert for any danger ahead.

The outskirts of Caracas were a series of rundown neighborhoods and cannibalized cars left to rot on the street. Piles of trash occupied every corner as if each block had decided to create its own dump. The air held the sharp stench of burning rubber and the sweet heaviness of decay.

A gang of children, ragged and dirty, with impossibly wide, dark eyes, watched them roll past. Dre guessed they were under ten years old, which meant what she was seeing now was the only life these kids had ever known.

She raised her hand, and one young girl, maybe five or six, waved back madly. Dre smiled at her, but then the little girl was behind them.

"Take the next left, Harrison," one of the men in the back seat said.

Harrison's gaze flicked to the rearview mirror. "Copy."

Dre recognized Tom Sellner and Andy Myers from the ETG office in Tysons Corner. In the hall, they usually nodded back at her if she said hello, but she'd never spoken to either man.

On the flight down from Andrews Air Force Base, Harrison had filled her in on "S&M," as the duo liked to be called. Both had a sterling resume: Airborne, Ranger school, and members of the 5th Special Forces Group. Their operational experience included two decades of fighting Salafist jihadi terrorist groups in the Middle East and northern Africa. After the Army, they joined the CIA Special Activities Division, a group of mostly former spec ops professionals who worked in a civilian capacity for the CIA. The team of S&M had transferred to Emerging Threats Group last year.

On the next block, Dre saw a US Army two-and-a-half-ton truck parked in a side street. An Army green field hospital tent emblazoned with a large red cross on a white background was pitched a few meters away. Soldiers were distributing food and water from the back of the truck, and a lengthy queue of people waited to enter the field hospital.

"Ramirez, what you're seeing here are the lessons of Iraq writ large," Harrison said.

"Amen, brother," said S&M in chorus.

Dre recalled having an Army colonel as a professor for a modern military history class at the Academy. One of his favorite sayings about lessons learned in Iraq and Afghanistan was: Amateurs talk tactics. Professionals talk logistics.

Only now was she really understanding what he meant. The success of the US operation in Venezuela would result not from military strength but from their ability to help the population of Venezuela to help themselves. The faster, the better.

She could hear the colonel's lesson in her head. *An unstable population will not yield a stable government. Take care of the needs of the people first. Stabilize the economy. Rebuild the infrastructure. Allow them to choose their path forward to a stable government,* their *version of a stable government.*

Dre knew little about Valencia Corazón, the latest rising star in

Venezuelan politics. Whoever she was, if she won the election, the woman had her work cut out for her.

She caught a glint of metal in the sky and craned her neck to see above them.

Dre had read about the use of drone swarms, but she'd never seen them in action. They were everywhere over Caracas, dozens of mini-drones barely the size of her clenched fist. They provided tactical overwatch and reconnaissance, feeding a continuous stream of integrated data back to a sector command post. Somewhere nearby, an Army officer was programming the drone swarm with an app on a ruggedized tablet.

What fascinated Dre about the use of swarms was that the user gave up decision-making at the individual drone level. Instead, the operator gave an area and mission and let the swarm make the individualized decisions based on local conditions like tree cover, population density, and weather. Dre would dearly love to get a look at the programming behind the drone swarms.

Distributed computing and cooperative threat engagement. DARPA stuff at its finest and very cool.

Sellner leaned forward between the seats and pointed. "There."

At the end of the street, Dre saw a large park with trees, a playground, and a scattering of picnic tables. As Harrison slowed, Dre saw the mangled wreckage of the downed Chinook helicopter.

As evidenced by the trail of destruction, the massive aircraft had been traveling in a southerly direction on impact. At the far end of the park, Dre could make out the dual stumps of the twin rotors still attached to the blackened body of the helo. The craft was on its side like some wounded creature, and the rear ramp hung halfway open. Her mind refused to process what it must have been like to be inside the craft as it crashed to the earth. A Chinook was capable of carrying fifty fully loaded combat troops.

Harrison parked the SUV on the street, and they approached the site of the wreckage on foot. A team of Army investigators wearing white clean-suits and carrying cameras worked the site, documenting the evidence. Harrison motioned for Dre to stay back. Sellner and Myers approached the officer in charge of the investigation.

Dre couldn't recall a time in the office when either of the former Delta operators had said more than two words to anyone—even each other—but out here in the field they were chatty and friendly.

The lieutenant colonel in charge of the wreck site greeted Sellner with a handshake and a hug.

"That guy was at Sellner's last command before he got out," Harrison said. "He's a battalion commander in the 101st now."

Dre watched the three men walk the length of the park and then huddle under a tent where two enlisted personnel were organizing pieces of metal on a series of tables. The officer drew a ballpoint pen from a breast pocket and pointed as he leaned over the table.

After twenty minutes, S&M rejoined Dre and Harrison.

"Well?" Harrison said.

Sellner's jawline was a ridge of muscle. "SA-29 MANPADS, complete with beamrider laser targeting. Confirmed. The friggin' things even have the factory label on them."

The Man-portable Air Defense System was a shoulder-fired surface-to-air missile. Versions of the Russian weaponry had been on the market for decades, but the SA-29 was the latest technology, equipped with the capability to integrate automated control over multiple units for coordinated kills. They were notoriously difficult to manufacture, and supplies were limited to only elite Russian frontline units.

Harrison swore. He peeled off his sunglasses and pinched the bridge of his nose. "SA-29s? They're sure?"

Sellner nodded. "Absolutely. They even got a damaged sample from the launch site." His voice had taken on an edge of anger that made Dre want to take a step back.

Harrison paced, his sunglasses dangling from his hand.

"This is not adding up," he said. "For starters, assuming the Venezuelans could buy this weaponry from the Russians, where did they get the money? We're talking top-dollar stuff here, worth millions of dollars. And that's not even the biggest question."

"Where are the little green men?" Myers said. His voice was deep and resonant.

Harrison stabbed at him with the sunglasses. "Exactly!"

"I'm not following," Dre said.

"There's no way the Russkies would airdrop this much primo firepower into a two-bit country and not send a whole company of mercs with it," Sellner said. "Just like Ukraine or Syria, the Russians like to have their own people on the ground pulling the strings."

"Maybe they got out before the US took control of the city," Dre said.

Harrison shook his head. "We would have seen increased signal traffic, from HUMINT sources, or something on satellite."

"Maybe they're still in Caracas," Dre countered.

"Possible," Harrison replied, "but not likely." He pointed at a pair of drones zipping through the air space above the park. "With these little guys all over the city, it's hard to believe we haven't seen any sign of them yet. My spidey sense says they were never here."

"Which means what?" Dre said.

"I don't know yet," Harrison said. "Saddle up, gents. Next stop: the hoosegow."

Harrison stayed silent as he navigated the SUV into downtown Caracas. The Palacio Federal Legislativo was a two-story white stone building with a gold-painted dome. It opened onto an open plaza the size of a city block.

In the center of the square stood a statue of a man on a rearing horse. Ancient spreading oak trees provided shade for a scattering of park benches. It should have been a peaceful setting, but instead it looked like a war zone.

Garbage can lids, pieces of doors, baseball bats, and plexiglass shields were scattered everywhere. Heaps of wood and metal that had been makeshift barricades were bulldozed off the street. A white tent with a red cross that had been erected in the middle of the square listed at a drunken angle. The stinging stench of tear gas still hung in the air.

Harrison parked on the cobblestone street. When Dre got out of the car, she almost stepped on a spent gas canister. She picked it up. *Made in the USA* was stamped into the side of the canister.

S&M surveyed the plaza with flat stares.

"This was ground zero," Harrison said. "Intel says there were almost ten thousand people in this plaza, mostly students and kids. The government gassed them—another gift from our Russian friends, I suspect—and rolled in."

Sellner picked up a spent gas canister. He noted the writing. Then he smelled the gas residue. The smell repelled him.

"Fire gas. We don't make this stuff anymore. My guess is this was another Russian trick to get these people to hate us."

Dre let her eyes roam over the detritus of the lopsided battle. "How many dead?"

Harrison blew out a breath and shrugged. "Who knows?"

The inside of the Palacio was like entering another era. Wide, airy spaces full of sunlight spilling over gleaming marble floors. Alabaster statues occupied niches in pale yellow-painted walls.

Harrison consulted an Army sergeant manning a desk inside the foyer and rejoined them.

"The main holding area is in the basement." He nodded to S&M. "You guys check the prisoners for any senior enlisted or officers who were involved with the weapons procurement." He nodded at Dre. "You and I are going to sit in on an interview with one Colonel Maldonado."

Harrison knocked on the door of the conference room where the Venezuelan colonel was being interviewed. The interviewer, a US Army captain, his hair shaved to the scalp, stepped outside. Harrison asked if he and Dre could sit in on the interview.

"No problem," the captain said, "but this guy's a phony. We're just cross-checking some details. Ask him anything you want."

Colonel Maldonado was a slumping man with a sizable paunch and a greasy pompadour. He had a nervous habit of running his fingertips along his thick black mustache. His green Venezuelan Army uniform tunic was unbuttoned at the neck, revealing a mat of chest hair.

Dre and Harrison took their seats, saying nothing. The Venezuelan officer studiously ignored them, even shifting his body position so he was half-turned away. Despite the air-conditioned room, the man was drenched in sweat, and his façade of bravado seemed stretched to the breaking point.

"Where did you get the surface-to-air missiles?" the interrogator asked.

"We purchased them on the black market," Maldonado replied.

The colonel was difficult to understand. Dre closed her eyes to try to tune her Spanish to the man's accent.

"You were involved in the negotiation?" the interrogator said.

"Of course."

"How much did you pay per unit?" Harrison asked in Spanish. "How many units did you purchase?"

The colonel pretended to consider the question. "Five thousand US dollars per unit."

Harrison snorted. "That's bullshit, Captain. This guy's useless. Lock him up with his troops and throw away the key. Let them deal with him." He tagged Dre on the arm. "Let's bounce."

The colonel wasn't fluent in English, but the word *bullshit* translated, and he got the gist of the rest.

"I don't know where the weapons came from," he said in rapid-fire Spanish. "The general had a meeting with an arms dealer."

"When?" Harrison demanded.

"One week before the US invasion," the colonel said. "And there was more. The arms dealer seemed to know the US invasion plans. He had a map and showed us exactly where to set up sites to ambush the helicopters."

"Were there any Russian advisers?" Harrison pressed.

The colonel shook his head. Thick strands of greasy black hair came loose and splayed over his forehead.

"There was no one. The dealer had a video that showed us how to use the missiles," the colonel said in a pleading voice. "We trained the men."

"Where did the general get the money to buy the weapons?" Harrison said.

"He said there was no payment," the colonel said. "He said the weapons were a gift."

"Who did the general meet with?" Harrison said. "Don't lie to me or I'll feed you to your men piece by piece."

"I don't know," the colonel said. "I only saw him for a second, and I didn't see his face. He had dark hair—that's all I know."

"Where is the general now?" Harrison asked.

"*Está muerto*," the colonel said.

"Suicide," the interrogator confirmed. "Why do you think I'm talking to this piece of shit?"

Harrison paced the room. Finally, he turned to the Venezuelan officer.

"How did the weapons get into the country?" he asked.

"By boat," the colonel said.

"You want to stay out of jail, Colonel?" Harrison asked. "You want freedom?"

"Sí." The officer's voice was quiet, his expression timid and fearful.

"You and I are going to the port," Harrison said. "I need you to find the name of the ship that carried the weapons into Venezuela. If you help me, I'll keep you away from your men. Can you do that for me, Colonel?"

"Sí."

Harrison turned to Dre. "Well, that's our best—"

Dre cut him off. "Did the general use a laptop?" she asked the Venezuelan officer. "Or have a mobile phone?"

"No computer," the colonel said in halting English, "but *celular, sí*."

The captain hooked a thumb over his shoulder. "Intel shop is at the end of the hall. If it exists, they'll have it."

24

Caracas, Venezuela

The intel shop had commandeered a large conference room. Whiteboards lined one wall, a series of large flat-screens lined the other. In the center, ten Army personnel wearing headsets hunched over computers. A thick bundle of cables met in the center of the table, then snaked to the floor. Some of the screens displayed aerial maps of the city, others showed head-shots of men, some in uniform, some in civilian clothes. On the white-boards, Dre read through a list of names in neat block lettering. About half of them had a line drawn through them.

Dre found the officer in charge and introduced herself. He was a fresh-faced second lieutenant with freckles and boyish good looks. He listened to Dre's request.

"Lieutenant, I'll be honest," he said. "Our primary mission right now is hunting down our most wanted list for questioning." He pointed to the whiteboard. "The general's body was bagged and tagged yesterday, so he's off the list. I'm sure our team gathered any devices and turned them in." He nodded toward a young woman hunched over the nearest computer. "Sergeant Palovski dumps the devices and uploads them to stateside servers. We're just first-phase exploitation down here. We don't have the manpower or the language skills to handle detailed analysis. If we have what you're looking for, you're welcome to it. You got your own gear?"

Dre slapped her backpack. "Right here."

The second lieutenant smiled. "Pull up a chair, ma'am."

Sergeant Palovski was a hyper-organized young woman from Tulsa, Oklahoma, with a quick smile and blazingly fast keyboard skills. It took her less than three minutes to find the general's file.

"He had only one device, ma'am," Palovski said. She spoke as quickly as she typed. "A mobile phone."

"Encrypted?"

The sergeant shook her head. "The man was a poster child for what not to do about cyber security. His passcode was one-two-three-four. I don't speak Spanish, so I have no idea what's in there."

Dre immersed herself into the digital life of the recently departed General Hernandez.

His email was a bust. The general appeared to prefer paper over a screen. He had an assistant who seemed to keep his inbox under control, and he sent very few outgoing emails.

She checked his text messages. She found a few from his wife about household topics, like when he was expected home. One text from two weeks ago was tagged with a phone number instead of a name. The message was two words: *Room 711.*

Perhaps a meeting about the weapons shipment?

She tried his photos. Pictures of an older woman, probably his wife. A series of photos of an attractive younger woman, dressed suggestively. Maybe a daughter?

The next photo made her reach for her own phone.

A Russian MANPAD lay in an open shipping crate. The date on the picture was ten days ago. She called Harrison.

"I'm in the general's phone, and I've got a picture of a MANPAD," she said. "Still in the crate, factory stickers and all." She read off the date on the photo.

Harrison sounded frustrated. "It's a shit show down here at the port. Do you know they still use Windows 95 to run their scheduling software? Every time I try to boot the friggin' thing up, we lose power and I have to start over."

"The Army's got a sweet setup down here," Dre replied. "Bring the computer in, and I'll take a shot at it."

"That'll work," Harrison said. "I'll be there in an hour."

Dre returned to the general's phone and dug into his WhatsApp files.

The younger woman in the photos file was most definitely not the general's daughter. The WhatsApp message thread between Hernandez and the woman who identified herself as Loredana made Dre blush. The pictures were even worse.

Palovski tilted her head at Dre's laptop.

"Flexible gal," was all she said.

Dre held back a chuckle, then went to the next thread, which was linked to a phone number in Belgium.

Jackpot.

The general had been communicating with a man named Dominik about the shipment of Russian weapons. She also turned up a transaction with a bank in Dubai.

Just as Dre finished sending the contact details and banking information to Michael back in Washington, Harrison arrived carrying an ancient desktop computer.

"What's the haps, Ramirez?" he asked.

Dre ran him through what she had found. Harrison chewed his lip.

"Our theory is that Dominik is an arms dealer for the Russians? Maybe Bratva?" he asked.

"I've got Michael running down the phone number and the bank account right now," Dre replied. She nodded at the desktop tower. It was crusted with decades of grime, and the fan was caked with dust. "Let's see what you have in there."

It took two hours to get the machine running and to dive into the scheduling system, but they finally narrowed the list down to a handful of two dozen likely candidates. The ships had originated from all over the world: Brazil, South Africa, North Korea, multiple ports in Europe.

"I was hoping we'd find a shipment signed off by Ivan Ivanovich on the merchant ship *Stalin*," Harrison said. "I'll start with the North Korean."

Dre laughed but said nothing. It felt good to be away from the office, doing real detective work in the field.

"Go back to the general's messages, will you, Dre?" Harrison asked.

She turned her screen to him and watched as his eyes scanned.

"This whole thing smells," he said.

Dre waited as the older man scrubbed at his chin.

"Arms dealers are not a charity," he said. "Why would this guy show up and just give weapons to the Venezuelan Army? What's in it for him?"

Palovski, seated to Dre's right, chimed in. "Maybe the Russians are paying him, sir."

"Sergeant, you might be onto something," Harrison said. "I think it's time we call out the big guns. Ramirez, I'll be right back."

Harrison walked into the hallway. Dre could see him pacing as he made a phone call. When he returned, he wore a smile.

"How about dinner, Miss Ramirez? My treat."

Harrison drove the black SUV with Dre riding shotgun. Sellner and Myers, ever silent, occupied the back seat. At a stoplight, Sellner opened his door and stepped out of the vehicle. Dre watched the man disappear into the evening foot traffic.

"Where's he going?" Dre asked. She got no answer. Ten minutes later, Harrison turned into a shady side street and parked the car.

Myers got out and walked down the block by himself. Dre was hungry, tired, and more than a little miffed that everyone except her seemed to know what was going on.

"I assume at some point you're going to fill me in on the larger plan, Harrison," Dre said. "I'm wondering why the silent Bobbsey twins know what's going on and I don't."

"We'll wait a few minutes before we go in," Harrison said. He opened the glove compartment and took out a small black container the size of a box for an engagement ring.

"Harrison, I'm sorry," Dre said in a mocking tone. "I just don't feel that way about you. I think we should just be friends."

The older man chuckled at her joke. "Trust me, I am not marriage material. Just ask my last three wives."

He opened the box and removed a black ethernet plug the size of his pinky nail. He slipped the device into his breast pocket. Dre recognized the adapter as a physical intrusion device for a network server.

"What are you planning?" Dre asked. "You gonna bug someone?"

"As a matter of fact," Harrison said, "we are."

Dre stopped laughing. "Don signed off on this?"

"My powers of persuasion are vast, young lady," Harrison said. "Stick with me and you just might learn something."

Harrison opened his car door, cutting off further inquiry.

"Let's eat," he said. "I'm hungry."

The Mezzanotte Ristorante was like a step back in time. If Dre hadn't just seen the carnage in Plaza Bolívar and the blackened hulk of a downed American helicopter in a city park, the restaurant might have convinced her that she'd imagined it all.

It was a beautiful evening. The setting sun lit up the side of the buildings above, but the street was shady and cool. Tables from the establishment spilled out onto a wide flagstoned patio surrounded by flowering vines. A gentle breeze floated mouthwatering smells from the kitchen. Dre's stomach reminded her that she hadn't eaten a thing since six a.m.

Myers sat at a table for two next to the street, a tall glass of pilsner in front of him. Harrison steered Dre toward the back of the restaurant. He held her chair for her at a table for two next to the garden wall. The seating was arranged so that they both commanded a full view of the dining area and the bar.

A heavyset man in a dark suit and open-necked white shirt approached the table. He needed a shave and was sweating despite the pleasant air temperature. A wide smile revealed the need for dental work.

"Harry!" he said in English, his arms opening wide before he even reached the table.

Harrison stood. "Carlos, good to see you, my friend," he replied in Spanish.

The two men hugged, and Harrison introduced Dre as a work colleague.

"Thank you for the table on such short notice," Harrison said.

Dre detected an unusual accent to Carlos's Spanish but couldn't place it. Possibly European?

"I'm always happy to help my friends," Carlos replied. He clasped his hands together. "I'm glad the Americans have come. Finally."

When Carlos departed, a waiter appeared, depositing two sweating mojitos and a plate of appetizers.

"Come to papa," Harrison said, taking a long sip of his drink. He speared a round breaded ball and dropped it on Dre's plate. He spooned tomato sauce over the appetizer.

"Thanks, Harry," Dre said in a teasing tone, "but I can feed myself, thank you."

"Bollos pelones," he said. "Meatballs in arepa dough. It's the house specialty. I think the secret ingredient is guinea pig meat."

Dre sliced into the meatball and took a bite. The meat inside was minced and spiced with enough heat to make her want her mojito but not enough to be uncomfortable.

"You're like Elvis down here," Dre said. "How do you know Carlos?"

Harrison's eyes strayed to the front of the restaurant as he chewed.

"I helped him out of a jam once," Harrison replied. "He owes me one... more like two or three, I guess." His eyes met hers. "We all have those things we can't talk about, right?"

Dre nodded.

Harrison smiled as the waiter approached. "Is the gnocchi still the best in South America?"

The waiter grinned at him.

"*Dos*," Harrison said, holding up two fingers.

Harrison checked a text on his phone. His gaze traveled to the entrance of the restaurant.

Dre followed his line of sight. A man sauntered in off the street and made his way to the bar. He was mid-thirties and slim, with slicked-back dark hair in a stylish cut. He wore a dark blue pinstriped suit and a white shirt with the first three buttons undone. His hands were jammed into his pants pockets, and he walked with an exaggerated roll in his step that looked like he was imitating something he'd seen in a movie.

The young man ordered a drink at the bar, then extracted a mobile phone from his jacket pocket and absorbed his attention in the glowing screen.

Dre noticed Sellner enter the restaurant and join Myers.

Harrison drained his glass. "I think you and I need another drink."

Without waiting for an acknowledgment, Harrison strode to the bar and ordered. Idly, he folded a bar napkin into the shape of a swan and placed it on the edge of the counter.

As the bartender placed two fresh drinks on the bar, Harrison's elbow bumped the figure. The swan dove to the floor.

If she hadn't been watching, Dre might have missed the handoff.

Harrison stooped to retrieve it. As he straightened up, his right hand moved the wiretap device from his breast pocket into the young man's coat pocket.

He returned with their drinks just as the waiter arrived with two plates of steaming gnocchi.

"Bon appétit," Harrison said, tucking into his meal.

The gnocchi was melt-in-your-mouth delicious, and Dre made short work of her meal. As they ate, the young man at the bar finished his drink and left.

Myers departed the restaurant a few moments later.

Harrison pushed his plate away. "I've done my part, Ramirez. Tomorrow it's all you."

Dre kept her voice low. "You mind telling me who your friend was?"

"Andrei is an IT professional," Harrison said. "He works here in the city." Harrison raised an eyebrow, then added, "At the Russian embassy."

Harrison's phone buzzed with an incoming text.

"Myers reports that our young friend is safely back home, unencumbered by followers."

Harrison waved at the waiter.

"Dessert?" he said. "I highly recommend the flan."

25

Don Riley's desk phone rang. He punched the speaker button with far more force than was necessary.

"Riley."

Mark Westlund's voice filtered through the speaker. "Don, we've got Dre on the line from Venezuela. She says it's important."

"I'll be there in five," Don said.

He sat back in his chair and blew out a long breath.

The daily intel brief read like a post-apocalyptic novel. Iran, India, Venezuela. He tried to arrange the disparate pieces of intel into a coherent narrative. Find some pattern in the madness. Was there a common thread? Or was he just seeing years of pressure building to a breaking point? If so, why now?

The computer screen provided him the grim facts. The United States military and diplomatic corps were stretched beyond the breaking point. Stop-loss policies were in effect across all the armed forces, preventing men and women from leaving the service as planned. Deployments were being extended or moved up to cover exigent circumstances. Ships and troops were being repositioned all over the globe to cover the emerging hotspots.

The Navy was scrambling to reposition assets. The Second Fleet, based out of Norfolk, was already stretched by the demands of the Iran campaign. Elements of the Third Fleet from San Diego were about to move through the Panama Canal to support Venezuela. It was a logistical nightmare with no end in sight.

Public opinion was building rapidly against further overseas commitments, but future commitments were not the issue. The United States couldn't cover the commitments that existed now.

And here he sat in his office in Virginia, doing nothing to help his country. His team had missed every single one of these flare-ups.

He wanted to sweep the mountains of paper off his desk in a rage and throw his computer against the wall, but it would do no good. Even with the benefit of hindsight, a thorough review of the intel did not show his team had missed anything of significance.

The clues simply weren't there to find.

Even as he thought it, he knew the idea made no sense. The signs were out there. He just needed to figure out where.

Don hurried to the meeting with Mark. On the videoconference screen, Dre and Harrison huddled together in front of a laptop in what appeared to be an elegant conference room. Mark and Michael had turned their chairs to face the monitor while still keeping an eye on their own computers.

Don plopped into an open seat. He was suddenly very tired. "What have we got?"

Dre's face had the flushed, excited look of someone who was deeply involved in her work. She was hot on the trail of some bit of critical intel and had the sense of satisfaction that came from making progress. It was a feeling Don did not share right now.

"Harrison planted a device inside the Russian embassy," she said. "I was able to hack their internal phone system, which allowed me to turn on individual desk phones in offices throughout the complex." Her voice had a note of pride.

"In other words, we have a listening device in every office in the embassy," Mark said.

"And?" Don asked. He knew his tone was peevish, but he was in no mood for a big reveal today.

"We have a recording between the Russian ambassador in Venezuela and the Russian foreign minister," Dre said. "Harrison can translate."

She tapped her laptop keyboard. Don recognized the husky laconic voice of the Russian foreign minister, a man named Sergey Irimov, from his frequent appearances on the news. He was a tall man who wore rimless glasses and an oily smile as he spouted assurances to the world that whatever awful thing had just happened, Russia was definitely not part of it. His unflappable composure in the face of aggressive reporters' questions was famous.

Only, at this moment, the Russian foreign minister sounded anything but composed. He sounded angry and under pressure, but also no match for the wrath of the Russian ambassador to Venezuela.

Harrison's voice as he translated was a calm counterpoint to the two men shouting at each other in Russian.

Foreign minister: "I promise you, Dimitri, I had no part in this. I'll speak to the president immediately. I promise you. I will get to the bottom of it."

The ambassador breathed like a wounded bull. They could hear him as he paced around the room. His speech was interspersed with muttered curses.

"The Venezuelan government wants to expel the entire diplomatic team!" Harrison translated the ambassador's voice. "My career is over."

Don made a motion for Dre to pause the recording.

"What's up?" she said.

"Why is he on speakerphone?" Don asked. "This is a secure conference call."

Harrison spoke up. "I'm pretty sure the ambassador has somebody in his office," he said. "If you listen carefully, you can hear somebody whispering. My guess is the ambassador's covering his ass with someone, maybe GRU, maybe someone in the Venezuelan government."

Don rubbed his face. "Okay, let's continue."

The foreign minister's voice again: "That's the Americans talking. They've invaded the country, now they tell the Venezuelan people what to do."

"How could you let this happen?" the ambassador screamed. "I should have been told that we were providing advanced weapons to the Venezuelan Army. You not only put this entire mission in danger, but we've lost a diplomatic presence here, maybe for good."

Foreign minister: "Dimitri, I swear to you, I knew nothing of this. I'll take this matter up with the president immediately."

Ambassador: "It's too late. The Venezuelans want to hold us responsible for the deaths of the Americans. We've already started destroying documents. I expect to receive official notification of expulsion of the entire Russian delegation by the end of the day."

"That's the gist of it," Harrison said. "There's a thick column of black smoke coming out of the Russian embassy, so he's not lying about burning documents."

Don tried to make sense of what he'd just heard. The foreign minister was the Russian president's closest confidant. The joke making the rounds was that if the president had gas, Irimov farted for him. Was it possible Irimov was out of the loop about a covert international operation of this magnitude?

"Do you believe the foreign minister is telling the truth?" he asked Harrison.

Harrison shrugged. "That man lies as easily as he breathes, but either we just witnessed a truly command performance of bullshit or he really does not know what's going on. When you couple his lack of awareness with the other suspect details about this operation, it just doesn't add up for me."

"Explain," Don said.

Harrison leaned into the camera. "The story we're getting is that an arms dealer, some guy named Dominik, provided the Venezuelans with state-of-the-art MANPADS. For free. Ignore the fact that these weapons are the latest and greatest Russian tech and they don't even have enough for their own troops. Even if you could swallow that line, the Russians had to know—no matter how successful the attack—they had to know that some of those MANPADS were going to fall into American hands."

Harrison's voice took on a cynical tone. "The Russians spend years and billions of dollars developing a new weapon system, and they just give it to Venezuela? In what universe does that make sense? That's the first point."

He ticked off a finger and raised a second. "Point two: Where are the little green men? If Russia was planning to use their latest tech to deliver a beatdown on the US, they would've deployed mercenaries. That's chapter one in the Russian playbook. As far as we can tell, the only people speaking Russian in this city are lighting bonfires over at the embassy. We have zero evidence showing mercenaries were ever in the country. Trust me, Army intelligence is all over that. They just got their asses handed to them by a third-world country. Any sign that the Russians were behind it would make them feel a whole lot better about the situation."

Harrison threw up his hands. "It doesn't add up, Don. None of it."

The flat-screen monitor adjacent to the screen containing Dre and Harrison was tuned to a muted CNN. Under the breaking news banner, a reporter stood in front of the White House.

"Hang on, Harrison," Don said. "We've got something going on here." He motioned for Mark to turn on the TV sound.

"...Pentagon has confirmed the president has placed the European Command on alert," the reporter was saying. He was a young African-American man with a slim-cut suit and skinny tie. Although he had a deep, resonant voice, he looked like he'd just graduated from high school. "While the conflict in Venezuela has grabbed international attention, it is the sudden resurgence of violence in the Balkans that has NATO leaders meeting at this hour. Sources inside the White House and the Pentagon both confirm that the US intends to redeploy troops from South Korea as part of a peacekeeping contingent."

Another crisis, Don thought. Even more troops getting spread more and more thinly over the planet.

"Speculate for me, Harrison," Don said. "The Balkans are in the Russian's backyard. They've been messing around in that sandbox forever. We found evidence of Russian tech at the site of the Iranian attack on the Navy destroyer. Venezuela has Russian fingerprints on it."

Don hoisted himself out of his chair and walked toward the monitor. "From where I'm standing, if it looks like a duck and quacks like a duck, then it must be a duck. Tell me I'm wrong."

Harrison ran his fingers through his short graying hair and shot a sideways glance at Dre.

"If somebody was setting this thing up," he said, "that's the conclusion they'd want you to come to, Don."

"You think this is a setup?" Don said.

Harrison shook his head. "What I have in mind is worse."

26

Singapore

The worst part about living as a deep cover operative was that Ian Thomas had a job.

A real job, a job that required him to actually work most of the time.

Although he had access to almost unlimited funds from the Minister, Ian was careful to live within his means in the expensive city of Singapore. His job as a maritime risk assessment manager for Global Risk Ltd paid well and offered him the perfect cover for travel almost anywhere in the world.

Normally, a risk assessment manager would not be at his desk at six p.m. on a Friday, but Ian was trying to make the demands of his cover job align with his latest tasking from the Minister.

Notification from the Minister had arrived in his spam folder when Ian perused his email first thing in the morning. Over his lunch hour, Ian ventured deep into the Chinatown section of Singapore to a small coffee shop. He ordered a hot tea and a sandwich. The server provided the login credentials for the secure router when she delivered his food.

Ian took a bite of the sandwich as his computer navigated the security protocols that gave him access to the secure message service from the Minister.

The brief was only one page of text and a photograph. He read the file quickly. He was to provide backup for a political assassination in Bosnia. A simple job. If all went according to the Minister's plan, he would have nothing to do.

After memorizing the details, he logged off and left the coffee shop.

The midday heat in the narrow streets of Chinatown was suffocating, but Ian walked anyway. He needed to clear his head.

Ian passed the ornate Buddha Tooth Relic Temple, the four-story pagoda towering over the squat dowdy structures surrounding it. On a whim, he turned left instead of heading back to the office. He walked into the lush greenery of the Pearl's Hill City Park. The park was built around a fenced reservoir, and Ian strolled the cracked concrete paths. Mahogany trees towered overhead, blocking the sun and littering the ground with their dead leaves.

It was time he faced facts. The Minister was acting erratically. In the past four months, he had used Ian more than in the last five years. Some missions required his expertise, but others—like the Bosnia job—were beneath him. Why?

Was the Minister angry with him? Was he punishing Ian for some transgression?

Or perhaps, Ian wondered, his latest orders were not from the Minister.

He considered the possibility, turning the thought over in his mind. If that was true, should it even matter? He was an instrument of the State, not a puppet of the Minister.

But it did matter to Ian.

He had done many deeds in the service of the State. Stolen secrets, blackmailed politicians, assassinated men and women for reasons he knew nothing about.

But he had never started a war before. Now Ian had started three: Iran, India, and Venezuela.

It was Venezuela that bothered him the most. The other two conflicts had been long-simmering affairs. If Ian hadn't started the latest installment of violence in Iran or India, it was just a matter of time until someone else did.

But Venezuela was different. The backlash from the Venezuelan arms shipment was both predictable and horrifying. Hundreds dead, the United States military industrial complex poised to wipe out hundreds more. The Minister's aim seemed to be to set the world on fire—and use Ian as the arsonist.

And now Bosnia...

As if to shut down this train of thought, Ian closed his eyes. There was nothing to be done. An operative of the State did not question his properly authenticated orders. He followed orders—to the letter, without hesitation.

That was his training. It was his reason for being.

He opened his eyes again, his mind clear.

From his office on the thirty-ninth floor of the Ocean Financial Center, Ian could see into the downtown core of the city-state of Singapore. The building had once been the tallest in Singapore, but now gleaming skyscrapers reached new heights all around him. At last check, the Ocean was only the eighth-tallest structure in this fast-growing city.

Friday evening traffic crawled through the crowded downtown streets. Singapore was an impressive city-state, an oasis of orderly government in the midst of the chaos that was Southeast Asia. Somehow this tiny island had managed to execute a balance between the ethnic tensions of the region and rampant capitalism.

Ian threw himself in his leather desk chair and flipped on the TV. CNN was continuing coverage of the US invasion of Venezuela.

An attractive reporter with long dark hair and a Spanish accent walked through the remains of a city park, blackened and routed with bomb damage.

"It was at this site, the United States Army claims," the reporter intoned, "that they were attacked by Venezuelan Army troops with shoulder-fired missiles. Those missiles claimed the lives of more than one hundred US soldiers." The reporter's voice deepened, and she gestured to her right. The camera followed. "Unfortunately, when the US responded, not all of the bombs found their mark."

A city block of what had been three-story tenements was nearly leveled. The bomb had landed on a street corner, and the blast blew inward. The resulting damage was like someone had scooped out most of the block in a sweeping arc of destruction.

The camera zoomed in, and Ian could see into living rooms and kitchens where the exterior walls had been sheared off, like he was looking into a macabre dollhouse.

Ian's stomach roiled at the sight. He flipped off the TV.

The phone on his desk trilled, a welcome sound of normality after the grisly TV scene. He snatched up the receiver.

"Thomas," he said.

"Hello, stranger." The tone was low, husky, and female. He recognized the voice instantly.

"Isabel."

After Panama, Ian had forced her from his mind, convincing himself that her sudden disappearance was a good thing. He did not need—or want —connections or commitments.

"I owe you an explanation," she began.

"You don't owe me anything," Ian interrupted. "The adrenaline was running hot that night, and we were caught up in the moment. I've already forgotten it."

"Well, that's disappointing," she said. "I was hoping I could see you again."

Ian felt himself grinning like an idiot. After the doubts of the day, it felt good to smile again.

"Look out your window," Isabel said. "What do you see?"

Ian slouched in his chair and put his feet up on the desk. Outside the golden sun was slipping toward the horizon, making the still waters of Marina Bay look like beaten gold. The distinctive three towers of the Marina Bay Sands casino were silhouetted against the glowing horizon.

"Friday evening in Singapore," Ian said. "The party is just getting started."

"You see the Marina Bay Sands?" Isabel said.

"Yes." How did she know that?

"Open your right desk drawer, Ian."

"Okay..." He shifted his feet and tugged the drawer open. A pair of Zeiss binoculars were sitting atop a stack of papers. His feet hit the floor. They were not his.

"Look at the rooftop of the Sands," Isabel ordered.

Using the binocs, Ian studied the long, sleek structure that spanned the three towers like the hull of a luxury yacht. With the magnification, he could make out the famous infinity pool and the gardens.

"Do you see the red umbrellas on the end?" Isabel said. "Your right side."

He made out a splash of red umbrellas hovering over tables. "Yes."

"I'm waiting for you there."

Ian squinted through the binoculars, warm excitement surging through him.

"You're here?" he said. "In Singapore? Right now?"

Her laugh tinkled in his ear. "I have a premier spot in the hottest bar in Singapore on a Friday night, and I must say the men in this city are quite attractive. If you don't get here within the next thirty minutes, I just might forget about you."

"Don't. Move."

Twenty-eight minutes later, a slightly winded Ian stood at the entrance to the CÉ LA VI Bar and Restaurant atop the Marina Bay Sands.

The light breeze that took the edge off the normal humidity faded as Ian angled his way into the crush of weekend tourists. He worked his way around the perimeter of the area.

He spotted Isabel at a table next to the balcony. Just seeing her again left a strange sensation in his gut, and he almost turned away. He could not have attachments in his life. It was forbidden.

She had her dark hair drawn back in a French twist that accentuated the delicacy of her features. Her face had a slight scowl as she studied her mobile, as if she were reading an annoying office memo.

Then she looked up and saw Ian. The scowl evaporated into a smile. Ian moved toward her.

Her kiss was warm and immediate. Any doubt he'd harbored about reconnecting with this remarkable woman disappeared in that instant.

"Sit," she said. "Enjoy the sunset with me."

The table was poised fifty-five stories above the teeming city, washed bloodred by the setting sun. Car headlights and taillights glittered along the roadways. In the harbor, massive cruise ships and container vessels looked like toy boats in a bathtub.

"Beautiful," Ian said, looking at Isabel. Her face was tinged red by the sunset.

"You're not looking at the horizon," she said.

"I've seen sunsets before," Ian replied. "Seeing you is better."

The sun slipped below the horizon, plunging the scene into darkness.

A server brought a dirty martini for Isabel and a vodka tonic for Ian.

"Grey Goose, right?" Isabel said.

Ian sipped the drink, tasting the bite of the tonic and the burn of the alcohol. "Perfect."

She wore a simple shift of loose off-white linen, belted at the waist, and no jewelry. The casual wear emphasized her slim frame, and the sleeveless dress showed off her toned arms and shoulders.

"What are you doing here, Isabel?" His senses were jangled, anxious, and intoxicated by this beautiful woman all at the same time.

"Do you know how many offers I've had in the last half hour?" She arched an eyebrow. "I could have had any man in this place." Under the table, she ran the toe of her bare foot along Ian's shin. Ian felt the electricity of her touch. "But I waited for *you.*"

"You also didn't answer my question," Ian said quietly.

Isabel looked out over the city, then at her drink, then—finally—at Ian.

"I owe you an explanation," she said. "About Panama."

Ian waited, not even daring to sip his drink. He studied her face, looking for signs that she was telling him the truth. His training would reveal deception, and if he found it, then this relationship was over. And he so desperately wanted it to continue. He stayed silent. The next move was hers.

"I should've been honest with you when we first met," Isabel said. "My client in Panama is a drug dealer. That's what I do: I help drug dealers hide their money."

She gulped her drink, faltering. "He wanted to mix business and pleasure. I said no. That's all true."

She signaled for another drink from the hovering server.

"What you didn't—couldn't—know is that on previous trips to Panama, I wasn't so careful. I guess you could say my drug dealer friend had reason to expect the level of intimacy that he didn't get."

The new drink arrived. She left it untouched. The server lit a small candle on their table, and the flickering light played across Isabel's features. Her dark eyes seemed to glow in the dim light.

"I'll just come out and say it," she continued, her voice strained. "The attack that night was not random. They were coming for me." She gave a short, mocking laugh. "You don't sleep with a drug dealer once, then suddenly get morality. You paid the price for my mistake. I'm sorry."

Her breath grew shaky, and she reached for his hand.

"That's why I left in the morning without saying goodbye. I was ashamed, and I'm sorry."

She withdrew her hand from his and picked up her drink.

"I wrote you off as a one-night stand, Ian Thomas," she said with a laugh. "A mysterious man I met in a bar and took to my bed, never to hear from again. Except..."

She let the word hang in the air.

"I couldn't stop thinking about you."

Ian drew a deep breath. She was telling the truth.

"I—I thought about you as well," he said. "Constantly."

Her smile blazed across the space between them.

"I knew it!" she said. "I took the week off from work and flew here to throw myself on your mercy. Either this works or not."

Ian's heart rose and sank in the same moment. The latest orders from the Minister...

He drained his drink. "Unfortunately, I have a flight out of Singapore in the morning, and I absolutely can't miss it."

"What time is your flight?" Isabel asked.

"Nine a.m."

The radiant smile never dimmed. Isabel raised her hand for the check. "Then I have exactly twelve hours to show you how sorry I am."

27

The Kremlin
Moscow, Russia

Russian President Vitaly Luchnik glared at the television on the wall of his office as if the force of his stare could alter what he was seeing on the screen.

The channel was CNN, the American version. He liked to see the same information his enemies were seeing.

A fire-engine-red breaking news banner flared across the screen. The chyron told the story:

Sarajevo mayor-elect assassinated.

A BBC reporter, dressed in a dark blue jacket, her blond hair pulled back into a hasty ponytail, was reporting live from the scene. She had a low, intense voice and seemed genuinely shaken by what she was describing.

A tall hospital rose up behind her, the modern building all sharp angles and edges against a pewter sky. The street in front of the edifice had been blocked off for an event. A dais with a lectern and chairs under a white awning occupied the front steps of the building.

The foreground was filled with police cars, lights flashing. Uniformed men clustered together. Misting rain beaded on the reporter's hair as she spoke into the camera.

"I'm at the site of what was supposed to be the grand opening of a new hospital here in Sarajevo. The celebration turned tragic when the mayor-elect of Sarajevo was assassinated. Hana Mulic, a devout Bosniak Muslim woman, was only thirty-two years old when she won the mayoral race in a landslide last month. She had been seen as the leader of the reconciliation movement here in Bosnia, but earlier today she was shot dead by a lone gunman in front of hundreds of people here at the hospital's grand opening. The entire assassination was captured by an onlooker on her mobile phone."

The screen displayed a shaky video. A young woman in a headscarf with a wide smile stood behind the lectern. A man, thin and bearded, appeared at the edge of the field of view. He raised a handgun and fired until the magazine was empty, then turned and ran. The woman clutched the side of the lectern, her eyes wide, then slid to the ground. The video ended.

"This video has gone viral in this once war-torn country," continued the reporter, "raising the specter of further violence. Already, we are seeing demonstrations all across the region and reports of armed paramilitary units being mobilized. Reporting from Sarajevo, this is—"

Luchnik muted the television and wheeled to face the two men standing at attention in front of his desk.

"How could you let this happen?" he shouted at Defense Minister Yakov. "I told you to stir up trouble, not start a war."

Ever the soldier, Yakov stared straight ahead, his eyes fixed on a spot on the far wall.

"Look at me, Yakov," Luchnik shouted, aware he was escalating more than was necessary for the situation. He tried to regulate his breathing and failed.

Yakov's head snapped in Luchnik's direction, and he met his president's gaze without flinching.

"Mr. President, it was not the military behind this attack," he said. "I am in contact with my men on the ground, and they knew nothing of this action." His eyes slid in the direction of the man standing next to him.

Luchnik fought for control. An assassination was messy, unnecessary, but what really bothered him was that he had not ordered the job. Luchnik turned his back on the pair.

"Get out of my sight, Yakov," Luchnik said. "Federov, you stay."

He waited until the door closed behind Yakov before he turned around to face Vladimir Federov.

The head of the FSB was arguably the second-most powerful man in the Russian Federation, behind only the president himself. Formerly known as the KGB, the Federal Security Service handled matters internal to the Russian Federation. Luchnik had engineered his rise to power from within that organization, and his protégé had absorbed the lessons of apprenticeship.

Security started at home. Without complete control within the State, there could be no security outside the State.

Federov's bald head gleamed in the sunlight streaming through the window. His hazel eyes glittered like crushed glass.

Luchnik had selected and trained Federov with care. The two men thought alike. They had the same instincts, the same world view. Federov was reliable. Federov was loyal—or was he?

"Well?" Luchnik said.

"It was not our people, Mr. President," Federov answered. His soft voice did not waver.

"You're sure?" Luchnik pressed.

"Absolutely." No hesitation.

Luchnik gestured to an armchair and sat down himself. "Is Yakov telling the truth?"

Federov shrugged. "As far as I know, but I can look into it if you wish."

"Yes." Luchnik scraped his chin with his knuckles. "If it wasn't us, who is responsible?"

"The attack appears to be a lone wolf." Federov indicated the muted television. "It could simply be what it looks like. Maybe we just got lucky, Mr. President."

Luchnik ignored the jibe. First a stroke of luck in Iran and now in Bosnia? No one was that lucky, not even him.

"Find out who is behind the assassination, Federov. If someone is free-lancing, I want to know who it is."

"Of course, sir." Federov nodded. He regarded the television with unblinking eyes. "While the world is captivated with this unforeseen event, I suggest we make a few adjustments to our external operations."

President Luchnik blew out a long breath, his mind still on the elusive subject of luck.

"Move some irregulars into the Donbass region," he said. "Let's put some pressure on Ukraine. See what happens."

Federov rose to leave. "What about Syria? Shall I move some contract fighters there as well?"

Luchnik nodded, his eyes still on the television screen.

The BBC reporter had managed to get her camera crew onto the stage where the young woman had been shot and killed. She had tears in her eyes as she knelt next to a bloodstain on the ground.

There is no such thing as luck, Luchnik thought.

28

Somewhere on the North Pacific coast

The secret base was listed in the naval registry as a radar station. Although owned by the State, the remote station was maintained by a series of private contractors.

It was located fifty kilometers from the nearest city of any size. More appropriate to the Minister at this moment, those fifty kilometers translated to an hour-long, bone-jarring car journey over potholed dirt roads.

He could've taken a helicopter, of course. But that might have aroused attention, and any sort of scrutiny was the last thing he wanted. The possible irony of one of the most secretive naval installations in the world being discovered because he wanted a more comfortable trip was too much to contemplate.

So, he endured the car ride.

As if the universe was reading his thoughts, the right front wheel slammed into a deep pothole. A scrape of metal sounded as the car bottomed out, then the vehicle lurched upward again.

The Minister experienced a jolt of pain in his midsection like the stab of an icy knife. Scanning the road ahead for upcoming obstacles, he released one hand from the handle over the window and fished in his suit jacket pocket for the small black pill bottle. Wrenching the lid of the pill bottle off with his teeth, he tongued one half of a pain pill into his mouth and dry-swallowed it.

Pain or not, half a pill was as much as he would allow himself for now. He wanted to be sharp for this next meeting.

That was what his existence was reduced to now, a balancing act between being distracted with pain or riding an opioid high.

The black pill bottle was his only defense against the disease that ate his body from the inside out. At night, when he lay in bed, floating on an opioid cushion, he imagined he could feel the cancer replacing his healthy cells with black death one cell at a time. Like black sand through an hourglass, he felt his life draining away.

Scarcely six months ago, he considered himself to be a healthy man with an unhealthy lifestyle. He had not seen a doctor in years. What finally drove him to seek a physician's opinion was not pain but an unusual fatigue in the late afternoons that often forced him to take a nap. He expected to be advised about a better diet, to stop smoking, and to lose some weight. Probably a lot of weight.

The doctor's diagnosis froze the Minister to his core.

Cancer. Stage IV pancreatic cancer. Treatment was useless. The disease had already metastasized throughout his body.

The Minister was a walking dead man.

The doctor gave him less than a year to live. Less than a year to close out his affairs and make his peace with death. In other words, a year to fade away into oblivion.

He had no family, no interests outside of work. No life outside of his service to the State. His carefully constructed existence as one of the most powerful spymasters on the planet was of zero use to him now. He could not scheme his way out of this dilemma.

The very next day, an intercepted report had come across his desk. A Canadian mining company had been contracted to analyze core samples for the presence of rare earth metals. On a normal day, he might have sent an operative into the field to verify the outlandish claims.

But instead, the report sparked an idea in the Minister's imagination. An idea so bold that he discarded it at first as outlandish. He had served for so long as a cog in the machinery of the State that the concept of an independent operation was terrifying.

The idea did not go away. What do I have to lose? he'd asked himself in the darkness of his empty bed.

Nothing, came the answer.

The pieces of the plan were already in his grasp. Ian Thomas was a trusted operative. He could easily buy the services of the North Korean shipping fleet and secure a temporary reduction in the fiery rhetoric of the country's brash young leader.

He smiled to himself. Every plan needed a fail-safe. In a few moments, he would see that asset for the first—and likely the last—time.

If the Minister believed in a Supreme Being, he might have suspected divine intervention. He did not, of course. The Minister believed in the religion of accumulated power. These assets existed at this time and place because he had seen fit to build them.

And now he would use them.

After a half century of service to the State, this would be his final act. This was his legacy.

The car rounded a bend in the road, endured another spine-shattering jolt in a pothole, and their destination came into view.

The radar station was perched high on a cliff, overlooking the ocean, which stretched away to a razor-sharp horizon. The installation consisted of a long, low-slung cinder block building next to a massive geodesic radome. A pair of parabolic communications dishes, angled upward, were mounted to concrete pads on the other side of the building. A dented, muddy truck was parked next to the door.

Eager to be out of the vehicle, the Minister opened his own door and stepped outside. A bitter wind cut through his thin suit jacket as he hurried to the door of the station.

His driver led the way. No one from the station staff came to greet him —that had been prearranged. He led the Minister to what might have been a storage closet except for the fact that it was a heavy steel door and secured by a keypad. The man entered a code, which the Minister knew was changed on a daily basis, and the door swung open.

Inside was an open elevator. The Minister entered and touched the only button on the elevator controls.

When the doors opened again, the Minister stepped into an underground submarine bay. The original cavern in the mountain had been enlarged and reinforced with steel trusses. The air in the space was still and humid, and the sound of the Minister's shoes echoed as he stepped out of the elevator onto the concrete pier.

The man waiting for him was dressed in heavy coveralls stained with grease and dotted with burn marks from a welding torch. He took the Minister's hand in both of his own and offered a short bow.

"Minister," the man said. "You honor me with your presence, sir."

"Thank you, Admiral." The Minister gestured with his free hand toward the cavernous space. "Show me. Please."

The water in the submarine bay was dark and still. Although large enough to house two ballistic missile submarines, the lagoon was empty except for a slim black craft tied up to the long concrete pier.

"This is the X1, Minister," the admiral said.

At barely forty meters long, the submarine lay low in the water. The conning tower present on a typical submarine was missing, replaced by a slight rise in the topside of the hull, like a pared-down dorsal fin.

Conning towers were used for sailors to stay above the water when the submarine was on the surface. The X1 had no conning tower because it didn't need one.

The submarine had no people.

The largest unmanned underwater vehicle in the world had been built and tested over the last two years under an iron curtain of security. Without a doubt, it represented the finest technology his country could muster.

The X1 had a range of ten thousand nautical miles and carried twelve weapons—a mix of heavyweight torpedoes and vertically launched anti-ship missiles. An automated cargo bay could hold mines or an array of smaller remotely operated vehicles for espionage work.

Unlike a shark that needed to keep swimming to stay alive, the X1 could go dormant for extended periods. It could be reactivated by a timer or by the use of an extra-low frequency code. The predator could lie in wait on the bottom of the ocean for weeks, even months before being summoned to service.

The sole hatch in the top of the submarine was open, throwing a cone of golden light into the dark cavern.

"The modifications I ordered are complete?" the Minister asked.

"It was a tight squeeze, but we managed to modify the cargo bay to hold the device." The admiral's feet shifted on the concrete, making a scraping sound in the still of the cavern.

"Your concern is unfounded, Admiral," the Minister said. "It is only a precaution."

"But if the device is discovered to be missing—"

"You will not be held responsible," the Minister interrupted. "I'd like a tour."

Like most submarines, the Xi had been constructed in sections, like slices of a sausage, and then welded together. Each section was densely packed with sensors, electronics, or the central computer that ran the entire operation. The interior of the Xi was not designed for human occupation. There were no berthing areas, no galley, no sanitation facilities. The passageways were a maze of sharp corners and claustrophobic spaces, meant only for infrequent maintenance access. Even a slim man would have had difficulty navigating the narrow passageways without turning to one side. At one point, the Minister was forced to get down on his hands and knees to crawl into the next compartment.

They began the tour in the front of the craft. The torpedo room contained a pair of round horizontal carousels, each containing four torpedoes.

"The launch system works like a revolver," the admiral said. "Once a torpedo is shot out of the tube, the command module automatically indexes the carousel and reloads the tube. The entire operation takes sixty-seven seconds."

"And the missiles?" the Minister asked.

"Vertical launch, sir," the admiral replied. "They are in a self-contained unit outside the pressure hull."

The Minister studied the sensor suite. The Xi sonar processor consisted of a separate computer the size of a small refrigerator and one tiny monitor used only for maintenance.

"How does the sonar perform under the ice cap?" the Minister asked.

The other man looked at him sharply. The ice environment was difficult for even the most highly trained operators.

"The X1 will perform," the admiral said.

The submarine had two power plants, he explained. A diesel engine for surface propulsion and charging the batteries. When submerged, a bank of fuel cells was used for supplemental power. With proper power management, also controlled by the central computer, the X1 could stay submerged for up to a month and achieve bursts of speed up to twenty knots.

The admiral paused aft of the power plant module. "All that remains is the cargo bay, sir," he said. "It's very a tight space."

"I'll take my chances, Admiral," the Minister replied.

A lone sailor went to work unbolting a hatch in the center of the narrow passageway. The smell of fetid seawater filled the air as the tech slid the hatch aside to reveal a narrow ladder disappearing into a dark space. The enlisted man unclipped an LED work light from his uniform and handed it to the Minister.

"The cargo space is unlit, sir," the admiral said.

The Minister squeezed past the admiral and squatted down. He lowered his feet into the dark space below and found the ladder. Then he climbed down.

The cargo area of the X1 was roomy, running at least fourteen meters along the belly of the ship and five meters deep. At the bottom, his foot splashed into a puddle of oily seawater. Although the massive clamshell doors of the hold kept out most of the seawater, the cargo hold was located outside the watertight pressure hull used to ensure a dry environment for the electronics. Only items capable of being submerged in seawater at depth could be stored in the cargo hold.

Normally, the cargo area contained a special forces mini-sub or remotely operated sensor submersibles. Today, the hold contained only one massive weapon.

The submarine-launched ballistic missile was held in place by three massive clamps along the body of the weapon. Measuring a full two meters in diameter and over thirteen meters long, the weapon just barely fit into the allowed space.

With a range of seven thousand kilometers and containing eight MIRVs, or independently targeted warheads, the weapon was the ultimate fail-safe option for the Minister's plan.

In the dim illumination provided by his tiny work light, the Minister reached out to touch the skin of the missile's watertight housing. It was damp to his touch, smooth white metal beaded with seawater.

He closed his eyes, imagining the future scene.

The Xi rising from the murky ocean depths like a leviathan. The clamshell doors opening with a burst of trapped air. Three short blasts as the explosive bolts on the clamps released the missile. The final launch order from the Xi...the missile ejecting out of the hold, righting itself, surging to the surface. Bursting free...

It was deadly. It was insane. It was magnificent.

"Minister," the admiral called down. "Is there a problem?" His face was framed in the circular hatch, pinched with worry.

"No," he replied. He drew in a deep breath of the trapped, salt-laced air. "No problem."

He watched the enlisted man replace the bolts on the hatch and tighten them to restore the watertight integrity of the Xi interior space.

Back on the pier, the Minister slid an envelope from his breast pocket and handed it to the admiral.

"Send the Xi to these coordinates."

The admiral ran his finger inside the envelope flap and extracted a single sheet of paper. He read the coordinates. His gaze flicked to meet the Minister's.

"The Arctic Ocean?" he said.

"When the Xi is on station," the Minister said, "place the ship in standby mode. Have it check in every eight hours via satellite communications link. I will provide further instructions."

The admiral came to attention and saluted the Minister. "It shall be done, sir."

"And now, Admiral," the Minister said. "The device, please."

The man unzipped his coveralls and extracted a slim black tablet from an interior pocket. He swallowed as he handed over the device.

"It's already keyed to your biometrics, Minister."

"And I have complete control over the X1 with this?"

The admiral's gaze flitted over the dark hull. "Yes, sir."

"Including," the Minister continued, "the modifications?"

The man nodded. "The launch codes are embedded in the software, sir."

"Excellent." The Minister stowed the device in his own pocket. He lowered his voice. "There's only one more matter to discuss. How many men know about the X1's new capabilities?"

The admiral stiffened. He licked his lips. "It is a tightly controlled group. Compartmentalized information protocols are in place. Less than ten people know the full extent of the project, mostly engineers."

"Good," the Minister said. "It is imperative that this information never become public. Do you understand what I'm saying, Admiral?"

The Minister saw the understanding in the other man's eyes.

"I understand, sir. Consider it done."

29

The Kremlin
Moscow, Russia

President Luchnik squinted at the laptop screen, studying his most trusted advisers using tiny cameras hidden all over the Security Council Meeting Room in the Kremlin.

The room was a cavernous space with a vaulted ceiling and dark stone columns set against contrasting alabaster walls. Four massive chandeliers of crystal and gold hung over the long mahogany table. At the far end of the room, three-meter-high double doors were guarded by a pair of polished soldiers handpicked by Luchnik himself.

The Russian president preferred to hold important cabinet meetings here because the room provided a powerful camera-ready backdrop for when he invited the press in afterward.

The room radiated might and majesty, evoking a time when the Russian empire ranked among the great powers of the world. Luchnik's presence in this room made a statement to everyone who saw him on television or in a photograph on a website or in a magazine.

The message was not subtle, and not intended to be so. These trappings of power and strength tapped into the lizard brains of the people watching him.

On the monitor, his cabinet members milled about, never more than a few paces from their seats, ready for his entrance.

Let them wait.

The hairs on the back of his neck prickled. Forty years of espionage experience told Luchnik he had a problem. A major problem. Common sense told him the problem originated with one of the men in the next room.

One of these men was false. He focused on the monitor as if he could divine the traitor by mere sight.

The attacks in Iran and India were not of his making, but also not unwelcome happenings. There were ample supplies of Russian armaments on the world market. Anyone could have procured what was needed for those two attacks. The results were both predictable and satisfying. Let the Americans squawk about Russian interference.

Federov had found no evidence of a Russian hand behind the Bosnian assassination. He was thorough. If Federov said they were clean, Luchnik was satisfied.

But the truth about Venezuela took Luchnik completely unawares. Someone had provided the latest in Russian MANPADs to the Venezuelan Army to use against the Americans. Yes, the Americans had gotten a bloody nose, but at what cost? The United States now possessed some of his country's most advanced field weapons, and Russia had lost an ally on the doorstep of the Americans.

And Luchnik was being blamed for the entire affair.

Any way he viewed this problem, *he* was the loser, and there could be only one reason.

Luchnik cast his gaze on the elaborately carved, gilded armchair at the head of the long mahogany table.

One of the men in that room wanted his job—no, they wanted his *head*.

Luchnik scowled at the monitor again. The candidates with both the balls and brains to attempt such a coup were few. He had made sure of that.

Minister of Foreign Affairs Irimov looked like he'd aged a decade in the past weeks. His jowls hung loosely, and the eyes behind the rimless glasses looked bleary. Irimov stood behind his chair, talking to no one. Still, he'd done what he could to push back the constant tide of criticism that was aimed at his country and his president.

An act? Luchnik wondered. Irimov was certainly the most gifted politician in the room. He would benefit no matter who ruled the Russian Federation.

But Irimov had been loyal for decades. Why would he turn on his president now?

As usual, Minister of Defense Yakov wore his emotions like a medal, and his blocky features radiated anger. The president doubted if Yakov had the intellectual capacity to plan the kind of operation that was unfolding across the globe. This was the work of a spymaster.

Federov, Luchnik thought. The head of the FSB was more than capable of such a task. He had the resources and the network to pull it off.

Federov was speaking to Prime Minister Mishinov, nodding his head, his bald pate gleaming by the light of the chandelier. When he smiled at something Mishinov said, the emotion of the gesture was confined to a bending of his thin lips.

Federov had the means, but did he have the motive?

Luchnik had guided Federov to his current position as the right-hand man to the president of the Russian Federation. Part of the reason he had nurtured Federov was because of the way the man handled power. Like a rich old miser who bought day-old bread to save a few rubles, Federov accumulated power but he never used it for his own personal gain, only for the benefit of the United Russia Party. Had something changed?

The president sat back in his chair, struck by a sudden thought: Had *he* changed?

Perhaps Federov believed that Russia would be better served by a new leader. The head of the FSB would never support a change in leadership for his own personal gain, but in the service of his beloved country...that was most definitely a possibility.

And there was one final candidate, but it was almost too painful to consider.

Admiral Nikolay Sokolov stood at the far end of the table, not talking to anyone.

Luchnik studied his nephew on the monitor, struck as always by the uncanny resemblance to his late sister. The president shook his head. It was almost impossible to conceive of his nephew—his own flesh and blood—as a traitor to both his country and his adopted father.

Almost impossible. Nikolay had the means and the intellect, but did he possess the motive?

Luchnik turned off the monitor and stood. His body man appeared, suit jacket in hand. The president slipped his arms into the tailored garment and allowed the young valet to smooth the jacket across his shoulders. He shot his cuffs and snapped his lapels into place.

The assembled cabinet came to attention when President Luchnik strode into the room, each man standing behind his assigned leather-upholstered chair. An aide held the president's chair for him as he sat—his gilded chair was larger, of course, and perfectly centered between the flags posted behind him. As a final touch, the coat of arms of the Russian Federation, a double-headed golden eagle on a bloodred background, was fixed to the wall above his head. When the men in the room looked at him, the backdrop reminded them of his power.

He waited a full second before gesturing for his cabinet to take their seats. There was a low chatter as the men dragged out their chairs, sat down, and positioned their notes.

"Enough," Luchnik said. Even though his voice was low, the sharp tone stilled the conversation in the room. At the far end of the table, a minister was just raising his teacup to his lips. He set it back down, careful not to make a clink as the cup touched the saucer.

The president savored these moments when all eyes were on him. He held the fate of these men, the fate of an entire nation, in his hands.

One by one, his gaze traveled around the table, focusing on each man until his opponent showed signs of discomfort. Only Federov met his eye without so much as a blink.

"Minister of Defense Yakov," the president said. "Please explain to me how our latest technology in shoulder-fired missiles found its way to Venezuela."

Yakov cleared his throat and shuffled a sheaf of papers. "Mr. President," he said in a gravelly voice, like rocks rattling in a tin can. "We don't know."

The room was absolutely still.

"You mean you haven't completed your investigation?" Luchnik asked.

"No, sir," he replied. "I mean there are no weapons missing."

Luchnik licked his lips. "We have solid intelligence that our state-of-the-art weapons were used against the Americans in South America. How did it happen?"

"We don't know, sir," Yakov said.

"Mr. President," Minister of Foreign Affairs Irimov began, "we need to make a public statement denying any involvement in the Venezuelan affair." A fit of coughing made him pause. "We need to tell the world that this was not our doing."

The president leveled his gaze at Irimov. Even the man's cough stilled.

"Why?" Luchnik asked. "You just heard your colleague tell us that we have no weapons missing from our inventory."

"But, sir," Irimov continued, "inventories can be manipulated—"

FSB Chief Federov cut him off. "The Americans got what was coming to them, Minister Irimov. Why must we apologize for something that is not of our making?"

"We didn't intend for this to happen," the foreign minister said, his tone incredulous. "We must condemn the action immediately and distance ourselves."

The Russian president's gaze made a trip around the room, assessing his opponent—whoever it was. If someone was playing him, they would expect him to deny the attack.

He would do the opposite.

"Foreign Minister," the president said. "You will say nothing."

"Sir, I hope this means that you will be making the statement personally. It would be so much more forceful coming directly from you." Irimov leaned over the dark wood table, his tone earnest, practically pleading.

"Yes, it would," the president said. "Which is exactly why I'm not going to do that. Your colleague is correct: the Americans got what was coming to them. I'm sure President Serrano is regretting his imperialist adventurism by now. Let the world believe what they want. We know the truth."

Irimov slumped back in his chair.

"Is there anything else?" Luchnik asked.

"Mr. President?" Admiral Sokolov asked.

"Yes, Admiral?" Luchnik said. His nephew had the same aquiline features and pale blue eyes as his mother. His blond hair was longer than regulations allowed, swept back from his forehead.

"There is the matter of the International Seapower Symposium at the United States Naval War College," Sokolov said. He spoke loudly and clearly from his junior position at the far end of the table, as if aware that most of the older men in the room were hard of hearing. "It's scheduled for two weeks from now. I recommend we withdraw from participation in the event. It will signal to the Americans that we are not about to let their aggressive actions go unanswered."

"An excellent suggestion, Admiral Sokolov," Luchnik replied. "Any objections?"

The head of the FSB twitched but said nothing. The president focused on his minister of foreign affairs. "Minister Irimov? Comments?"

Irimov barely raised his chin off his chest. The man was beaten, and he knew it. "No, sir."

"Very well, then, Minister Irimov, please advise the Americans that we will not be participating in their little party in Newport."

The president stood. The rest of the men in the room leaped to their feet. "You all have work to do."

He strode out of the room, directly to his secret monitor to watch who talked to whom after the meeting.

His body man fussed over his jacket and brought him a cup of tea, but the president's eyes never left the screen.

One of these men had made the fatal mistake of going against his leader.

He sat back and raised the tea to his lips.

Your move, traitor.

30

New York City

Ian Thomas's flight from London Heathrow Airport touched down in New York City at precisely three o'clock in the afternoon. As a first-class passenger, he was one of the first people off the plane, and he cleared customs in less than ten minutes.

Ian passed through the baggage claim area without stopping and entered the crowded Concourse 4 of JFK International Airport. He spotted his connection immediately. Asian-American woman with hair cut in a shoulder-length bob, wearing a dark blue suit with a canary-yellow scarf. She walked toward him from the opposite direction. Their paths crossed at the entrance to a crowded Wolfgang Puck restaurant, and she executed a textbook-perfect brush pass.

Ian deposited a key in his pants pocket and continued walking.

Luggage storage services were located next to the Arrivals hall. The key fit locker 169. Ian removed a leather computer bag and a set of car keys. A sticky note attached to the keys read: Blue 4-10.

Without bothering to check the contents, Ian slung the bag strap over his shoulder and strode out of the terminal to the parking area. Thirty-six minutes after touching down at JFK International Airport, Ian drove a black Acura TLX sedan out of the Blue daily parking lot and turned toward New York City.

The destination preloaded in the car's GPS navigation system took him to an address on Atlantic Avenue. He passed the one-story, graffiti-covered brick building, then doubled back after four blocks.

The neighborhood was mostly small shops located in one- and two-story buildings. Even though the weather on this late September afternoon was pleasant, the sidewalks were mostly empty. Atlantic Avenue was a busy four-lane road, split down the center by an elevated train line.

As Ian approached his destination on the return trip, he triggered the garage door opener on the key fob. A graffiti-covered steel door rolled open, and Ian drove inside. He waited for the overhead door to close behind him, then shut the car off and waited for his eyes to adjust to the dim interior.

Ian rested his hands lightly on the steering wheel of the car. This setup was unlike any job he'd done for the Minister before. Normally, his assignments were briefed in advance, so he knew what he was getting into before he arrived on location. But the exact nature of this assignment had not been disclosed yet. Still, the dead drop at the airport, the pre-staged vehicle, and the warehouse all indicated a large-scale operation.

The warehouse was silent save for the ticking of the car engine and Ian's footsteps as he walked the perimeter of the ten-meter-square space. Besides the overhead door through which he'd entered, there was a pedestrian door in the back of the building that opened onto an alley. A line of dirty opaque glass windows set high in the back wall offered minimal light.

Against one wall was an army surplus cot and a folded blanket. A cheap card table stood a few feet away, containing a hotplate and a coffeemaker. A small refrigerator was tucked under the table. In the center of the room, an IKEA computer table held three brand-new flat-screen monitors, arranged in a U-shape in front of a cheap office chair.

Ian took the computer bag from the car and plugged the laptop into the monitors. Before he booted up the computer, he noted it had no way to connect to the internet and was equipped with a removeable, encrypted solid-state hard drive. An air-gapped device was another indication of a major operation. He turned the computer on and opened a file directory. Ian selected Mission Brief.

Fifteen minutes later, he sat back in the office chair, still unwilling to comprehend what he had just read.

The plan was bold. It was brilliant. It was also mass murder on a breathtaking scale.

And Ian was assigned to pull the trigger.

He closed his eyes, drew in a deep breath, and held it. He counted to fifteen, then let it out slowly, feeling the thud of his heart in his chest.

He opened the attachments and set the pictures on slide-show mode. Large limestone buildings topped with copper roofs green with age. A massive bridge arcing over a waterway. Visual landmarks on either bank of the channel, highlighted with red arrows. Careful instructions about what were called "rules of the road" for navigating a boat in United States inland waters. He committed the brief and the pictures to memory.

The final file was a program labeled Simulator. When he opened it, the screens offered Ian a 360-degree view of a control room of a small boat. He familiarized himself with the controls: speed, helm, a clickable button for sounding the ship's horn.

In the computer bag, he found a game controller and plugged it into a USB port.

Run simulation? the computer prompted.

Ian clicked YES.

Immediately, the boat simulation began moving. The speed controls registered ten knots, and the course showed 020. In the windows of the boat, he recognized the image of a small island with a lighthouse that had been part of the briefing. Dead ahead, a suspension bridge towered far above his simulated ship. He passed under the bridge, then steered into the center of the waterway. Carefully, he noted his visual landmarks as he practiced the simulation multiple times.

When Ian satisfied himself that he had the task mastered, he shut down the computer. The windows in the back wall had gone dark, and his stomach rumbled with hunger.

He pulled out his phone. Nine p.m. The tiny glowing screen beckoned him to take the next step.

Isabel Montez lived in New York City. She was only a phone call away.

His fingers sought the mutilated flesh of his right earlobe as he considered his options.

Since the Minister's orders had been vague, Ian had not warned Isabel he would be in the city. But now that he knew the exact mission and the timeline, there was time in his schedule.

He had a perfectly legitimate cover story for being in New York. What was the harm?

Ian answered his own question: His life was a lie. There was no way he could have a meaningful relationship with Isabel.

But he still wanted to see her. Damn the consequences.

Ian dialed the phone quickly, before he changed his mind.

"Hello?" Her voice was a jolt of energy up his spine.

He forced a calmness into his tone that he did not feel.

"Isabel," he said. "It's me."

"Ian?"

"I'm in New York," he said.

There was a long pause, and he wondered if he had made a terrible mistake. She'd withheld information from him before. What if she was married or lived with someone?

Ian stilled his racing mind. None of that mattered now. He wanted to see her—he *had* to see her.

"Where are you?" Her voice was breathy.

"I had to see a client in Brooklyn, but I'm free now."

She told Ian her address. "I want you to stay with me tonight."

Isabel's apartment was on the sixtieth floor of a building called Manhattan View.

She met him at the door, dressed casually in yoga pants and a faded T-shirt that spelled *Harvard* across her chest. She pulled him inside, pressed him back against the closed door, and pulled his head down to meet her eager lips. Ian's body responded.

He ran his hand down the muscles of her back, and she moaned.

"I haven't stopped thinking about you since Singapore," she whispered.

"I know," Ian said into the tender skin behind her right ear. The intoxicating scent of her skin made him tremble with need.

She took him by the hand and led him deeper into her apartment. She favored a minimalist design approach, and the living room held only a single white sofa on a matching deep pile carpet, facing a bank of floor-to-ceiling windows.

The Manhattan View lived up to its name. The bejeweled nightscape of Manhattan provided the only light in Isabel's apartment. Ian spotted the Empire State Building and the gleaming waters of the Hudson River.

"It's beautiful," Ian said.

Isabel stripped off her T-shirt and threw it at him. The dappled light of the nightscape played across her smooth skin.

"I'll show you the sights tomorrow." She kissed him deeply, then fit the curve of her hip against Ian's body. "I promise."

Ian woke precisely at five a.m.

For a second, he forgot where he was. Then the memory of the previous night flooded back in vivid, delicious detail. Isabel breathed softly beside him, her lithe body lost under the down comforter. The sound of another human, vulnerable, intimate, felt oddly comforting.

He stretched, careful not to wake Isabel, then slid out from under the covers. Still naked, he padded into the living room.

The coming dawn limned the horizon with a shade of deep rose. The city beneath him was coming awake. Car headlights moved along 42nd Street, and a brightly lit ferry pulled out of the West 39th Street Terminal into the dark waters of the Hudson River.

Ian stood in the center of the dark room, feet firmly rooted to the ground, hands at his side.

The view of the waking city blurred as he focused his attention inward. The mantra echoed in his mind.

My mind is my sword. My body is my shield. My existence is not my own.

Without opening his eyes, Ian let his body slip into the familiar routines of his morning ritual. The mental chaos he had felt last night faded in the muscle memory of his movements. Serenity flowed through him like water.

His arm swept up, every tiny muscle tightening in perfect harmony. He drew up his right knee and pivoted. He felt the movements transporting him to a state of inner and outer balance. The kick flowed from his coiled body, and he landed on the ball of his foot.

Everything in perfect alignment, everything in harmony.

Thirty minutes later, his body shining with sweat, his soul at peace, Ian opened his eyes to find Isabel watching him.

Ian startled, a ripple of unease in his pool of serenity.

"How long have you been there?" he asked.

"The whole time," she said.

She had his dress shirt wrapped around her body like a robe. Isabel's slow smile held an emotion behind it that made Ian catch his breath.

"Your control is impressive," she said, her eyes drinking him in. "Powerful."

Ian's eyes narrowed. "Do you have a practice?"

Instead of answering, Isabel let the silk dress shirt slide from her shoulders.

Her skin was sleek, the color of sun-bleached sand. Her muscles rippled like water as she moved. She twisted her sleep-tousled hair into a knot and stood before him so close that Ian could feel her heat.

Isabel took his hand, lacing her fingers into his.

"Together," she whispered.

Their bodies flowed as one. Ian wondered that the presence of another being in his space should have felt awkward.

It wasn't.

Isabel's body matched his, movement for movement. Intimate, yet distinct. Her naked form was close to his, but never touching apart from their fingers. He could feel the heat of her body, the sigh of her breath.

Close, but an ocean away.

They both returned to a standing pose, facing each other like images in a mirror.

Ian felt her breath pushing into the center of his chest. Steam rose from her shoulders in the chill of her cool apartment. The musky smell of her sweat filled his head like a drug.

Ian couldn't stop himself. He reached for her.

31

Barking Sands Tactical Underwater Range (BARSTUR)
Kauai, Hawaiian Islands

"*Idaho*, this is *Zumwalt*. How do you copy?"

Captain Lannier lifted the VHF handset from the radio base. "*Zumwalt*, *Idaho*. Read you five-by-five. Over."

"*Idaho*, *Zumwalt*. Stand by to take control of *Orca*," came the reply.

The USS *Idaho* was at periscope depth. Janet watched the video monitor where the USS *Zumwalt* rode the calm waters of the Pacific Ocean only two thousand yards distant. The angular tumblehome hull and geometric silhouette made the futuristic destroyer look like something out of a science fiction movie.

Bobbing between the *Idaho* and the *Zumwalt*, a slender mast poked out of the water. If she looked closely, she could see faint heat waves from the diesel engine exhaust of the *Orca*.

"Status, Lieutenant Everett," Lannier said.

Janet scanned her screen. One of the fire control stations had been converted to a command and control station for the *Orca*.

"Ready to assume control, Captain," she said.

Lannier said into the microphone, "*Zumwalt*, *Idaho*. Ready to take control on your mark."

"Acknowledged, *Idaho*," the radio squawked. "Shifting positive control of *Orca* to *Idaho* in three...two...one...mark."

The signal strength monitor on Janet's user interface was a round dial ranging from zero to ten. The dial swung all the way to full scale.

"I have positive control of *Orca*, sir," Janet said.

"*Zumwalt, Idaho*, we have control," Lannier reported over the radio.

"Acknowledged, *Idaho* has the ball. Break. *Warner*, this is *Zumwalt*. How do you copy?"

Janet ignored the noisy back-and-forth over the ship-to-ship radio. She was more concerned with her new charge.

The *Orca* was the US Navy's most advanced XL-UUV, or extra-large underwater unmanned vehicle. Today was the first stage of operational tests for the newest addition to the Fleet. The basic test plan was for *Idaho* to control the underwater drone using a laser comms system, then simulate a coordinated attack on a submerged hostile target.

In the future, the *Orca* would be equipped with her own torpedoes, but for now, all attacks had to be conducted from the *Idaho*, the host platform.

"This is good. This is very good." Henry Patel, the technical rep from the defense contractor responsible for the new laser comms system, was seated at the fire control station adjacent to Janet. Since ownership of the *Orca* had been transferred to the Navy, he was strictly there as an adviser.

The *Idaho* had spent a painful month in dry dock while her sail was fitted with the new comms system. During that time, Janet had gotten to know the tech rep pretty well. He was a short, dark, intense man who spoke with a clipped British accent and had any number of nervous mannerisms that drove her crazy. Even now, before they had done anything, the man was simultaneously tapping one foot and twirling a pen in his right hand.

Janet had been both elated and disappointed to be named the technical lead on the new comms system. She enjoyed the technical challenge of overseeing the installation of the laser system and the subsequent integration with the *Idaho*'s weapons systems. If everything worked as planned, someday submarines might have underwater "wingmen" they could use to extend their sensor range or even launch tandem, coordinated attacks.

But those future scenarios were years, maybe decades, away. Right now,

Lieutenant Janet Everett burned to be part of a frontline warfighting effort. She had not transferred back to the Fleet to sit on her ass in Hawaii while the rest of the world burned.

Just yesterday, Janet had gotten a secure email from Dre Ramirez. Dre had been in Venezuela only days after the US invasion. Naturally, most of her work there was classified, but Janet could read between the lines. There had been some kind of covert effort by the Russians to equip the Venezue-lans—anyone could connect those dots—and Dre had been part of the team to track down the bad guys.

Janet fidgeted with the controls on the console, doing her best to keep her frustrations in check. Had she been at Emerging Threats, she would have been on the ground in Venezuela. Instead, she was here, overseeing a science project.

The radio chatter ceased. Lannier raised his voice. "Attention in the control room."

Background chatter died away as everyone turned their eyes on the captain.

"This is the first operational scenario for the *Orca*, and it's important. We will submerge the drone and establish an underwater comms link. For the next few hours, we'll run some basic tests."

He grinned. "Then the real fun begins. At 1600, we will transition to a new water management area shared with our old friends on the USS *Warner*. The *Idaho* will operate three hundred feet and above. The *Warner* will have all the water three hundred fifty feet and below. Our job is to use the *Orca* to find and simulate an attack on the *Warner*. Last time we went up against the *Warner*, we won. Let's do it again, people. Any questions?"

There were no questions, but the watchstanders shared knowing smiles all around. Captain Lannier was an intensely competitive man. During their last encounter with the *Warner*, the two captains had wagered a bottle of Macallan 18, a four-hundred-dollar bottle of whiskey, on the outcome. It was rumored that for the *Orca* exercise today, their captain had upped the stakes to a bottle of Macallan 25. Janet had looked it up online. The "Rolls Royce of Single Malts" went for upward of two grand a bottle.

"Officer of the Deck, match course and speed of the *Orca*," Captain

Lannier said. "Put her five hundred yards off our starboard beam as a starting position."

"Captain, steady on course one-eight-zero, six knots, still at PD," the OOD said after a few moments. "The *Orca* is five hundred yards to starboard."

"Very well." Lannier looked at Janet. "Order the *Orca* to submerge. New depth two hundred feet."

"Two hundred feet, aye, sir," Janet replied. She tapped at her display. "Securing snorkeling, shifting to battery power." She clocked a look at the visual monitor, which had been turned to high magnification. The telltale diesel exhaust plume was gone.

"Ordering new depth and lowering the mast on the *Orca*," she said, touching her display.

On the monitor, the slender mast disappeared beneath the surface of the ocean, and her signal strength monitor dropped to zero.

"That's normal," Henry Patel interjected.

"I know that," Janet said. She raised her voice. "Captain, temporary loss of comms with the *Orca*. Transitioning from surface to subsurface comms link."

"Very well," the captain said. "OOD, make your depth two hundred feet. Hold course and speed."

The visual of the outside world slipped underwater as the OOD lowered the optical monitoring mast. Janet waited until they passed one hundred feet before she turned on the underwater laser communications system.

"Bringing the laser comms online," Janet announced.

"Keep the power below fifty percent," Patel said. Both his feet tapped nervously on the deck with an annoying *tic-tic-tic* sound.

"The O&M manual says I can safely operate the laser at ninety percent power on a continuous basis and up to one hundred percent for limited periods." Janet set the power to fifty percent.

"We agreed on a seventy-five percent max power for this test," Patel said.

"No one agreed to limit power for this exercise," Janet said. "Should I take it up with the captain?"

Patel hesitated. "That's not necessary."

"Establishing the laser comm link, sir," Janet said. She touched the button labeled Transmit and sat back. The laser array ran a wide scan to attempt to find its target. Once established, the system would shift to a tight beam pattern for a continuous link.

A minute passed with no result.

"Lieutenant?" Lannier asked.

Janet shot a look at Patel. "Increasing laser power to sixty percent, sir."

A few seconds later, her signal strength monitor needle swung to three, then climbed slowly as the laser link focused a tight beam on the target.

"I have the *Orca*, sir!" Janet said. She could almost hear the collective sigh of the control room watchstanders.

Next to her, Patel's nervousness bordered on manic. In addition to tapping both feet, he now had a pen in each hand, and they spun like propellers on an airplane.

"Calm down, Patel," Janet muttered.

"I'd be calmer if you operated at a lower power on the laser," he snapped back.

Janet bumped the power up to sixty-five percent and was rewarded with a signal strength of eight. She ran the short diagnostic routine and received a green board—all systems go—from the underwater drone.

"Good signal," Janet reported. "*Orca* reports a green board. Drone is in station-keeping mode, sir. Ready for testing."

Lannier nodded. "Very well. OOD, come left to new course zero-nine-zero."

As the *Idaho* slowly turned, the *Orca* mirrored her movements, always maintaining position five hundred yards off the *Idaho*'s starboard beam. Janet breathed a sigh of relief, and even Patel put down one of his spinning pens.

For the next three hours, the *Idaho* ran a series of maneuvers with the *Orca*. They changed depth and speed in station-keeping mode, then maneuvered the drone around the submarine, mindful of the submarine's screw and towed array. The only position where Janet lost contact with the *Orca* was when the drone was directly beneath the hull of the larger submarine.

For the final hour, they sent the drone on an autonomous route, then met at a rendezvous point and reestablished the laser comms link.

At 1600, the *Idaho* and her drone partner were at the designated starting point for the search-and-destroy exercise with the *Warner*.

Janet joined the captain and OOD at the nav plot. The quartermaster had laid out the exercise grid on the table with their position plotted in the direct center of the area.

"We've got an acoustic layer at four hundred feet, sir," the OOD said. "That's going to make it hard to track the *Warner*."

Lannier pinched his chin as he contemplated the navplot. "I want you to come northeast for five miles, increase speed to ten knots. If we don't pick anything up, then turn south and run all the way to the end of the box."

"Aye, sir," the OOD said.

Lannier turned to Janet. "Is your data link with the *Orca* good enough to transmit sensor data?"

"If I increase the power, I can up the data rate," Janet said. "What are you thinking, sir?"

"The *Warner* knows we're capped at twelve knots with the *Orca* in station-keeping mode," Lannier said, "but they probably don't know about the SAS on the platform."

The synthetic aperture sonar on the *Orca* was typically used for highly accurate underwater measurements, such as bottom contour mapping of the ocean floor. It was not much good for long-range tracking like they were doing as they hunted for the *Warner*.

"I don't follow, sir," Janet said.

Lannier offered a wolfish smile. "If we can just get a sniff of the *Warner* on the towed array, I'll send the *Orca* in for a closer look. We can use her sensor data to get a firing solution on *Warner*, then we have him."

Janet nodded. It was a bold plan, but this was why they were running the exercise: to determine the real capabilities of the underwater drone program.

She went back to her station. The link with the *Orca* was holding steady at signal strength of seven.

"OOD," the sonar supervisor reported. "Possible submerged contact bearing two-nine-zero, designate new contact Sierra one-nine. Establishing track."

Janet listened as the OOD and the captain conferred with the sonar team.

"It's pretty weak, sir," the sonar supe said. "It fades in and out. The layer is killing us."

The OOD ordered a new course that aligned the sonar contact perpendicular to the long line of the hydrophones embedded in the towed array that streamed behind the *Idaho*.

"Contact faded, sir," sonar reported. "Last good bearing two-six-eight."

The captain convened another powwow at the navplot with Janet, the OOD, and the sonar supervisor. He circled a broad area of water with his index finger.

"I think he's in this area," the captain said. "My guess is he's using a sprint-and-drift search pattern. He knows we're speed limited with the *Orca* in tow, so he'll try to exploit that advantage. If he thinks he knows where we are, he'll pop over the layer, confirm his fire control solution, and try to take us out."

The sonar supe frowned at the plot. "If we're the speed-limited platform, he's got the drop on us, sir."

"That's what I want him to think, chief," the captain replied. "I intend to turn our handicap into a benefit. Everett can program the *Orca* to run a search pattern here." He tapped the far side of the area of interest. "Meanwhile, we sprint to the south and set up our own search pattern. We rendezvous with the *Orca*, integrate her sensor data into our firing solution, and take them out." Lannier turned to Janet. "Can we do that?"

"Setting up the search pattern is no problem," Janet said. "The trick is reestablishing contact with the *Orca* and getting a strong enough signal to download all her sensor data. Once we have her data, we have two independent tracks on the same contact. The *Warner's* dead meat, sir."

Lannier grinned. "Music to my ears, Lieutenant. Make it happen."

The next hour passed swiftly as Janet programmed and dispatched the *Orca* on her recon mission. As the *Idaho* ran south at high speed, Patel's nervous antics increased.

"You're expecting a lot out of this platform," he said to Janet.

"I'm expecting to get what the US Navy paid for," she replied. Janet was used to the defense contractor teams being conservative about their new systems, but Patel seemed more anxious than normal. Or maybe that was just his nature.

"Conn, I have reestablished contact with Sierra one-nine!" the sonar chief announced. "The signal's weak, but it's there, sir."

"OOD, stay on this course for another ten minutes, then come left to one-eight-zero." Lannier looked at Janet. "How long until we rendezvous with the *Orca*?"

Janet consulted her monitor. "Eighteen minutes, sir."

"Very well." Lannier bounced on the balls of his feet as he paced between his command console, the sonar team, and Janet's station. Next to her, the fire control team worked on a firing solution with little success.

"Firing solution has thirty percent confidence, sir," the lead tech reported to the OOD.

At the appointed rendezvous time, Janet put the laser comms system into acquisition mode.

Five long minutes dragged by as she attempted to will the machine into finding the *Orca* in the vast Pacific Ocean.

"Anything?" Lannier asked.

Janet shook her head. She bumped the laser power up to seventy-five percent.

"No more," Patel said. "And if you find the *Orca*, lower the power, please."

"You mean *when* we acquire the *Orca*," Janet replied acidly.

"Yes, when," Patel said. His entire frame quivered with nervous energy.

The signal strength meter bounced to three, wavered for second, then moved to five.

"I have her, sir!" Janet all but shouted in the quiet control room.

Lannier and the OOD crowded behind her.

"Please tell me she has useful sensor data," the captain said.

The *Orca* slid into station five hundred yards off *Idaho*'s beam. Janet queried her sensor logs.

"Oh, yeah," Janet said. "She has good track data. Downloading to our fire control system now."

She saw the signal strength dip from five to four. The data transfer rate slowed accordingly. Janet increased the laser power to eighty-five percent.

"No!" Patel said. "You need to dial it down."

"We need this sensor data," Janet replied.

"How much more time do you need, Everett?" Lannier asked.

Janet looked at her monitor. "Thirty percent downloaded, sir. Looks like another five or six minutes."

"Conn," the sonar chief said. "Sierra 19 signal is increasing. He's coming above the layer, sir!"

"Fire control," the OOD snapped. "Status of our firing solution."

"Fifty percent confidence, sir. Not good enough. We need the *Orca* data to lock in range."

Lannier swore under his breath.

"I'm on it, sir." Janet boosted laser power to one hundred percent. Patel tried to stop her, and she shook him off. The data transfer rate pegged high. "Two minutes left."

"Make tube one ready in all respects," Lannier ordered.

"Tube one ready, sir," the OOD replied. "Firing solution confidence is still less than fifty percent."

The signal strength meter on Janet's monitor snapped to zero.

"You burned out the laser!" Patel hissed. "I told you—"

"Launch transients, bearing two-seven-five!" the sonar chief announced. He looked at the captain. "It's the *Warner*, sir."

Janet heard Captain Lannier sigh behind her.

"This one's on me, team. They got us fair and square," he said. "Preserve all the data for the postmortem. We have a lot of work to do." He eyed Janet. "And if Everett's cursing is any indication, we're going to need some repairs as well."

Janet's face flushed with embarrassment. She had just bought her ship another trip to the dry dock.

"OOD," the captain said. "Take the ship to periscope depth."

32

United States Naval War College
Newport, Rhode Island

Rear Admiral Thomas Sharp stood at the open French doors looking out onto Narragansett Bay. With the passing of each hour, he could feel the tension easing out of his shoulders.

The Naval War College in Newport, Rhode Island, put on the International Seapower Symposium every two years. Hosted by the US Navy's Chief of Naval Operations, it was the most prestigious maritime conference on the planet. It was also an apolitical event, meaning that the heads of all the world's navies, coast guards, and major maritime commerce organizations were invited to attend regardless of their political relationship status with the host nation.

This year, the Russians had declined at the last minute, which irked Sharp, but the Chinese were well represented—albeit at a lower echelon of power than he would have liked. To his eye, the Chinese admirals were all too young and inexperienced, not a gray hair among them as far as Sharp could tell.

A bit like the Chinese naval forces, he thought. Young and bold, but inexperienced.

Of course, when the Chief of Naval Operations says he "hosts" the Symposium, that doesn't mean that he participates in any of the planning for the event. He appoints a "volunteer" to attend to the details so that the largest gathering of naval military brass in the world comes off without a hitch.

And this year, that lucky man was Rear Admiral Thomas Sharp. Sharp was coming back to DC after a brilliant tour as J2 for the US Indo-Pacific Command. As the newest—and most junior member—of the CNO's immediate staff, he was the logical choice.

Even at the highest levels of power, Sharp mused, the laws of gravity still apply. Shit still rolls downhill.

Sharp stepped through the open doorway onto the gallery overlooking the water. Across the array of small standup cocktail tables—those had been his idea—uniformed officers mingled, chatting in any number of languages. He caught a snatch of Mandarin to his right; to his left a torrent of Hindi was in verbal combat with a wave of French.

The breeze off the bay was fresh and brisk. Sharp drew a deep breath and forced himself to relax. This was the third and final day of the Symposium. They were on the midmorning coffee break. Just one more session, then lunch, then a closing dinner, and he was free to go back to some real work.

A young lieutenant appeared at his elbow. Jill Bowers had a round face, stocky physique, and a pageboy haircut. She had terrible PT test scores, but the woman was an organizational genius. As his aide-de-camp, she was the one who had marshaled an army of contractors and enlisted personnel to make sure that the event came off flawlessly. Her boss, Admiral Sharp, was just the suit from Washington to make sure it was done to "Navy standards" —whatever that meant.

Bowers had done an amazing job. The best in years, he had heard from several longtime participants. Her fitness report would reflect her hard work.

"Sir." Bowers cleared her throat. "May I suggest you mingle?"

Sharp realized he was just standing in the center of the patio, gawking at the water like a doofus while the symposium attendees milled around him.

"You may, Lieutenant," Sharp replied.

"The Chinese look unattached, sir," she said. "They might appreciate some face time after the morning session."

Sharp had chaired the morning session, leading off with some pointed remarks on regional security in Southeast Asia. As J2, or intelligence chief, for the US Indo-Pacific Command, the South China Sea had been his front yard and his number one headache. Everyone in Washington focused on Russia, but the real long-term threat to US hegemony was China. While Congress argued about how many ships should be in the Navy, the Chinese constructed manmade islands so they could claim the South China Sea as inland waters. The Russians, on the other hand, couldn't even be bothered to show up at the Symposium.

Sharp sighed. As a student of history, he was fascinated by the way countries were always so desperate to fight the last war instead of focusing on the threat coming at them with both barrels loaded.

Still, Bowers was right. His comments about the South China Sea had been very pointed, aimed at the Chinese. The PLA Navy contingent of four admirals had sat through the entire discussion without a single comment, their faces still as stones. The Singaporean admiral, on the other hand, had led a lively counterpoint to Sharp's comments, drawing the Vietnamese and the Filipinos into what amounted to a verbal fracas at a typically staid event like this one.

Maybe he should try to normalize relations with the Chinese. Sharp headed for the youngest officer in the Chinese contingent, who happened to be standing a few meters away at a high-top coffee table. The man looked to be in his early forties, but these days everyone looked young to Sharp. A cup of tea steamed on the table as he stared across the water at the Claiborne Pell Newport Bridge.

"Good morning, Admiral," Tom said in Mandarin. Sharp spoke passable Mandarin and hoped his attempt to use the man's native tongue might buy him some good will.

"Good morning, sir," the Chinese man said in flawless Oxford-accented English. "Your talk this morning was very provocative."

Sharp let out an inner sigh. Strike one for normalizing relations.

"I don't believe in beating around the bush," Sharp replied. "I think allies should be direct with one another."

"Are we allies, then?" the Chinese officer asked. His lips showed the ghost of a supercilious smile.

"You know what I meant," Sharp said. "The sea lanes are open to all. There is no such thing as inland waters of the People's Republic of China. The First Islands claim is baloney."

The officer turned to his tea. "Reasonable minds may disagree, Admiral Sharp," he said. "But I also believe there is an American saying that applies here: possession is nine-tenths of the law."

Sharp had to agree. The man might be an arrogant asshole, but his point was rock solid.

An awkward silence ensued as both men studied the water. Sharp noticed a tugboat making good time in their direction. It was magnificent autumn weather. What he wouldn't give to be out on the water today.

Maybe it was time to put aside self-righteousness and just talk to this guy for a while.

"This is the best time of year in Newport," Sharp said. "It's too hot in the summer, too cold in the winter, but in the fall, it's just right. Warm, sunny days. Crisp, clear nights."

Sharp winced. He sounded like a friggin' travel agent. The younger man seemed to accept the change in conversation.

"I appreciate the weather," the Chinese man said. "I grew up in Xiamen, an island. We had weather like this once a year."

The awkward silence returned. Sharp decided to end their conversational suffering.

"Excuse me, Admiral. There are some details I need to see to before the next session."

He headed toward Bowers but was intercepted by the Singaporean admiral. The man was classic Singapore: Western façade on an Eastern mind. He was short and fit, his uniform custom tailored and massed with brightly colored ribbons and medals.

"Admiral Sharp." He possessed a Midwestern accent that Sharp recalled came from his undergraduate education at the University of Minnesota. "I've been polling my neighbors in Southeast Asia, and we would like to continue the conversation about regional security in our part of the world. You took great care to 'thread the needle' with your comments. Is that the correct saying, sir?"

Sharp gritted his teeth at the man's feigned display of ignorance. He knew perfectly well that was the saying. His schooling in the English language was probably better than Sharp's. The Singaporean twisted the conversational knife ever further.

"While the United States has provided some assistance in the region, my neighbors and I believe that the US should be more forceful in their response with our Chinese partners." He smiled, revealing a row of even, pearl-white teeth. He beckoned to a Vietnamese admiral to join them.

The Vietnamese man was short, dark, and slight. He had slicked-back hair, and his uniform jacket was baggy on his thin frame. He shook Sharp's hand and offered a half bow. "My English is not so good," he said.

Sharp gave his standard reply. "Your English is better than my Vietnamese, sir."

The Singaporean began to hold forth on all the things that the United States should spend money on in Southeast Asia. Sharp's attention wandered. He had heard this speech before and had worked hard to avoid this conversational rabbit hole during the morning session. He saw now that all he had done was delay the inevitable.

At least he could ignore this idiot in some beautiful weather. His eye wandered over the sun-blasted water. The tug was drawing abreast of their position now.

The Naval War College was located on a hundred-acre island, the only connection to the mainland a causeway. The historic stone buildings, like Luce Hall behind him, had stood on this piece of land for nearly 150 years.

The tug was hauling ass in the channel, Sharp thought. In a hurry to get somewhere. The heavy, padded bow rode out of the water, and a thick white wake trailed behind it. A canvas-covered mound filled the fantail on the back of the craft.

Sharp checked his watch. In eight hours, all this schmoozing would be behind him and good riddance, as far as he was concerned. The next time he was asked to "volunteer" for something like this, he'd resign his commission. Sharp was more than happy to show up and drink his ass off in the evenings with admirals from all over the world, but he was damned if he was going to organize an event like this again.

The tug made a sharp turn toward the shore. It was only a few hundred yards distant now.

What the hell was this guy doing? Sharp wondered. The tug looked deserted. Sharp shielded his eyes against the sun, trying to see into the wheelhouse of the ship and failing.

Out of the corner of his eye, he saw the Coast Guard patrol boat assigned to this sector speeding toward the tug.

A sudden gust of wind flipped up a corner of the canvas tarp covering the cargo on the tug's fantail.

Sharp spied a row of oil drums lashed together.

The Singaporean admiral was still talking, his voice excited as he held forth on how much the US should budget for additional freedom of navigation operations in the South China Sea.

The tug was less than a hundred yards from shore, running at full speed.

Tugs carried oil drums all the time, Sharp told himself, but his mind rejected the attempt to normalize what his eyes were seeing. The hump of material under the canvas...that was not shaped like an oil drum.

People on the patio noticed the tug. They pointed. A few of them even laughed.

"Get inside!" Sharp shouted. He picked up the still-talking Singaporean and threw him through the open French doors.

The tug ran up on the shore, less than fifty yards from the patio. It had enough speed that it traveled up the rocky beach, the bow of the tug coming to rest on the manicured lawn. The powerful propellers continued to churn even as the vessel grounded.

Sharp's sense of time slowed to a crawl. People streamed past him in slow motion. The little Vietnamese admiral stumbled as he turned, then righted himself and disappeared inside.

A second passed...then two.

Glorious sunlight flooded the patio, warming Sharp's face. A gentle breeze brushed his cheek. This was truly the best time of year in Newport. The very best.

The detonation was a white-hot burst of light, too bright to look at, happening too fast to give Sharp time to even blink his eyes shut.

The shockwave that followed picked up Rear Admiral Thomas Sharp. The blast smashed his body against the historic, hewn stone exterior of Luce Hall. The walls at his back dissolved like melted butter.

Then all went black.

33

Emerging Threats Group
Tysons Corner, Virginia

The FBI agent on the secure videoconference had gone down a technical rabbit hole about the use of secure bar codes on ammonium nitrate fertilizer, a detail that felt far removed from the reality of the Naval War College bombing. The improvised explosive device on the tug had delivered a blast three times the size of the 1995 Oklahoma City explosion, the only comparable terrorist event in recent American memory.

As Don tried to refocus on the briefing, a voice from his past called out. *What's the Butcher's bill?*

Don Riley had lasted less than a year as a midshipman at the Naval Academy. Never a natural athlete, Don remembered in vivid detail the toll plebe year had taken on him physically and emotionally. On the other hand, as a gifted student with an excellent memory for detail, his recollection of academics at the storied institution on the Severn River was just a blur—except for one course.

Introduction to Naval History was a required course taught by Lieutenant Commander Harold Watkins, a surface warfare officer with an aggressive mustache and a wry smile. He was a man truly in love with his subject matter. Many of Don's classmates made fun of the officer as he strode around the lecture hall, coffee cup in hand. They whispered about how he'd settled for a dead-end job teaching a useless subject to plebes who didn't care about anything except making it through the next meal in King Hall. To them, Watkins was a washout.

But to Don, Lieutenant Commander Watkins's class was a respite from the tornado of plebe year. Don had never been much of a liberal arts type, but to his surprise, he found naval history fascinating. Watkins could talk for hours on obscure Greek battles and Phoenician trade routes, but his favorite topic was the Napoleonic Wars.

Now, as Don sat in his office at ETG, the image of Lieutenant Commander Watkins popped into his head. The walrus mustache, the ever-present coffee cup, the way his voice rose when he wanted to make a point. When he spoke of Admiral Nelson, Watkins would often strike a pose, hand on hip, and call out Nelson's famous phrase.

"What's the Butcher's bill?"

The Butcher's bill in Nelson's day was the accounting of dead and wounded from battle. Watkins delved into gory detail about what a cannonball could do to a wooden ship, how the splinters from the projectile strike caused as many deaths as the projectiles themselves. The surgeons in those days, he claimed, were often called butchers. They operated without anesthetic or antiseptic in less-than-ideal conditions. Even if the men lived after being treated by a surgeon, they often died from infections.

What's the Butcher's bill? Don thought.

The terrorist attack at the Naval War College in Newport, Rhode Island, had a Butcher's bill that defied comprehension.

A full third of the most senior officers in the United States Navy and Marine Corps were dead. Another third were spread among the intensive care units of hospitals in Newport, Providence, and Boston. The Chief of Naval Operations was dead, and the Vice CNO was in a medically induced coma. The Pacific Fleet commander was deceased, and at least half of the other numbered fleet commanders were injured in some way.

The deputy commandant of the US Coast Guard had attended the International Seapower Symposium instead of the commandant, who had presided instead over the commissioning of the newest polar national security cutter entering Coast Guard service. The deputy commandant was among the dead.

And that was just the United States. The body of the United Kingdom's First Sea Lord had already been loaded on a plane back to London, while the Operations Commander of Northwoods and the Commander-in-Chief Fleet were in intensive care in a Boston hospital. They would both live, but it was unlikely either of the two men would ever return to service.

The list of countries who had incurred naval leadership losses spanned the globe. France, Germany, Australia, Norway, Sweden, Finland, Spain, Brazil, Singapore, Indonesia, Malaysia, China, Japan, South Korea, Vietnam.

And no Russians. It was impossible to ignore that fact. The Russian president, a famously cold-hearted man, had immediately sent his personal condolences to each nation who had suffered a loss but offered no official statement.

There had been no claim of responsibility for the bombing, but the tide of global public sentiment ran strongly against the Russian Federation. After decades of international meddling, surreptitious assassinations, and any number of heinous acts, it seemed that President Luchnik might have finally gone too far.

Except, of course, for the fact that they had not a shred of proof supporting any Russian involvement.

The FBI's investigation was painstakingly slow, but they had made some progress. The crew of the tug was missing, and there was a twelve-hour block of time between their last radio communication and the explosion.

The day of the bombing, the tug had been remotely controlled, as had the detonation. That set of facts indicated a technologically sophisticated plan and an operator within line of sight of the explosion.

FBI and local law enforcement had combed the Newport area for days, going house to house to find anyone who might have seen something. So far, their efforts had yielded no leads. A separate team worked on the theory that the tug had been controlled via an unmanned aerial drone relay.

Don logged off the videoconference and slumped back in his chair. His head pounded, a dull aching throb that started at the base of his neck and radiated up into his skull. He pressed his palms against his eyes until he saw red splotches in his vision.

The answer would be in the details, he told himself. It would take time.

His desk phone sounded. Without opening his eyes, he reached out and felt for the speaker button. "Riley."

Mark Westlund's voice filtered into the room. "Don, we may have something."

Without bothering to respond, Don punched the speaker button to end the call and stood. His chair rolled back into the wall with a solid thunk.

The center wall screen in the young officers' bullpen-style office showed a map of the world. The existing conflict hotspots were tagged with red dots: Iran, the Balkans, Kashmir, Venezuela, and now Newport, Rhode Island.

Dre, Michael, and Mark stood when Don entered. He nodded at Dre, realizing he'd barely spoken to her since her return from Venezuela.

"Tell me," Don said.

Like everyone in the building, Mark's face looked haggard from lack of sleep, but his eyes held a spark of excitement.

"It's something," Mark began. "We know that the tug from the bombing was flagged in Dominica."

Don nodded. "The Dominica Maritime Registry Incorporation. We knew that on day one."

It was common for US maritime shipping companies to establish their fleets under "flags of convenience" for tax and regulatory reasons. The Republic of Dominica in the Caribbean had built a thriving cottage industry of flagging foreign vessels. One of their largest customers was Consolidated Tugs, an American company with a tugboat fleet in all major East Coast ports.

"Correct," Mark continued. "We poked into their finances and found a suspicious cash transaction about ten days ago."

Don felt his pulse quicken. "How much?"

"Ten thousand dollars," Dre said, speaking for the first time.

Don frowned. "That's not much." He tried not to sound as irritable as he felt.

"It's not," Mark replied. "But where the money came from is interesting."

Don felt his impatience growing. "And?"

"A bank in Dubai," Dre said. "And the account matches the information we took off the Venezuelan general's phone. But it gets better."

A connection between Venezuelan weapons and the Naval War College bombing? Don was all in now.

Dre continued. "The general was a WhatsApp junkie," she said. "Most of it was filled with absolutely filthy talk with his mistress, but there was a short exchange between the general and the arms dealer—only it wasn't an arms dealer."

"I'm not following you," Don said.

"We assumed that the Venezuelans were buying the MANPADS from the arms dealer," Dre said. "That's not what happened. The arms dealer paid them. And the money came from the same account that sent ten grand to the Dominica Maritime Registry Incorporation."

Don dragged a chair from the wall and sat down. "What do we know about the account?"

"It's with a bank in Dubai," Michael said. "Numbered account that's been in place for more than a year. Even if we could hack it, there's no way we can tell who owns it."

"And the mobile number on WhatsApp?" Don asked. "Anything there?"

Dre shook her head. "Another dead end."

"I've compiled a list of disbursements from that account since it was established," Michael said. He touched a button on his keyboard, and the second wall screen sprang to life showing a spreadsheet containing a dozen transactions. Don scanned the column of information. Oman, Brussels, Pakistan, Switzerland, Mali, Panama, Cairo. The amounts ranged from $10,000 up to a few hundred thousand US dollars.

"I'm working on identifying the owners of the recipient accounts," Michael said, "but most of them are numbered accounts as well."

Don massaged the back of his neck. "So, all we really have are the locations and amounts to go on."

"What about the dates?" Mark asked.

"Michael," Dre said, "let's add a column of the dates of all the conflicts since the account was established."

Working together, it took Michael and Dre five minutes to update the spreadsheet.

"Let's work with the assumption that a single entity is behind all of these attacks," Don said. "What does this data tell us?"

"A week to ten days before each conflict, we have a disbursement from the Dubai account," Dre said. "Some of the deposit sites make sense. For example, Oman and Pakistan could be correlated with the Iranian attack on the USS *Black* and the Kashmir separatists, right?"

Before Don could answer, Harrison Kohl appeared in the office doorway.

"I've been looking all over for you, Don," Harrison said. "I have something you should see."

"Join the party, Harrison," Don said. "We have something you should see."

Barbara Goldstein accompanied Harrison. In her mid-fifties, Barbara looked more like an elementary school teacher than a CIA analyst. The woman had a penchant for bright scarves and bland pantsuits. Today's ensemble was a navy-blue pantsuit and a bright red, white, and blue scarf with a matching pin on her lapel.

Don watched Harrison's face as Mark briefed him on the financial connection between the Venezuelan weapons and the tug. When Mark finished, Harrison nodded gravely.

"That's some good work." He leveled a look at Don. "I suppose you're back on the Russian hobbyhorse?"

He didn't say it in a pejorative way, but Don felt his face getting hot. He bit back a sharp answer.

"I've been giving some thought to how the Russians could take advantage of this chaos," Harrison said. "If they're out there stirring up the shit, then they must want to get something out of it, right?"

Don, swallowing his anger, nodded. "That stands to reason."

Harrison motioned for Barbara to take one of the workstations. "I asked Barbara to run some OpIntel reports for me. She used to work at ONI back in the day."

Dre frowned. "OpIntel?"

"Operational intelligence," Barbara said crisply, as if she were lecturing a fifth-grade class. "Real-time assessment of operational moves as compared to historical data. Every large military in the world is a bureaucracy, and bureaucracies are based on procedures and routines. Name a country, and I can tell you what their operational and training patterns are based solely on OpIntel.

"Unless they're up to something. Then their patterns change. If we overlay current movements on historical patterns, we can spot anomalies. Anomalies usually mean trouble."

She finished typing and swiveled to face the screen. What played out on the viewscreen was a map of Russia and surrounding countries.

"The historical data is in blue," Barbara said, "the last four months in red." The red dots, representing Russian military units, made little racetracks on the screen.

"By tracking operational movements of Russian forces, you can see that they have been relatively static over the last four months. No pattern changes."

Don felt his headache returning. "Which means what?"

"Which means," Harrison said, "we're not seeing any indication that the Russians are prepositioning forces to take advantage of all this chaos. When in the history of the world has that happened?"

Don wanted to put his head in his hands. He was so tired. "If it's not the Russians, who is it?"

"I didn't say it wasn't the Russians," Harrison replied. "What I'm thinking is worse."

Don's head snapped up. "Explain."

"The same guy has been running Russia for over twenty-five years," Harrison said. "He knows where all the bodies are buried because he buried them. He will own that country until his dying breath. But suppose someone wanted to get rid of him. How would you do it?"

The room was silent. Finally, Mark spoke.

"You'd get him overextended," Mark said. "Make him responsible for an international crisis that he can't worm his way out of."

"Or more than one crisis," Harrison said. "All at the same time."

Don sat back down. The pieces fell into place in his mind. The pattern he had been looking for was right there in front of him.

"You think the Russians are doing this to themselves," Don said.

"Worse," Harrison replied. "I think we're seeing a coup."

34

Arctic Ocean
120 miles northwest of Prince Patrick Island, Canada

Control the Arctic. Control the world.

Captain Sergei Zaitsev considered the coin in his palm. It was a bit of cast metal with the slogan printed on one side and the emblem of the Russian Pacific Fleet on the other. The cheap gold paint was already beginning to wear off. Admiral Sokolov had ordered thousands of them made up and distributed to every sailor in the Pacific Fleet. Ships were ordered to paint the slogan in a prominent place in the crew's mess and in the officers' wardroom to remind everyone of their important mission to the future of Russia.

He wished he could trade in every one of these stupid coins for a bigger maintenance budget. The Arctic was a brutal playground. Even though his command, the *Sovershennyy*, was barely three years old, she badly needed a refit.

In the Mediterranean, a major maintenance problem meant a tow to a nearby port. Here, in the Arctic, it could mean death.

Control the Arctic. Control the world.

Sergei came from a family of sailors. He could trace the Zaitsev family military service to Mother Russia from present day all the way back to the 1917 Revolution. He could remember his father and grandfather talking about the Arctic in respectful terms, but they had never sailed these waters.

When Papa served some thirty-five years ago, it was a different world. His father was an officer on the *Kirov*, a Soviet nuclear-powered battle cruiser. It was a beast of a ship, named after a real Bolshevik hero.

Sergei slipped the coin into his trouser pocket and tried to get comfortable in the captain's chair on the bridge of the *Sovershennyy*.

Papa would have been so proud to see his son become the commanding officer of a Russian Navy vessel. But compared to the *Kirov*, this *Steregushchy*-class corvette was a toy of a ship. A touch over one hundred meters long and only eleven meters wide, his command had none of the firepower or the brute strength of a battle cruiser, but Sergei was confident the *Sovershennyy* could hold her own in any fight.

He would order his executive officer to run more action station drills this afternoon. What his ship lacked in maintenance funds, he would make up for in better training.

Sergei sighed. Not that there was a lot of fighting these days. In fact, his mission was to monitor the activity of Canadian military vessels in the Arctic waters of the Beaufort, Chukchi, and East Siberian Seas.

It was boring, demoralizing work for a warship. Their orders were to get close enough to identify the Canadian ship, then hang back and report their movements to fleet headquarters every six hours. Every fourteen days, the *Sovershennyy* sailed off station to resupply and returned to her post within three days.

Even their resupply point was a joke. A tender based at Wrangel Island, a desolate bit of rock and snow that had a Russian radar station and nothing else. The crew wasn't even allowed to go ashore in Wrangel—not that there was anything to do on shore, but that wasn't the point.

The thing that really galled him, really made Sergei angry at his lot in life, was that when his ship came off station after fourteen days of religiously reporting the position of every Canadian warship to Pacific Fleet HQ every six hours, no one replaced them.

"Captain," the young officer of the deck interrupted Sergei's mental ramblings. "The noon report, sir."

"Very well." Sergei paged through the clipboard. Fuel reserves, fresh-water levels, food, readiness status. He noted they had lost a third PK-10 decoy launcher. He waved the OOD over and pointed to the entry.

"Corrosion, sir," he said. "Shorted out the firing circuit."

Sergei signed off the report and handed it back. He left the comfort of his command chair and strode out to the bridge wing. The enlisted lookout greeted him with respect, then stepped away.

The crew knew that Captain Zaitsev liked to brood alone.

On the bright side, the weather for this stint on station was spectacular. A cloudless sky, a balmy zero degrees Celsius, and gentle winds left the sun-flooded sea calm and ice-free.

The lack of ice was what made the Arctic so important these days. On the Russian side of the pole, there were now entire months where tankers and cargo ships could transit the Northern Route entirely ice-free. Sergei had seen the numbers. A cargo ship sailing from Shanghai to New York could cut off two weeks of transit time, a savings of nearly a quarter of the shipping costs. For Russia, this new shipping lane in their backyard was a gold rush they intended to protect at all costs.

On the Canadian side of the pole, there was a similar ice-free passage, but it was tricky to navigate and therefore not as profitable. The Russian government understood information was power, so Captain Zaitsev and the fearless crew of the *Sovershennyy* were here to show the flag and gather information.

Sergei picked up his field glasses and scanned the empty horizon. The HMCS *Ottawa*, a Canadian frigate visible only on radar, was some fifteen nautical miles ahead carving a wake into the calm Arctic waters.

He wondered about the captain of the Canadian ship. Based on his position reports, his mission was to patrol the edge of his own country's exclusive economic zone, a responsibility about as useful as Sergei's own mission.

The Chinese were in the mix now, too. Unlike the Americans, the Chinese poured money into their Arctic program. For the last ten days, the latest ship in the Chinese fleet, the icebreaker-research ship the *Snow Dragon*, had been fifteen miles behind the *Sovershennyy*.

The Russian ship shadowed the Canadian ship, and the Chinese ship shadowed the Russians. Like the blind leading the blind.

The OOD appeared at Sergei's side.

"Position report for your signature, sir."

Pen poised for approval, Sergei studied the message. "What happened to the *Snow Dragon*?"

The OOD shrugged. "About four hours ago, she turned west and left the area, sir."

The Chinese ship had been trailing them ever since they came on station almost thirteen days ago.

"Resupply, I suppose, sir," the OOD prompted as if reading his captain's thoughts.

Sergei grunted and scribbled his signature to release the message. Only twenty-four more hours and this season would be over. They weren't headed back to Wrangel this time; they were headed home to Petropavlovsk.

Sergei recalled his father's tales about going head-to-head with the Americans during the Cold War. This was a different time, and the Arctic was a different theater. One that favored the Russians.

Here the Americans were nothing. They might be the richest country in the world, but they still possessed only one functioning icebreaker. The world was changing. Global warming was a boon for Mother Russia. And the *Sovershennyy* was on the front lines.

Control the Arctic. Control the world.

He surveyed the open ocean ahead of the ship with his binoculars. The Arctic, Sergei decided. This was where he belonged, protecting the future of his great country.

In the distance, he heard a *pop*, like the sound of champagne cork.

His lookout yelled, making Sergei turn toward the stern of the ship.

The young man had his glasses up, his arm outstretched, index finger pointing aft.

The pop noise turned into a hiss, then a roar.

Sergei stood rooted to the deck, the binoculars dangling, his mind refusing to believe what he was seeing.

Fifty meters behind the *Sovershennyy*, just as the white wake of the ship started to blend back into the slate blue of the Arctic Ocean, a massive cloud of smoke and vapor boiled on the ocean.

A missile rose from the cloud, the exhaust a fiery trail.

A second missile followed.

The pair of missiles arced over the *Sovershennyy* so closely that Sergei could smell burned fuel. Droplets of mist rained down on Sergei and the lookout.

The missiles raced toward the horizon.

Toward the Canadian warship.

Sergei grabbed the doorframe and launched his body into the bridge.

"All ahead flank," he shouted. "Right full rudder."

The combat information center was reporting a missile launch. Using the ship-wide intercom system, Sergei cut them off.

"This is the captain," he said. "All hands to general quarters."

The gong signifying action stations pulsed through the ship like a heartbeat. An enlisted man handed him a flak jacket, a flash hood, and a steel helmet. As he put them on, Sergei mashed down the intercom button to connect with CIC.

"Captain Lieutenant Krikov, are you in Combat yet?" he said.

"Yes, sir," came the crisp reply. "Indications are the missiles were launched from a submarine."

Sergei glanced at the spinning compass. "Helm, steady new course one-eight-seven. All ahead two-thirds." He waited for a repeat back of the order, then said into the intercom, "Go active on sonar, Krikov. Find that sub."

He felt the ship slow to a speed that was conducive to a sonar search.

Less than fifteen seconds had elapsed, but it might as well have been yesterday. Things were moving too fast.

"Time to missile impact on the Canadian ship is thirty seconds, Captain," Krikov reported.

"Find the sub, Krikov," he replied.

Less than a minute. At this range, that's how long the Canadian ship would have to respond to the incoming missiles. He could imagine his Canadian counterpart being woken up or pulled away from the wardroom by a report of incoming missiles...

From the Russian ship.

Sergei cursed out loud as he threw himself at the VHF radio. The Canadian captain would react the way any warrior would if he were attacked.

He would counterattack with everything he had.

Sergei crushed the press-to-talk button on the VHF handset. He closed his eyes, trying to form the words in English.

"*Ottawa*, this is Russian corvette *Sovershennyy*. We did not fire on you. I repeat, we did not fire on you."

The VHF radio was always filled with static. On a chaotic bridge, would anyone even hear him? Even if they did, would it even matter? Would they believe him?

As if in answer to his question, an explosion formed on the horizon, then a second.

"Missile impact," Krikov reported.

Sergei raised the binoculars to his eyes.

Out of the smudge of dark smoke on the horizon, he saw pinpoints of light arcing in the sky. He counted them to himself.

One...two...three...four.

"Incoming missiles, Captain," Krikov said, his voice ramping with tension. "We are tracking four, sir. Targeting now."

"Very well," Sergei replied. "Stand by to launch VLS interceptors. All of them."

A precious second passed.

"Missiles ready."

"Fire."

The vertical launch system forward of the bridge came to life. Clamshell doors popped open. Fire and smoke poured out of the deck. The Vityaz interceptor missiles streaked away in a blaze of incandescent light.

"Quadrant four failed to launch, Captain," Krikov reported from Combat. "We have eight active missiles on an intercept course...Correction: seven missiles. One splashed."

Sergei swallowed. Seven missiles to take out four incoming weapons. The odds sounded good, but he knew the physics of the problem were akin to shooting a bullet out of the air using another bullet.

He strode to the bridge wing and raised his binoculars.

"One incoming missile destroyed," Krikov reported. "Two!"

Sergei saw a burst of smoke and light, like a fireworks shell bursting in the air.

"Three missiles destroyed!"

A pause that stretched on for a very long time.

"Fourth missile is still active."

"Stand by to deploy countermeasures," Sergei said. With a sickening thought, he realized the PK-10 launchers were out of commission.

"I have men standing by for manual launch of the PK-10, Captain," Krikov reported.

Sergei wanted to weep with relief. Krikov would get a medal for this if it was his last act as a captain. But all he said was: "Very well, Mr. Krikov. Deploy countermeasures."

He heard the *pop-pop-pop* of the launchers. A massive cloud of metal confetti filled the air. Flares burst.

He could see the missile now, running so close to the ocean that it left a trail of vapor behind it.

As the *Sovershennyy* drew away from the chaff cloud, he saw the missile alter course to follow the false target. Then his heart dropped as the missile corrected.

The Kortik close-in weapons system engaged the incoming target. An ear-splitting *BZZZZT* filled the air above him as the Gatling gun of the point-defense system spewed out a steady stream of 30mm rounds.

Less than a hundred meters behind them, the incoming missile exploded.

Chunks of shrapnel, carried by the momentum of the missile, slammed into the ship. Sergei felt the *Sovershennyy* lose power.

But they were alive.

He wanted to cry and throw up and dance all at the same time.

"Missile destroyed, Captain."

"Very well, Mr. Krikov."

He heard the background noise of the damage control teams being deployed to fight the fires, but dammit, they were *alive*.

"Engine room reports the main engines will be back online in three minutes, sir."

"Very well, helm," Sergei said. "Mr. Krikov, let's find that sub. Communications Officer, flash message to Fleet headquarters—"

"Captain!" It was the lookout's voice, the same kid who had spotted the missile launches only...what had it been? He looked at his watch. Only four minutes ago.

He moved to the railing, his eyes following the pointing finger of the lookout.

"There, sir!"

At first, Sergei thought it was a whale. The hull was low and sleek and black, but it did not have a conning tower like a normal submarine.

But whales did not have masts sticking out of their backs. The top of the mast glinted with an optical sensor. Someone was watching them.

He saw two white fingers lance out of the bow of the strange submarine. They sped right at the *Sovershennyy.*

"Torpedo in the water!" Krikov yelled over the intercom.

Sergei lowered his glasses.

"I know, Mr. Krikov."

35

The Kremlin
Moscow, Russia

When Vitaly Luchnik strode into the Kremlin meeting room, his steps had the precision of a metronome. His eyes snapped to the faces of the men standing at attention behind their own chairs.

Not a single man looked their leader in the eye. None of them dared.

Luchnik had made all of them rich beyond their wildest imaginings. Given them power that had not existed in their motherland since the time of the tsars.

And all he asked for in return was one simple, nonnegotiable thing:

Loyalty. To him and their country—in that order.

One of the men in this room had betrayed him. Iran, Bosnia, Venezuela —those transgressions were challenging to manage, but not fatal to Luchnik's grip on power.

But a terrorist attack on United States soil followed by sinking a ship of a NATO ally?

Unforgivable. Potentially unrecoverable for Luchnik.

Of course, his successor would simply let the sins of Luchnik's reign become part of the historical record—as long as he promised to do better.

Luchnik's facial features remained impassive as he took his seat, leaving the entire cabinet standing at attention.

Inside, he seethed. Someone in this room had beaten Luchnik at his own game. The student had bested the master, and for that, the master was paying the price.

"Seats," he barked.

Still silent, the two rows of ten men pulled out their chairs and settled in.

Luchnik felt every throb of his own heart, the rush of blood in his veins, the crash of new thoughts in his consciousness as every sense he possessed sought out the answer to this puzzle. The sad truth for the Russian president was that he felt more alive at this moment than he had in years, maybe even decades.

His opponent had awakened a lion. Luchnik was a fighter of the first order, and he had not yet begun to fight back.

But first, he needed to find his opponent.

"Minister of Defense Yakov," the president said. "Report."

"Mr. President," he said in his harsh voice. "Before the Canadian frigate sank, she sent a message claiming that she was under attack by a Russian warship. The *Sovershennyy* was trailing her. We believe the Canadian ship launched a counterattack and sunk the *Sovershennyy*. She went down with all hands."

"Did we have satellite coverage?" the president asked.

"No, sir."

"Did the Americans have satellite coverage of the incident?"

Yakov hung his head. "Probably."

Luchnik snapped a look at Federov, who gave a slight nod. The president wrinkled his nose as if the news had left a bad odor in the room.

"We have visual confirmation of sinking?" he asked.

The defense minister nodded. "We've done flyovers and found evidence of two wrecks. No survivors on either side."

"There was no message from the *Sovershennyy*?" the president said. "No explanation for his behavior?"

Yakov looked down the table to where Admiral Sokolov stared at his notes. He clearly wanted Luchnik to direct his fire onto his adopted son.

"Is there a problem, Defense Minister?" Luchnik asked.

"The Pacific Fleet commander is looking into it, Mr. President, but at this point we have no explanation for the incident." Yakov stared at his papers.

"Were there any other ships in the area?" the minister of foreign affairs asked. Even Irimov's voice sounded like he'd aged. "Is it possible the missiles were launched from another ship?"

The defense minister shook his head. "The only other ship within three hundred nautical miles was the Chinese icebreaker *Snow Dragon*. She does not carry anti-ship missiles, and she was out of range anyway."

"A submarine?" the foreign minister pressed.

The defense minister's mournful look deepened. "No, sir. We have accounted for every foreign submarine. Every capable platform from every nation is either in port or we have positive confirmation of their general location. None of them were in the Arctic."

"A rogue ship captain, then?" the president said. "That is your conclusion, Defense Minister?"

To his credit, Yakov looked him in the eye. "Yes, sir."

"May I make a suggestion, Mr. President?" Prime Minister Mishinov said from the far end of the table. All eyes turned to the man.

In most countries, the office of prime minister is the apex of political power. Not so in President Luchnik's Russia. The man derisively called "Little Mishi" was widely considered as President Luchnik's political doormat, the man Luchnik stood on while he wielded real power. The president had selected Mishinov from his post in the former KGB for his political flexibility in all matters of state.

Now, Luchnik looked at Mishinov with new eyes. The prime minister was in his mid-sixties and spare of frame. The president noticed the man's complexion appeared sallow, and the area under his deep-set eyes looked dark with fatigue.

"Of course, Prime Minister," Luchnik said. "I value your opinion in these matters."

At a normal cabinet meeting, this sentence would have drawn secret smiles from the more favored ministers. But today, with every action under such obvious scrutiny, not a single man dared crack a smile.

"I believe I have the support of the minister of foreign affairs that we must make a strenuous disavowal of any involvement in these attacks," the prime minister said. "But I also think that you should make an internal statement to the people of Russia that these events are being perpetrated by Western imperialist forces who wish to harm the *Rodina*."

To Luchnik's right, Irimov sat up in his chair. "I absolutely agree, Mr. President," the foreign minister said. A fit of coughing made him pause. The president was suddenly painfully aware of the advanced age of most of the men in the room.

Luchnik leveled his gaze at Irimov until the man stopped coughing.

"Why?" he asked.

"This is clearly the work of outside forces," the foreign minister said, his tone incredulous. "Perhaps they incited a mutiny. We must distance ourselves in the eyes of the world."

"And this attack on the US Naval War College?" the president asked. "We had nothing to do with that, either?"

Irimov's mouth gaped open. "Of course not, sir. That was an act of terrorism. Probably Islamic State or al-Qaeda."

"A brazen act of terrorism that no one has claimed, Minister," Luchnik snapped back. "Doesn't that strike you as odd? On 9/11, when al-Qaeda attacked New York City, Osama bin Laden claimed his victory immediately. But for this attack...nothing. The Seapower Symposium at the Naval War College." The Russian president's gaze made another trip around the room, looking for a reaction. "The Russian Federation was the only major country who did not participate."

The silence in the room crackled with tension as Luchnik bored in for the kill.

"I believe you were in full agreement not to send our naval representatives to Newport, Foreign Minister?"

Irimov licked his lips. "I—I was, Mr. President."

The shape of his opponent was coming into focus now, Luchnik decided. What had transpired was too complex for one man. He was facing a conspiracy, a team of traitors operating in tandem, using their collective knowledge of their leader to exploit his weaknesses.

They were good. He would give them that much, but that just meant that Luchnik needed to be better.

They were playing him. These men had studied Luchnik, and his playbook in the face of hard evidence was well known: deny the facts, attack the veracity of the source of the allegations, flood the zone with counterfactuals and disinformation. Then, sit back and wait for the storm to pass. It was the mother's milk of his KGB training, his go-to maneuver.

In this scenario, Luchnik realized, he was playing against himself. The traitor behind this conspiracy had been trained by Luchnik himself. They were driving him like a wild animal into the hunter's field of fire.

If he reacted as they expected, he would be cut down by enemy fire.

No, Luchnik decided, he needed to do the opposite. Force his opponents to react to his new tactics. Wrongfoot their plans against him.

"Foreign Minister," the president said. "You will say nothing."

The light in Irimov's eyes flickered. Was it fear or something else? His foreign minister's shoulder sagged, but he stayed silent. He knew from Luchnik's tone that his president's mind was made up.

"Let the Americans believe what they want," the president said. "A Russian warship has been sunk by the Canadians. We will deal with this act of aggression from a position of strength."

His gaze rifled over to Yakov.

"Minister of Defense, I want all ships ready to sortie immediately. And send out an order putting all our air and ground forces on twenty-four-hour standby."

"Aye-aye, sir," Yakov said. His aged frame sat erect in his seat. "It shall be done."

Luchnik continued, his gaze searching the faces in the room, weighing reactions. "If the West wants to make a move against us, let them come."

"But, Mr. President," Prime Minister Mishinov began. The president cut him off with a glare.

"I'm not finished yet, Prime Minister."

Little Mishi bowed his head.

"I will be making a public address to the nation," Luchnik declared. "Not to apologize for acts of war against us but to ready our people for the coming battle.

"Our enemies will seek to destroy us from within, using cyber warfare," the president said. "But I will not give them that opportunity. From this moment, *suveren dannyye* is in effect."

The announcement caused a stir in the room. *Suveren dannyye*, or sovereign data, was the plan to isolate the Russian internet from the rest of the world. Years in the making, the FSB had developed the capability as a way to preempt cyberattacks on the homeland.

While highly effective at protecting Mother Russia from cyberattacks, it had severe side effects. An internet lockdown meant no exports or imports, a devastating blow to Russia's fragile economy. Inflows of food, medicine, cash—all desperately needed to keep the country afloat—would cease. Over time, an internet stoppage would cause public opinion to turn against the leadership.

But there were other reasons for the reaction, less apparent to the ordinary Russian citizen but hugely important to the men in the Security Council Meeting Room. Every one of them had foreign bank accounts, flush with dollars and Euros, which were far more stable than the Russian ruble.

Denied access to their all-important cyberweapons, the Americans and the European Union would freeze those assets, trapping everyone inside the Russian Federation. Luchnik had warned his closest supporters to ensure they had all their resources safely locked away in Russian banks, but he knew they kept billions in currency stashed away outside the country.

Irimov stirred in his seat. He, perhaps better than any man in the room, knew that there were only two possible paths out of this crisis: violence or a backdoor negotiation with NATO. With an internet blockade and a heightened Russian defense posture, Irimov's ability to negotiate a peaceful resolution was made monumentally more difficult.

No, Luchnik decided. Impossible—and that was exactly the plan.

Would the traitor be willing to risk destruction of the country just to unseat Luchnik?

"Foreign Minister Irimov," the president said, "you have something to add?"

"I do, Mr. President." The voice belonged to his nephew, Admiral Nikolay Sokolov.

Luchnik's gaze locked onto the younger man's pale blue eyes. He saw no deception there but took no comfort in that thought. His love for his nephew was a weakness he could not afford in this moment of peril.

"Yes, Admiral?"

"I want to apologize, sir," Sokolov said. "For making the recommendation that we withdraw from the International Seapower Symposium. That action made us look culpable in the eyes of the world. For that, I am sorry."

The ministers froze. The admiral was displaying weakness in the face of his president's obvious and escalating rage.

In the space of a thought, Luchnik weighed the situation. His typical response would be to destroy the messenger, but today he was all about throwing his adversaries off-balance.

Do the opposite of your instincts, he decided.

Luchnik smiled. "You are forgiven, Admiral. You made the recommendation to the full cabinet. Did any of these men disagree with you?" He turned his gaze on Irimov. "Foreign Minister?"

Irimov shook his head. "No, sir."

"See?" Luchnik spread his hands. "You are a young man and a military man, Nikolay. If your idea was truly bad for the *Rodina*, I would have expected your elders to say so. They were silent."

"Thank you, Mr. President."

Luchnik searched the face of his nephew, so like his mother. Every time he saw the man, he was reminded of Natasha. His mind wanted to say the words, but his lips stayed locked together:

Kolya, are you with me or against me?

36

In the moments before the president joined any meeting of the National Security Council, there was always a buzz of talk in the room.

Not so today. The seating at the main table had been rearranged to provide four open seats along the right-hand side. The power players at the table eyed the change in their surroundings with suspicion.

The mystery was solved when President Serrano made his entrance. The House and Senate majority and minority leaders followed the leader of the free world into the room with Chief of Staff Wilkerson bringing up the rear.

As everyone stood, all eyes locked on the four politicians.

None of Don's positions thus far in his career had required him to report to Congress. As a result, he did not know any of the House and Senate leaders from personal interaction, only from their frequent appearances on television.

The four—two men and two women—looked around the unfamiliar surroundings with awkwardness. On television, they appeared polished and sure of themselves as they spoke from prepared comments. But here, under the lights of the White House Situation Room, they seemed deflated and out of their depth.

President Serrano, aware of their discomfort, took his seat quickly and called for everyone in the room to do the same.

What a difference a few months could make in a man, Don mused. The president had been in office less than ten months but the job had taken its toll. Heavy lines carved the skin around his mouth, and dark circles had formed under his intense brown eyes. Even his trademark Hollywood hair seemed dull and tired.

But the Serrano smile was still warm, and he showed energy as he flipped open his leather portfolio. The facing page was covered with dense handwriting.

"I am pleased to welcome the House and Senate majority and minority leaders here today. My aim is simple: full transparency. This country is going through a series of crises that will require the full and complete cooperation of our civil, political, and military leaders. Rather than offer our legislative leaders a meeting summary, I extended an invitation for them to see how the sausage is made." He smiled at the four and nodded. "Welcome, ladies and gentlemen."

Serrano's grin turned off. His gaze panned around the room, his expression dead serious.

"Enough niceties. The situation that faces the country is serious and multifaceted. I owe everyone here a clear statement of priorities so we can plan for success.

"Canada, a neighbor and trusted NATO ally, has invoked Article 5 of the NATO treaty. We will do everything in our power to support NATO, including the use of force against the Russian Federation, if necessary. I intend to act under the existing Authorized Use of Military Force until Congress advises otherwise."

The military leaders at the table side-eyed their political counterparts. The AUMF was the perennial congressional football. The Constitution of the United States gave Congress, not the president, the power to declare war. Following the terrorist attacks on 9/11, Congress passed the 2001 Authorization for Use of Military Force. Subsequent presidents used that authority to enter into new conflicts, in new countries, against new entities that did not even exist at the time of the original AUMF.

Yet the politically radioactive legislation had never been updated, and presidents had continued to use it for nearly three decades, just as Serrano was doing now.

"Let's talk priorities." The president held up his index finger. "First and foremost, Russia will be held to account for her actions in the Arctic, promptly and forcefully. If we can prove her involvement in other disasters, such as the Naval War College bombing, she will pay for those as well. State will be laying out a menu of economic sanctions, but today I want to focus on the military response."

The president raised a second finger. "We will retain our position in Venezuela."

Serrano paused and surveyed the room, anticipating resistance.

"Was it a mistake in timing for us to engage in Venezuela?" He shrugged. "Perhaps, but that's my responsibility to bear. The operation has transitioned from establishing security and stability to providing aid and a national rebuilding operation. We will withdraw fighting forces as quickly as possible, but I want to make it clear that we will not abandon what we started in Venezuela. When we emerge on the other side of this crisis—and America will get through this—we will have made our own hemisphere significantly safer."

A third finger ticked up. "To the maximum extent possible, we will employ unmanned assets to limit the risk of American deaths."

The president's fourth finger snapped to attention. "Finally, we need to get our cyber capabilities back. I've left that one for last, but in many ways, all of the other three don't even matter unless we can get that done."

He rested his hands on the table.

"Our capabilities are not unlimited, so we're going to have to think strategically about our military assets.

"I've already directed the DoD to deemphasize the effort in Iran," Serrano continued. "Two of the three aircraft carriers will be available for other duty. Same thing with North Korea. We have twenty-eight thousand troops on the Korean peninsula and a diminishing threat scenario in North Korea. I'll let Secretary Howard talk specifics."

Secretary of Defense Howard's pantsuit of the day was classic dark blue with a silvery scarf. She nodded to her aide to start the presentation. The first image Don saw was the world map.

"Let's start with naval assets, sir." Howard's tone was businesslike. "Our initial strategy with Russia is one of containment. Intel says the Russian fleet is making preparations to sortie, and we want to be on top of them the moment they enter international waters. NATO allies will handle the Arctic coverage, including the Barents Sea and the Russian Northern Fleet out of Murmansk. The US will handle the Bering Sea. We have formed a three-carrier strike force for this task, headed by Admiral Sharratt on the USS *Enterprise* out of Seventh Fleet in Japan. *Enterprise* will be joined by *Nimitz* and the *Teddy Roosevelt* as soon as we can transfer them north from Third Fleet."

Her laser pointer flashed to the Persian Gulf. "The USS *Ford* and the *Bush* will be redeployed from the Gulf to the eastern Med to cover the Russian Black Sea Fleet. We intend to cut off the Russian access to the Mediterranean."

She circled the North Atlantic. "The GIUK gap presents a challenge for us. We are speeding up repairs of the *Eisenhower* to put her into service off Iceland, but we are running out of escorts as well. To fill that need, we propose to transfer a surface action group from San Diego through the Panama Canal."

Howard paused. "Normally, we only allow ships to pass through the Canal one at a time, for security reasons. Based on the heavy commercial usage of the Canal, it will take us nearly a week to get the necessary assets moved to the Caribbean and on to the North Atlantic. If we send the surface action group through all at once, we can make the transit in a day. That operation requires presidential authorization, sir."

The new Chief of Naval Operations was Admiral Norman Tanaka, a fourth-generation Asian-American man with a blocky physique and square facial features. Serrano focused his attention on the CNO.

"Admiral Tanaka," he said. "Welcome."

"Thank you, Mr. President." Tanaka had a surprisingly deep voice.

"The Navy was hit hard by the tragedy at the Naval War College,"

Serrano said, "but we will need to lean on our naval forces now more than ever."

Admiral Tanaka nodded curtly. "We'll be ready, sir. Moving the full SAG through the Canal is a risk, but it is also the fastest way for us to get ships on station. I support the secretary's request for authorization."

"Granted," Serrano said.

"We'll make it happen, Mr. President."

From his peanut gallery perspective, Don had the luxury of analyzing the military movements. Without a doubt, this was the largest mobilization of US forces across services since World War Two. In contrast, the US military engagements in the Middle East had been large but limited in geography and focused on land and air assets. This new action was truly global in nature and spanned all the services, with special strain on the Navy.

The room was silent when the Secretary of Defense stopped speaking, as if everyone else in the room was echoing Don's thoughts about the scope of the undertaking before them all.

"I'll ask the chairman to speak to our use of unmanned assets, Mr. President," Howard concluded.

General Nikolaides stood for his presentation, his tall frame towering over the people seated at the table.

"Sir, I'll get right to the damn point," the general began. "With the exception of UAVs, that's unmanned aerial vehicles, our capability in the use of unmanned assets is piss-poor, in my opinion. The Air Force has used Reapers and such for years, but they're all controlled stateside from Creech Air Force Base in Nevada. What we really need are assets under the local control of theater commanders."

He flashed an image on the screen of an aircraft that looked to Don like a V-2 rocket. "This is Skyborg, the Air Force version of a UCAV, or unmanned combat aerial vehicle. The Navy and Marine Corps have the X-47. Both platforms perform as wingmen. They act as extensions to a manned warplane. However, both platforms have an AI component and could be used in an independent mode."

He paused to allow his comment to sink in.

Valentina Flores, the National Security Advisor, spoke for the first time.

"Are you suggesting that we allow an AI to make kill decisions on the battlefield, General?"

"I'm suggesting that we might not have enough goddamn planes and pilots to go the distance, ma'am," the chairman replied. "I want to make sure we keep all options on the table."

The Secretary of State made motions like he wanted to weigh in, but the president stopped him.

"Let's table that discussion for now, Mr. Chairman," Serrano said. "Tell us about unmanned capabilities in other domains."

The general changed the screen to show a long, sleek trimaran ship. "This is the *Sea Hunter*, an unmanned surface asset capable of anti-submarine, electronic warfare, and surveillance. Range of ten thousand nautical miles and upwards of a month at sea. Capable of autonomy and well tested. We've got an even dozen of these ready to deploy around the world. The *Sea Hunter* has been in the press."

He flashed a new image of a jet-black sailboat. "No one knows about this platform yet."

"Is that a sailboat?" the president asked.

"Yes, sir. This is the *Sea Skate*–class recon platform. Uses wind power for transportation and to power the batteries. Twenty-five feet long, stem to stern, and damn near invisible once it's in the water. Completely silent, completely autonomous. It relays intelligence reports via satellite. You could sail this baby right through a carrier strike group and nobody would ever know it was there."

"What about subsurface drones, Mr. Chairman?" the president asked.

Nikolaides sighed.

"We're testing the *Orca* in Hawaii right now, sir, but our abilities in this area are limited. The USS *Idaho* is trying to make an underwater comms system work so we can use the *Orca* as an underwater wingman for our submarines." Nikolaides shot a look at the National Security Advisor. "The discussion about autonomous operations is even more critical for underwater ops."

Don noticed that Flores did not take the bait.

"Kathleen," the president said to the Secretary of Defense, "I want you to do everything you can to accelerate the deployment of unmanned assets.

The defense contractors have enjoyed trillions of taxpayers' dollars over the last fifty years. We need them to step up."

Serrano turned to Samuel Blank, the CIA director. His personality and appearance fit his name. Pale of face and white-haired, Blank was soft-spoken and unassuming.

"Mr. Director, please tell me you have a plan to break through the Russian internet blockade."

Director Blank shook his head slowly. "There are no easy answers on this problem, sir. Russia's ability to isolate themselves from the global internet is much more extensive than we had originally anticipated."

He motioned to an aide to show a slide on the wall monitor. The country of Russia showed boldly on the screen. Dots flashed at various border points.

"We are going to launch six teams of operators simultaneously. We've drawn from all resources to get the best possible mix of language skills, local knowledge, and technological ability."

Don listened in amazement as his boss laid out plans to penetrate Russia via Ukraine, Belarus, Turkey, Kazakhstan, and Finland. His team surely could have added to the talent pool for this effort, but he had not been included.

"The Finns are on board with this?" the Secretary of State asked.

"We think ignorance is the best policy in this case," Blank replied. "If it works, they benefit. If we get caught, they can honestly say they didn't know. Plausible deniability."

Secretary Hahn's face indicated he did not agree, but he let the matter ride.

"The internet blockade isn't perfect," Blank continued, "but unless we can establish a reliable access point that we can come back to again and again, there's no way we can launch a coordinated cyberattack. I'm confident that one of these operations will be successful."

Don stewed as the meeting drew to a close. When the president adjourned the meeting and left the room, he pushed through the staffers toward Samuel Blank.

"Sir," Don began, "can I speak to you for a moment?"

"What's on your mind, Don?" Blank's bushy eyebrows drew together in concentration.

"I'm wondering why Emerging Threats isn't part of the Russian internet operation."

"That was my call, Don," Blank said. "I'll be honest. I'm concerned about ET these days. I don't know that you're helping us get ahead of the problem like we had anticipated."

Don stepped back, stung. He was hard on himself in private, but to hear the same blunt criticism come at him from his boss was like a slap in the face.

"Sir, I—I..."

"Look, Don," Blank said, putting a hand on Don's arm. "We're in this thing for all the marbles and I need the A-team on deck. Your group will back up the NSA, if they need it. Meanwhile, focus on the future. I need to know what's gonna bite me in the ass next week."

As the room emptied around him, Don returned to his seat next to the wall to consider his boss's words.

37

USS *Enterprise* (CVN-80)
250 miles south of Attu Island, Alaska

Fat drops of rain pelted the thick glass of the flag bridge on the USS *Enterprise*. In the pitch darkness below, Rear Admiral Chip Sharratt saw dim shapes move along the darkened flight deck. Occasional flashes of light flared, red-tinted to protect the night vision of the flight crews.

He knew that two F-35 strike fighters were loaded on the catapults, pilots ready to launch on a moment's notice, the so-called "alert-five" status.

As was now his habit, Sharratt listened with half an ear to the open comm circuit in Battle Watch. The background of familiar voices was his constant companion, even on when he slept—not that he did much sleeping these days.

The USS *Nimitz* had joined the *Enterprise* carrier strike force during the night, swelling their complement to twenty-five US Navy warships. Three aircraft carriers—the *Enterprise*, the *Nimitz*, and the *Theodore Roosevelt*—formed the backbone of the force. Their escorts consisted of three guided missile cruisers, six destroyers, three frigates, and three supply ships.

Somewhere under the dark waters of the North Pacific Ocean lurked three submarines: one in the Bering Sea to the north, one operating to the west, and one assigned for direct undersea support of the carrier strike force. Submarine operations were opaque to him. The nuclear-powered boats were assigned a few hundred square miles of ocean and let loose to do their work.

Sharratt hardly knew what to make of the final six ships assigned to the strike force. They were *Sea Hunter*–class USVs, or unmanned surface vehicles. Three of the ships were outfitted for submarine detection, two for electronic warfare, and the final one for intelligence and surveillance missions. Although the ships were designed to operate autonomously, Sharratt had placed them all under positive control and positioned them as outer pickets, thirty miles to the west, between the strike force and the Russian coastline.

The ships were all named *Sea*-something: *Sea Hunter*, *Sea Shadow*, and so on. Sharratt was skeptical of the wisdom of naming a robot ship at all. What was the point? The name of the ship was mostly a reflection of the pride of the crew. On a USV, there was no crew.

The USVs were not the only unmanned assets in his arsenal. The F-35 pilot on combat air patrol had a UCAV as a wingman. The unmanned aircraft and his meatsack flying companion would more than likely be refueled in the air by an MQ-25 Stingray, a refueling drone.

Sharratt checked his watch, then gripped the handrail and peered into the eastern darkness, trying to discern any lightening of the horizon. They hadn't seen sunshine for three days, and today's nonexistent sunrise indicated more of the same.

The shitty weather did nothing to dampen Sharratt's mood. He was a man at peace, well aware that everything he had done since his first day as a midshipman at the United States Naval Academy was in preparation for this job.

The Naval War College bombing had gutted the senior ranks of the United States Navy. Among the dead was his friend and mentor, Vice Admiral Sal Mondelli. In private moments like this one, staring out over a vast dark ocean, Sharratt felt the loss most keenly.

And he was here to do something about it.

Russia, if you're listening, he thought. Payback is a bitch. I guarantee it.

He checked his watch again and decided that seeing the sun rise was a lost cause. Sharratt gave up and headed down the ladders for Battle Watch.

"Morning, Tom," Sharratt greeted his chief of staff as he joined him next to the BattleSpace holographic display.

"Not that you could tell from looking outside, sir," Zachary replied. "Dark as the devil's own asshole out there."

"So it is." He studied the graphical representation of the strike force's layered defenses. The escorts were mostly positioned along the northwest threat axis of the major Russian naval base at Petropavlovsk on the Kamchatka Peninsula. He indicated to the lieutenant running the plot to expand the range.

To their north, the Aleutian Island chain swooped south from the Alaskan coast for 1,100 miles. To their west, the Russian Kamchatka Peninsula poked down from Siberia, eventually dissolving into the Kuril Island chain and then into Japan. To their south and east was nothing but thousands of miles of open Pacific.

The *Enterprise* strike force sailed a few hundred miles due south of the final island in the Aleutian chain. Attu Island was the westernmost point in the United States, so far west that the island was actually part of the eastern hemisphere. It was easy to find on a map: look for the point where the international date line jogged to the left for no apparent reason.

"We'll be at McMorris Station by midday, sir," Zachary commented, referring to the site of the World War Two battle where Admiral McMorris held the line against the Japanese Imperial Navy forces in the Battle of the Kormandorski Islands. "You know that was the last naval battle fought entirely with naval guns?"

"Is that so?" Sharratt mused, thinking about how many unmanned platforms were part of his strike force today. "Remind me to never play Trivial Pursuit against you, Tom."

As strike force commander, his orders were to establish a substantial US naval presence in the North Pacific, carry out reconnaissance patrols, and counter any Russian aggression with proportional force.

It was the last part that gave him heartburn. The definition of *proportional* was slippery at best. Too little and the US risked looking weak. Too much and some future historian would be naming this point in the Pacific

Ocean Sharratt Station, in recognition of the naval battle that had sparked World War Three.

The rules of engagement had been loosened to allow preemptive strikes in self-defense. Basically, if a ship or aircraft detected a lock from an enemy fire control radar, that platform could strike first. Radar locks were considered an act of hostility—period. Sharratt fervently hoped that the US diplomatic corps had been clear with their Russian counterparts about the situation. His strike force contained a lot of sensors, a lot of hardware, and a lot of US sailors anxious for some payback over the Naval War College terrorist attack.

"What's our status?" he asked the Battle Watch Officer, a surface warfare–qualified Navy captain.

"*Teddy* has the CAP this watch, sir," the man answered, referring to the combat air patrol from the *Theodore Roosevelt*. "Per your orders, the CAP is an F-35 with a UCAV as wingman. We've got a rock-solid data link with the Hawkeye and a fresh Stingray on station for aerial refueling."

He pointed to the Bering Sea, above the Aleutian Island chain that dotted the blue ocean like a necklace. "The Air Force is running a pair of F-15s out of Adak to our north as backup."

"Subs?"

The watch officer pointed to the west of the strike force. "*Topeka*'s last position was here—that was three hours ago. She reported no subsurface contacts. Not even a sniff."

"What about the *Sea Hunters*?" Sharratt asked, pointing at the six dots to the west of the strike force representing the unmanned surface vessels.

"Still under positive control, sir." The watch officer hesitated. "I'd like to switch them to autonomous when we get on station. See what they can do."

"Lemme think about it," Sharratt replied. "Maybe we use the ASW units for some additional sensor capacity."

By training, Sharratt was a weapons systems officer for an electronic warfare aircraft. He understood air threats, and to his line of thinking, surface ships with missile capabilities were just another form of air threat.

Submarines were another matter. Those quiet bastards were the greatest threat to his strike force. Stealthy and deadly, your first sniff of a submarine might very well be your last sniff on this earth.

And now the Russians were developing unmanned, autonomous submarines. The thought chilled him to his core. The latest intel reports were chock full of sketchy intel about a new subsurface nuclear-powered drone with a two-megaton warhead. The "apocalypse torpedo," as some analysts tagged it, was launched from a specially equipped submarine based out of Petropavlovsk.

The trouble with the Russians was that they were always talking up big weapons systems and offering up just enough detail to make intel analysts take them seriously.

"The Russians sortied a small surface force out of Petropavlovsk late yesterday afternoon, sir," the watch officer continued, "but they're sticking pretty close to shore. That said, we're seeing increased air activity." He pointed out two red contacts.

"These two are MiG-35s," he said. "Looks like their job is to mirror the movements of our CAP. They keep their distance, but they're always there."

He indicated another pair of air contacts. "About fifteen minutes ago, this Su-57 showed up to the party."

Sharratt was familiar with the fifth-gen multirole fighter, the Russians' weak answer to the US F-35 and the Chinese J-20.

"His wingman is a UCAV, sir." The watch officer threw an image from his tablet to the flat-screen. The flying wing design was reminiscent of the X-47 UCAVs his strike force was using, but the Russian version was much larger.

"S-70 Okhotnik is a big son of a bitch, Admiral," the watch officer continued. "Twenty-meter wingspan and weighs as much as an F-15 Eagle."

The new air contact traced a lazy racetrack seventy-five miles off the peninsula coast. The *Enterprise*'s CAP was just reaching the bottom of their own patrol area, three hundred miles to the southwest.

"The Air Force CAP is headed back to Adak, sir," one of the enlisted technicians called out to the Battle Watch Officer. "We'll see a gap in coverage of about an hour."

That was the last update Sharratt heard as he glanced at his watch. Nine a.m., time to call his new boss.

Vice Admiral Kale Bumpers had received his third star and his position as Commander, Seventh Fleet, as a result of the Naval War College massacre. Sharratt had only met his new boss once in person and had yet to solidify an opinion of the man. Bumpers was a big guy, broad of face and body, with a booming voice. To Sharratt, the bluster felt out of place after Mondelli's normally calm, even manner.

Sharratt grinned, remembering his last meeting with Mondelli when his friend had chewed him out for the Strait of Taiwan near miss.

The tech nodded as he finalized the secure connection with Seventh Fleet HQ and stepped out of the small conference room.

"Morning, Chip," Bumpers's voice boomed through the speakers. "How's life up north?"

The USS *Blue Ridge* was located six hundred miles to the southeast of Sharratt's strike force. The ship had departed Yokosuka, Japan, the day after the Naval War College incident.

A Navy ship pierside was a sitting duck, the saying went, while a warship at sea, surrounded by escorts and guarded by submarines, was a much more challenging target for an enemy. In every wargaming scenario Sharratt had ever been involved in, the first action of the Seventh Fleet was to go mobile.

"So far, so good, sir," Sharratt replied. "*Nimitz* arrived last night, right on schedule, and we'll be on station by midday. I'm told this crappy weather is par for the course, so I might as well get used to it."

Bumpers belly-laughed. "Well, just remember, if you can feel the weather on the bridge of an aircraft carrier, just imagine what it's like on one of those teeny-tiny frigates."

Sharratt's new boss liked to remind everyone that he'd come up through the ranks the old-fashioned way, via the surface fleet. Sharratt had spent six weeks on a destroyer out of Diego Garcia on his youngster cruise at the Academy and had forsaken surface warfare as a service choice. He'd spent most of the cruise hurling his cookies over the side—and that had been in relatively calm waters.

"It's a dirty job, sir," Sharratt said, "but someone's got to do it." He paused, impatient with the small talk. "Any clarification on the rules of engagement?"

To Sharratt's mind, the current ROE scenario left something to be desired when combined with the parallel order to preferentially use unmanned assets.

What was the "proportional response" if an unmanned asset was attacked? Was he permitted to take the fight to a manned enemy asset if it got in the way? The resulting debate had raged for three days between the State Department and the DoD. Sharratt understood the stakes and wanted to make sure that Washington, DC, understood the complexity of the problem they were creating on the battlefield.

"The updated ROE will be out later today, but here's the upshot: if an unmanned asset engages in hostile action against the US Navy, the first priority is to return fire. If possible, use an unmanned asset to engage, but —and this is important—any firing decision has to have a human pull the trigger. In other words, automated self-defense actions by unmanned assets are not authorized. Clear as mud?"

Sharratt held back a sigh. "Yes, sir. You realize that all this does is put another link in the decision chain? That doesn't make us safer."

"Hey, ours is not to reason why, and so on," Bumpers replied.

With a pang of regret, Sharratt recalled Mondelli using the same phrase at their last meeting. He finished the saying in his head: *ours is but to do or die*. That's what he was worried about.

From the corner of his eye, he saw the Battle Watch Officer lean over the BattleSpace display. A rigidity in the man's posture told Sharratt that something was up.

"Sir," he said. "I may need to call you back. We've got some activity."

Sharratt hung up the phone without waiting for an answer and stepped back into Battle Watch.

"Admiral, we've got a situation brewing," the watch officer reported. Sharratt studied the holographic display as the man spoke.

"The Su-57 and his UCAV are inbound at high speed."

Sharratt saw the problem immediately. The Air Force F-15s were off station and their own combat air patrol was far from the strike force and still being shadowed by their Russian counterparts. The Russians had apparently been studying the US habits and were going to poke the beast.

"Any fire control radars detected?" Sharratt asked.

"Negative, sir. Alpha Whiskey launched the Alert Five CAP." As the watch officer spoke, two new friendly contacts showed up on the Battle-Space display—another F-35 and his UCAV wingman.

Sharratt did the math in his head. At their current supersonic speed, the incoming Russian fighter and escort would reach the hundred-mile red line around the strike force in about five minutes.

"Screwdriver Five, this is Alpha Whiskey." AW was the air defense coordinator for the strike force, the commanding officer of the guided missile cruiser USS *Port Royal*. "Set heading three-five-five. Angels three-five, buster. Intercept bandit on your nose at angels three-two. Probable Russian Su-57 with Su-70 UCAV as wingman."

"He's breaking off!" the Battle Watch Officer said. "Wait...stand by."

One of the incoming Russian contacts broke hard left and angled back toward land. The second contact stayed on course for the *Enterprise* strike force.

Sharratt would have bet a paycheck that the incoming contact was the Russian UCAV.

"Screwdriver Five, this is Alpha Whiskey. You are authorized to engage your bogey."

"Roger, Alpha Whiskey—"

Sharratt snatched up the nearby handset.

"Alpha Whiskey, this is Alpha Bravo. You are authorized to engage using the UCAV only. Do you copy?"

The captain of the *Port Royal* scarcely missed a beat.

"Copy all, Alpha Bravo. Break, break. Screwdriver Five, you are weapons tight. Engage bogey via tinman, over."

"Copy all, Alpha Whiskey. Tinman has the shot."

The whole engagement took less than a minute. The incoming drone never deviated off course or fired a shot. The F-35 pilot directed his UCAV to release a single AIM-260 missile. The Russian Su-70 was no match for the Joint Air Tactical Missile.

The bogey disappeared from the display.

"Splash one bad guy," the pilot reported.

In Battle Watch, as the room erupted with cheers and high fives, Sharratt studied the BattleSpace display.

They'd just splashed a few hundred million dollars' worth of Russian hardware. It had been so easy.

Too easy.

He squinted at the pixels but found no answers. Try as he might, Rear Admiral Chip Sharratt felt like someone had just made a very big mistake.

He only hoped it wasn't him.

38

Pearl Harbor, Hawaii

Janet Everett looked up from the computer screen and stretched her arms over her head. She eyed the coffee pot in the wardroom of the USS *Idaho*. It was after nine in the evening, but her day had started at four a.m. and her body ached from lack of sleep.

Maybe just one more cup...

Bad idea, she decided. As soon as she did her duty officer rounds at midnight, she intended to hit the rack for a solid six hours. On a typical duty night in port, she could expect to be woken a few times for all sorts of pressing issues or maintenance sign-offs. But this was their first night back in Pearl after two weeks underway, and the submarine was empty of anyone who didn't absolutely need to be there.

Janet had risen at four a.m. to make sure she reviewed the docking procedures for Pearl Harbor and was ready to assume the duties of OOD promptly at six a.m. The captain had watched her bring the *Idaho* pierside. He made a few comments but mostly let Janet run the evolution on her own. Captain Lannier didn't show a lot of emotion, but when the *Idaho* was tied up and the Maneuvering Watch secured, he smiled at her.

"Little different from Groton, eh, Lieutenant?" he asked.

Janet, still riding the euphoria of her successful docking, grinned back. "I'll say, sir," she replied.

It was true. Bringing a submarine into port on the East Coast was a marathon. By procedure, submarines surfaced at the hundred-fathom line, usually six to eight hours away from port on the East Coast of the United States. Submarines were underwater vessels, not designed to perform well on the surface. If the weather was rough, the ship rolled like a log in the surf.

But Hawaii was an island. The hundred-fathom line was only a few miles offshore. A submarine could surface and be tied off at the pier in Pearl Harbor in under two hours.

The captain, Janet, and an enlisted sailor who had stood lookout watch on their way into port occupied the cockpit at the top of the conning tower on the *Idaho*. As soon as the brow was lowered to the back of the sub, the pier was swarmed by *Idaho* crew rushing to complete their final duties before they went on liberty.

Thick black shore power cables ran across a bridge from the pier to the engine room hatch so the engineering team could shut down the reactor. Another team connected hoses allowing potable water to flow into the ship and wastewater to be pumped off. The deck division rigged temporary stanchions and safety lines topside to ensure no one slipped overboard.

"Permission to lay below, Captain," the petty officer said.

Lannier nodded. "Lay below."

The captain watched the sailor disappear down the ladder beneath them.

"When you showed up on my ship, Lieutenant," the captain began. "I wasn't sure what to make of you. Your service jacket is unusual."

Janet shifted on her feet. The operations in North Korea and in Sudan were redacted from her record, and she was not able to speak about them even with her new commanding officer. Her service record merely stated that she had been involved in a classified operation. The classified FitReps were stored in a secure facility in Millington, Tennessee.

She knew from prior experience that senior officers often chafed at not knowing something about a new member of their wardroom. Janet couldn't blame them. Men like Lannier had responsibility for a multibillion-dollar submarine, over a hundred crew, and top secret missions. They needed to trust their officers completely. Telling a captain that they were not cleared to hear about the background of one of their junior officers could be viewed as an issue of trust.

"You're a good officer, Janet," Lannier said. "Whatever you choose to do in the Navy, you'll do it well."

Janet blushed. "Thank you, sir."

"I should be thanking you," Lannier said with a chuckle. "Before you came on board as Weapons Officer, I'd about given up hope for our torpedo room. The XO wanted to clean house from the chief on down."

"They just needed some TLC, sir," Janet said. It had been far more complicated than that, but she was not about to break the confidence of Chief Cabe, the torpedo division chief.

As she'd learned at the Academy, leadership came from the top. Once she'd got some help for her chief's personal issues, he had gotten his head back in the game.

"I just wanted you to know that I appreciate the work you've done for this command." Lannier paused before he started down the ladder. "Enjoy your liberty, Lieutenant."

"I've got the duty tonight, sir."

"Hmmm," was Lannier's reply as he disappeared down the hatch into the ship.

Janet sighed. Without thinking, she poured herself a cup of coffee. She was already adding creamer before she realized what she had done.

I need to get a life, she thought.

Janet Everett had grown up on the East Coast and been stationed there for her entire career, first at the Academy, then at the sub base in Groton, and finally at the CIA Emerging Threats Group in DC.

The choice of Pearl Harbor for her next duty station was deliberate. If she really wanted to focus on her career as a submarine officer, she needed to make a clean break. Get away from home, her friends, her job at the CIA.

All of those friendly reminders that might pull her away from her chosen profession.

But she was lonely. Apart from a few casual work relationships with the other officers in the wardroom, she hadn't made a single friend in her six months in Pearl Harbor.

She always volunteered to be duty officer for the first night in port. This was a rare move for a department head. The assignment was usually given to the most junior officer in the wardroom, but she knew the rest of the wardroom was either married or in serious relationships and anxious to get ashore to see their loved one.

When first aboard the *Idaho*, she took the unpopular watch as a way to earn a measure of respect from her new shipmates. Now, after six months, she did it out of habit. The ops officer didn't even bother to ask for volunteers anymore; he just assigned Janet.

Janet didn't mind, not really. She kept a small one-bedroom apartment in town, but it was more of a crash pad than a home. She still had a wall of boxes from her move that she hadn't unpacked. The refrigerator held only an untouched six-pack of beer, a half case of diet soda, and a block of Parmesan cheese that she had bought one weekend for a reason she couldn't remember.

She was happy. Well, more like content. She missed Michael and Dre terribly, and she wondered how Don was doing without her. Sometimes, she thought about Mark Westlund, and a spiteful part of her personality hoped that Mark wasn't as good as he'd seemed in his first few days at ETG. She hated herself for feeling this kind of jealousy, but she supposed it was normal.

Enough, she told herself.

She focused her attention on classified intel reports on her computer screen. It read like disaster porn. The attacks on civilians in India were horrible. The Iranian situation looked to be at a standoff for now, but still volatile.

She devoured the update on the Russian internet blockade, chafing at the thought of what was happening back at ETG. Don and the team would be all over this, kicking ass and taking names. Meanwhile, she was sitting in a submarine wardroom drinking coffee at ten o'clock on a Friday night, feeling sorry for herself.

Janet caught a look at her reflection in the laptop screen. Her cheeks were hollow and her complexion sallow. She reached back and removed the scrunchie holding her hair in a rough ponytail. Strands of ragged, dirty blond hair framed her face.

Janet grimaced at her image. She needed a haircut. Hell, a good start might be washing and blow-drying that mop. She dragged a finger across her forehead. The atmosphere of a submarine underway left an oily residue on her skin that could only be removed by a long soak in a tub.

She slapped the lid of the laptop shut and stood with a sudden burst of anxious energy. She'd do her midnight rounds early. In her stateroom, Janet's eye caught on a book stuffed into a narrow cubbyhole in her fold-down desk.

Blind Man's Bluff, a gift from her father after she had been accepted into Annapolis.

She opened to the title page to see her father's inscription. It made her smile. Her old man was a lot of things, but subtle was not one of them.

Someday, he wrote in his bold block letters, *I expect you to have your own chapter. Love, Dad*.

Janet remembered reading the book for the first time and being fascinated by the daring undersea adventures, the cat-and-mouse back-and-forth between the Americans and the Russians during the Cold War.

That all felt like another era, like an old movie. The situation with the Russians today felt urgent and dangerous.

She flipped through the book to the picture section, studying the black-and-white photographs of submarines and their crews. A name caught her eye: Operation Ivy Bells.

Janet searched the index to refresh her mind on the details.

In 1971, the *Halibut* went through a refit to mount a Deep Submergence Rescue Vehicle, or DSRV, onto her hull. In fact, the protrusion affixed to the submarine was not a rescue vehicle at all but a divers' decompression and lockout chamber. In one of the most daring and dangerous submarine operations in history, the *Halibut* entered the Russian-held Sea of Okhotsk, located an underwater telephone trunk line, and tapped the line for top secret intelligence. The CIA operation ran for years until a disgruntled NSA employee sold the information to the KGB.

Janet closed the book and started her rounds. She took her time walking the spaces of the submarine. When she arrived at the hatch where the *Manta* had docked, Janet paused.

A lot had changed since 1971, she thought, but the use of underwater cables had only increased. She had studied the technical specs on the *Manta*, and dexterity of the mechanical arms was fine enough to allow SEAL teams to defuse underwater mines. The mini-sub prototype was sized to be able to fit inside a C-17 for transport anywhere in the world. Even with the *Manta* attached to her hull, a submarine out of Holy Loch, Scotland, could make the transit up to the Barents Sea inside of a few weeks...

Janet smiled. Now that would be an operation for the history books for some lucky East Coast submarine.

When she arrived back at her stateroom, Janet opened her secure email connection.

Dear Don, she began.

I have a wild idea for you to think about.

39

Panama Canal, Panama

Captain Ronald McCoy, commanding officer of the USS *Cape St. George* (CG-71), was nervous. In his twenty-one years in the Navy, he had transited the Panama Canal six times, but never as a commanding officer. That distinction made all the difference.

A CO was responsible for everything that happened on the ship. Everything, without exception. Some seventeen-year-old down in the bowels of the engine room trips off a main engine and the ship loses power, it was his problem.

During high-risk evolutions like this one, he felt the weight of command like a stone on his back. Add to that stress the fact that he was in command of the surface action group that was following the *St. George* through the locks, and his blood pressure was off the charts.

And so, Captain McCoy paced the bridge of his ship, constantly rechecking the actions of the maneuvering watchstanders and making a general pain in the ass of himself.

His ship was almost through now. For the last ten hours, the civilian pilot had patiently guided the *St. George* through the Panama Canal locks system. The final leg of their journey started as they entered the Chagres

River. McCoy heaved a sigh of relief. A few more kilometers and the *St. George* would be in the open waters of the Caribbean.

McCoy stopped at the chart table to check on the rest of the ships in the SAG.

Allowing US Navy ships to transit the Panama Canal at the same time was a security risk, but desperate times called for desperate measures. After the Naval War College bombing, it was difficult to know who was making the calls back in Washington or how much vetting they had received. These days, it seemed like everyone was operating under new rules.

The *St. George* was the lead ship in a replacement surface action group transiting from San Diego, California, to relieve the Fourth Fleet assets off the coast of Venezuela. The Norfolk-based ships being relieved were slated to resupply and head to the North Atlantic.

The world was a dumpster fire, and the only firetruck seemed to be the US Navy. The Navy's carefully constructed numbered fleet system had been thrown into shambles as they tried to put the right assets—sometimes the only assets—on the most pressing problem.

The Russian attack in the Arctic had been the final straw. Just before they left San Diego, McCoy had placed a call to his Naval Academy roommate, who was stationed with the Seventh Fleet staff. Between their guarded conversation and the message boards, McCoy knew that the barn was empty in the Seventh Fleet home port of Yokosuka, Japan. Every available asset in WestPac was either in the Arctic or off the coast of Iran.

In a quarter century of active duty, he'd never seen it this bad. Not even close.

McCoy shot a quick glance out the bridge windows. Thick green jungle ran to the water's edge. The air was hazy with humidity, and the white-hot sun blasted down, turning the water the color of quicksilver. The Chagres River was narrow here, but a few more kilometers and it would begin to widen.

And he'd be able to breathe again.

He turned his attention back to the chart table. The flat computer screen automatically updated the position of other ships in his SAG.

In addition to the *Cape St. George*, there were three destroyers, the

Decatur, the *Stockdale*, and the *John Finn*, as well as two littoral combat ships, the *Montgomery* and *Charleston*.

The *Stockdale*, an *Arleigh Burke*–class guided missile destroyer, was the last ship in the column. She was in the Miraflores locks now. According to the readout, she'd clear the lock in another hour.

The block of stone on his shoulder shed a few pounds. McCoy nodded at the first-class petty officer running the chart and stepped away.

They really don't need me here, he reflected. They're pros, and they know what they're doing.

Another man might have chafed at the thought of being unnecessary, but McCoy took it as a point of pride.

In his diary, he kept a tally of the days since he'd assumed command of the *St. George*. Today was Day 792—twenty-six months and a few days. The daily count reminded him to take the job one day at a time, to make each day a building block for the next one and always make forward progress every day.

He squinted at the sun-hammered river ahead of the ship. His O-6 command tour was winding down, and he was ready for a new posting. Before the world turned to shit, he'd been on track to pick up his first star as an admiral. His detailer in Washington had been talking up a post as Flag Aide to Commander, US Naval Forces Europe and Africa.

Now? Who knew?

Like all his peers, he wondered about the impact of the Naval War College bombing on his career. It was crass, and he felt guilty even thinking about it, but the questions remained. His detailer had said the Navy promotion process was "fluid" for the foreseeable future. A lot of vacancies had opened up at the upper echelons of command.

As much as he wanted a new command, with a possible war with the Russians looming, the Navy needed every qualified commanding officer in place on a major combatant platform like the *St. George*.

Would they extend his sea tour until the world stopped shooting itself in the face?

McCoy sighed. Sometimes it was better to let the elephants in Washington, DC, finish dancing before trying to figure out what it all meant for his future. Flag rank had been his career goal, but if he was needed here right now, that was just fine with him.

The civilian pilot they'd brought on board for the Panama Canal transit approached him. He was a short, dark man with a torso like a barrel and a perpetual scowl. McCoy didn't wonder at the man's expression. Boarding a new ship every day to transit the Panama Canal with an antsy commanding officer looking over your shoulder every three seconds was no picnic.

"Captain, my ride is here," the man said. He spoke in thick English with a heavy accent. "Request permission to bring the tug alongside and disembark, sir."

McCoy stuck out his hand. "Thank you. My only hope is that the rest of my Navy colleagues have pilots as skilled as you. You may disembark, sir."

The moment the two men clasped hands, McCoy felt a rumble in the deck beneath them. A split second later, geysers of water shot into the air on either side of the bridge. The USS *Cape St. George*, all ten thousand tons of steel and weapons and sailors, rose in the air as if the ship was taking flight.

McCoy was thrown against the roof of the bridge by the explosion. He heard a tremendous crack as the keel of the great ship broke in two.

For the smallest fraction of a second, amid the smoke and fire and mist and thundering noise, everything stopped, as if the mighty warship was suspended on the point of a knife.

Captain Ronald McCoy couldn't feel his legs—hell, he couldn't feel anything. He couldn't speak, either.

But he could think.

The *St. George* crashed down into the Chagres River, her broken hull filled with water, and sank, blocking the channel access to the Caribbean.

There would be no Day 793, McCoy thought.

40

Singapore

Breaking News. The two most useless words in the English language, decided Ian Thomas.

If any of his colleagues at Global Risk Ltd had peered into his office on the thirty-ninth floor of the Ocean Financial Center, they would have seen Ian lounging, feet on his desk, watching TV. Had they looked closer, they might have noticed the vacant stare, his slack expression.

But they would have detected no trace of the storm raging inside the mind of their colleague.

The TV on the wall opposite Ian's desk was tuned to CNN. A man in his mid-twenties with dark hair and a blue dress shirt reported from Panama. In the background of the shot, the gray hull of a US Navy ship jutted skyward. Oil shimmered on the slack water as a barge maneuvered along-side the wreck.

The reporter put the appropriate somber look on his face, but his rolled-up sleeves and open-necked shirt gave him a contrasting stylish feel. He walked as he talked:

"Officials estimate that the Canal could be closed for months while they clear the debris and ensure the area is safe for commercial traffic.

"At this hour, the United States Navy is saying very little about this latest attack, which comes only a month after the horrific bombing of the Naval War College in Newport, Rhode Island. Two US Navy warships were sunk in a coordinated attack as they transited the Canal. The Pentagon has not released a list of casualties, but sources say the death toll is likely to be in the hundreds. Experts we've interviewed say an attack like this one could only be from mines, but who placed the deadly explosives in the Canal and when is unknown. For that reason, the other four US Navy ships, while undamaged, remain anchored until the Navy sweeps the entire Panama Canal for additional explosives."

The image of the reporter cut away to an aerial view of the Panama Canal. Red *X*s marked the detonation sites.

Ian switched off the TV but continued staring at the blank screen.

The Minister had done this. No...*he* had done this. The mines were *his* work, not the Minister's.

The Naval War College and now this. Ian had blood on his hands. The Minister had turned him into a mass murderer.

Why? What was the Minister's end game?

Ian had served the Minister for decades. He knew the man—or thought he knew him. These were not the actions of the man who had trained him.

He surged to his feet, nervous energy tingling in his veins. This line of thought led to a dark place for Ian Thomas. The Minister had practically raised him. If he couldn't trust the Minister, then...

He placed both hands on the plate glass window and breathed deeply, willing the disturbance from his mind—another skill the Minister had taught him.

Ian Thomas was not a man, he told himself. Ian Thomas did not exist. The man who called himself Ian Thomas was an entity of shadow and lies.

That man had taken an oath.

That man was an instrument of the State. The State had given him everything, and in return he owed the State his very life.

Orders were orders, not guidelines, and he would follow them to the letter without interpretation.

He dropped his hands to his sides, his mind steady again. Outside his window, dusk fell on the magnificent lights of Singapore at night.

His mobile phone rang. Ian slipped the phone from his pocket and checked the caller ID.

Isabel Montez.

He answered with her name.

"I was thinking about you," she said, her voice cool. "And how much I want to see you."

Ian closed his eyes. He wanted that too.

"Meet me in London," she whispered. "I'll text you the address."

Then she hung up.

Forty-three Wilton Crescent was a stately address in the Belgravia section of London, equidistant from Buckingham Palace, Hyde Park, and the River Thames.

Each block consisted of solidly built, limestone-faced houses that formed a four-story wall of porticoes, balconies, and windows. Number 43 was fronted by a wide flagstone walk leading up to two marble steps that were flanked by elaborate wrought iron fencing. The exclusive address faced a small park, and Ian noted several of the other residences in the area had been converted to foreign embassies. Security would be high in this section of the city.

As the limo drew to a stop, Ian opened his door and stepped onto the sidewalk while the driver retrieved his overnight bag from the trunk. The late afternoon air held a hint of fall crispness. A man wearing a plaid scarf with his suit jacket walked a jet-black Scottish terrier along the flagstones.

Isabel appeared in the doorway of Number 43. Her hair was pulled back into a ponytail, and she wore shorts and a T-shirt. She hurried across the sidewalk in her bare feet and threw herself into Ian's arms. Her eyes flashed with excitement, and her lips were soft and warm. Ian lifted her off her feet in a hug.

"Are you happy to see me?" she said.

He kissed her back. "Yes," he said, and he meant it.

"What's the matter?" Isabel pulled back, placing her hands on either side of his face and looking deeply into Ian's eyes.

"Nothing. Let's go inside."

Isabel wouldn't let it go. She led him through the front door, then took his overnight bag and placed it next to the stairs.

"Something's happened." She took his hand. "Tell me."

Ian felt a surge of discomfort. Was it possible she was able to read him that easily? He put extra effort into his smile this time and drew her close. He ran his hand down her back to where the firm muscles swelled into her hips.

"Work stuff," he said, kissing her. "And I did not come to London to talk about the intricacies of risk management in international shipping."

Isabel sighed. "Well, you've ruined my plans by getting here early. I was going to take a shower and slip into this brand-new little black dress I just bought."

Ian cocked an eyebrow. "Shower? I can work with that. As we say in the insurance business, sometimes you just need to go with the flow."

Isabel slid a bare foot up the side of Ian's leg. "I don't think they say that in the insurance business, Ian."

"What did I tell you about talking shop?" he replied in mock sternness. He stooped and swept Isabel into his arms. She wrapped her arms around his neck.

"Are you going to teach me about risk?" she said.

Ian headed for the stairs. "School is in session."

Dawn grayed the windows in the vast master bedroom of 43 Wilton Crescent. Although he should have been exhausted the previous night, Ian had not slept well.

The shower with Isabel had turned into an extended lovemaking session, then dinner at Simpsons on the Strand. The two-hundred-year-old establishment, with its leather booths and signature carving trolleys, reeked of class and elegance. Isabel's little black dress was spectacular, and she flirted with the stately waiter about their relationship status. With mock sternness, the man advised Ian to "put a ring on it," as they said in America. On the long, slightly tipsy walk home, they had joked about the waiter and done their best impersonations of his British accent.

Ian had a modest hangover from the cocktails and the wine with dinner, but that was not the cause of his insomnia. Every time he closed his eyes, he saw the fruits of his labors for the Minister.

Bloated bodies floated in oily water. The scorched ruins of the Naval War College building. A flattened neighborhood in downtown Caracas. Some of them came from TV reports, others from the dark depths of his own mind. All of them pricked the conscience he'd never before known was there.

In the dim light, he studied the curves of Isabel's sleeping face. His gaze traced her cheek, the slant of her eyelid, the wisp of hair that cut across her brow.

Had she done this to him, changed him somehow? His relationship with this remarkable woman had sparked something in him...Call it humanity, call it a soul, call it a curse. It all led to the same conclusion: he was in love with Isabel Montez.

Even as he allowed the thought, he knew it could never happen. He was not the man she believed him to be. Eventually, she would figure that out.

No, it was up to him to end it. Now.

Ian slipped out of the bed and padded across the plush carpet to the window. Gooseflesh prickled his bare skin in the morning chill. He peeked around the edge of the blind.

The sun was just rising over the city. Overnight, a hard frost had fallen, riming the world with a gauzy white.

Isabel stirred, and Ian hurried back to bed. The big four-poster dominated the room like a stage. He burrowed under the comforter until he found Isabel. She responded by pressing Ian onto his back and sliding on top of him. She rested her chin on his chest and stared into his eyes.

"Who are you?" she asked. Her dark eyes were soft, but they bored into his with intensity.

"What's the matter?" Ian forced himself to stay calm. "You know who I am, Isabel."

"I actually don't know anything about you," she said. "Every time we talk about you, somehow the subject changes."

Ian moved his hips under her. "And that's a bad thing?"

She returned his smile but would not be deterred. She touched his right earlobe, running her fingers along the jagged scar where the flesh had healed.

"This," she said. "How did that happen?"

Ian's mind flashed to the exact moment seared into his memory forever. His first mission for the Minister, a simple exchange of money for a thumb drive. He could still see the man's face. A government official in Bulgaria, his Slavic features doughy with soft living.

The man had taken one look at Ian's youth and decided the payoff was insufficient. The argument escalated quickly, too quickly—another sign of Ian's inexperience. The man's gun was a Makarov. The weapon discharged next to Ian's right cheek, rendering him temporarily deaf and blind on his right side and blowing off the lower part of his right earlobe.

In hindsight, the man had probably only wanted to send a message, but Ian reacted on instinct. Deadly instinct.

When he returned with the thumb drive and a report that the Bulgarian source was dead, the Minister had only smiled.

"He had outlived his usefulness," the Minister said. "You did well."

Have I outlived my usefulness? Ian wondered.

Isabel's fingers still stroked his damaged flesh.

"Well," she said, "how did this happen?"

Her gaze probed him, and for a split-second Ian considered telling her everything. Then reality returned.

"I was mugged when I was a kid," he said. "A stupid accident that reminds me every day to be careful."

Isabel sighed.

"I don't believe you," she replied. "And that's a problem, because I'm in love with a man that I don't know anything about."

"What?" Ian sat up in the bed, wrapping his arms around Isabel.

"That's right. You win. I said it first: I love you."

He rested his forehead against hers. Their breaths mingled in a warm pocket between their bodies. A shaft of morning sun penetrated the space between the blind and the windowsill, lighting the room and casting a glow on Isabel's face.

"I love you, too," Ian whispered.

In that moment, anything felt possible. He could—he would—find a way to be with this woman. Somehow.

"I never said I love you to a man before," Isabel said. "It's hard work. I want coffee and a good breakfast." She kissed him. "Then we'll come back here for a while."

They threw on clothes and left 43 Wilton Crescent hand in hand. A few blocks of brisk walking took them through Hyde Park and into the Mayfair neighborhood. Isabel navigated using her phone as Ian strolled at her side, enjoying the rush of emotions that coursed through him. A cocoon of confidence enveloped him.

His gaze automatically checked the reflection in a shop window as they passed. Pure habit, born through years of countersurveillance training.

A man hurried along the sidewalk, half a block back and on the other side of the street. He was wearing a hat and dark glasses, but his gait caught Ian's attention. Memories clicked in place like tumblers on a lock.

He had seen the man walking a dog in front of the house where he and Isabel were staying.

He had seen the man in the doorway of a pub as he and Isabel stumbled home after their dinner at Simpson's.

Different clothes, different circumstances, but the same man.

Ian was being followed.

41

Whoever coined the saying "There are no bad ideas" never worked at the CIA.

After he received Janet's email about the Ivy Bells idea, Don took a full twenty-four hours to think about it. Although Don had been only peripherally involved, the operation to physically penetrate the Russian internet—dubbed Operation Net Neutrality—was well beyond the idea stage. It was a full-fledged mission with presidential sign-off.

And it was a massive effort. Using a combination of US Army 10th Special Forces Group, JSOC, and CIA operators, Operation Net Neutrality consisted of six teams poised to penetrate the Russian internet in six different locations at the same time.

The mission was more than difficult. The US needed to establish at least one permanent, undetected backdoor access to the Russian network. Their target objectives were internet exchange points, IXPs, physical infrastructure where internet traffic was routed between networks. It was in these buildings full of equipment that Russia had managed to sever her links with the worldwide internet.

Operation Net Neutrality aimed to gain back a tiny sliver of that capability.

Over the past weeks, the covert operation had inserted five teams onto Russian soil. The sixth team, ODA 0222, a twelve-man "A" team from 10th Special Forces Group, had a rapid insertion protocol in place if the other teams were not successful.

Stealth was the key. If the Russians suspected a site had been compromised, they could reroute traffic or shut down the facility temporarily for a thorough search. All insertion teams were comprised of highly skilled linguists, military, and technical operators, capable of blending into their environment.

At this late stage of planning, Don presumed any leader of an operation of this scale and complexity would not entertain another option. Because he personally knew the man leading Operation Net Neutrality, he was absolutely certain of that fact.

Nevertheless, Don felt obligated to raise Janet's idea with the leader of the operation.

It was Friday morning before Don was able to schedule fifteen minutes on Dylan Mattias's calendar for a secure videoconference.

The deputy director of the CIA took the call from his office. Mattias had risen through the ranks as a case officer before taking over the powerful position of Operations and Resources Directorate, which was where Don had met him. A shrewd political operator, the man on Don's video screen was equally cool and confident in a congressional hearing or in an interrogation room with a terrorist. He was widely mentioned as the next director of the Central Intelligence Agency.

He even looked the part of an espionage agent. His dark hair swept straight back from his forehead, containing just enough product to hold it in place but not enough to make him look like a used car salesman. When Don had first met Mattias ten years ago, the man had sported just a hint of silver at his temples. Today, Don saw the silver had crept up his sideburns, making him look even more distinguished. They were the same age, but Mattias looked ten years younger. Don sat up straighter in his chair and sucked in his gut.

"Don Riley," Mattias said with a smile that did not reach above his cheekbones. "What can I do for you?"

"I know you're busy, Dylan—"

"Yes, I am," Mattias snapped back. "And you are very persistent. I scheduled fifteen minutes for this call, but I'm hoping to be done in five. What have you got, Don? You told my assistant it was urgent."

"I have an idea for penetration of the RuNet that we haven't considered yet," Don said as an opener.

Mattias gave a theatrical sigh. He looked like he wanted to roll his eyes.

Don was painfully aware that the background of his video image consisted of piles of paper festooned with multicolored Post-it Notes. Mattias's background was camera ready for an appearance on *Meet the Press*: American flag, CIA seal, a row of books, and an antique-looking globe.

"Look, Don," Mattias said. "I know this is tough for you. Emerging Threats was a worthy experiment, but I think its usefulness is coming to an end. The director and I have talked, and once this Russia crisis is over, we'll schedule some time to discuss how we can reposition ET assets within the Agency. You've got some good people. We'll find a place for them to land, including you as well."

Don stared at the screen. This idiot thought he was trying to make a power play.

"This call has nothing to do with Emerging Threats or my job," he said. "I have an idea that has not been considered yet."

"Don," Mattias replied, "listen to me. We have this under control. We have six teams—six!—executing simultaneous physical intrusions of the Russian internet. There is no way the Russians can counter that."

"You don't even want to hear what I have to say?" Don wanted to swear and rant at the screen, but he kept his face immobile.

Mattias's gaze cut away to someone off screen, and he gave a curt nod.

"Tell you what, Don," Mattias said. "This thing goes off at five o'clock this afternoon. Why don't you come by the Ops Center and watch the show? As my guest, of course."

Don stared at the screen. He suspected the only reason why Mattias was inviting him was to put a final nail in the coffin of Don's career, but he didn't care. The success of the operation was all that mattered, and Don wanted to be there.

Dylan Mattias could take his perfect hair and his perfect video background and go screw himself.

"I'll be there at four thirty." Don ended the conference call.

———

His guide for the afternoon was a junior analyst named Lynn Lydell, a sturdy blonde with thick glasses and a generous smile. She wore dark blue slacks with an untucked men's blue Oxford shirt and sensible shoes. She shook Don's hand with a firm grip.

"I'm a big fan, Mr. Riley," she said. "I think what you do at Emerging Threats is brilliant." She spoke with a vague British accent.

She noticed Don's pause. "My accent?"

Don nodded.

"I was a foreign diplomat brat and spent my life being dragged around the world. International schools have a lot of British teachers, and I thought the accent made me sound sophisticated." She grinned at him. "Old habits die hard."

"I have you on the clearance list for the operation," she continued. "And I've been involved in the planning, so I can fill you in on what's going on."

Don decided he liked this young woman. "Call me Don," he said.

She smiled again. "Then you shall call me Linny, Don. That's what my friends call me."

Linny led Don to the glassed-in gallery overlooking the Langley Ops Center. The entire space had been commandeered for Operation Net Neutrality. The room had been reconfigured into six working groups arrayed around a central desk manned by Dylan Mattias and two technicians.

The intended information flow was obvious to Don because it was exactly how he would have arranged it. Each working group consisted of four people. They ran their own field team and reported in to Mattias. Mattias ran the "big board," the name given to the massive configurable screen that spanned the front of the room.

Mattias looked every bit his confident, in-charge self. Wearing khakis and a plain white button-down shirt with the sleeves rolled up on his muscular forearms, he stalked from team to team getting final updates and delivering instructions. Don tamped down a little surge of envy at Mattias's command presence.

You're better than this, Don, he told himself.

"Do you know Director Mattias well, Don?" Linny asked.

Don considered the most diplomatic answer, then chuckled.

"Dylan and I go way back, Linny," he said. "He's not a fan of our work at Emerging Threats and has let me know that on multiple occasions."

"I noticed that none of your team was involved in the planning," she said. "I was hoping to meet some of them."

Mattias finished his rounds and mounted the two steps up to his central desk. He spied Don in the gallery and gave him a mock salute. Don felt his face get hot.

Mattias gave a nod to his tech to broadcast his voice through the room. He had a strong baritone that radiated authority.

"Listen up, people," Mattias said. "We are about to kick off what might be the most audacious operation in the history of the CIA. Six teams in four different time zones are on the same mission: to penetrate the Russian internet and regain access to our cyberweapons."

Mattias was a compelling speaker. Next to Don, Linny bit her lip as she watched him.

"Everything is at stake here. If this conflict with the Russian Federation continues on its current trend, we will be at war soon. Maybe not next week, or next month, but it will happen. In any conflict, our success relies on our ability to operate freely in the cyber domain of the Russian Federation."

CIA Director Samuel Blank entered the gallery and sat down in the same row as Don and Linny. He nodded at Mattias.

"We have final authorization from the president," Mattias said. "By midnight tonight, I expect our cyber teams will be back inside the Russian network where we belong. Let's go around the horn with a go-no go on your team's readiness."

"Belgorad is ready," reported the first team.

"Kursk is a go, sir."

"Vyasma is a go."

"Stavropol reports ready to move, Director."

"Samara is standing by, sir."

Mattias turned to the final station.

"Chelyabinsk team is approaching the drop zone, sir."

Don watched the map of the Russian Federation on the big board as each city lit up. Two across the border with Ukraine, one outside of Moscow, Stavropol and Chelyabinsk in the south. Samara was deep inside Russian territory on the Volga River.

"The Chelyabinsk team is performing a HAHO drop," Linny whispered, referring to a high-altitude, high-opening parachute launch. Disguised as a commercial airliner, the special forces "A" team would open their chutes high in the atmosphere and drift up to forty miles across the border into Russia.

"Chelyabinsk and Samara are backup plans to the four primary sites," she continued. "Director Mattias expects the teams entering from the Ukraine to be successful early."

Director Mattias was wrong. The team in Kursk reported their local operative had been picked up by the local police off the street. With their cover likely blown, Mattias ordered a withdrawal.

Mattias received an update from Belgorad and ordered the live feed put up on the big board. Don watched a street view of a four-story concrete building surrounded by at least a company of armed soldiers. Mattias ordered the Belgorad team to fall back as well.

The two lights on the map nearest to Ukraine changed from green to red.

"Satellite images show increased military activity around Stavropol, sir," another team reported.

"Tell Stavropol to stand down," Mattias ordered.

The green dot north of the border with Georgia switched to red.

"Status on Vyasma," Mattias said. Don was impressed that Mattias's voice still held a calm edge after three early setbacks.

"Team is making an entry via the sewer system," came the report.

"On screen," Mattias ordered.

The bodycam footage was shadowy.

"Go to IR," Mattias said.

The screen switched to grayscale. The white silhouette of a man crouched in front of a door lock. The sound of heavy breathing from the team lead came over the intercom.

"We're in the maintenance level of the building," the voice whispered. "Making an entry now."

The door swung open, and three men went through in stacked formation.

"Clear!" Three voices called back.

The team lead stepped into a wide hallway. The space was dark save for a brightly lit exit sign over a door at the far end. The team moved down the hallway with swift steps, weapons up.

"Proceeding to the main access—" the team lead began.

"Grenade!" came a shout. Don caught a glimpse of the exit door cracking open and an object rolling down the shiny linoleum floor. A brilliant white explosion saturated the screen, and the connection went dead.

Mattias's face paled.

"Samara is coming online, sir!"

"On screen!" Don could hear the relief flooding Mattias's voice.

"We only have audio," the tech reported.

"Samara is a CIA team," Linny said. "They were supposed to be a last resort."

"Homebase, this is Volga. Device is in place."

"Test it," Mattias said.

"We have a signal!" the Samara team reported. "We're in."

Mattias rested his hands on the back of his chair and lowered his head.

"Great work, Volga," he said.

No answer.

"Volga, this is Homebase. Do you copy?"

Silence. The team lead for the Samara team shrugged and bent over his keyboard. He sat up straight in his chair.

"We just got a text," he said.

"Well," Mattias barked. "What does it say?"

"Jackrabbit."

"They're on the run," Linny said, her voice a whisper.

Don sensed the uneasiness in the men and women on Ops Center floor. The United States was the dominant cyber power in the world. It was not supposed to be this hard. Mattias's increasing agitation wasn't helping matters.

"Sir?" the Samara team lead called out to Mattias.

"What?" he replied sharply.

"The Samara access point is offline."

Don checked his watch. In the space of less than two hours, Operation Net Neutrality had gone from six teams to one final chance for success. That didn't happen by accident. Somewhere in the extensive planning phase, the operation had been compromised.

The Russians knew they were coming.

Down on the floor, Mattias was arriving at the same conclusion.

"Get me eyes on the Chelyabinsk team," Mattias ordered.

The satellite infrared video showed the twelve-man special forces team making their way through sparse forest.

"What's their ETA to target?"

"Three hours."

Mattias paced behind his desk in the center of the room.

"Order the Chelyabinsk team to divert to secondary objective," he said.

"That's bad," Linny said.

"What is the secondary?" Don asked.

"They are going to dig up a fiber optic line and try to tap it," she replied. "There are all kinds of logistical issues with that plan, starting with the fact that it's not covert at all."

"I see," Don said. Out of the corner of his eye, he saw Director Blank stand and head for the door.

"Director." Don stood. "I need to talk to you, sir."

42

Moscow, Russia

Vitaly Luchnik ran his hand across the red seal and the Top Secret/Eyes Only markings covering the report on his desk. He wondered if his visitor could see the very slight tremor in his fingers.

Admiral Nikolay Sokolov, ensconced in a leather armchair on the other side of Luchnik's desk, stirred. The younger man watched his surrogate father intently. A glass of vodka sat at his elbow, untouched.

"Uncle?" The tentative nature of the whispered voice spoke volumes to Luchnik.

He imagined Nikolay saw weakness, indecision, cowardice. If Luchnik could not inspire faith in a family member, how was he supposed to lead a country through this crisis?

"*Da*," Luchnik replied sharply. He forced his mind to concentrate on the contents of the report. Yet his mind rebelled at the facts the report told him.

The mines in the Panama Canal were Russian-made. The Americans knew it, which meant it was only a matter of time before the rest of the world found out.

They would blame him for this. Not Russia. Not the military. *Him.*

In normal times, he would be able to weather the storm. Let the Americans prattle on about war crimes and UN resolutions, he was a survivor. No one dared bet against Vitaly Luchnik.

But the report laid bare the facts of the case, and it did not bode well for Luchnik. Just like the MANPADs that had been used in Venezuela, someone had stolen premier Russian war technology for their own purposes. The *Chort* stealth mines used in the Panama Canal attack were the result of years of research and testing.

Just like the MANPADs, there was no record of any missing inventory. It was as if they had never existed. Whoever had done this not only possessed an intimate knowledge of the Russian military's latest technology but also a thorough understanding of their manufacturing base.

"You are certain about these conclusions?" Luchnik placed his hand on the report, the only copy in existence. He had tasked his nephew with the investigation.

"I checked the inventory myself, Uncle," he said. "There are no missing units. I would stake my life on that."

Or my life, Luchnik thought, and immediately regretted it. He needed an ally now more than ever. His nephew was the only one in his inner circle he could trust.

Nikolay shook his head. "We have intel that the Americans recovered a mine from the bottom of a lock and are examining it."

"How could this happen?" Luchnik asked.

Nikolay shrugged. "Possibly someone found a way to manufacture additional units off the books in the assembly plant in Vladivostok. That would be very risky, but with enough bribe money and the right connections, it could be done."

Vladivostok. Luchnik stared at his nephew. Nikolay was in charge of operations there. He had access to the right people. Nikolay could have done this thing—

His thoughts were interrupted by the ringing phone on his desk. The president's gaze snapped to the clock on the wall. It was after one in the morning. He touched the button to activate the speakerphone.

"Mr. President." Federov's soft voice filled the room. "We've intercepted attacks on internet exchange points." Despite the hour, the head of the FSB spoke with energy.

"Where?" Luchnik launched himself out of his chair, striding to the map of the Russian Federation that covered the wall of his office. His nephew followed.

"Vyasma," Fedorov replied.

On the map, Luchnik tapped the city two hundred kilometers west of Moscow as Federov continued.

"A team came up through the sewers into the basement of the building. We killed two in a firefight, but the rest got away. We'll find them, sir."

"You said there was more than one attack," Luchnik snapped.

"We received word through an informant of an operation in Kursk," Federov said.

Luchnik turned his attention to the town bordering the Russian-Ukrainian border. That was to be expected. The Americans would use the fluid situation in Ukraine to infiltrate their people into Russia.

"We picked up a local man who was rumored to be part of the operation. He gave us the address to a safe house—eventually. By the time we arrived, the place was empty."

Luchnik nodded, feeling his spirits rising. He was forcing his enemies to react to his actions. That meant the blockade was working.

"There's one more, sir," the head of the FSB said. "Samara."

The city along the Volga was deep in the heart of Mother Russia. During World War Two, it had been the site of Stalin's bunker against the invading Germans. For an enemy to attempt to breach the Russian internet blockade in Samara suggested either extreme desperation or confidence.

Luchnik picked up on Federov's tone. "How bad was it?"

"They successfully breached the facility. As a precaution, we have shut the exchange point down, and we are conducting a search for implanted devices." He hesitated. "We have found one so far."

Luchnik tried to check his anger and failed.

"Did you capture anyone?" he shouted.

"No, sir. We suspect they had external surveillance—possibly a satellite. By the time we arrived, they were gone. We will find them, sir."

No, you won't, Luchnik thought.

"The men you killed in Vyasma," he said. "Do you have identities yet?"

"I'm confident they're Americans," Fedorov said. "But I can't prove it yet. That will take some time."

"Time is a luxury we do not have right now, Vladimir," said Luchnik. "The Americans are getting desperate. The internet blockade is having an effect."

"I agree, sir," Fedorov said. "I will inform the prime minister."

"*Nyet!*" Luchnik replied. He turned to Nikolay, a new plan forming in his head as he spoke. "I am calling an emergency cabinet meeting for eight o'clock tomorrow morning. You need to get me identifications of the dead terrorists by then."

"It shall be done, sir."

Luchnik charged back to his desk and killed the speakerphone without another word.

He returned to the map, surveying the expanse of Mother Russia. Maybe he had been too hasty. His plan was working after all. His enemies were reacting to him now.

He scanned the northern border, the snow-covered islands scattered across the Arctic Ocean.

Luchnik paced in front of the map, the greens and browns passing through his peripheral vision. He channeled the rising confidence he felt into his thought process. In order to master his opponents, he needed to break new ground, make an unexpected maneuver that would force his adversaries to play defense.

When he reached the blue of the Pacific Ocean, he wheeled around to face his nephew. The younger man straightened under his surrogate father's attention.

"Yes, Uncle?" he asked.

"I need you to go home, Nikolay," Luchnik said. He placed his hand on the admiral's shoulder and looked him full in the face. "As soon as the meeting is over tomorrow morning, I need you to get back to the Pacific Fleet. You are my eyes and ears on the eastern front. The Americans will try to divide us, but we must not let them. They will try to draw us into a war and use it as an excuse for NATO to move against us."

"But the report," the admiral began. "The mines."

"I will deal with that in my own time," Luchnik said. "My enemy is not the Americans—not yet. My enemies are within our midst."

He studied his nephew's face, looking for any hint of betrayal. He looked so much like his mother, it pained Luchnik to doubt his own flesh and blood.

If betrayal was there, would he see it? If he saw it, would he believe it?

"I understand, Uncle," Admiral Sokolov said as he placed his hand over Luchnik's. "You can count on me."

I hope so, Luchnik thought. Or I am a dead man.

⋯⋯⋯⋯⋯

At precisely eight o'clock the next morning, Russian President Luchnik strode to his chair at the head of the long mahogany table and ordered his ministers to take their seats.

In the silence that followed, Luchnik stared them down one by one.

Little Mishi, his prime minister, looked pale and weak. Was he sick or just hung over?

Federov's pale scalp gleamed in the light. He met his president's glare with unblinking complacency. Minister of Foreign Affairs Irimov looked on the verge of a nervous breakdown. The sallow skin of his face sagged, and his fingers nervously tapped the table. Only Minister of Defense Yakov seemed chipper at this early hour.

The traitor was in this room. Luchnik felt it in his bones. They had played the game well, even caused Luchnik to doubt his own skills, but that moment had passed.

Russian President Vitaly Luchnik was back and spoiling for a fight.

He relaxed in his chair and folded his hands across his belly.

"In one hour," Luchnik began, keeping his voice cool and even, "I will give a press conference. I intend to tell the world about the bodies of two Americans who attempted to infiltrate Russian internet facilities last night. They had accomplices. Even now, we have a nationwide manhunt underway. They will not escape. Federov will find these men."

Federov passed out pictures of the two dead men from the raid in

Vyasma. Although he had not been able to positively identify the corpses, he was content to follow the lead of his president.

"These fugitives are not prisoners of war," Luchnik continued in the same conversational manner. "They are spies, and they will be executed."

Irimov moved his hand, but then put it down again. He hung his head.

Luchnik ignored the weak gesture. "Since the Americans are unable to respect the sovereign borders of the Russian Federation, I have no choice but to respond accordingly."

"Minister of Defense." Luchnik's gaze rifled over to Yakov. The man quivered with anticipation.

"Sir!" he barked.

"You will place your troops on the western front on highest alert. Ukraine, Latvia, Estonia, Poland—anywhere there are NATO troops. I want to remind the West that we will not stand by while they desecrate our borders."

Irimov cleared his throat. "NATO will take these actions as signs of hostility, Mr. President." His voice was thin and tired, resigned.

"Yes, they will," Luchnik replied evenly. "What is your point?"

"I question the wisdom of goading the Americans like this, sir."

Luchnik gave him a wolfish smile. "Then you will truly hate my next announcement, Foreign Minister."

"The Russian Federation will expand our northern border out to the Lomonosov Ridge in the Arctic Ocean. We will defend this area as sovereign waters."

"Sir," Irimov protested, "that's two hundred miles!"

"I'm aware, Minister Irimov," Luchnik replied, "but if the Chinese can claim the entire South China Sea as part of their First Islands strategy, we can exercise equivalent rights in the Arctic."

"Mr. President," the prime minister said. The pale skin of Little Mishi's throat worked with anxiety. "How do you expect to defend that claim?"

The room turned to the far end of the table where Prime Minister Mishinov sat. He rarely spoke in these meetings and never challenged the president.

Instead of answering, Luchnik turned back to the Minister of Defense.

"How soon can the *Sarov* be ready to sail?" he asked.

The room froze. The *Sarov* was a special purpose submarine, modified to carry Poseidon underwater drones. Nicknamed by the Western press as the "Doomsday Drone," the unmanned vehicles were nuclear powered, which gave them virtually unlimited range—and could carry a nuclear warhead as their payload.

"Defense Minister," Luchnik snapped. "I asked you a question. How soon can the *Sarov* be ready to sail?"

"I—I'll find out, sir," Yakov stammered. "Perhaps a month, maybe less."

Luchnik surveyed the room, and his eyes came to rest on Mishinov.

"Make it less, Defense Minister," Luchnik said. "Much less."

43

White House
Washington, DC

Don paused inside the West Gate of the White House grounds. His phone had been buzzing nonstop since he'd gotten out of the National Security Council meeting a few moments ago. He stepped off the sidewalk and opened up the screen. He'd missed three calls, six texts, and had eight news alerts.

President to seek congressional authority for use of military force.

Don stared at the screen in disbelief. That decision had been made less than thirty minutes ago inside the Situation Room at the White House where everyone had been admonished to stay quiet until the afternoon press briefing. How in the hell was it already on the *Washington Post* website?

He scanned the article. The "highly placed sources speaking on condition of anonymity" could have been any of the two dozen people in the room.

He clicked further. Rapidly following the actual news came the hastily written opinion pieces that ran the gamut from President Serrano being a spineless coward running from a fight to being a national hero who understood the true purpose of military force.

Don breathed a sigh of relief. None of the articles mentioned the other bombshell from the recent NSC meeting: the mines in the Panama Canal were of Russian origin. The so-called "smart mines" had fiberglass shells and were programmable to use a wide variety of sensors to attack: time delays, magnetic detonators, contact detonators, the list went on. The Navy EOD teams had discovered an undetonated mine in the Canal and were working to render it safe so a full analysis could be conducted.

He clicked the phone screen off and slipped the device back into his pocket. Don shivered as the raw December wind cut through the flimsy material of his suit jacket. In his haste to leave this morning, he'd neglected to bring his overcoat. The leaden sky and dampness in the air threatened snow. Another dismal low point in what was shaping up to be a dark week indeed.

He headed for the gate, already calculating his drive time back to the ETG office.

"Mr. Riley!" A young enlisted Marine was hurrying toward him. He handed Riley a black leather portfolio. "You left this, sir."

The folder wasn't his.

"Wait," he began. "This isn't—"

"Sorry, sir. I was told to deliver it to you." The young man turned on his heel and strode away.

Don flipped open the portfolio. The yellow legal pad inside had a scrawled message.

Return to the meeting room.
 – SB

SB. Samuel Blank, Director of the CIA. Don tucked the leather folder under his arm and hurried back into the building.

Four people waited for him in the Situation Room. The door shut behind him, the heavy magnetic lock slamming into place with a solid clack.

"Have a seat, Don," Director Blank said.

Don took a chair next to Blank, facing National Security Advisor Valentina Flores and the new CNO. At the head of the table, Chief of Staff Wilkerson sat in the chair normally occupied by the president.

In the ensuing silence, Flores clicked her long, red-painted fingernails on the tabletop. Wilkerson's attention was absorbed in reading a thin printed report. Don spied an SCA logo on the top of the page.

Special Compartmented Access.

Wilkerson looked up and nodded at Flores. The national security advisor smiled at Don. She was a stunningly attractive woman, but her smile was anything but warm or convivial. As her dark eyes scanned his face, Don was left with the distinct impression that he was being assessed.

"The director says you have a suggestion that could address our cyber problem," she said finally.

Don looked at Director Blank, then back at Flores.

"I did," Don said. "In the meeting we just had, the topic of tapping an undersea cable was discussed and acted on, ma'am. The decision was made to use the USS *Jimmy Carter*. That's the Navy's best platform for the task."

"Your original idea that you pitched to Sam was different, though," Flores replied.

"A former colleague of mine is based in Pearl Harbor. She has experience with a new mini-sub program for the SEALs. The *Manta* program. Her idea was to use the *Manta* to tap a cable. It's never been tried, though. The *Carter*, on the other hand, has experience with this kind of operation."

"You know what my job is, Mr. Riley?" Wilkerson asked. He had a mild voice that matched his grandfatherly appearance. He peered at Don owlishly through his glasses.

Don had no idea where this was going.

"You advise the president, sir," he said. "Help him set priorities, manage his schedule." Even Don thought he sounded like an idiot.

"I do all those things, of course," Wilkerson replied. "But my main job is to give the president options. And what he needs right now are some better options. What would it take for you to lead a team and tap the cable in the Sea of Okhotsk?"

"Sir, the Sea of Okhotsk was never my idea," Don said. "Just look at a map. After the Black Sea, it's probably the most heavily protected body of water in the Russian Federation."

"Yes, it is," Wilkerson agreed. "Which is exactly why I want to go after it."

"But, sir, the risk—"

The CNO spoke for the first time. "I've made some inquiries, discreetly. And the consensus is that a *Virginia*-class boat could get into the Sea of Okhotsk undetected."

"What do you say now?" Flores asked.

Don looked around the room. "I'd say if the Navy believes they can get the mini-sub within twenty miles of a cable, I think we have the technical capability to tap that cable. I've made some inquiries as well. Discreetly, of course."

Wilkerson sat back in his chair. "Here's what I'm thinking, Mr. Riley. You know the USS *Jimmy Carter* is a cable-tapping boat, and I know the USS *Jimmy Carter* is a cable-tapping boat. Furthermore, I'm betting the Russians probably know the USS *Jimmy Carter* is a cable-tapping boat. She's in dry dock in Norfolk, Virginia, as we speak."

He looked at his watch. "I'd say right about now, SUBLANT is sending an army of contractors to that ship to get her ready to go to sea as soon as possible. The Russians are going to see that, and they will respond with an all-hands-on-deck counterintelligence operation."

He thumped his elbows on the table. "While we have their undivided attention on the front door, what if we had a small team slip into the Russians' backyard and get inside their network? What do you think of that idea?"

"We'd have to handle it much differently than we did with Operation Net Neutrality, sir," Don replied immediately.

Wilkerson steepled his hands and tapped his closed lips with his index fingers. "Continue."

"The land penetration operation was massive," Don said. "Six teams, each with anywhere from five to twelve people per team, plus logistics and planning. Hundreds of people knew about that op before those specialists ever set foot on Russian soil. We went after the obvious target, internet exchange points, which were heavily protected.

"For this to work, we need to keep the operation as small as possible. The Russians don't know about the *Manta* program capabilities, and we need to keep it that way. No major intel briefings, and we limit who in the Navy chain of command absolutely needs to know."

"Admiral?" Wilkerson directed his question at the CNO.

"I know just the man for the job," the CNO replied. "The J2 at INDOPAC is a personal friend of mine, Mike Stoddard. I'll put him in charge of it. He'll keep the operation locked down tight. We'll use the *Idaho* and the existing crew of the *Manta*, since they're familiar with the platform. They've been putting to sea on a regular basis for some platform testing. Perfect cover for a near-term departure."

"One of the officers on the *Idaho* used to work in my shop, sir," Don said. "She has the clearance and the experience to handle any cyber work once we're inside the Russian network."

Don paused, realizing he had just assumed success. Wilkerson and Flores exchanged glances. They'd heard it, too. With the full realization that his boss's boss was sitting next to him, Don plowed ahead.

"One other thing we need to sort out up front," he said.

"Name it," Wilkerson said.

"Any intel we glean goes through my shop first so we can make sure we protect the source," Don said. "The mini-sub crew will be sitting on a cable miles away from her host ship. If anything leaks that could indicate the source of the cable tap, the *Manta* is a dead duck."

"Director?" Wilkerson asked Blank.

"Riley makes a good case, sir," Director Blank replied. "We will run all the data through Emerging Threats and release it on a need-to-know basis to the rest of the national security teams."

"I have another suggestion, sir," the CNO added. "Riley makes a good point about the security of the mini-sub. The *Idaho* is also the test platform for the advanced *Orca* program, that's an unmanned underwater drone. If we got into a tight spot, it would make sense to use the drone as the fighting platform, rather than the *Idaho*."

Wilkerson considered the suggestion, then shook his head.

"I'm going to leave that call to the captain of the submarine, admiral," he said. "We can give him guidance, but he gets to make the final judgment."

"Fair enough, sir," the CNO replied. "I'll make that clear."

Wilkerson turned back to Don.

"Mr. Riley, go get us back inside the Russian network."

"Aye, sir," Don replied. He could hardly stop the smile spreading across his face. "I won't let you down."

"Speed is essential, Riley," Wilkerson said. "Between the military force authorization in Congress and the feint with the *Carter*, you've got a window of a few weeks to make this happen."

Don paused.

"Something on your mind, Riley?" Wilkerson asked.

"The news about the AUMF came very quickly after the meeting ended, sir."

Wilkerson grinned. "You think there's a leak in the NSC, Don?"

Flores smiled, but the CNO looked as clueless as Don.

"There is," Wilkerson continued. "Me. I leaked the story."

He laughed at Don's puzzled look. "Politics is the art of postponing decisions until they are no longer relevant, Mr. Riley," Wilkerson said with an impish grin. "Congress will tie themselves in knots as they try to avoid being responsible for taking the country into another war. When the president is good and ready—and we have access to our cyberweapons again—we'll release the information about the Russian mines, and Congress will stampede into line."

He looked at his watch. "All you need to know is that I'm giving you space to do your job. Time's a-wasting, young man."

44

Pearl Harbor, Hawaii

Janet was midway through her morning bowl of Cheerios when a new message popped up on her unclassified email.

A meeting request from the J2 at US Indo-Pacific Command for 0800 at Camp HM Smith. The subject line read *BRIEFING,* and there were no other attendees listed.

It had to be a mistake. Why on Earth would the director of intelligence at INDOPACOM, a man who was well outside her chain of command, even know who she was, much less want her in a meeting?

As if anticipating the question, a personal note was appended to the email.

LT Everett —
  Attendance is mandatory.
  RADM Mike Stoddard, USN

. . .

An interesting way to start a Monday, she thought as she accepted the meeting request. Janet did a quick calculation in her head. There was not enough time for her to stop by the boat and still make it out to Camp Smith in time for the meeting.

After finishing her cereal, she hurriedly changed from working khakis to summer whites and left her apartment.

She took Kamehameha Highway for the drive out to Camp HM Smith. It was a little longer but more scenic.

Janet rolled down the car window and let her free hand dangle in the fresh ocean breeze. She couldn't ask to live in a more beautiful place, and yet, she'd gladly give up the sunshine and the fresh air to be underway on the *Idaho*. Give her a real mission—something that mattered to the fight her country was involved in—and not seeing the sun for months would be a welcome relief.

The Pearl Harbor National Memorial passed by the left side of the car. She spied the sleek gray shape of the *Bowfin*, a World War Two *Balao*-class submarine that was part of the exhibit. She squinted into the glare of the morning sun reflecting off the harbor water for a glimpse of the USS *Arizona* memorial.

For the United States, World War Two had started here in Pearl Harbor. She'd seen pictures of this area after the Japanese bombing, but it was still hard to imagine that scale of destruction. Now the world was hurtling toward a new conflict.

Janet's mind drifted to her former life with the Emerging Threats Group. Don Riley and his team would be up to their necks in action. For the thousandth time, she wondered if she had made a serious mistake by giving up that career path.

She put the thought out of her mind as the entrance to Camp HM Smith came into view. The Marine sentry at the gate directed her to the Nimitz-MacArthur Building, the home of INDOPACOM. The United States Indo-Pacific Command, one of six Unified Combatant Commands, was responsible for a vast part of the globe. From the West Coast of the United States to the western border of India and from the Antarctic to the North Pole, the INDOPACOM region encompassed fully half of the globe.

The Nimitz-MacArthur Pacific Command Center was a six-story building of brown stone and glass with a multi-tiered green-tiled roof. She'd heard the C4I capabilities in the Joint Ops Center were state-of-the-art, and she wondered if maybe she could wrangle a tour...

Or maybe she was getting ahead of herself.

The civilian receptionist took Janet's name and handed her a preprinted blue visitor badge. "You're in Conference Room 119, ma'am, basement level."

Janet checked in with a Marine sergeant at the entrance to the conference room.

"The room is set up as a SCIF, ma'am," he informed Janet. "I need you to leave all electronics with me, please."

Janet dutifully deposited her mobile phone and laptop in the proffered plastic container and stepped inside.

The subterranean secure conference room was set up to seat a dozen people in a U-shaped table arrangement. A large wall screen with the INDOPACOM crest stood at the open end of the U.

"Everett? What are you doing here?" Captain Lannier, her commanding officer, was waiting inside the conference room with the XO.

"I'm not sure, sir," Janet answered. "I got a meeting notice this morning from the J2. No explanation, just a note that said attendance was required."

Lannier glanced at the XO, who shrugged.

"That's about the same amount of notice we got." Lannier shot a look at the commodore of Submarine Squadron 7, who was in deep conversation with another officer a few paces away. "The commodore doesn't know either."

"Let's take seats, everyone." Admiral Mike Stoddard, the INDOPACOM J2, was a solidly built, dark-haired man with naval aviator wings pinned on his summer white uniform.

"Apologies to all for the short notice on this meeting, but we are being tasked with an operation vital to our national security. Time is tight, so we'll get right to it." He nodded to the back of the room. "Mr. Riley, the floor is yours."

Janet's head snapped around to see Don Riley at the back of the room.

He caught her eye and winked as he strode to the front of the room. Janet suddenly had a bad feeling about this meeting.

"I don't need to remind anyone here about the string of attacks that have been waged on the United States in recent months," Don began. "As we speak, we have naval forces engaged in containment actions against the Russian Federation in the Arctic, the eastern Med, and the North Pacific." He flashed a world map on the screen showing US Navy assets ringing the vast expanse of the Russian Federation.

"What you may not appreciate is that all of this activity is a holding action, a stalling tactic, if you will, for the main event."

"The main event?" The commander responsible for US national interests across one half of the world's surface was a four-star admiral and did not appreciate Don's tone.

"Yes, sir," Don continued. "The Russian internet blockade has been very effective. So effective, in fact, that our ability to implement *any* of our cyber assets inside Russia is compromised. I am talking about years of work rendered useless. I can say without exaggeration that if we do not regain access to those assets, our ability to defend our national interests is gravely at risk."

Don let his news sink into the audience, then continued.

"The CIA has been engaged in an operation to regain access to the Russian internet. A week ago, six teams operating at six different locations in the Russian Federation attempted to penetrate the Russian blockade. They all failed.

"One special forces 'A' team is still in place. They are attempting to dig up and tap a fiber optic cable at a remote location. That effort looks doubtful at this juncture. In the meantime, President Luchnik is not slowing down. His latest move to expand his territorial waters out two hundred nautical miles in the Arctic seems designed to force a confrontation. In short, ladies and gentlemen, time is running out."

The image on the monitor changed to plain block letters: OPERATION LOCKPICK.

"Today, I'm here to brief you on a new plan. If we can't tap into the RuNet on land, we're going underwater."

"I don't understand, Mr. Riley," the theater commander interrupted. "If you want to tap an undersea cable, you want the USS *Jimmy Carter*. Last time I checked, she was in Norfolk."

The *Carter*, a *Seawolf*-class submarine, was specially modified to conduct submerged covert ops, like cable tapping, using divers.

"You know that, sir," Don said. "And I know that. And we're very confident the Russians know that, too. In fact, we're counting on it. We want Russians to be all over the fact that the *Carter* is going to sea next week and heading north to the Barents Sea."

The monitor changed to a chart of the Sea of Okhotsk.

"Meanwhile, the USS *Idaho* is going to be right here." He used his laser pointer to circle the inland sea between the Siberian border and the Kamchatka Peninsula. To Janet, the body of water looked very small next to the vast blue of the Pacific Ocean.

"You want to do Ivy Bells all over again," the admiral said, shaking his head.

"That's exactly right, sir," Don replied. "When Lieutenant Everett came to me with the idea, I thought it was crazy, but I've checked with the experts, and it can work."

Janet heard her XO take in a sharp breath at the mention of her name. The squadron commodore, seated two chairs down next to Captain Lannier, leaned over and glared at her.

Janet's mouth went dry. The XO hated surprises. Captain Lannier? Well, if there was anything left of her dignity after the XO finished chewing her out, the CO would finish her off. By the time she got to the commodore, she'd probably be busted down to ensign.

"This is nuts," the theater commander said.

"It's not, sir," Don said. "I've consulted with the design team for the *Manta* submersible program. The mechanical arms on that platform have enough fine motor control to defuse an underwater mine. If the *Idaho* can get the submersible within driving distance of the cable, we have a shot."

Silence settled on the small group as each considered the risks of such an operation.

The admiral spoke up again. "You're talking about taking a US Navy submarine through the Kuril Islands and four *hundred* miles into enemy territory. I assume you'll want her to stay on station for..." He looked at Don. "A week? Maybe more?"

"We estimate it could be two weeks, sir," Don said. "Maybe longer."

"Captain?" The admiral looked past the commodore to Lannier. "It's your ass that's going to be hanging out to dry if this plan goes sideways."

"The *Idaho*'s ready, sir," replied Lannier without hesitation.

"Take a beat, Captain," the admiral continued. "If the *Idaho* is discovered in the Sea of Okhotsk, the Russians will hunt you down like a dog in the street. You will not have backup."

"Sir," Captain Lannier said. "I think it's a pretty simple choice. We need access to the Russian network, and the *Idaho* is the only way to achieve that goal. We've trained with the *Manta*. If Mr. Riley says it can be done, then the *Idaho* is our only option."

"Sir," Janet said. "We do have backup. The *Orca*. We've tested the platform, and we know how it works."

"You're asking me to arm an underwater drone?" the admiral asked.

"Yes, sir, I am," Lannier said. "It might give us an edge if things get dicey."

Don Riley was reading the room.

"Now that we've gotten the preliminaries out of the way," he said briskly. "I'd like to ask Dr. Hector Delgado to give us a briefing on the modifications he's made to the *Manta*."

For the next two hours, Janet watched as her spitball idea turned into an operational reality. When the meeting finally broke, it was nearly eleven o'clock in the morning. Janet waited outside in the warm Hawaiian sunshine for her commanding officer. When he emerged, Janet hurried over and saluted.

"Sir," she said. "I'm really sorry. I never thought the idea would become...well, become real. I should have told you before I sent the note to Don."

Captain Lannier extracted a pair of sunglasses from his breast pocket and cleaned them using a handkerchief. He held them up and inspected the lenses for spots, then put them on. The XO's face was unreadable.

"Everett," he began. "First of all, you should have told me before you sent that email. Don't ever do something like that again or I'll bust your ass."

He held out his hand.

"Secondly, you have singlehandedly gotten the *Idaho* into this fight in a big way. Well done."

45

USS *Enterprise* (CVN-80)
400 miles southeast of Petropavlovsk, Russia

Rear Admiral Sharratt had never been more tired in his entire life. His eyeballs felt like they'd been rubbed with sandpaper. His nerves quivered like piano strings. He'd lost at least ten pounds since they'd been on station.

And yet, at the same time, he'd never felt so alive. His mind would not shut down.

The morning briefing team gathered around the eight-person conference table in Sharratt's quarters. Flag officer quarters on the Navy's newest aircraft carrier were small but comfortable. In addition to the conference table, which doubled as a dining area, the room contained his desk and a sitting area with two armchairs and a sofa. The space was decorated in Navy chic: blue-and-gold carpet, brass wall sconces for lighting, and prints of naval battles on the walls. A seventy-inch flat-screen occupied the wall adjacent to the conference table.

Next to the door, a small black box was tuned to the Battle Watch open circuit.

The strike force commander liked to keep his early morning briefings short and to the point. They were his way of resetting his brain for a new day—something increasingly difficult after fifty-six days on station.

Sharratt managed by exception. The other commanding officers in the strike force knew their jobs and were expected to act within his standing orders and the rules of engagement. If the members of his staff were able to handle a routine problem, they did so. His valuable time was reserved for the big picture and emerging issues.

In addition to Tom Zachary, his chief of staff, his six a.m. briefing included his N2, Commander Jerry Sorenson, a professorial-looking intel officer who liked to use his reading glasses as a pointer, his N3, Captain Lacie Trent, a Black woman from the Bronx who spoke at New York speed no matter the topic, and his meteorologist, Lieutenant Commander Trish Langhorne, who understood weather like nobody's business but scarcely looked old enough to be Sharratt's daughter.

Rounding out the team was Captain Roy "Mongoose" Collins, a Montana farmer who looked and talked like a real-life cowboy. Although technically not part of Sharratt's staff, the commander of the *Enterprise* air wing, or CAG, served as Sharratt's eyes and ears for the entire strike force air contingent.

They always began with the weather report. The Bering Sea between Alaska and Siberia was known as "The Cradle of Storms." The area was home to a weather pattern called the "Aleutian Low," which meteorologist Langhorne explained was a "region of low pressure where sub-polar cyclones reached their maximum intensity." During the winter months, the weather front moved south of the Aleutian archipelago—where Sharratt's strike force was currently operating—and had caused no end of maintenance and operational issues.

"Merry Christmas, Admiral," Lieutenant Commander Langhorne said brightly.

Sharratt broke off from his study of the swirling, multicolored arrows on the monitor.

"What?"

"It's Christmas Day, sir," Zachary said.

"I'll be damned," Sharratt said with a self-conscious laugh. "Merry Christmas, everyone."

He dimly recalled being served Christmas Eve dinner the prior evening, but the detail had come and gone. Food was fuel, not something for enjoyment. Between the perpetually bad weather and his irregular sleep schedule, the days seemed to melt together. He existed, he ate, he processed information, and he gave orders. In the spaces in between all those actions, he took naps. The soundtrack for everything in his life was the Battle Watch intercom.

"Do the Russians celebrate Christmas?" Sharratt asked his N2.

Sorenson removed his glasses and chewed on the earpiece. "I'm not sure, sir. I mean, they do have religion in the Russian Federation, and it's a worldwide commercial holiday, so I guess so." He shot a look at the chief of staff, then amended his answer. "I'll find out, sir."

"What are you getting at, sir?" asked Zachary.

"When George Washington sailed across the Delaware on Christmas Eve and surprised the Hessians," Sharratt said, "that was a turning point of the Revolutionary War. I'd hate for us to be the Hessians in this scenario."

Sharratt rubbed his burning eyes. He sounded like an idiot. "Continue, Trish," he said.

Langhorne, with her customary enthusiasm, delivered a concise summary of the gloomy forecast. More rain, less snow, heavier seas. The strike force had already lost one destroyer to maintenance problems in heavy weather, and Captain Trent reported another was teetering on the edge of readiness.

Russian President Luchnik's recent extension of Russian sovereign waters two hundred miles into the Arctic Ocean drove a hard lesson home for Sharratt. The United States was not prepared to take the fight to the Russians in the north.

Apparently, Luchnik knew that.

Sharratt brooded as he listened to CAG query Langhorne about the weather details. The strike force was able to keep a combat air patrol on station, but thank God for the Stingray unmanned refueling drones. Although the force had not lost a pilot, twice they'd diverted the CAP to Alaska when the weather got too rough. That was only possible because he was able to risk launching an unmanned unit to refuel his pilots in midflight.

CAG said to Sharratt, "I don't see any issue with us flying in this weather, sir. We'll be able to maintain the CAP." He shot a look at Ops. "I just hope the supply officer has lots of deicer on hand."

"Always, CAG," Trent replied.

"What's the latest from INDOPACOM, Lacie?" Sharratt asked.

"The strike package is ready, sir," Trent replied. "Still no word on when or if we're going to use the damned thing."

Four days ago, Indo-Pacific Command's J3 Operations Directorate had sent down a massive air tasking order for Sharratt's strike force to plan. An ATO provided a detailed listing of targets to be destroyed, the composition of the force of aircraft, flight altitudes, and timing of the attack.

All pilots not actually flying or on a mandated rest period had turned the ATO into an operational document, planning every action of every aircraft from launch to recovery. Since the strike package had gone up the chain of command, nothing had returned.

Next to the weather, the biggest pain in Sharratt's ass was his own chain of command. Be aggressive with the Russians, but not too aggressive. The response to his act of shooting down the Russian drone a few weeks back had been alternately condemnation and congratulation, depending on who was talking.

"Any change on Russian air tactics?" Sharratt asked CAG.

"Same CAP, same tactics," CAG replied. "They're running Sirius high-flyers on a racetrack west of the escorts." The Sirius high-altitude surveillance drone was the Russian version of the US-made RQ-4 Global Hawk UAV.

"What about the Russian SAG, Jerry?" Sharratt asked. "Any changes?"

The Russian Navy had sortied a small surface action group out of Petropavlovsk. The Varyag, a guided missile cruiser, served as the flagship and was accompanied by three destroyers and three corvettes. The small force spent most of their time operating inside the twelve-mile territorial waters of the Russian Federation.

"Same-same, sir," Sorenson replied. "We're due for a drive-by in the next day or so."

Every few days, the Russians would point their ships east and sail within a hundred miles of the strike force escorts. After a half day of maneuvers, they would return to their territorial waters.

Like their airborne counterparts, the Russian SAG was always present but never threatening enough to cause the Americans to take action.

The air and surface threats were the ones Sharratt and his strike force could detect readily. Unsaid, but never far from top of mind, were the threats under the surface of the heaving ocean. Petropavlovsk was mostly a sub base, homeport to four *Akula*-class nuclear fast attacks and ten *Kilo*-class diesel subs. Satellite imagery showed exactly one of each currently in port.

To counter the Russian undersea threat, Sharratt had unmanned *Sea Hunter* surface ships running constant ASW patrols. His escorts all carried ASW helos with dipping sonars, and daily visits from P-8 maritime patrol craft out of Adak added to his comfort level.

But Sharratt knew the very best way to find an enemy sub was with a friendly sub. Three US nuclear attack subs patrolled to their north and west of the strike force. Submarines operated using the concept of "water space management," meaning each sub was assigned an area of water to patrol. Since US submarines were not assigned overlapping areas, by process of elimination, any subsurface contact encountered was a hostile.

Real-time communications with a submarine were always an issue. Submarines ventured to periscope depth only a few times in a twenty-four-hour period, when they were able to communicate with the strike force using satellites. The rest of the time they spent deep in the ocean, hunting.

In emergencies, submarines were capable of launching small communications units, called SLOT buoys, or submarine-launched one-way transmitters. These units floated to the surface and accessed a satellite to deliver a message. Of course, there was no way to reply to the message.

"Any sign of subsurface threats?" he asked Sorenson.

"The *Sea Hunters* keep reporting occasional hits," Sorenson said, putting the unmanned surface vessel patrol areas on the screen, "but by the time we get a helo onsite, we can't confirm the sensor readings. The *Texas*, that's the *Virginia*-class boat to the west, has reported some intermittent contact in their area, but they don't have anything concrete yet."

Sharratt considered the screen glumly. The patrol space assigned to the

Texas was over a thousand square miles. Sharratt knew the underwater environment was a complex three-dimensional space rife with acoustic features created by temperature, salinity, and depth that bent and blocked the sound waves the hunters used to find their prey.

"I recommend we move two of the *Sea Hunters* to the *Texas*'s op area," Trent said in her rapid-fire New York accent. "See if these ASW drones are actually finding something or just feeding us baloney to make us chase our tails."

Sharratt considered the idea. He still had an instinctive distrust of the unmanned platforms, but his ops officer's idea was a simple way to test the platform's capabilities.

"Do it, Lacie," Sharratt said. "Coordinate with Alpha Xray."

"Aye, sir," she replied.

"Anything else?" Sharratt asked.

"Sir." Sorenson tapped the eyepiece of his glasses on the tabletop. "I have the update on the *Sarov*, sir, if you want to hear it now."

"Is that what you call a Christmas present, Jerry?" Sharratt said with a wry laugh. As Sorenson called up a satellite image on the viewscreen, Sharratt recognized the harbor at Petropavlovsk.

"Since the Russian president announced the expansion of Arctic territorial waters, there's been much more activity on the *Sarov*," Sorenson began.

The laughter faded as everyone studied the image of the black hull of a submarine surrounded by scaffolding.

"You can see here"—Sorenson pointed to the aft section of the ship— "they've patched the hull, and it looks like they're removing some of the scaffolding. Both of those indicate they're getting her ready for sea."

When Sharratt got up from his chair, it seemed like every muscle in his body screamed with discomfort. He walked to the screen for closer view.

The *Sarov* was what the intel community called a "special purpose submarine," a one-off hull modified to support a specific mission. In this case, the *Kilo*-class diesel submarine had been outfitted with a supplemental nuclear reactor. Diesel submarines operated on batteries when submerged. When it came time to recharge the batteries, required every two days or less, the submarine had to return to the surface to access the large volumes of air necessary to operate a big diesel engine. The small nuclear reactor was used to recharge the submarine batteries while submerged, extending the operating time from days to weeks.

But the *Sarov* had other, more sinister modifications. She was built to carry Russian Poseidon drones, unmanned underwater vehicles that were both nuclear powered and capable of carrying a nuclear warhead.

In other words, a Russian underwater weapon with unlimited range and a devastating destructive capacity.

Like most Russian weapons systems since the fall of the Soviet Union in 1991, the platform claims were long on hype and short on reality, but the consequences of being wrong about the Poseidon were unthinkable.

The drone could swim into New York harbor and detonate a nuclear payload. Or into the middle of a carrier strike force, Sharratt thought.

"Have they loaded any weapons?" he queried Sorenson.

"No, but these arrived yesterday." The N2 tapped three rectangles parked in a nearby lot. Tractor-trailers, Sharratt realized.

"The area is cordoned off and under heavy guard, sir. They are the right size for a Poseidon underwater drone, but nothing's confirmed."

Sharratt swore under his breath.

"How much time before they can get underway?" he asked.

"Best estimates are two to three weeks. Maybe more."

"That'll do for now," Sharratt said. He went back to his chair and sank into the cushions, suddenly exhausted.

Chief of Staff Tom Zachary waited until the room emptied out.

"Sir, if you want to grab a few hours, I'll stay in Battle Watch," he said. "I don't think Ivan will pull anything on Christmas Day, George Washington notwithstanding."

Sharratt laughed. "Do I really look that beat up, Tom?"

"Compared to a man who just came off a three-day bender, you look great, Admiral."

"Okay," Sharratt said. "I'll take a nap. Maybe I'll call home and wish Suki and the girls a Happy Christmas. Tell the MS to bring me some coffee at noon."

"Aye-aye, sir."

After Zachary departed, the only sound in the room was the murmur of voices from the intercom box on the wall. He listened to the sound of crewmembers as they turned over their stations to the incoming watch. The mood was light, Merry Christmas was said more than a few times, and someone hummed "White Christmas."

Sharratt let his chin drop to his chest. He should call Suki. It would be good to hear her voice. The girls might be over.

But he was too tired. His forearms felt like they were glued to the chair arms. He would call them later. Maybe after lunch.

Sharratt hauled himself to his feet and pointed his body toward his sleeping quarters. He paused, walked over to the black intercom box, and switched it off. The sudden silence rang in his ears. He stumbled as he crossed the threshold into his dark bedroom. Without removing his clothes, or even his shoes, Sharratt crashed onto the bed and fell fast asleep.

In his dream, Christmas dinner stretched across the table. Like all the food in the Sharratt home, it was a mix of his American heritage and his wife's Japanese upbringing. Sushi and mashed potatoes, dried seaweed and stuffing, all of his favorites were there.

Suki sat at the other end of the long table, beaming at him. She wore a tight red dress with a high collar, and her hair was pinned up, revealing her nape. He loved the way his wife shivered when he kissed that spot on her neck.

His girls were there, too, but they were older, and they had kids of their own. A boy, maybe six years old, who looked just like Sharratt's daughter Jen at that age, was seated to his right.

"Merry Christmas, Chip," his wife said. Her voice was like a cold beer on a hot afternoon, so satisfying, so rich. He just wanted to drink her in.

"Papa," the boy said, "Papa." He grabbed Sharratt's arm and shook it.

Then he said, "Admiral."

Sharratt snapped awake. The brilliantly lit Christmas dinner vanished, the insistent child evaporated.

But the shaking remained.

"Admiral," the voice said. "You're needed in Battle Watch, sir."

Sharratt careened through the hall, bouncing off walls like a drunken man as he ran to Battle Watch.

Tension snapped in the atmosphere of Battle Watch. Someone had put a garland over one of the monitors, and there was a discarded Santa hat on the floor. Sharratt joined his chief of staff at the BattleSpace display.

"Submerged contact, sir. Twelve thousand yards," Zachary said. "Classified as the *Kuzbass*, hull number K-419, *Akula*-class Russian submarine. We've got helos in the air."

Sharratt squinted at the holographic display. Twelve thousand yards was well within torpedo range for a modern sub.

"First contact was from a *Sea Hunter* drone, Admiral," Zachary continued. "We were repositioning them to the western side of the strike force when one of them registered a hit."

"Contact has gone deep, sir," the watch officer reported. "Looks like he's clearing out."

"Tom," Sharratt said.

"Sir?"

"Reposition the *Sea Hunters* inside the picket line. If they're that good, let's use them."

"Aye, sir."

Sharratt gripped the railing around the BattleSpace display.

"Something else, sir?" Zachary asked.

"No," Sharratt replied. "That'll be all."

But he could not contain his thoughts. On this Christmas Day, was he George Washington, or was he the commander of the Hessian army?

46

RFS *Kuzbass* (K-419)
North Pacific Ocean

Captain Anatoly Renkov glowered at the depth gauge. The red LED numbers, which had been falling fast, slowed.

317...318...319...

"Depth three-two-zero meters, Captain," his conning officer said.

"Very well," he muttered, without taking his eyes off the depth gauge.

The red zero flickered, and Renkov heard a sharp intake of breath.

But the number 1 never appeared. The last digit of the depth gauge returned to a solid 0.

Every man in the control room—every man on board the *Kuzbass*—knew that if the conning officer allowed the ship to overshoot by even one meter, he would be relieved of duty. Captain Renkov was a man of exacting standards and brooked no sloppiness in how his orders were followed.

Which made the fact that he had just been detected by the Americans all the more embarrassing.

"Increase speed to thirty knots," Renkov ordered. "Steer course one-one-zero." The new course and speed would rapidly take him in the opposite direction of the American strike force.

Away from his mission.

Not a man in the control room dared look at their captain. Instead, they studied their instrument panels or plots with great care.

"Steady new course one-one-zero," the conning officer reported. "Speed thirty knots."

"Very well," Renkov growled.

He began to pace in the few square meters of polished linoleum adjacent to the periscopes, the only open area in the cramped control room that wasn't packed with equipment.

Renkov's path made a box around the greased silver periscope barrels that disappeared into the darkness of the periscope well at his feet. The long metal masts ran vertically from the keel of the ship to the top of the conning tower.

Three paces across, right turn, one pace forward, right turn...

The repetition helped him think.

His mission was to shadow the Americans, maintaining a constant firing solution on the carriers. In the event the enemy launched a strike on the mainland naval bases at Petropavlovsk or Vladivostok, he was to execute a subsurface attack. While Russian missiles rained down from above, he would put as many torpedoes as possible into the massive aircraft carriers.

Admiral Sokolov's orders had been delivered personally and were crystal clear.

Be ready. Be silent. Above all, do not fire on the Americans first.

The admiral had been so adamant on the last point that Renkov was not even permitted to load torpedoes into the torpedo tubes. If the *Kuzbass* was called on to attack the carriers, he would first have to waste precious minutes loading weapons.

The admiral had especially selected the nuclear-powered *Akula*-class submarine for this mission because he wanted to ensure the ship would be able to stay on station indefinitely. A *Kilo*-class diesel sub would need to leave the area every day or so to recharge their batteries with their noisy diesel engines.

Kuzbass was also the only submarine assigned the mission to shadow the Americans. For twenty-seven days, Captain Renkov and his crew had performed their mission admirably.

And now, in one blazingly stupid act by Renkov himself, they had been discovered.

The captain retraced in his mind every action he had taken in the last eight hours, searching for where he had made his mistake.

Normally, he ordered his conning officer to take the ship to periscope depth under his watchful eye, but today he had decided to do so himself.

He had slowed the ship to seven knots and ordered a depth of fifty meters. Renkov turned the submarine in a wide, slow circle to allow his sonar operators to listen for any enemy vessels, a maneuver known as "clearing baffles."

He had studied the sonar screens himself. Renkov had slipped past the American destroyers and frigates acting as pickets for the three carriers, positioning his ship between the outer ring of escorts and inner ring of guided missile cruisers that rode herd on the massive flattops.

The main force was a mass of white noise on a bearing of three hundred degrees, only twelve thousand yards away. A simple trip to periscope depth to access his satellite and the *Kuzbass* would return to the safety of the deep. Depending on the weather conditions, from this distance he might be just able to see the top of the carriers' superstructures.

Renkov reviewed the sonar images in his mind. The screens had not displayed anything of concern. The sonar technicians had not heard anything unusual.

And they were all wrong. The next few minutes would be seared into his brain forever.

Renkov had activated the hydraulic lever that raised the periscope. The silver barrel gleamed as the scope extended from the conning tower into the frigid waters of the North Pacific. When the eyepiece was at a comfortable height, Renkov snapped down the handles and peered into the scope. At this depth, the image was black. Using the hydraulic assist on the handles, Renkov walked the periscope barrel in a circle so he could get a full view all around the submarine.

"Conning Officer," he'd ordered. "Make for periscope depth."

The deck beneath his feet angled upward as Renkov continued his methodical searching turn, never taking his eye from the periscope. The black lightened to gray, then the top of the periscope emerged from the water.

He'd seen gray skies, watery sunshine, heaving swells like liquid pewter—

"Captain!" his ESM operator had said. "G-band radar, signal strength high!"

Just as he'd heard the words, he'd seen the ship. It was a small vessel, dead in the water, with a raked bow and what looked like an outrigger on one side.

And it was less than a thousand yards away—a naval close call in normal times. A disaster in these times of heightened tensions.

"Emergency deep!" Renkov had shouted. He slapped the extended handles back into place against the periscope barrel and slammed the hydraulic lever to lower the periscope. Rivulets of water streamed down the glistening barrel as the shaft dropped into the periscope well.

The emergency deep procedure called for an immediate increase in speed and a crash dive.

How had he not detected the ship in advance? Why was it just sitting there?

"Captain, we're cavitating!" the sonar chief called out.

The words dragged Renkov back into the moment.

"Conning Officer, reduce speed to seven knots, make depth two hundred meters, come left to new course—"

"Submerged contact!" The sonar chief's voice jumped a full octave. "Bearing three-zero-zero, range four thousand yards. American submarine, sir! I'm getting transients!"

The report froze Renkov to his core. An American Mark 48 torpedo fired from a range of four thousand yards was unbeatable.

"Launch countermeasures," Renkov snapped. "Flank speed, make your depth three hundred meters. Cavitate!"

The deck angled steeply downward. His only hope was to put as much distance between his ship and the Americans as quickly as possible. The countermeasures, small seawater-activated noisemakers, would create a sound barrier behind the *Kuzbass* and hopefully attract a torpedo—if one had even been fired.

At this speed, his passive sonar was useless. If the US sub had fired on them, his ship would never hear the torpedo until it hit them.

Renkov paced around the periscopes like a caged animal while his mind made calculations. A torpedo, which can move at fifty knots, is fired at an enemy submarine from four thousand yards away. The enemy submarine can travel at thirty-five knots. How long before the torpedo reaches the enemy submarine or runs out of fuel?

Renkov watched the clock. When the *Kuzbass* was still alive after seventeen minutes, he said, "Reduce speed to seven knots. Conning Officer, conduct a sonar search."

Another quarter hour crawled by as his sonar team searched the oceans for any sign of their enemy.

Nothing.

Renkov listened to the sonar recording of the American submarine. He closed his eyes as he heard the *chunk-chunk* transient that had been reported by the sonar operator. It might have been a torpedo tube door, or it could have been the American captain launching a communications buoy to report the position of the *Kuzbass*.

If the Americans had been trailing the *Kuzbass*, it made sense for them to release a comms buoy when the Russian sub was at periscope depth where her sonar was cluttered with surface noise. On the other hand, the US had already fired on a Russian aircraft that had come within missile range of her carriers. The *Kuzbass* was well within torpedo range of the carriers. Did the American captain have orders to fire on Russian subs within a certain distance of his carriers?

Renkov would never know the answer to the question, but he did know one thing: if his torpedo tubes had been loaded, he would have fired on the American submarine in self-defense.

He, Captain Anatoly Renkov, might have started World War Three.

A cold sweat broke out under his coveralls. His stomach turned nauseous. He looked around for his cup of tea and took a swallow. The lukewarm water tasted faintly of diesel oil, and his stomach rebelled. He spit the tea into the trash can, barely able to control himself from vomiting.

The eyes of his crew felt like pinpricks of heat all over his body. He glared back at them, seeing only boys, some barely old enough to shave. Did they realize how close to dying they had come today?

Of course not, he thought, they were sailing with the great Captain Anatoly Renkov. He caught his tortured reflection in the glare of a glass panel.

They trusted him to keep them alive.

He thrust his mug at the nearest sailor. "Get me a fresh cup of tea. Now."

"Right away, Captain."

An uneasy silence settled over the control room.

"Captain?"

The conning officer shifted on his feet, clearly uncertain whether he should disturb his commanding officer when the man was in one of his famous moods. He extended a color printout. When Renkov took the document, there were two smudge marks from the young officer's sweaty fingers.

It was the image Renkov had seen through the periscope of the drifting surface ship that had surprised him.

"I enhanced the image to allow for a better identification, sir."

Definitely a US Navy ship, but a small one and unlike anything Renkov had encountered before. He had seen an outrigger. In fact, the ship was a trimaran.

"What is it?" he asked.

The young man cleared his throat and gave a shy smile. He never would have volunteered the information if he had not done his homework.

"It's a *Sea Hunter*, sir," he said. "An unmanned vessel. It was probably doing a sprint-and-drift search—"

"A drone?" Renkov asked.

The conning officer nodded.

Renkov chewed on the inside of his cheek. As a submarine officer, he had one job: to remain undetected. In one maneuver, he had been unmasked by both an enemy submarine and by a fucking drone.

He handed the page back to the conning officer. "Write this into an intel report. We'll send it off in the next radio transmission."

"Aye, sir."

Renkov turned to the sonar operator, a senior noncommissioned officer. "Well done, *michman*. You and your team performed admirably today."

The man beamed. "Thank you, Captain."

Renkov crossed his arms, considering his next step. The answer was not difficult. The *Kuzbass* was the only Russian submarine assigned to track the American carrier strike force. He needed to clear datum, ensure he had lost his American submarine shadow, and reapproach the strike force from a new direction.

Renkov glowered at the depth gauge.

And this time do it without being detected.

47

Sea of Okhotsk
50 miles east of Okha, Russia

Janet adjusted her headset, positioning the microphone close to her lips.

"*Idaho*, *Manta*, comms check," she said.

"Check sat, *Manta*," came the crisp reply.

"Standing by to take positive control of *Orca*," she said.

"On your mark, *Manta*."

"Three...two...one," Janet said. "Mark!"

Her display filled with data from the *Orca*'s sensors.

"I have the baby, *Idaho*."

In the seat next to her, a Navy SEAL lieutenant named Tony ran through his preflight checklist for the *Manta*. He acted with deliberation, speaking softly to himself as he reviewed each item, then marking it from his digital list. She waited until he was finished.

"I'm ready when you are, Captain," she said. "*Orca* is in station-keeping mode on us."

"Very well." Tony grinned at her. "What do you say we get this party started?" Tony twisted in his seat to look at their passenger. "You ready to rock and roll, Hector?"

Dr. Hector Delgado, the submarine cable expert, was a thin Black man with a graying mustache and a perpetually mournful expression. In addition to a parka, Hector wore long underwear, two pairs of socks, and bright red mittens that he told everyone had been knitted for him by his granddaughter. Hector's deep voice issued from inside a parka hood.

"I'm ready whenever you are, Lieutenant."

Hector sat in a makeshift seat between two racks of computer equipment that had been added before their departure from Pearl Harbor. If they were successful at tapping the Russian communications cable that ran between Okha and Ust-Bolsheretsk on the Kamchatka Peninsula, Janet would need all that equipment.

When they were successful, she reminded herself.

From the comfort of dry land, the concept of tapping an undersea communications cable hundreds of miles inside Russian territorial waters seemed simple. After all, the US had done it once before, why couldn't they do it again?

So. Many. Reasons. Once Janet immersed herself in the complexity of the problem, she was embarrassed to have proposed it at all.

There were the technical problems. Operation Ivy Bells had taken place before the use of fiber optic cables. They had been able to "tap" the undersea electrical signals using inductive methods, without penetrating the watertight skin of the cable. Operation Lockpick had to establish and maintain a clean, water-free operating chamber to access the fiber optic cables.

Even if they managed to achieve all that, the amount of information that ran through a modern communications cable was massive. Just storing and analyzing the data was a huge task. Some of it could be accomplished in a makeshift computer lab set up inside the torpedo room on the *Idaho*, but most needed to be uploaded to the Emerging Threats Group back in Washington, DC.

The logistical challenges threatened the operation from the start. *Idaho* had to transit 3,700 miles underwater with two prototype systems in tow: the *Manta* attached to the hull of the submarine and the *Orca* swimming alongside. The trip had taken fourteen days.

Once they arrived at their destination, the *Idaho* and her precious cargo penetrated the heavily trafficked Kuril Island chain that guarded the entrance to the Sea of Okhotsk.

That had been three days ago. Before the *Idaho* made her way into Russian territorial waters, Captain Lannier had called an all-hands meeting in the crew's mess, the only space large enough to house more than twenty-five people.

The area was standing room only for the captain's briefing, the low-ceilinged room stuffy with the heat of that many bodies crammed together.

The *Idaho* carried a complement of one hundred twenty-seven men and women for Operation Lockpick. With the exception of current watch-standers, they were all present, waiting to hear what their ship was about to do.

The average age of the crew was twenty-three. Janet had never really considered that fact, but staring across the sea of faces, it was all she could think about.

Captain Lannier spoke in simple terms, outlining the purpose of the mission and what they hoped to accomplish. He left nothing out—that had been his one demand from his chain of command. If he was going to ask his crew to risk their lives, he was damn sure going to tell them why.

"Tonight," Lannier said, "we are going to take the *Idaho* into Russian territorial waters. We're going to pass through a deep channel south of Simushir Island and into the Sea of Okhotsk."

The navigator put a bathymetric image of the Sea of Okhotsk on the monitor, and the captain pointed to the island chain that guarded the mouth of the inland sea like jagged teeth.

"You can think of the Sea of O as a bathtub." He sketched out a rough rectangle on the shaded blue map. "Down here where we enter is the foot of the bathtub, the deepest part called the Kuril Basin. That transitions into the Okhotsk Basin. Our target is here."

He tapped the northern end of Sakhalin Island on the left side of the chart. "Four hundred and fifty miles into Russian waters. Lieutenant Everett will take over from there and execute the mission."

Lannier stepped away from the chart and held his palms up. "Why am I telling you all this?" he asked. "Anyone?"

"Russian boomers, sir," said a voice from the crowd.

Lannier pointed. "Petty Officer Reston is exactly right. The Sea of O is where the Russians like to hide their ballistic missile subs—lots of 'em. There's a very good chance we're going to meet up with a few along the way...and we're going to quietly back away and keep to our mission.

"The reason why I'm telling you all this is because you—every one of you—can make a difference. Our mission relies on stealth. If we get discovered, the Russians will come after us with everything they have. We are in *their* backyard, people. They will hunt us down."

The room was deadly still. Every eye in the crew was trained on their captain, hanging on his every word.

"When we cross into the Sea of O tonight, this ship will be rigged for ultraquiet, and it will stay that way until we reenter international waters. Are there any questions?"

A murmur of whispered "no, sirs" swept the room.

"I'm going to level with you," Lannier said. "Our country is under attack. The Panama Canal, the Naval War College bombing...we are closer to war with the Russians than at any time since World War Two. This operation is the difference between winning that war and losing it. *We* are the difference. When the history books are written, the USS *Idaho* and her crew will be there as the ship that put it all on the line for her country."

He paused, and Janet remembered how the room took in a collective breath.

"Who's with me?" Lannier said.

The crew's mess erupted in cheers, high fives, fist pumps. The captain let it ride for a full minute, then he held up his hand for silence.

"But before we enter the belly of the Russian beast, I believe the supply officer has a surprise?"

"Surf and turf tonight, Captain!"

Janet's earpiece crackled, interrupting her trip down memory lane.

"*Idaho*, this is *Manta*," Tony said over the circuit. "We are ready for undocking."

"Proceed, *Manta*." Janet recognized Lannier's voice. "We'll see you right back here in about twenty hours. Good luck."

Tony touched his panel. Downward-angled lights lit the black hull of the *Idaho* and shafted off into nothingness. Janet caught her breath as the mini-sub lifted off the hull and turned west toward the coast of Siberia.

It took them more than three hours to transit away from the deep water of the Deryugin Basin that abutted the coast of Sakhalin Island into shallower coastal waters. The sea floor in this area was polished clean by the strong underwater East Sakhalin Current that ran north to south along the coast.

The oceanographers had concluded that the strong current would also serve to uncover the undersea cable. What they hadn't bargained for was the effect of the current on the *Manta's* navigation system. Since there was no way to get a GPS fix underwater, the *Manta* had to rely on dead reckoning to ascertain her position. The strong current meant the computer's assumptions for course and speed were only as good as her estimates on the varying current.

After six hours of searching, Janet came to the conclusion that the nav computer's assumptions were shit.

The *Manta* hovered a meter from the sea floor, fighting the current, her work lights illuminating a cone a few meters in diameter. Visibility was marginal, with bits of floating debris carried by the current winking as they passed through the work light. A magnetometer was mounted on one of the *Manta's* extended mechanical arms to sense for the steel armor on the exterior of the undersea cable. So far, it had turned up nothing.

Tony had taken to using a sprint-and-drift methodology to execute a zigzag search pattern. He surged into the current for five minutes, then backed off the power and let the craft ease backward.

The immensity of the problem settled on Janet. They were looking for a one-inch-thick black cable that might or might not be buried in a low-visibility environment, and they were not sure where they had started. It was like using a tiny penlight to find a black soda straw in a football stadium while wearing a blindfold.

"This is crazy," Tony said finally. "We don't even know if we're searching in the right area."

"I have an idea," Janet said. "But you're not gonna like it."

"Oh, boy," intoned Hector, "that doesn't sound good."

"Let's get a GPS fix," Janet said.

Tony stared at her. "You want to surface off the coast of Russia and get a GPS fix?"

"Not us," Janet replied. "*Orca*. We ground ourselves and send her up to PD. It'll take her twelve seconds to get a satellite fix. She beams it to us, and we know where we are."

It sounded simple, but there were many ways that plan could go wrong.

"Hector?" Tony said.

"Why not?" Hector replied. "Otherwise, I might die of boredom."

Thirty minutes later, they had the answer they were looking for. The *Manta* had been searching almost six miles south of the target area.

Three hours later, the reading on the magnetometer spiked. Tony held position while Hector scanned the area. He peeled off the parka hood, exposing wiry, close-cropped salt-and-pepper hair.

"Right there!" he said, pointing at the screen.

Janet squinted. It looked like a garden hose, half-buried in silt.

"Which way, Hector?" Tony asked. In order to tap the cable, they needed to find a repeater, an amplifier inserted into the cable every twenty to fifty kilometers to boost the fiber optic signal.

"Let's go east," Hector said. "Away from the coast."

They followed the cable for two hours before Hector stopped them.

"If we go any deeper, I can't be sure we'll be able to maintain the water-tight enclosure," he said. "We'll have to turn around."

They made their way back toward the coast and finally found the repeater a hundred meters past their starting location. The search had consumed another two hours of mission time.

Tony positioned the *Manta* perpendicular to the cable and settled the craft on the ocean floor. The repeater was a one-meter-long steel capsule, shaped like a lozenge with flexible tapered tails that merged into the cable.

"It's all yours, Hector," he announced and climbed out of the pilot's chair. "I'm gonna take a nap."

Janet positioned the *Orca* between their position and the coast to the west, programming the unmanned submarine to remain fixed in place, its sensor suite on full alert for any Russian submarines or surface ships. She confirmed the laser communications link was strong, then she stole a glance at the mission clock. They had six hours left.

Clad only in a T-shirt, sweat glistened on Hector's forehead as he worked quickly but efficiently. Janet assisted the scientist as he positioned the repeater into a watertight "coffin." They burned another hour as the enclosure failed to achieve a watertight seal. They finally used the mechanical arms to lift the entire coffin and drop it. It worked.

"Mechanical persuasion," Hector said with a laugh. "Works every time."

Two hours later, Hector had drilled into the steel repeater housing in two places using remote mechanical tooling. He inspected the interior using a tiny camera lens. Eight fiber optic lines, each one connected to an amplifier, were laid out in two rows of four.

"Now for the fun part," Hector said. He threaded a tiny probe through the second hole in the steel housing. "This is a three-dimensional MEMS device, basically a tiny machine. When I turn it on, it will burrow through the cladding until it finds a light signal. Then it uses a mirror to reflect a tiny portion of the light signal to us."

"Won't they notice a signal loss?" Janet asked.

"If they're watching when I connect it, yeah, but signals vary all the time. I'm tapping right at the amplifiers, where the signal is the strongest, so..." He paused. "Unless the worst case happens."

"What's the worst case?"

"The little micro-auger cuts right through the line and kills the whole signal." He grinned at her. "Then we're screwed."

"That's not funny, Hector," Tony said from a reclined position in the back of the mini-sub.

"Hey, man," Hector shot back. "You're the one who signed up for a life of adventure. I'm just here for the science."

They all shared a strained laugh. They'd been confined to the tiny submersible for more than sixteen hours, and nerves were fraying. Hector looked at Janet.

"I'm ready when you are, Ms. Everett."

Janet traded places with Tony in the rear of the mini-sub and began to power up her computer equipment. The added load on the *Manta*'s batteries would eat into the mission clock.

Minutes passed as Hector worked on his remote tooling console. Janet saw his shoulders relax.

"Sending you a signal now," he said quietly.

Janet's monitor had eight channels, all showing a flat green line. One spiked.

"I've got it!" She diverted the signal to the processor. As expected, the data stream was encrypted. She sent it to storage for later analysis.

Over the next hour, Hector tapped the seven remaining fiber optic lines. As Janet processed each one, they found unencrypted voice and email traffic mixed in with the secure messages.

Tony sank to the deck next to her workstation. He smelled of sweat, seawater, and the reconstituted beef stew he'd eaten two hours ago. Or maybe she was just smelling herself.

"Now what?" he asked.

Janet cued up a series of emails. Her computer program had analyzed the traffic and would inject them seamlessly into the data streaming across the fiber optic line when she gave the command.

"Now we go hunting," she said.

"Big game?"

"I'll settle for a few sheep," she replied. "I just need a few people to click on a perfectly innocent link in an email, and my little computer virus will do the rest."

"Hit the button, Everett," he said. "I need a shower, and we've got a long drive back."

Janet tapped the keyboard. The list of emails disappeared one by one.

"It's a phone-home program," she said. "If our cyber payloads are still alive, this tells them to send me a beacon signal."

Hector joined them. "How many cyberweapons are out there?"

"Lots," Janet replied. "We need computer programs to manage our computer programs. That's how many."

"And all this stuff I read about cyber warfare," Hector said. "Is it true? Do they have just as many buried in our systems?"

"I suspect they do," Janet said.

She checked the screen where the processor had queued unencrypted voice and email traffic. Responses to her beacon program would show up there as innocuous unclassified emails.

The first one arrived. Janet felt a surge of hope. They had done it. They had completed the mission.

A second beacon response arrived in her inbox, then a third. She pumped her fist.

"It's working," she said. "The payloads are still out there."

"I don't know whether to be happy about that or sad," Hector said as he pulled on his sweater. "Makes me long for the days when all we worried about was nuclear weapons. At least we knew where they were."

"That cheery note is my cue to start the preflight checks," Tony said. He checked the mission clock. "You've got another forty-five minutes, Janet, then I'm pulling the plug."

"Aye-aye, sir," Janet said, still high from the win.

She clicked on one of the voice calls. The sound of two men speaking in Russian filled the cabin of the *Manta*.

Janet flipped back to the rapidly filling screen showing email responses to her polling program. She snugged her wool cap over her ears and settled down to watch the show.

48

USS *Enterprise* (CVN-80)
400 miles southeast of Petropavlovsk, Russia

The illuminated tablet on the table in front of Sharratt bore the words OPERATION RED SUNSET in bold letters, followed by Top Secret-SCI markings.

They'd been emailed the package only an hour ago—just enough time to skim the document before the secure videoconference with the Seventh Fleet Commander, which was to take place in the next five minutes. Sharratt surveyed his staff as they finished reading their copies.

Intel officer Commander Sorenson was slapping his reading glasses in his palm while he stared off into space. Chief of Staff Tom Zachary's face was as inscrutable as ever. Captain "Mongoose" Collins nodded at Sharratt.

"They hardly changed a comma, sir," he said. "This is the strike package we submitted two weeks ago."

"Be careful what you wish for," said Ops Officer Lacie Trent, her flat Bronx accent adding an extra syllable to the word *for*.

Mongoose chuffed. "As long as we can put planes in the air, we'll get the job done."

Sharratt raised an eyebrow at Meteorologist Langhorne.

"If you give me a time frame, sir, I'll give you a forecast," she replied to the unasked question. "I'm going to be more accurate inside of forty-eight hours."

"C'mon, Trish," Collins said, "all your forecasts are just varying degrees of shitty weather. It's going to suck. We already know that, and we embrace it."

But CAG said the words in a kindly way. They had all more or less adopted the newly minted lieutenant commander. She worked hard, delivered solid work, and never complained.

"That's enough," Sharratt said quietly, stilling the laughter. "Jerry, what's your take on the rest of the operation?" he said to the intel officer.

Sorenson put his glasses on, then took them off again.

"It's a bold move, sir," he began. "If our strike is convincing enough, it just might give our forces in the north the edge they need to make the difference."

"Hmmm," Sharratt replied.

From the very beginning, he'd wondered why the United States had put three carriers in the North Pacific. One made perfect sense, even adding the second was a wise move, but three had just seemed like overkill. He told himself that the US wanted to send a strong message to Russia in this part of the world by showing the flag—or three flags.

Turns out, the Joint Chiefs knew exactly what they were doing: Sharratt's carrier strike force was bait for the Russians. A shiny object to distract the enemy from the real goal, which was the Russian Northern Military District.

The flat-screen at the end of the table changed from the seal of the US Seventh Fleet to the fleshy features of Vice Admiral Kale Bumpers.

Sharratt still had not quite made up his mind about his new boss. Not that it mattered. You don't get to choose family, and in the Navy, your chain of command was your family. Complain all you wanted, they weren't going to change unless the Navy deemed it so.

"Morning, sir," Sharratt said.

"How's life up north, Chip?" came the reply.

"Living the dream," Sharratt said.

The two men had spoken every day since Bumpers had replaced Sharratt's old friend and mentor Sal Mondelli as Seventh Fleet commander. Their conversations always started the same way.

Bumpers laughed right on cue, but it sounded forced and uncomfortable.

"You've had a chance to review the op order?" he said.

"Yes, sir," Sharratt replied. "We're ready to do our part."

Sharratt noted the sizeable number of staff officers surrounding Bumpers in the background on the VTC. One thing the USS *Blue Ridge* did not lack was space for staff officers, thought Sharratt.

"For anyone who didn't know, this is the Russian New Year holiday," Bumpers continued. "They take off a week in the beginning of January so they can sit around and drink vodka, I guess. Despite the heightened tensions, we expect their military posture to be somewhat relaxed. The end of the holiday is our window.

"Timing is everything here. This is a tightly coordinated strike, ladies and gentlemen. Once we knock over the first domino, it all follows like clockwork. Two days from now, we are going to unleash holy hell on the Russian Federation. The first wave is rolling cyberattacks on military installations and major infrastructure. As soon as they go dark, Chip, your carriers will execute an alpha strike on the Far Eastern Military District. Targeted strikes on Vladivostok, the Kamchatka Peninsula, and Sakhalin Island to take out communications, command-and-control infrastructure, and destroy any planes still on the ground."

Sharratt's strike package called for a three-phase attack. Cruise missiles and hypersonics went in first, followed closely by two of his three carrier air wings supported by Air Force AWACS and refueling tankers out of Alaska. The Air Force was also responsible for striking northern Russian bases across the Bering Strait, especially the Anadyr-Ugolny Air Base, which was home to a fleet of UAVs.

The third air wing in the *Enterprise* strike force would be held in reserve for rotating attacks, to neutralize any Russian counterattacks, and combat air patrol protecting the valuable carriers.

On the screen, Bumpers was hitting his stride in the briefing. His features flushed as he continued.

"While you have Moscow's attention in the east, the main event is happening in the Arctic. Special operations teams will take out major command centers while the 173rd Airborne Brigade launches out of Norway to seize bases at Alakurtti, Pechanga, and the crown jewels, the headquarters of the Northern Fleet in Severomorsk. Submarines will seal off the chokepoint at the entrance of the White Sea. Any ships in the port of Archangel will be contained."

"Sir," Sharratt said finally, "it may not be my place to say, but how do we prevent this from escalating? How does this not lead to a nuclear response?"

"President Serrano is calling the Russians out," Bumpers replied. "Just before the cyberattacks roll, he will make an address to the American people. He's going to tell them that we have hard evidence that the Naval War College terrorist attack and the bombing in the Panama Canal were done by the Russians. They drew first blood.

"He's drawing a red line in the Arctic. The push to extend their territorial waters is a step too far. The United States will not stand by and let a two-bit punk like Luchnik decide our future. If the Russians want a fight, then we're gonna grant that wish."

"What about the congressional hearings on authorized use of military force?" Sorenson asked.

Bumpers shrugged. "Not our fight, Commander. We follow the lawful orders of our civilian leaders. When the commander in chief says go, we go. Besides, once the president tells the country about what the Russians did, do you really think any politician is going to miss that train?"

Sharratt recalled the AUMF vote after the 9/11 attacks and silently agreed with Bumpers. Not that it mattered. What went on in Congress was not his concern.

Bumpers switched topics. "There's a few things beyond our control, though. The weather, for example. How does the forecast look over the next few days?"

Sharratt shot a look at Langhorne, who nodded. CAG joined her in silent approval.

"Terrible, as usual, but nothing we can't handle, sir," Sharratt replied. "I just thank Christ I'm not on one of those combatants out there. Being on one of the destroyers is like living on a roller coaster. Hell, even the Chinese fishing boats that were following us decided to go home for the Chinese New Year holiday."

Like the Russians, the People's Republic of China maintained a signals intelligence collection capability on their civilian distant-water fishing fleet. Unlike the Russian AGI fleet, which had a reputation for aggressively pursuing their targets to the point of harassment, the Chinese kept a respectful distance from the US Navy ships. Still, the Chinese had maintained between two and five "fishing vessels" close to the strike force since they had left Japan. The last one had departed just that morning.

"There's still some fine-tuning going on with the timing," Bumpers continued. "The computer jockeys are still dotting their *I*s and crossing their *T*s. This Russian internet blockade has proved to be a colossal pain in the ass, and that's been the weak link in the chain for this op. What that means for you is that I need you to keep this quiet for another day while we get the details nailed down. As soon as I know, you'll know."

The videoconference ended, and Sharratt let silence hang over the room as the impact of what they were about to embark on sank in.

This was a path to war, plain and simple. The next few days could very well thrust the world into a global conflict. Sharratt didn't shrink from the thought—it was what he had trained for—but he didn't welcome it either. These were political decisions, and he was a military officer who took orders from those civilian politicians. It was just that simple.

Sharratt thought of his two daughters. What would this do to their lives? He thought of the nearly twenty thousand men and women in his strike force getting tossed around by the rough waters of the North Pacific. The mean age of the crews was not that much older than his daughters. In the next few days, some of them, possibly all of them, could be dead.

"Set EMCON Condition Alpha," Sharratt said. "Secure all calls and emails off all ships immediately."

The other aspect of having a strike force full of young people meant you had to anticipate youthful tendencies. It was a given that someone some-where in the fleet was going to say or write the wrong thing to a loved one. The old adage "loose lips, sink ships" was never more appropriate than right now.

"I assume you want to postpone the briefing on the Chinese joint exercises, sir?" Sorenson asked. "They start in about ten days."

Sharratt considered the question. Ten days from now seemed like an impossibly long time in a very murky future. Watching a bunch of Chinese troops pretend to go to war was off the priority list.

He noticed Tom Zachary and CAG were ignoring the conversation. Both sat erect in their chairs, their attention focused through the window into Battle Watch.

"Looks like something's going on, boss," Zachary said, rising from his chair.

Inside the computer-chilled atmosphere of Battle Watch, Sharratt felt the snap of electric tension and noted the rigid posture of the watch team.

The watch officer looked up as Sharratt's staff entered.

"I was just about to call you, sir," he said. "Looks like we've got a runner. Alpha Whiskey is on the net."

He pointed to the BattleSpace display. The Russian air patrol, which normally mirrored the *Enterprise*'s combat air patrol, followed the typical racetrack pattern alongside the Russian coast. The strike force CAP and their shadows were at the base of the patrol area, off the Kuril Island chain.

A single red triangle, signifying an enemy air contact, headed northeast. If it maintained its current course, it would pass directly over the strike force.

"The new bogey came in from Dolinsk-Sokol about a half hour ago, sir, and entered the Russian patrol pattern at twenty-seven thousand feet, five hundred knots. We have it classified as a Sukhoi S-70 Hunter drone—same model that tried to make a run at us before."

Sharratt studied the holographic display. "Where's his wingman?"

"Doesn't have one, sir. He's solo," the watch officer said. "He entered the patrol pattern, then broke toward us unexpectedly. Assuming constant course and speed, he'll be overhead in seven minutes."

"Fire control radar?" CAG asked.

"None, sir. He's dark."

The Russians had timed the attack perfectly, Sharratt thought. The airborne CAP would have to burn hard to close the bogey, and that assumed they had the necessary fuel.

"Alpha Whiskey already launched the Alert Five CAP, Admiral," the Battle Watch Officer said, then paused. "Stand by, sir. The UCAV launched, but the cat with the F-35 went down. They're moving the F-35 to the operating catapult now."

CAG charged out of Battle Watch en route to Pri-Fly, where flight operations were managed.

Sharratt did the math in his head. A direct flyover of the strike force was four minutes away. He seized the handset.

"Alpha Whiskey, this is Alpha Bravo actual. Light up the target with fire control radar."

"Alpha Bravo, Alpha Whiskey, WILCO."

Sharratt watched the display. He saw contact data change as the missile targeting radar achieved a missile lock.

"No deviation in course or speed," the watch officer reported.

It was the same as the last Russian drone attack, a head-on rush at the US carrier strike force...except this time, the Russian drone might be armed.

"The standby CAP is airborne, sir," the watch officer reported.

"Time's short, Admiral," Chief of Staff Zachary said. "Recommend we splash this bastard."

Sharratt had flown back seat in the EA-18 Growler for his entire Navy flying career. He knew what it felt like to be in the vortex of a rapidly unfolding combat situation where everything hung on your next reaction.

In those moments, his senses keyed on tiny changes in his surroundings. He had learned to listen to his body, follow his instincts.

"Alpha Whiskey, this is Alpha Bravo actual. Confirm visual ID on bogey before engaging, over."

"Alpha Bravo, this is Alpha Whiskey. Acknowledged. Break, break. Dragonrider 5, Alpha Whiskey, vector 270, buster. Bogey on your nose at angels 27. Weapons tight."

"Sir," Zachary said in a low voice. "That delay puts the bandit within weapons range."

Sharratt kept his eyes on the three-dimensional holographic display, willing the blue dot representing the F-35 and its pilot to merge with the red arrow of the incoming Russian bogey.

"Alpha Whiskey, this is Dragonrider 5!" came the voice of the F-35 pilot. "Contact is a Korean Air Airbus 330. Repeat, this is a civilian aircraft!"

"Dragonrider 5, Alpha Whiskey, copy civilian flyover. You are weapons tight."

A collective gasp whistled through the silent Battle Watch as the full impact of what might have happened crashed down on every person in the room, from the petty officer manning the backup sound-powered phones to the admiral himself.

Sharratt gripped the steel railing around the BattleSpace display so hard he heard his knuckles crack from the strain.

49

Emerging Threats Group
Tysons Corner, Virginia

Don Riley entered his office and shut the door quietly behind him. Leaving the lights off, he navigated to his desk by the dim glow from his computer screen and collapsed into the leather armchair.

His head reeled from too much caffeine and too little sleep. His eyes ached from squinting at screen after screen for far too long.

But he knew the real source of his tension was rooted in a deep-seated worry that gnawed at his subconscious. It was just another incarnation of the doubt that had hounded him for months.

The fear that he was missing something.

Try as he might, Don could not name this elusive element. It floated like a shadow just beyond his senses, but it was there. Always.

The cache of communications Janet had sent them from Operation Lockpick was nothing short of a treasure trove. In addition to the unencrypted emails and voice communications, they had been able to exploit enough of the encrypted comms to paint a complete picture of their Russian adversary. His presentation at the National Security Council meeting in—Don checked his watch—less than ten hours was going to make a lot of people very, very happy.

The Russian Federation was not ready for war. The junkyard dog that had antagonized the United States for the past year was all bark and no bite.

Even as Russian President Luchnik gave speeches to his people about the American aggressors and isolated his internet from the rest of the world, what was going on behind the digital curtain of secrecy was nothing short of chaos.

While Luchnik raised the stakes, personal communications between senior ranking officials in the Russian Federation read like cries for help. No one seemed to have any clue what was going on.

And yet, even Luchnik had limits. His orders to his force commanders were crystal clear: Do not, under any circumstances, start a shooting war. He'd even gone so far as to forbid submarine commanders from loading torpedoes in their tubes for fear that they might be tricked into firing a shot.

The general in charge of the aerial drone program at Dolinsk-Sokol Air Base had been relieved of command after an Su-70 Hunter UAV strayed too close to the US carrier strike force near the Aleutians and was shot down. He was currently being held in Lefortovo Prison awaiting trial. Even now, the internal communiques revealed, the drones and warplanes that were flying near the American carrier strike force were unarmed.

On the face of it, this was undoubtedly welcome news to the US war planners, but it raised the question that only fed Don's latent concerns.

Why?

Why would the Russian president go to extraordinary lengths to destabilize the world order, then show weakness within his own borders? Why wasn't he preparing to take advantage of the chaos for his own gain?

The obvious answer—that he had overplayed his hand—seemed hollow to Don. Luchnik had been in power for nearly three decades. He knew how to wield influence the way a maestro knew how to coax beautiful music from an orchestra.

It made no sense. There was more to this analysis, Don was sure of it, but time was running out.

In frustration, he tapped his keyboard to bring his computer monitor to life and scanned his email inbox. There were dozens of unread classified messages in his queue. He sorted them by priority, and two jumped to the top of the list.

Analysis of Russian Black Sea Submarine Missile Capabilities

Foreign Materials Exploitation Analysis—Russian SA-29 MANPAD

Christ, Don thought, even his inbox was being overrun by the Russian Federation.

As was his habit, he forwarded both reports to his admin to print hard copies. Don expelled a long breath and leaned his head back until he was staring at the ceiling.

Everyone on his team had been working nonstop for days analyzing the Operation Lockpick data. He was sure the conclusions they had developed would support a go decision on Operation Red Sunset—despite Don's lingering concerns.

A draft of his NSC presentation was waiting in his email queue. He could send everyone home right now or...

Don sat up straight and logged in to the internal message system he shared with his direct staff.

War Room – 10 mins.

He stopped by the kitchen and charged his coffee cup before he entered the meeting room.

Everyone was in their seats, waiting. Don took his chair at the head of the table. Dre and Michael sat to his immediate right, facing Mark West-lund and Harrison. The monitor with the seal of the Emerging Threats Group glared at him from the opposite wall.

He surveyed the faces around him, seeing curiosity, fatigue.

Second thoughts crowded into his consciousness. They were as tired as he, but unlike them, he had to give a presentation to the president of the United States in a few hours. He should be sleeping now.

"Tomorrow morning, I'm supposed to brief the National Security Council on our findings from Operation Lockpick. We have good news. Janet and the team on the *Idaho* have verified at least eighty percent of our cyber arsenal is in place inside the Russian Federation and ready for action.

We can send her the execute codes. All Janet needs to do is hit return on her keyboard from the mini-sub."

Don took a sip of coffee, thinking about how he wanted to frame the next bit.

"I was not in the intel community when the US invaded Iraq," he began. "But I've worked with a lot of men and women who were. To be blunt about it, they were scarred by the experience. A lot of them blamed the politicians for not believing what the intel was telling them about weapons of mass destruction, but the truth is more complicated.

"If you shared a beer with one of the survivors from that time, they tell a different story. Some call it groupthink, some call it confirmation bias, but it's the same problem."

"You think our analysis is missing something, Don?" Harrison asked.

Don shook his head.

"I'll be honest with you, I don't know," Don replied. "When I look at the data, I get an answer, and that answer says Russia has gone too far this time. They set in motion a chain of events that has gotten away from them. The answer I come to is that President Luchnik is about to get what's been coming to him for a long time."

"And you think that's the wrong answer?" Dre asked.

"No," Don said, "I think maybe we're asking the wrong question."

"And what's the right question?" Michael asked.

Don sighed. "I don't know. That's why I called you all here. Take two giant steps back from the problem and look at the intel again. Start from the beginning. Is there something we've overlooked?"

"Sure," Dre said. "Go back to the attack on the USS *Black* in the Strait of Hormuz. The Iranians were behind it, not the Russians."

Don chuckled in spite of himself. "With all due respect, Dre, I think maybe your past experiences with the Iranians might be clouding your judgment."

"Fair enough." Dre managed a slight smile. "But I still think they did it."

"It's the Russians, but not the Russians we're used to dealing with," Harrison said. "I still think this is a coup. President Luchnik is being played. As soon as the shit hits the fan, they're gonna pop him in the back of the head and steal the throne."

"A useful theory," Don said. "But who is behind it, and why now?"

"I can't answer that," Harrison said. The CIA and NSA had entire platoons of analysts working on that exact question. They couldn't answer it either.

"There's another thing that's bugged me," Dre said. "The Russians have thousands of cyberweapons deployed across America, but they haven't used a single one. Every attack, even the one on US soil, has been kinetic. Why?"

"Two reasons," Harrison said. "Digital weapons leave digital signatures. Physical weapons go through cut-outs, arms dealers. We have yet to link a single weapon to an actual Russian operative for any of the attacks."

"You said two reasons," Don said.

Harrison frowned. "A cyberattack requires signoff from President Luchnik. If someone is staging a coup, they don't have the authority to use cyberweapons."

Silence settled around the table.

"If this is a coup," Mark said, "then there should be evidence that the attacks were coordinated through a single person or group. We don't have that."

"Maybe we're not looking in the right place," Michael asked. "What if we expand our data set?"

"Explain," Don replied.

Whereas the rest of the room looked ragged from lack of sleep, Michael seemed calm, his gaze thoughtful.

"What if there was something before the incident with Iran in the Strait of Hormuz?"

"Like what?" Dre asked.

"If we go back to the beginning of the year, the first unexpected event was not the USS *Black*. It wasn't even an attack," Michael said. "After eighty years, the dictator of North Korea suddenly decides he wants to be a peaceful nation. That's not normal, right? Before the *Black*, North Korea was all anybody was talking about."

"Everything else we've analyzed was an attack, though," Mark said. "The Naval War College, the Canal, Bosnia, Venezuela. How does North Korea fit that pattern?"

"If you assume the goal was an attack," Michael said, "it doesn't. But what if the goal was simply to destabilize the world order in a way that put maximum pressure on the United States. The outcome of the attack is secondary to the US response."

Don experienced a surge of adrenaline-fueled hope.

"If Michael's right," he said, "how do we prove it?"

"I've done some work on North Korea," Mark said. "If we're saying that the Russians bribed North Korea to start a peace offensive, there's only one person in the country that has the power to do that."

"The Supreme Leader," Dre said.

"Exactly," Mark replied. "And it would be an in-person meeting. There's no way anyone leaves a paper trail on that kind of decision."

"So, we're looking for evidence of a meeting between the Supreme Leader and a Russian operative sometime before mid-March of last year," Mark said, looking at Don. "That's our starting point."

It took three hours and a one a.m. call to the Director of National Intelligence before Don was given access to the files for North Korea. Human assets inside the Hermit Kingdom were highly valuable and took years to develop. Any raw HUMINT was secured and sanitized before it made its way into analyst reports, even highly classified ones.

After describing what he was seeking to the DPRK analyst on duty, Don received a one-page summary of a visit matching his parameters. The details were thin, but they supported Michael's theory.

Two weeks after the Lunar New Year celebration, the Supreme Leader had received a foreign visitor. He was described only as medium height with dark hair, dressed in a Western-style business suit. He spoke very rudimentary Korean.

Don read on. The man met with the Supreme Leader and his sister, but no other advisers, which Don inferred from the report was unusual. The topic of the meeting was listed on the Supreme Leader's calendar as "international trade," but due to the lack of advisers and the short length of the meeting, this topic was likely a euphemism.

It wasn't until the very last line of the report that Don saw a possible connection.

The unknown visitor had arrived by private jet from Vladivostok.

Don's hope was short-lived. An investigation into the private jet yielded a tail number and a flight plan, but no further details about the passenger.

Another dead end.

The effects of the all-nighter were weighing on his body now. Don checked his watch and calculated he could get a two-hour nap before he needed to take a shower and head to the White House.

"I need to get some shut-eye before my meeting," he announced. "I think we've beaten this thing to death. Everyone go home and get some sleep. If we get another data dump from Janet, we'll send out a group text."

His office was still dark as Don made his way to the couch and collapsed. His eyes slid closed, and finally, his mind allowed him some peace from the hounding doubts.

"Don." The voice sounded like an echo, someone shouting down a long tunnel at him.

"Don," the voice insisted. "Wake up. We found something."

It took a long time to open his eyes. Mark Westlund bent over the couch, shaking Don's shoulder.

"I'm going to turn on the light," he said. "Okay?"

Don struggled to sit up, nodding. Bright light stabbed into his brain, and he screwed his eyes shut.

"What is it?" he asked. His tongue had the consistency and taste of a well-used litter box.

Mark's eyes were ablaze with new energy. "You need to see it, boss. You're a genius."

Don heaved his body upright. "Let's go."

His feet had swollen, making the short trip to Mark's office a painful walk. He managed to focus on his watch and saw he'd been asleep for over an hour. It felt like much less, and he actually felt worse than before he'd laid down.

"Morning, sunshine!" Dre called brightly as he reached the door of the bullpen office. She and Michael had the same glow of second-wind energy as Mark.

Oh, to be young again, Don thought.

"We thought we were at a dead end," Mark said, "but then I remembered you asked me to do a 5G analysis of North Korea last year. I went back to the NSA database and put in the exact time frame that our mystery Russian was on the ground in Pyongyang." He grinned at Don.

"We got a match," he said. "Our guy was carrying a 5G phone, and he registered on the network."

"It's a burner," Michael said. "No way to know the ID of the guy carrying it."

"Then we decided to run it through the NSA database for any geolocation matches," Dre continued. "Here's what popped up."

She put an image of a world map on the wall monitor. Red pins highlighted where the phone had been over the past twelve months. Don studied the screen. Asia, India, South America, Europe...The owner had taken the phone all over the world.

"If we restrict the search to dates around major attacks," Mark said, "we get this."

The screen cleared, leaving only clusters of red.

"They match perfectly," Mark said. "This is our guy. We find him, we get the answers we need."

Don was wide awake. "Is the phone still active?"

Dre nodded. "It's in Singapore right now."

50

Singapore

Ian Thomas ended his phone call in front of the picture window in his apartment. The Singapore Flyer, the brightly illuminated five-hundred-foot-high Ferris wheel in the downtown core of the city, rotated slowly against the dark horizon, each capsule like a jewel on a giant bracelet.

He considered his mobile phone, the handset still warm from his call with Isabel.

When she returned to Singapore, he would take her on a tour of the city. They'd ride the Flyer and do a dozen other tourist things, like a normal couple.

He spoke to Isabel almost every day. He called her during his evening, when her day was starting twelve time zones away in New York. It was during those precious few minutes that Ian was able to suspend reality. They talked like a normal couple in a healthy relationship.

Good morning...Good night...How did you sleep, darling?...How was your day, dear?

In these moments after he ended a call with Isabel, as the sensation of her voice in his head faded, shame gripped Ian's body like a flash of fever.

It wouldn't last. It couldn't last. There was no way his future was expansive enough to include both the Minister and Isabel. Yet every evening like clockwork, Ian dialed Isabel's number and deepened the lie.

His phone buzzed with an incoming text. He stared at the characters, his brain decoding the message hidden in the innocuous-looking advertisement.

A new mission from the Minister. Encoded in the message was the location to download the mission brief through a secure connection. He recognized the place as a small coffee shop off Temple Street in Chinatown.

His training kicked in. Ian didn't bother to speculate on what the Minister had in store for him. After the last year, nothing could surprise him. He quickly changed into a dark polo shirt and jeans and scooped up his slim laptop.

In the elevator, Ian decided to walk to the coffee shop. It was about a kilometer away, and the exercise would clear his head.

The Singapore evening was warm; the air close and humid. He hurried along Bridge Street, crossing the Singapore River on Elgin Bridge. The white painted structure glowed yellow in the streetlights. To his right, the lights of the Clarke Quay tourist area nestled at the feet of the downtown skyscrapers. Even late on a weekday evening, music and the laughter of diners carried across the water.

Perspiration beaded on Ian's forehead, but the exercise felt good, his muscles loose and warm.

A few blocks further, the streets narrowed as he entered the Chinatown district. In this older section of the city, three-story colonial buildings lined narrow streets. The upper two stories were apartments with tall arched windows covered by louvered shutters. The street level was a mix of eclectic shops sandwiched together that extended deep into the building.

Narrow, dimly lit alleys, scarcely wide enough for two people to pass side by side, branched off at random intervals between the shops. Ian ducked into one of the alleys and emerged on Temple Street.

This throughfare was quieter and mostly empty this time of night. Parked cars crowded close to the curb, leaving just enough room for a single vehicle to travel down the center of the street.

Ian arrived at his destination and was surprised to find the door locked.

A handwritten notice in Chinese Hanzi characters was taped to the inside of the glass door. Ian had to squint in the dim light.

Closed due to family emergency.

Impossible, Ian thought. The Minister was a man with excruciating attention to detail. There was no way he would have assigned this location for a priority mission download without verifying the status of the establishment first.

New details flooded Ian's senses.

The businesses on either side of the coffee shop were also closed, leaving the area in which he was standing in shadow.

A man walked along the narrow sidewalk in Ian's direction. Despite the heat, a jacket hung across his heavily muscled shoulders. His right hand was thrust into his jacket pocket.

From the other direction, another man emerged from a storefront fifteen meters distant and hurried in Ian's direction.

Hesitation kills. The lesson had been drummed into Ian's psyche from his very first hand-to-hand combat lesson.

Commit and win.

Ian knew the knife was there before he saw the glint of steel in the closest man's right hand. His opponent moved with fluid grace, a confidence born of long practice.

But Ian moved first. He stepped inside the man's reach, blocked the blade with his laptop, and shot his knee into the other man's groin. He felt the point of his knee dig deep into soft flesh.

His opponent had at least ten kilos on Ian and a lower center of gravity. He connected with Ian's midsection, driving him back against the glass door. The door buckled under their combined weight and shattered.

As they fell onto the coffee shop tile floor, Ian felt the razor-sharp edge of a blade run down his rib cage, the man trying to lever the point of the knife into Ian's chest. Ian brought the thin edge of his laptop down on the back of the man's neck. He felt the flesh between the vertebrae give way, and he wrenched the laptop sideways.

His opponent's body went rigid. Ian heaved the dead man off him, leaving his laptop buried in the man's neck. Slick blood ran down his right side.

The second adversary loomed in the doorway and dove at Ian. The new opponent was just as quick and strong as the first man. Ian tried to blunt the new assault with a metal chair from a nearby table, but the man swatted it away. He landed a kick in Ian's injured side, then he pounced. He hammered a fist between Ian's eyes that smashed his head back against the floor and left him stunned.

Then he drew something out of his pocket...A black cloth. A hood.

They were going to kidnap him, Ian realized.

His fingers scrabbled in the wreckage of the glass door. He closed on a piece of glass. Heedless of the sharp edge cutting into his fingers, Ian stabbed at the man's face again and again.

Sightless blows rained down on Ian's chest and face, but he pressed his attack. When his blood-soaked fingers began to lose their grip on the glass, he buried the long shard in the man's cheek and pushed him away.

Ian got to his feet, snatching up the knife as he rose, and staggered to the door.

The street was empty, but the headlights of a van turned the corner and accelerated toward Ian.

The rest of the abduction team.

He could not outrun a car. Ian turned back toward the coffee shop, intending to escape through a rear entrance. The second assailant staggered to his feet, his face a bloody horror show. He tackled Ian, slamming his body back against a car parked next to the curb. A car alarm shrieked in the night.

Ian's feet left the ground. The center of his back impacted the top of the car window frame. A blinding bolt of pain ran up his spine.

But the man, mostly blinded by Ian's prior attack, had smashed his own face into the car window. His knees buckled, and he sagged to the ground.

The lights of the oncoming van flared in Ian's peripheral vision. He was completely exposed, his strength flagging.

Ian gripped the man under the arms and flipped him back against the car just as the van rolled up and the side door opened. The muzzle of a suppressed weapon snapped into focus.

Blam...blam...blam...blam.

The gunshots sounded like muffled rimshots in the empty street.

Ian ducked behind the body, feeling slugs tear into the man's flesh. One round penetrated the torso, spraying him with blood and bits of flesh. The round creased his own trapezius muscle.

When he heard the shooter change magazines, Ian popped his head up and threw the knife. He heard a grunt, and he knew that was his chance.

He charged into the open doorway of the coffee shop.

The first rule of clandestine operations is to always have an exfiltration plan. That mantra had been part of the standard espionage training.

During his personal tutelage with the Minister, Ian had learned a corollary to the first rule.

Trust no one. Your safety is your own responsibility.

Ian's interpretation of the Minister's teaching was to develop his own escape plan, one separate from whatever the State provided for him.

It had taken him six months of careful planning to put the necessary pieces in place. Singapore was a tightly controlled society. One could not just buy a car or a gun on a whim, and he wanted his purchases to remain secret.

Ian used the twisting side streets of Chinatown to his advantage. Once he was convinced he had lost his attackers, he purchased a dark jacket and a baseball hat from a stall on the edge of a night market. The vendor had startled at Ian's bloody appearance, but a fistful of Singapore dollars ensured his silence.

Singapore was also a city with thousands of cameras. He had to assume his attackers had access to the surveillance data.

He stayed to the shadows and took his time as he made his way across the city to a storage site near the docks. Despite the stifling heat in the tiny garage, Ian rolled the steel door down before he switched on the overhead lights.

The garage he had rented was barely large enough to hold the tan Toyota Corolla Altis. The late-model vehicle was the most popular brand in Singapore, and tan was the most common color.

He edged his way to the back of the garage and opened the trunk.

Clothes, cash, first aid kit, weapon, three burner phones, and new identities were sealed in plastic pouches under the carpet. As he stripped off his bloody clothes, his mobile from the Minister clattered to the floor.

His hands shook as he picked the phone off the floor.

The fingers of his free hand teased the missing flesh of his earlobe as his mind put the pieces of the last hour into focus, analyzed the results.

The men who had tried to take him were a trained team. He knew these kinds of men, recognized their training and the way they fought. In another time and place, he had been one of those men.

He swallowed hard, unwilling to believe the truth.

There had been no new assignment. The fact that the coffee shop was closed was not a mistake. The Minister did not make mistakes.

The Minister had sent the team to take him—or to take him out.

I am an instrument of the State...

The oath echoed in his mind. He had served faithfully and to the best of his ability, but his usefulness had reached an end.

The Minister was tying up loose ends. Ian Thomas was the biggest loose end of all.

His hands were steady as he removed the battery and the SIM card and destroyed the phone. He put the pieces into a paper bag with his bloody clothes.

Working quickly now, he used a surgical stapler to close the wound in his side and apply a bandage. The bullet crease wound across his trapezius got the same treatment, as did the cuts on his hand from the glass shard.

He popped four Advil and drank a full bottle of warm water from the stash in his trunk.

Ian dressed slowly, careful not to get any blood on his fresh clothes. He opened the garage, pulled the car out, and then shut and padlocked the overhead door again before he slid behind the wheel. Ian left the car headlights off. Icy air conditioning played across his sweaty skin.

There was one more task left to do before Ian Thomas disappeared.

He powered up a burner phone and dialed a number from memory. It rang once, twice, three times.

"Isabel Montez." Her voice was firm and professional, but it caused an avalanche of emotion in Ian's chest.

He screwed his eyes shut and took a deep breath.

"Isabel," he said. "It's me. I need you to listen to me carefully. Your life is in danger."

When the conversation was over, he powered the phone down, removed the battery and SIM card, and broke the device in half. He tossed the wreckage into a storm drain and drove into the night.

51

White House Situation Room
Washington, DC

"That's what I'm talking about, dammit." The Chairman of the Joint Chiefs hammered his fist on the mahogany table of the White House Situation Room.

General Nikolaides, realizing he had said the quiet part out loud, straightened in his chair and turned to the president of the United States. His face reddened, the color reaching all the way into his iron-gray crew cut.

"My apologies, sir," he said, "but it's about damn time we caught a break in this mess. Having access to our cyber arsenal again relieves a huge amount of pressure from the rest of the operation."

Don Riley watched the interaction play out from his place at the briefing podium in the front of the room. President Serrano had streaks of silver in his mane of dark hair that hadn't been there before, and his face had taken on a hollowed-out quality.

But he still had the same penetrating "Serrano stare." If anything, the impact of his gaze was heightened by the new sharpness to his facial features.

The chairs along the wall of the room were empty. Attendance at this highly classified briefing was intentionally sparse—only the president's immediate advisers, no staff—and tension hummed in the atmosphere. Everyone knew the stakes of the next twenty-four hours and felt the weight of their responsibilities coloring their every thought.

"I understand your enthusiasm, General," Serrano said with a bemused smile. "I share your elation, but I find it is tempered by the seriousness of the topic."

Serrano turned his gaze on Don. "Could you repeat the last part, Mr. Riley?"

Don turned back to the flat-screen that displayed a map of the Russian Federation. It was littered with red dots, each one indicating an active cyber payload that had been verified by Janet's work on Operation Lockpick.

"Approximately ninety percent of the cyberweapons inside the Russian Federation have reported back as active," Don said.

"What about the other ten percent?" National Security Advisor Valentina Flores asked. "Does that mean the Russians found them?"

Don shook his head. "Not necessarily. All it means is that they haven't reported in yet. I can say with confidence that we have more than enough assets in place to support Operation Red Sunset."

General Nikolaides nodded in satisfaction.

Don, on the other hand, felt a twinge of queasiness. Cyber had been much of his career at the CIA and at US Cyber Command. Many of the exploits in each red dot on the map contained code that he had personally developed or approved, which meant he knew their destructive potential.

Every red dot represented an attack on a critical node of infrastructure. It might be as simple as disabling the traffic lights outside a major military installation or locking a drawbridge that spanned a major river in the open position. It could also be as destructive as shutting down a power grid in the middle of winter or opening the sluice gates on a major dam to cause downstream flooding.

The coordinated cyberattack planned for Red Sunset was designed to cripple the Russian Federation and create chaos across the country. Meanwhile, NATO forces would penetrate the northwest corner of the country and take over the Russian Northern Fleet. In the words of the chairman, NATO was about to "do a little Crimea action on their Russian asses."

"How do we activate these weapons, Mr. Riley?" the president asked. "And control them?"

"The only reliable access we have through the Russian internet blockade is using the undersea cable tap executed by the USS *Idaho* in the Sea of Okhotsk," Don replied. "The *Manta*, that's the submersible, needs to travel to the surveillance site and physically plug into the network. The attack needs to be manually initiated by the operator on board the *Manta*."

"How long does that take?" Secretary of Defense Howard asked.

"Depending on currents, it's up to ninety minutes travel time once the *Manta* undocks from the *Idaho* and moves into shallow water to access the surveillance site, ma'am," Don said. "During that time, she's out of communication with the *Idaho*."

"And out of communication with us?" Howard pressed.

"Yes, ma'am," Don said. "That's correct."

"If I understand your point, Mr. Riley," the president said, "we need to give a go signal to the *Idaho* at least two hours before the operation starts, and we can't rescind the order. Is that what you're saying?"

Don nodded.

"Can we control the cyberweapons once they're released?" the Secretary of State asked. Hahn's voice was slow and purposeful, his question laden with meaning for Don.

"Not really, Mr. Secretary," Don replied. "The sheer number of attacks that need to happen in tandem means they need to be coordinated by a computer program. We can interrupt the program, of course, but that's only part of the picture.

"The types of weapons we're talking about have never been deployed before. How they will react in the real world, where they will spread, what other systems they will attack—these are all unknown factors. In this case, the Russian internet blockade works in our favor. We can't get in, but these weapons can't get out either. That should limit the collateral damage."

"What happens when the Russians drop the blockade?" Hahn pressed. "Will these viruses infect computer systems of our allies, maybe even our own systems?"

"Absolutely," Don said. "There are many case studies going back to Stuxnet in 2009 of our own cyber exploits causing damage to our own commercial infrastructure."

The room was silent.

"Thank you, Mr. Riley," the president said. "Are there any other considerations we need to be aware of?"

Don clocked a glance at CIA Director Blank and then to the Director of National Intelligence. He was about to go off script in a big way.

"There is one other aspect of the analysis that needs to be emphasized," he said. "The message traffic we've uncovered shows the Russian Federation is in a state of internal chaos, sir."

Director Blank cut in. "Sir, this is highly speculative and not really pertinent to the operational planning effort that we're focused on today."

Serrano turned his gaze on Don, giving him an unexpected surge of confidence.

"Considering how Riley's team managed to get us access back inside the Russian system, I think that makes his analysis worth listening to," Serrano said. "Tell us your take on what's going on inside the Russian Federation, Don."

"I think it's fair to say we do not fully understand the internal situation of our adversary, Mr. President."

"What are you getting at, Riley?" Flores asked, her eyes narrowed to slits.

Don took a deep breath. "The external posture of the Russian Federation and their internal actions don't add up. For example, submarine commanders have been ordered to unload all their torpedo tubes while at sea. Although the Russians have moved units along the border with NATO, they are not distributing ammunition in anywhere near the quantities necessary for an imminent attack. The Air Force general in command of the air base that launched the UAV we shot down was relieved of command and is in prison. These actions are not consistent with a nation on the verge of war."

"We know all that," the chairman said. "They're being careful. They don't want to start anything they can't finish."

"With all due respect, General," Don said, "I think it's more than just caution."

"You have a theory, Don," the president said.

"I do, sir." Don ignored the glares from Director Blank. "An alternative explanation for this behavior could be an internal struggle for political power."

"You mean a coup," Flores said.

"Yes, ma'am," Don said. "Someone is trying to start a war so they can overthrow President Luchnik."

A silence settled on the room as the president's cabinet absorbed this new twist.

"You have evidence for this theory, Mr. Riley?" Flores asked.

"No," interrupted the CIA director, "he doesn't. It's all circumstantial nonsense."

"Sam," the president said. "I don't see Mr. Riley as a loose cannon. Let's hear his case."

All eyes turned to Don. His mouth felt pasty and his underarms hot. What the hell was he doing?

"Director Blank is correct in that this theory sprang from the anecdotal reports we received from Lockpick," he began, "but they are compelling. Personal emails, phone calls, and the like. These are high-ranking people who do not have a clue about what's going on.

"But the most convincing aspect of what has transpired over the last year is what has *not* happened. All of the attacks have been kinetic. If anything, Russia has pulled back on their cyber intrusions against the US. This is one of the most advanced cyber operations on the planet, sir, and we haven't heard a peep from them."

"Why does that matter?" the chairman said. "The bastards bombed the goddamned Naval War College, for Christ's sake!"

"Because deployment of cyberweapons requires President Luchnik's signoff," Secretary of State Hahn said. "In Riley's theory, the coup plotters don't have access to those weapons. It's a neat theory, Riley, but can you prove it?"

"I think I can, sir," Don replied. He showed a graphic linking all the attacks to a single mobile phone.

"Based on the odd Russian behavior, we went back and looked at each unattributed attack over the last year. One of my analysts had the idea to include the sudden change in attitude by the North Koreans as part of the mix. That netted us a phone number that is linked to all of these attacks. It is our belief that one Russian operative was in charge of the entire operation."

"Do we know who this mysterious Russian operative is?" Flores asked, her tone dripping with sarcasm.

"The last location of the phone was Singapore, but the number's dropped off the grid." Don watched the room as they digested this new bit of information.

"This operative," Don said. "If we find him, we know who's behind the coup."

The president pinched his lip as he thought. "How long do you need to find him?"

"It's not an exact science, sir, but a few days might make all the difference between having a complete picture to the internal Russian situation and going in blind."

"Mr. President," the chairman said. "I've been dealing with Luchnik's bullshit for almost thirty years. If he's gone, I don't see that as a downside."

Secretary of State Hahn cleared his throat. "President Luchnik is an evil man, a devil. But he's also the devil we know. I don't need to remind anyone in this room what happened after the Soviet Union collapsed in 1991. Political uncertainty, economic chaos, loose nuclear weapons. Add unrestricted cyberweapons to that mix, and we may find ourselves wishing Luchnik was back in charge."

"Be that as it may, sir," General Nikolaides said. "We cannot afford to delay this attack. Mr. Riley's briefing tells us that the Russians are in disarray. We have them right where we want them. If we wait, we could be giving up the element of surprise."

National Security Advisor Flores weighed in. "I agree with the chairman, Mr. President."

The president's gaze rifled over to the Secretary of Defense.

"I'm afraid that given the intelligence we have to date, sir," Howard said, "it would be foolish for us to delay the operation."

"I find this rush to war most troubling, sir," Hahn said without being prompted by the president. "If we do not understand the internal situation in Russia, we could destabilize the entire globe. We could be looking at World War Three."

Don studied Serrano as his eyes moved from advisor to advisor. The president fixed his gaze on each speaker as if assessing the person as much as their input.

The pressure on Serrano to make the right call was beyond enormous. His intervention in Venezuela, no matter how well intentioned, had been a disaster. No matter how many Venezuelan lives he had saved—and there were many—the price in the lives of American soldiers had cost him personally and politically. Even worse, his decision further overextended the US military when the US could least afford it.

In short, President Rick Serrano had taken a bad situation and made it much, much worse. But if history judged Serrano harshly for the Venezuelan decision, it would pale in comparison to how he would be judged on the call to invade Russia.

The stakes were astronomically higher. Tens of thousands of lives were on the line. Maybe hundreds of thousands. If Operation Red Sunset failed because President Serrano hesitated, the consequences could be catastrophic.

When Serrano leaned back in his chair, Chief of Staff Wilkerson moved forward and whispered in his boss's ear. The president closed his leather portfolio and rested his folded hands on top.

"The timetable for Red Sunset is unchanged. Move the remaining assets into place, Mr. Chairman, and stand by for final authorization. I'll be addressing the nation tonight at nine o'clock."

52

USS *Enterprise* (CVN-80)
North Pacific Ocean, 300 miles east of Petropavlovsk, Russia

Wrapped in cold-weather gear, Rear Admiral Chip Sharratt rested his elbows on the steel railing of Vultures' Row and looked down on the beehive of activity that was the flight deck of the USS *Enterprise*.

The weather was uncharacteristically beautiful for the North Pacific. The normally heavy swells had shrunk to only a meter or so in height, almost glassy for this part of the ocean, and the air temperature hung at a balmy forty degrees Fahrenheit. The skies were clear, and the few clouds gathering on the western horizon turned a gorgeous scarlet color.

Red skies in morning, sailors take warning.

Red sky at night, sailors delight.

Sharratt hoped the old saying spoke true. In twelve hours, the entire air complement of his strike force was headed into battle. They needed the weather to cooperate. Flight ops in the North Pacific were a dicey proposition on a normal day, but trying to launch upwards of seventy-five aircraft in the space of an hour was nothing short of logistical sorcery. If the weather was on their side—for once—that would be one less headache to deal with.

On the flight deck, crews were hard at work outfitting the F-35s with their ordnance loadout for the upcoming alpha strike. Air-to-air missiles and GPS-guided munitions were affixed to hard points in the internal bomb bay area and on the wings. Each plane had a custom ordnance load-out designated for specific targets, and all maintained air-to-air engagement capability in case any Russian fighters decided to get in their path.

Sharratt sucked in a lungful of fresh sea air. His mood was surprisingly light, almost jovial.

Execute, execute, execute—that was the name of the game now.

A quarter century of Navy life had schooled Sharratt to focus on the things he could control—solid plans, trained personnel, effective logistics —and leave the rest of the baggage on the pier.

Besides, he laughed to himself, no plan ever survived first contact with the enemy. He'd have more than enough to worry about by the time the first plane shot off the cat tomorrow morning.

The carrier strike force steamed into the light southwest wind. A thousand yards off the starboard quarter, the USS *Antietam*, a guided missile cruiser, cut through the light seas. From this height above the water, Sharratt was able to pick out the superstructure of one of their *Arleigh Burke*-class destroyer pickets against the backdrop of the deep red sunset.

Close to the horizon, Sharratt spied a thin vertical puff of spray and smoke. He squinted. A waterspout, maybe?

Another appeared, and another. A spark of light flared, like someone had lit a match in a dark room.

Sharratt realized what he was seeing just as the intercom over his head blared to life.

"Vampire, vampire, vampire, bearing two-six-zero!"

The heavy pulse of the general quarters alarm rang in his ears as teams on the flight deck raced to secure the live ordnance. Sharratt charged into Battle Watch, not stopping until he reached the railing of the BattleSpace display.

"Multiple incoming missiles, Admiral," the watch officer shouted. "Four bogeys—make that six bogeys! Probable classification Russian SS-N-19 Shipwreck missiles."

Shipwreck missiles, Sharratt realized, were launched from a submarine. They were under attack from an enemy sub.

"All stations, Alpha Whiskey," came the report over the intercom, "taking incoming vampires with missiles."

The BattleSpace display filled with data as the escorts launched interceptor missiles.

A new contact popped into the BattleSpace data stream, a subsurface hostile.

"There he is," Sharratt said.

"All stations, Alpha Xray," said the ASW commander for the strike force. "New subsurface contact. Mystic two-four, you are weapons free."

Every second stretched into minutes as information flowed into Battle Watch from all over the strike force.

The pilot of the anti-submarine helo reported in: "Alpha Xray, Mystic two-four, dropping torpedoes now, now, now."

The Battle Watch Officer, monitoring the incoming airborne threats, called off downed missiles in an excited voice.

"Splash four!...Five—"

A new report stopped all traffic on the net: "Torpedo in the water! Active homing!"

The deck of the mighty *Enterprise* rumbled as the big ship began evasive maneuvers. He heard the anti-submarine coordinator order the launch of multiple ASROC anti-submarine rockets.

From far away, Sharratt heard a sound like a door slamming.

"*Antietam*'s been hit, Admiral."

Battle Watch descended into shocked silence.

"Alpha Bravo, Alpha Sierra, request permission to launch on the Russian SAG."

"Tell him to stand by, Tom," Sharratt said to his chief of staff. He turned to the watch officer. "What's the Russian surface action group doing?"

"No change in status, sir," the watch officer replied. "We're only seeing navigation radars, and their helos are on the deck. No change in course and speed, either."

Sharratt studied the display, adding up the data points in his head.

"And the Russian CAP?"

"Nothing, sir," the watch officer said. "Same number of aircraft up. No change in posture. It's like they don't know what's happening, sir."

And yet the Russians send in a single submarine to launch a suicide mission against three heavily protected carriers?

"What are you thinking, sir?" Chief of Staff Zachary asked.

Sharratt checked his watch. Although it felt like an hour had passed since he'd seen the gorgeous sunset, only eight minutes had elapsed.

By now, the CRITIC flash-precedent message that had been automatically sent as soon as the strike force was attacked would be on the president's desk. The national security apparatus in Washington, DC, would be launching into action...

But out here, in the middle of the North Pacific, what happened in the next few minutes depended on him.

His assessment of the facts, *his* judgment. *His* orders.

"What's the status of the *Antietam*, Tom?"

"Torpedo detonated on her starboard bow, Admiral. Her bow is a mess, but by some miracle there were no secondary explosions. VLS is offline, but she has power, and they've isolated the flooding. She'll make it, sir."

"Casualties?"

"Yes, but no accurate numbers yet," Zachary replied. "It could have been a lot worse."

"Admiral," the watch officer said. "The Russian SAG has increased speed and changed course. They're headed back to port, sir."

"Very well," Sharratt mumbled.

Zachary stepped beside him at the BattleSpace display. "This doesn't smell right, sir."

Sharratt's mind raced. Why would the Russians pick a fight, then run away?

A rogue submarine captain had finally reached his limit? Was it possible the Russian Navy was in such disarray that individual commanders were taking matters into their own hands?

"It most definitely does not smell right, Tom." Sharratt reached for the handset.

"Alpha Sierra, Alpha Bravo actual, strike request denied. Restore EMCON Condition Alpha. Bravo, out."

Sharratt hung up the handset, aware that all eyes in Battle Watch were on him.

"Listen up, people," he said. "The United States Navy will respond in a manner and time of our own choosing. And that time will be in"—he made a show of checking his watch—"ten hours from now. Let's make that strike count!"

Sharratt turned to the watch officer.

"Get me an uplink to Seventh Fleet," he said.

No battle plan ever survived first contact with the enemy, Sharratt mused. But it would be nice if he knew who he was fighting before the bullets started flying.

53

RFS *Kuzbass* (K-419)
North Pacific Ocean, 21 kilometers south of *Enterprise* strike force

"Captain to Control!"

The shipwide announcement caught Captain Anatoly Renkov in the wardroom, a spoonful of borscht midway between his lips and the bowl. Crewmembers flattened their bodies against the walls of the narrow central passageway to make way for their captain. Renkov took the hallway at a run and threw his body up the steep stairwell to the upper deck of the submarine.

The watch officer, standing next to the broadband sonar display, began his report as soon as Renkov entered the control room.

"Launch transients, bearing three-zero-zero, Captain," he said. "It's another submarine."

He pointed at the monitor. The green gray "waterfall display" represented the sounds of the ocean around the *Kuzbass* using color intensity similar to a thermal image. Louder sounds showed up as bright yellow, weaker background sounds faded to dark green.

When the display updated, the most recent information appeared at the top of the screen. Continuous loud noises, like the screw of an American aircraft carrier churning through the water, showed up as a bright vertical line on the display. The Russian submarine was close enough to the carrier strike force that individual ships showed up as a series of vertical lines.

The watch officer indicated a series of bright blips of color between two bright lines. Renkov counted six.

"Submarine-launched missiles, sir," he said. "Someone is attacking the Americans."

Renkov took two steps to the fire control plot where his team was maintaining a constant firing solution on every American ship. His mind translated the abstract details of the sonar display to the geographical picture of the carrier strike force.

Another submarine had crept inside of the American destroyers that were acting as outer pickets and launched an attack.

But the *Kuzbass* was supposed to be the only Russian submarine in the area...What was happening?

"Conning Officer, make your depth five-zero meters," Renkov said. He stood next to the periscope barrel as the deck beneath his feet angled upward.

"Sonar, report all contacts," Renkov said.

As the sonar operator reeled off the contact designations and bearings, the captain updated his mental picture of the situation on the surface. He didn't actually need the refresher, but it gave him time to think. The electromagnetic spectrum would be alive with American radars capable of detecting a periscope, but he needed to gather more intel before he made a decision about his next moves.

"Depth is five-zero meters, Captain," the watch officer reported. "Course is three-zero-zero," he added, as if to remind his commanding officer that they were still driving directly at the American force that had just been attacked by an unknown assailant.

"Reduce speed to six knots," Renkov said. "Raising the scope."

Renkov energized the hydraulics to raise the periscope. He squatted next to the periscope well as the silver shaft pushed upward into the ocean above them. When the periscope controls appeared, he flipped down the handles and pressed his eye against the optics. He began a slow rotation of the scope.

"Take the ship to periscope depth."

As the submarine angled upward, the picture in the periscope optics changed from black shadows to a watery red. Seconds later the scope broke the surface of the ocean. To the west, Renkov saw a fiery sunset. He swung the optics to the north. The scene was anything but peaceful.

From the overhead, the intercom broadcast the warbles and chirps of search radars, reminding the captain that every second the periscope was above the waves, he was exposing his ship to detection by the enemy.

He switched to high magnification and swore under his breath.

Ghostly trails of smoke looped across the horizon from the attacking submarine and the interceptor missiles from the American strike force. He counted six American helicopters, some hovering, some moving across the horizon.

"Multiple periscope detection radars, Captain!" the ESM operator said. "Sir, I'm detecting a P-700 missile in active homing. Captain, the missile is one of ours."

Over the horizon, Renkov saw a brilliant flash and puff of smoke.

"The signal is gone, sir," the operator reported.

"Lowering scope," the captain said. He folded the handles flat against the periscope barrel and engaged the hydraulics. The sound of the search radars stopped.

Renkov went back to the fire control tracking plot. The American strike force was arrayed in concentric rings. The valuable carriers were in the center, closely surrounded by guided missile cruisers. The smaller destroyers and frigates made up the outer ring, which ranged from five to twenty miles in diameter.

The watch officer had drawn a red X on the chart to approximate the location where the mystery submarine had launched its attack. It was old information, of course. The attacking submarine had surely gone deep and cleared the area immediately after launching its missiles. The American ASW helicopters would scour the area for their attacker. To remain would be suicide.

"Bring me the latest message traffic of ship movements," Renkov said.

He reviewed the document. There were no other Russian submarines assigned to this area. The *Kuzbass* was supposed to be alone.

A secret mission? he thought. They had detected the radar signature of a Russian anti-ship missile. Why would Moscow send a second submarine and not tell him?

"Launch transients, Captain!" the sonar supervisor called out. "Multiple torpedoes launched on bearing two-nine-three! They're firing on the Americans."

Renkov studied the sonar display. What was this submarine captain playing at? A second attack when the Americans were on full alert was a death wish.

"We've been at periscope depth for four minutes, Captain," the conning officer reminded him.

They were vulnerable this close to the surface, Renkov knew, even with the periscope lowered. If an American helo ventured too close, they might detect the submarine's steel hull.

"Torpedo impact, Captain!" the sonar supervisor reported.

"Radioman to Control," Renkov called.

The captain dictated a short message to the senior enlisted man, who disappeared back into the secure radio room. One minute later, he reported over the intercom.

"Captain, radio. Message ready to transmit."

"Very well," Renkov replied. "Raising periscope."

He folded down the handles and put his eye to the optics. The whine of enemy search radars blared out of the intercom over his head.

"Multiple search radars, Captain!" the ESM operator reported.

On the horizon, thick black smoke billowed into the clear sky. It was difficult to tell for sure, but it appeared one of the carrier escorts had been hit and not one of the carriers.

The Americans launched another brace of missiles, smoke trails lancing into the sky. He watched them arc downward toward the water.

Submarine killers, he thought. That submarine captain was either very brave or very, very stupid. Either way, he was dead.

"We have satellite acquisition, Captain," the radioman reported. "Ready to transmit."

"Transmit. Tell me the second you have an acknowledgment."

Amid the barrage of enemy electromagnetic noise, Renkov heard a blip of static as the burst transmission launched off to a satellite.

"Multiple periscope detection radars, Captain! Signal strength is increasing!" The ESM operator's voice skipped a full octave.

"Radio, did you receive a satellite acknowledgment?" Renkov demanded.

"No, sir."

"Transmit again. Now!"

The transmission blanked out the buzzing of the enemy radars for a split second.

"Captain," the conning officer said. "I recommend we—"

"Satellite acknowledgment received, sir," the radioman reported.

"Down scope!" Renkov slapped up the periscope handles and engaged the hydraulics. As the barrel sank down into the periscope well, the sound of enemy radars cut off.

"Conning Officer, make your depth two hundred meters," Renkov said. The deck sloped down, toward the safety of deep water. "Increase speed to twelve knots. Come left to new course one-eight-zero." The submarine banked slightly as it made the long, slow turn.

Renkov stood behind the sonar supervisor, studying the broadband display over the man's shoulder. The white traces of the American ships angled across the screen as the submarine changed course. The noncommissioned officer shifted the headphones off his ears.

"Anything, *michman*?" Renkov asked.

"The helos are up there, but none are hovering." A hovering helicopter meant the aircraft was lowering its dipping sonar, a sure sign that they suspected a submarine was close by. "Yet," the sonar supervisor added.

Attacking a submerged contact that had just fired weapons at you was an easy decision. Renkov was banking on the fact that the Americans did not know the exact locations of their own submarines, so they wouldn't launch weapons on an unidentified submerged contact. Like the *Kuzbass*.

"I don't plan on staying to see what the Americans do next," Renkov said. He clapped the man on the shoulder. "Good work today."

The sonarman beamed. "Thank you, Captain."

"Steady new course one-eight-zero, Captain," the watch officer reported.

"Increase speed to twenty knots," Renkov replied. "Stay on this course for two hours, then clear baffles and take the ship to periscope depth to receive our message traffic."

He waited for the order acknowledgment, then stalked out of the control room to his stateroom. Once inside, he closed the door and sank into his desk chair. Renkov breathed deeply, clenching his fists to stop his hands from shaking.

He caught a glimpse of his reflection in the mirror over the tiny sink. Pale and wild-eyed, he needed a haircut, and his ragged beard did little to cover his hollowed-out cheeks. He looked more like an inmate at a mental asylum than a commander of one of his country's premier fast-attack submarines.

On impulse, he dug into his shaving kit for a razor. He would wash and shave and put on a fresh uniform—anything to consume the next two hours. Still, even as he busied himself with the task at hand, his thoughts raced ahead.

When the *Kuzbass* next raised her periscope above the waves, what kind of world would she find?

54

Sea of Okhotsk

The *Manta* submersible drifted in the underwater current. The sea bottom looked gray-brown in the glare of the work lights. Janet watched bits of sediment spark as they flitted through the sphere of illumination the lights carved into the dark waters.

Tony, his eyes on the locator beacon signal, made a slight course adjustment.

"And that should do it," he muttered.

The pill-shaped undersea cable-tap station appeared in view. Tony worked the propulsor controls to slow their progress and cut power. The mini-sub settled to the bottom of the sea with a gentle thud.

"Perfect landing," he said. He checked the mission clock. "And a new submerged speed record of forty-nine minutes, fourteen seconds. Thank you very much."

Trips between the *Idaho* and the undersea cable tap had become close to routine for Tony and Janet. This was the fourth trip over the last three days—and hopefully their last. In addition to the mental strain of operating a US submarine inside heavily patrolled Russian waters, Janet was physically exhausted. She and Tony returned to the *Idaho* long enough to recharge the batteries on the *Manta* and get some sleep and sustenance before they set off again.

Janet forced a smile. "Congratulations, Speed Racer."

"You guys always like this?" On each trip to the surveillance site, they brought with them a single passenger. Today their passenger was Timothy Singh, a Russian language specialist, who would monitor real-time unencrypted communications. Tim looked to be in his late twenties and had the physique of a bodybuilder. He looked uncomfortable wedged into the seat between the computer racks that filled the back of the *Manta*.

"We like to keep it light," Janet replied without looking around. "No sense worrying about things we can't control."

Janet watched Tony use the manipulator arm to connect the *Manta* to the cable tap. He ran a purge and vacuum cycle to evacuate moisture from the connection, then initiated a conductivity check.

Janet pulled up the controls for the *Orca* on her own console. She had programmed the unmanned attack sub to run a surveillance perimeter around the *Manta* when they were on station. If the UUV made a detection, it was programmed to return to laser comms range with the *Manta* and seek further orders.

"I'll have it check in every forty-five minutes," Janet said.

"I think you just like having a robot you can order around," Tony said.

Janet grinned at him. She knew he was trying to take her mind off the grim task at hand, and she appreciated the effort.

"Well," she said, "*Orca* certainly listens better than you do. I could get used to that."

She got out of the copilot's chair and climbed into the back.

"I'm going to need that seat for a few minutes, Tim," she said. "World War Three's not gonna start itself. I need to program it first."

Tim moved his bulky frame out of the chair and sat on the deck with his back against the bulkhead.

Janet powered up the computers and established a connection with the cable tap.

"The tap has eight channels," she said to Tim. "We have the ability to store about eighteen to twenty hours of data locally, depending on the volume of traffic." She started the download and handed him a pair of headphones and a tablet.

"I'll send you a live feed. The computer will automatically sort encrypted and unencrypted data. Anything that's unencrypted will show up in a queue on your screen for you to review." Janet gave him a wry smile. "I'm guessing after what happened with the *Enterprise* strike force last night, the phone lines between Moscow and Petropavlovsk will be burning up."

Tim shifted on the cold metal deck. His musclebound thighs did not allow him to sit cross-legged, and there was not enough room to stretch his legs out straight. He eyed Janet's chair.

"What are you going to do?" he asked.

"Mayhem," Janet replied.

The program she called up was known as TRON, an acronym for Tailored Remote Ordnance Navigator. To call the initiation of a cyberattack using thousands of payloads buried deep inside the infrastructure across a country as vast as the Russian Federation a complex problem was the understatement of the century. If certain malware was initiated before others, they might close down avenues of attack. By the same token, if a first wave was more effective than expected, other payloads might be reserved for future attacks.

The answer to the problem was TRON, a real-time virtual cyberwarfare commander. Normally, a program as sophisticated as TRON would be controlled from Cyber Command at Fort Meade, but with the advent of the Russian internet blockade, they had developed a field-deployable version.

In other words, a cyberweapon was going to initiate a cyberattack from inside the Russian Federation. The robots were controlling the robots. The first wave of US-initiated cyberattacks would disable the Russian internet blockade, enabling TRON to phone home to Cyber Command for further instructions.

At least that was the plan. Janet wasn't sure how much testing they had been able to perform before shipping the field version of TRON to her.

The TRON screen prompted: *Begin asset mapping?*

Janet typed YES and sat back in her chair.

As TRON polled each potential point of access for status and received a response, data spooled down the screen. Janet clicked on the tab labeled Strategic Assessment.

Mesmerized, she watched as a map of the Russian Federation filled with red dots of varying sizes. She hovered her cursor over a large dot in the vicinity of Moscow, and a pop-up field flashed on the screen:

MOESK, electric transmission and distribution
    Physical impact: high
    Political impact: high
    Civilian collateral impact: medium

Janet sampled red dots across the map. TRON had access to banks, railroads, tollbooths, dams, water treatment plants, the list went on and on.

"Welcome to Armageddon," she muttered to herself.

While the *Idaho* was deep in Russian waters, every satellite communication with Washington, DC, risked discovery. Along with the download of the TRON program, Janet had received a short email from Don Riley describing the analysis of the surveillance she had sent back to ETG. Even in those few sentences, she could tell he was troubled by what they had uncovered.

When it came to intelligence matters, Don was the smartest man she knew. If he was concerned, she was concerned.

And yet they really had no choice. The Russian submarine attack on the *Enterprise* strike force just a few hours ago had sealed the deal. The United States was going to war, and she was about to fire the first shot.

TRON beeped at her. The program had accumulated enough responses from embedded cyberweapons to formulate a plan of attack. As more data came in, TRON would adapt the plan to achieve the desired blend of infrastructure damage and political chaos inside the Russian Federation.

Tony climbed over Tim and squatted next to her. "How's it going, Einstein?"

"It's alive," she replied.

Janet experienced an odd mix of elation and horror at what she was about to do. On the one hand, she wanted to pinch herself to prove the adventure was real. The technical achievement of tapping a fiber optic cable on the bottom of a Russian inland sea was the kind of stuff she had read about in declassified mission briefs. Now, with the push of a virtual button, she had the power to take down an entire nation.

But at the back of her mind, she could not ignore the cataclysmic consequences of those actions. Hospitals without power, homes without heat or running water, open dams flooding broad swaths of populated land...Her mind flashed to American disasters like Hurricane Katrina or the Texas blackout in 2021. Those had lasted only a few days, and the rest of the country had been able to lend immediate assistance.

Multiply that sort of damage by a factor of a hundred...a thousand.

"Remember Panama and the Naval War College," Tony said. "They started this fight. It's up to us to finish it."

"I know that," Janet said. "I also know what this program is designed to do. One push of a button and a lot of people are going to have a really bad day. It just seems too easy."

"That's why I became a Navy SEAL," Tony said. "I prefer the personal touch."

"You're not wrong." Janet considered how much the military had changed just within her short career. Cyberweapons and unmanned platforms were making warfare safer for the combatants, but was it making the world a safer place?

She believed in what she was doing. She believed in her country and took her oath seriously. But somehow, pressing a button on a computer, knowing that it might kill thousands of people, seemed too easy.

Tony checked the mission clock. "In another two hours and forty-seven minutes, it's out of our hands. We drop your cyber bomb, bust ass back to the *Idaho*, and get the hell out of Dodge. Who knows? Maybe I can break my own speed record on the trip back."

"Roger that," Janet said. For all her misgivings, her mission was crystal clear.

Once she uploaded TRON to the Russian network and initiated the attack, her job as a cyber expert was done. After that point, Janet was a submarine officer again and the *Idaho* had a new mission.

The Russian Federation had long used the Sea of Okhotsk to hide a portion of their ballistic missile submarine fleet. What the Russians did not yet realize was that they had a hunter loose in their protected waters. The Russians would never know what hit them.

"Guys?" Tim asked. He stared at his tablet, his face screwed into a frown. He slipped one headphone off an ear. "I just heard something that you might want to listen to."

Without asking, he unplugged the headphones and put the conversation on speaker. The sound of Russian voices filled the cabin of the *Manta*.

Tony nodded in mock seriousness. "I can see what you mean, Tim. I had no idea the caviar harvest was down this year. Very interesting."

Tim ignored the humor. Janet noted his fair skin had taken on an ashen cast.

"I want you to hear the voices while I translate," he said. He restarted the conversation at the beginning.

An older male voice began, angry, shouting.

"I gave you one task, and you failed me. What the fuck is going on out there?" Tim translated. He stopped the recording.

"Do you recognize the voice?" he asked.

Janet and Tony looked at each other.

"It's the Russian president!" Tim said. "That's Vitaly Luchnik."

Tim restarted the recording. A younger voice, also male, responded in equally heated terms.

"Sir, we did not fire on the Americans," Tim translated. "I have spoken directly with the submarine commander we had on station. He swears it was not us."

"Who's the other guy?" Tony interrupted. "The admiral?"

Tim ignored him as he translated Luchnik's response: "What about the rest of the submarines? Have you accounted for all of them?"

The younger voice hesitated.

"We have two submarines who have not yet checked in, Mr. President. Based on their last position reports, it's highly unlikely they could be responsible—"

"But not certain?" Luchnik interrupted.

A long pause. "No, sir, not certain, but—"

"But nothing!" Luchnik shouted. "Tell me the truth. Are you part of the conspiracy against me? There is still time to stop this if you tell me the truth."

A shocked silence. Then the younger man continued in a quiet, firm voice.

"Uncle, I swear to you. I had nothing to do with this attack. It was not a Russian submarine that attacked the Americans. I would stake my life on it."

Tim stopped the recording.

"The second voice belongs to Admiral Nikolay Sokolov," he said. "Not only is he the commander of the Russian Pacific Fleet, but he is the son of Luchnik's late sister. Luchnik raised him as his own."

"Play it again, Tim," Janet said. She closed her eyes, concentrating on the intensity of feeling behind the voices as Tim translated the words.

"Again," she said when he had finished.

After the third time, she quizzed him about possible alternate meanings to key words.

Satisfied, Janet turned her attention on Tony.

"I know that look," he said.

"Don Riley needs to hear this," she said. "It could make all the difference."

Tony shook his head. "We have a little more than two and a half hours left. My superior driving skills notwithstanding, that's not enough time for us to get back to the *Idaho*, send a message, wait for a response, and then get back here."

"You're right," Janet said.

Her copilot's console pinged, indicating the *Orca* was back in comms with the *Manta*.

"We're not going anywhere," Janet said. "*Orca* is going to send the message for us."

55

White House Situation Room
Washington, DC

Don Riley's fingers tightened on the edge of the lectern as the members of the National Security Council listened to the recording for the third time. Don didn't speak Russian, but he had listened to this recording so many times he could have repeated it verbatim.

The wall screen next to his podium showed the translated words of the conversation between President Luchnik and Admiral Sokolov.

"This is definitely Luchnik?" President Serrano asked. "No question about it?"

"Voiceprint analysis confirms the identity," Don said. "The older man is Luchnik, sir."

"I've met President Luchnik dozens of times," Secretary of State Hahn said. "That voice is his, and the emotion is genuine, in my opinion."

"And the other man?" the president pressed. "Can we definitely confirm that's Admiral Sokolov?"

Don shook his head. "We don't have the intel to be certain, but two independent sources agree that it's very likely him."

"Mr. President," Hahn said. "The relationship between Luchnik and Sokolov is like father and son. I think this phone call is genuine."

The president sat back in his chair, his lips twisted into a grimace. He shot a look at the CIA director.

"Could this be a setup, Sam? Is that possible?"

"It's always possible, sir," Director Blank said, "but the likelihood is small. The only reason why we have this intel at all is because Sokolov phoned from the base in Petropavlovsk using a nonsecure line. If he'd been in Vladivostok, we'd never have intercepted this call. I don't believe this is a setup."

"Does this phone call confirm that the Russian Federation is in the midst of a coup?" the president asked. Nervous glances angled around the room.

Chairman Nikolaides cleared his throat. "Sir, we have forty-seven minutes to make a firm decision on Operation Red Sunset. There's a lot of moving parts to this plan, and the consequences of delaying by even a few—"

"It's the consequences of making the wrong call that I'm talking about right now, General," the president snapped. "We could be looking at World War Three—maybe worse. I will not be forced into a decision."

"I understand, sir," the chairman pressed, "but this is not like flipping a switch. We have the element of surprise on our side. We can end this quickly and with humanity. I am reminding you that we have assets in place, some in exposed positions. These men and women are in danger. Their lives are in our hands."

"Thank you, General," Serrano said. "Your counsel is valued, but sometimes the best way to win a war is to not fight one in the first place."

"Agreed, sir," Nikolaides said.

"If it is a coup," the president asked National Security Advisor Flores, "what should our response be?"

"We should hold off," the Secretary of State said firmly. "Luchnik is using us to flush out his competition. Let the Russians get their own house in order."

"With all due respect, Mr. President," Flores said. She cast a withering look at Hahn for interrupting her. "I agree with the chairman. Screw

Luchnik. That guy's been a pain in our ass for thirty years. The only reason we're in this spot is because he put us there."

Don's attention drifted from the political back-and-forth. In another forty minutes, it wouldn't matter anyway. Janet had her orders to launch the cyberattack. There was no going back from that move. Based on what he was seeing here, the United States was staggering toward a decision to begin Operation Red Sunset.

An air of defeat settled on him like a shroud.

From the very beginning, he had done his best to find the truth in the analysis, but it had eluded him. Still eluded him now. In this moment of honesty, he was too tired to care.

His eyes drifted down to the screen embedded in the lectern that showed his next slide.

A map of the world, red dots clustered around the conflict zones. His gaze followed the crimson trail.

Venezuela, India, the Persian Gulf, Bosnia, the East Coast of the United States, and the Arctic. The US was like a team of exhausted firefighters trying to stop a wildfire in a windstorm.

Over the years, he'd seen the same red-dotted map a million times, but always in reverse. Usually, the red was clustered in the Middle East and the South China Sea...

His mind froze. A moment of crystal clarity sliced through the tiredness and the noise and the clamoring voices all around him.

"It's not a coup," Don said.

Shocked silence descended on the room. All eyes turned on Don, and he realized he must have shouted the last part.

"It's not a coup, Mr. President," Don said again.

"I heard you the first time, Mr. Riley." Don felt the full effect of the president's gaze on him. The man wanted an answer that didn't involve touching off a global conflict. Don experienced a surge of energy. For the first time in a long time, he felt like he was seeing clearly again.

"I'm not sure I understand your point, though," Serrano prodded Don.

But Don's mind was leaping forward as the puzzle pieces snapped into place.

It was the right answer. It *had* to be the right answer. It was the only answer that made any sense.

But could he prove it?

"We've been asking the wrong question from the very beginning. We asked what do the Russians have to gain from all this? That answer is obvious. Almost every conflict on this map is straight out of the Russian playbook. It all makes perfect sense."

Don put the world map on the wall screen. The red dots glared back at him.

"But the Russian reaction makes no sense. They've expended all these resources to turn the world upside down, so why haven't they taken advantage of any of them? Our working theory is that we're witnessing a coup. It's the Russians, but not the Russians we're used to dealing with. But we're wrong.

"All of this happened"—Don slapped his hand against the wall screen —"because we failed to ask the right question."

"And what is the right question, Mr. Riley?" Serrano said. There was an edge to his tone now.

"Instead of asking what do the *Russians* gain from this, we should have asked *who* gains from this?"

Don pointed to red dots in Venezuela, the Gulf, the Naval War College, the Panama Canal. Each one represented American lives lost and even more in harm's way.

"Every time there was an attack, we responded. We moved forces from somewhere else in the world to the new conflict. But our resources are not unlimited. Take an aircraft carrier from Japan and put it in the Arctic, and you've left a big hole where that carrier used to be. Instead of looking at where the conflict *is*, we need to look where the conflict *isn't*."

"Oh my God," the chairman said. "He's right."

Don's brain raced ahead of his words, looking for the thing, the piece of conclusive evidence, that he still did not have.

He had a nice theory but needed *proof*.

The answer struck him so hard, he stopped speaking.

"Mr. Riley," the president said. "Are you okay?"

"I can prove it," Don said.

His computer bag was at his feet. He plopped it onto the lectern and rummaged through the contents.

"Mr. Riley—Don," Director Blank said.

Don pulled out the printed report from his bag and flipped to the executive summary. His finger trembled as he ran down the text. What he was searching for appeared in the second-to-last paragraph. He looked up at the room, but not at the people. He looked at the clock.

Thirty minutes...

"This report is the foreign materials exploitation analysis on the Russian SA-29 MANPADs we found in Caracas. Basically, it's a technical assessment of the next-gen shoulder-fired missiles that surprised us in Venezuela."

Don held his finger on the line of text.

"Here's what it says: The production of this weapon system was outsourced to a third party. It was not manufactured inside the Russian Federation."

Don met Serrano's gaze.

"Mr. President, the Russians never outsourced these weapons. The Russians never even knew they existed."

He dropped his gaze back to the page and read the line above his finger.

"Based on the manufacturing techniques and metallurgy analysis, this weapon was manufactured in the People's Republic of China."

Don slapped the report closed.

"Sir, I recommend you call off the attack. There is no coup, Mr. President. There never was. It was the Chinese the whole time."

56

Beijing, China

The National Center for the Performing Arts, better known as the Beijing Opera House, stood across the street from the Great Hall of the People in the Xincheng district of Beijing.

To Minister of State Security Fei Zhen, these two buildings represented the past and the future of his beloved homeland.

The Great Hall was a vast, imposing limestone structure with sweeping steps and fronted by a dozen massive stone columns. The interior was all marble floors, gold chandeliers, and crimson carpets. It was strong, solid, a tribute to China's power and wealth.

The Beijing Opera House was a modern structure, often called the "giant egg" for its ellipsoidal shape and color. The exterior was covered with tens of thousands of titanium metal plates specially oxidized to give it a metallic luster that shone like a silvery egg at night. It changed color depending on the time of day and angle of the sun.

Its power was not in its solidity but rather in its elusive beauty. When a visitor to Beijing saw the Opera House, they saw in form and function a representation of the future of China.

The Minister viewed the familiar landmark from the back seat of a black Hongqi limousine. The brand was made only in China and favored by Party dignitaries. Normally, he eschewed such status symbols as beneath him, but tonight it provided a useful cover.

The Minister was not at the magnificent Beijing Opera House to see a performance. He was here for a secret meeting with the most powerful man in the country, the General Secretary of the Chinese Communist Party and President of the People's Republic. During the second act, when the rest of the audience returned to their seats, the president had agreed to give his Minister of State Security ten minutes of his valuable time before he took in the rest of the performance.

"Turn the heat up, please," the Minister said to the driver.

He shifted in his seat, unable to find a comfortable position to alleviate the gnawing pain that had settled in his lower back. In the night, he imagined his cancer as a living, breathing tiger that was eating his guts from the inside out. The pain migrated inside his body from place to place depending on the day. Today, the tiger had chosen his kidneys, making it nearly impossible for the Minister to sit for any length of time.

As the driver turned into the employee parking garage underneath the Opera House, the Minister allowed himself half of a pain pill. A steel gate rattled shut behind them. The Minister picked out armed men dressed in business suits scattered throughout the mostly empty parking garage.

The limousine drew up next to glass double doors. When the driver opened the rear door, damp air flooded the warm cabin. Cold, stale, smelling of car exhaust. The Minister tucked a slim leather valise under his arm and exited the vehicle.

"This way, sir," said one of the suited men, leading the Minister inside.

The interior was a plain marble hallway with an industrial-grade carpet that dead-ended at a single elevator with open doors. Inside, his escort waved a key card over a sensor and punched a button.

When the doors opened again, the Minister looked down a long hallway lined on both sides with dressing room doors. From a wall speaker, a soprano was singing a familiar aria.

"Madame Butterfly," the Minister whispered to himself. "How appropriate."

As his escort hustled him down the hallway, the doors grew closer together, indicating smaller dressing rooms. He stopped at the last room, knocked once, and opened the door.

The tiny room contained a cheap card table, a desk with a mirror ringed with LED lights, and two folding chairs. On the cinder block walls, the glossy white enamel paint was almost completely obscured by graffiti. Signatures, fragments of poetry, and crude drawings in black ink were a testament to the former occupants of this transient space.

In his dinner jacket, the General Secretary of the Communist Party of China looked sleek and well fed. His expressionless face studied the Minister. He wore a white silk scarf around his neck, and he toyed with the fringed end.

The Minister, ignoring the stabbing pain in his lower back, bowed.

"Thank you for seeing me on such short notice, sir," he said, "and under these unique conditions."

The General Secretary's face wrinkled into a frown.

"Your message was cryptic," he said. "I trust your explanation will be worth my time."

Instead of answering, the Minister took a copy of a bound report from his valise and placed it in front of the General Secretary. The exterior bore crimson Top Secret markings.

"This report is almost a year old now," the Minister said. "It is the only copy remaining. I had all the others destroyed and the digital files erased."

The General Secretary opened to the title page. "Analysis of the Rare Earth Metals Deposit in Wutai, Taiwan, China."

He cocked an eyebrow at the Minister. "You say this is a year old? Why am I just hearing about it now?"

China had spent thirty years cornering the global market on rare earth metals, investing billions in both mining and refining capacity. They enjoyed a market share of more than eighty percent, but more importantly maintained a hammerlock on the elements used to produce all manner of high-tech electronics, from smartphones to X-ray machines to hypersonic missile guidance systems.

"When this report arrived on my desk a year ago," the Minister began, "I was dismayed. The quality of the discovery combined with latest Western mining practices described a severe threat to our dominance of the world market. It would give Taiwan another link with the Western powers."

The General Secretary slapped the report. "And why did you not act on this information?"

The Minister's spine seized with pain, but he smiled all the same.

"I did," he said. "You have to understand that this report arrived on a day of great personal meaning to me. I saw its arrival as a sign, a calling for me to make a great sacrifice for my country."

The General Secretary got to his feet. "You're not making sense. This meeting is over."

"Sit down, sir!" the Minister said sharply. He moderated his tone. "Five minutes. That is all I ask."

The leader of the People's Republic of China looked at his Rolex, then sat back down.

"Over the past year," the Minister continued, "I received regular reports on the secret development of the Taiwanese mining operation. It has gone very well. They expect to make their first shipments to the United States in a few weeks, right after the Lunar New Year."

"I have received no such reports," the General Secretary said.

"I suppressed them," the Minister replied. "All of them."

"Why?" the General Secretary demanded, his placid face flushed and creased. "You are not making any sense, Minister Fei."

"I suppressed the reports so that you would be forced to order an immediate invasion of Taiwan," the Minister said. "Immediately. Tonight."

"That's ridiculous. An invasion takes weeks, maybe months of planning."

The Minister smiled. "The annual People's Liberation Army war games start tomorrow. I have been working with a small cadre of generals and admirals to ensure we could change the joint exercises into a live invasion of the island of Taiwan. All you have to do is give the order, sir."

The General Secretary's mouth gaped open. Then his jaw snapped shut, and his face darkened.

"That is treason," he thundered. "I could have you shot tonight."

The Minister laughed. It was not the response the other man expected.

"What's so funny, Fei?"

The Minister tapped the report. "The day this report arrived on my desk, I was diagnosed with stage-four pancreatic cancer. You could have me shot, Mr. President, but it would make no difference. I am already dead, but to my last breath I will serve the State. Whether I draw that breath tonight or next month, it makes no difference to me. What I have done for my country, I did out of love."

He sat down, the pain in his back all but forgotten.

"The Russians and the Americans are at each other's throats," the Minister said. "Our forces are ready to pounce. We will never have a better opportunity than right now."

"Now is not the time, Minister," the General Secretary responded. "We are seeing the benefits of the Russian-American conflict in an increase in trade. This is not the time for us to embark on nation-building just because the Russians decided to pick a fight with the Americans. Now is the time for us—"

"It wasn't the Russians, Mr. President. It was me."

The General Secretary stared at the Minister. In the hallway behind them, a soprano's voice soared in song.

"What have you done?" the leader of China said in a whisper.

"For the past year," the Minister said, "I have engaged in a covert operation to draw the Americans away from the South China Sea. All for this moment. All to give my country this historic opportunity."

The General Secretary looked at the report. The Minister could see him fitting the pieces of the puzzle together. The rare earth metals threat, the upcoming war games, the Russian conflict...

"There are two ways to kill a tiger," the Minister said softly. "You can drive a spear through his heart in a single killing thrust, or you can stab him over and over and over again and watch him bleed to death slowly."

The General Secretary's eyes grew wide.

"*Lingchi*," he whispered. "It's brilliant, Fei."

The Minister's chest flooded with joy, the euphoria beating back the gnawing pain.

"Yes, sir," he whispered back, unable to keep the rush of pride from his tone. "*Lingchi*, death by a thousand cuts."

"All of the attacks? That was you?"

The Minister nodded.

"Venezuela, the Panama Canal?"

Another nod.

"The Naval War College?" the General Secretary said. "We had people there!"

The Minister bowed his head.

"Sacrifices had to be made, sir. It is unfortunate but true."

But the General Secretary was not finished yet.

"What about the attack in the Arctic?" he asked. "And the attack on the American carrier strike force yesterday?"

"An unmanned submarine, sir," the Minister said. "One of ours." He leaned across the table. "Mr. President, you miss the point. Those actions are in the past. They have given us—given *you*—the opportunity of a life-time. The opportunity of ten lifetimes. You will be the man who reunited greater China. The man who brought Taiwan back into the fold of the People's Republic. But you must act now."

The General Secretary was quiet for a long time. The Minister gave the man his space.

This was the moment, the Minister knew. If the General Secretary said he wanted to consult with his advisers or conduct an analysis before he made a decision, then the Minister had lost.

The man possessed the power. Over the last twenty years, he had care-fully manipulated the bureaucracy to give him, and only him, the ability to do what the Minister was asking.

If he seized the moment, the invasion would succeed, the Minister was sure of it.

But only if he committed right now.

"The invasion," the General Secretary said finally. "How long will it take?"

"Ten days," the Minister said. "Before the end of the Lunar New Year, we will be in complete control of Taiwan. The Americans will still be engaged with Russia. They will protest at the UN and puff out their chests, but they will fail."

"You're sure you can conceal our involvement in deceiving the Ameri-cans?" the General Secretary asked.

The Minister's breath came quick and fast. He was so close now.

"Absolutely, sir," the Minister said. "All of the operations were carefully compartmentalized. Apart from me, there is only one man who had enough access to put the pieces together. He is a trusted operative who has been in deep cover in the West for years. I trained him myself. I would trust him with my life."

"And you will make sure these secrets die with him?"

The Minister nodded. He knew what the General Secretary was asking.

"Already done, sir," the Minister said.

The Minister rose as the General Secretary of the People's Republic of China got to his feet, but he was not prepared for what happened next.

The General Secretary embraced him in a crushing bear hug.

"Well done, Minister. Well done."

57

USS *Enterprise* (CVN-80)
North Pacific Ocean, 300 miles east of Petropavlovsk, Russia

"Alpha Bravo, this is Alpha Papa, last aircraft is off the cat." The voice of the strike warfare commander was steady.

Sharratt glanced at the mission clock. Thirty-seven minutes was all it had taken to put nearly one hundred aircraft in the sky over the strike force. Using multiple catapults on all three carriers, flight deck crews had put the Stingray refueling drones up first, followed by the support craft, such as E2-D Hawkeyes and EA-18G Growlers, then the strike force itself, manned and unmanned warplanes ready to rain holy hell down on the Russian Federation.

Everything was proceeding with flawless precision. Even the weather was cooperating for once.

Sharratt felt the cold steel of the railing surrounding the BattleSpace tabletop under his fingertips. The holographic display showed a sea of blue arrows in the sky that represented the friendly aircraft.

The only red arrows on the screen were the Russian CAP flying 250 miles to the southeast and a pair of high-flyer overwatch drones. Surely, the Russian forces understood that an alpha strike was about to happen.

"Any response from the Russians?" he asked the Battle Watch Officer.

"No sign of increased activity, sir," the officer replied.

"Looks like our cyberattack worked, sir," Tom Zachary said. "We got these bastards with their pants down."

"Let's hope so, Tom."

Sharratt looked up. The eyes of every man and woman in the Battle Watch were on him. The atmosphere quivered with tension. He smelled fresh wax on the floor, the acrid scent of ozone from the electronics, the ever-present scent of steam found in every warship.

Sharratt clenched the steel railing with all his strength.

"Alpha Papa, this is Alpha Bravo actual." Sharratt's voice boomed in the quiet room. "Launch cruise missiles."

The attack on the Russian Federation was planned as three waves. Tomahawk cruise missiles launched from ships and submarines were first, followed by a wave of hypersonic weapons. The aircraft were the third wave. The F-35s and their UCAV wingmen carried precision weapons and pinpoint location data to ensure complete destruction of all the designated targets.

There would be formidable resistance from the Russians. The S-400 surface-to-air missile batteries were deadly accurate—as the US Navy knew well from the recent experience in Iran. By sending in two waves of missiles in advance of manned aircraft, the US forces hoped to deplete or degrade the Russian defensive response.

That was the plan, Sharratt thought, knowing full well that some of the pilots that were in the air now would not be alive come nightfall.

"Alpha Bravo, Alpha Papa, copy launch cruise missiles," came the reply.

Sharratt studied the BattleSpace display, waiting to see the telltale launch signatures show up on the screen. Over his head, the intercom issued a stream of orders from the strike warfare commander.

He spotted the first launches from USS *Port Royal*.

"Admiral!" the shout came from SUPPLOT, the top-secret area adjacent to Battle Watch. Commander Jerry Sorenson stood in the doorway, his eyes wild. He gripped a sheet of paper in his hand as he bounded across the room.

"Flash message traffic! The operation is canceled, sir." He thrust the paper at Sharratt, who stared dumbly at the single-line message:

Operation Red Sunset canceled. Stand by further orders.

Sharratt seized the radio handset. "On the net, this is Alpha Bravo actual, abort cruise missile launch. I repeat, abort launch. Weapons tight."

"Alpha Bravo, Alpha Papa, aborting Tomahawk launches."

On the BattleSpace display, thirteen blue traces had separated from the mass of aircraft over the strike force and were already winging their way toward the Russian coastline.

"We've got thirteen missiles in the air, sir," Zachary said.

Sharratt cursed savagely, but there was no way to recover Tomahawk missiles once launched.

"Alpha Papa, this is Alpha Bravo actual, splash all cruise missiles. Splash them now."

"Copy splash all cruise missiles."

Sharratt watched the blue traces disappear from the display one by one. The sea of blue arrows circled over the carrier strike force like angry hornets. Not only had he wasted about $25 million dollars of US taxpayer money, he had depleted a precious weapons resource for his strike force and given up the element of surprise.

"Tom?"

"Sir."

"Get me Seventh Fleet on the line," Sharratt said. "Now."

He strode into the conference room, taking care not to slam the door behind him.

What seemed like hours, but was actually less than two minutes, passed before Vice Admiral Bumpers's fleshy face appeared on the screen.

He held up a hand. "Before you start, Chip, I don't know anything more than you do."

"I've got a hundred fully loaded aircraft in the air," Sharratt said, "and I just splashed thirteen Tomahawks. If we're trying to lose this war, we're doing a damn fine job of it."

"I can't even begin to guess," Bumpers said. "Maybe Serrano lost his nerve or—" He looked past his screen for a moment, then held out his hand. His forehead creased as he studied a sheet of paper.

"Sir?" Sharratt asked.

"New message traffic," Bumpers said. "*Blue Ridge* to make best possible speed to Hawaii. Prepare to embark Commander Pacific Fleet. What the hell is going on?"

Sharratt felt a chill run up his spine. In his quarter century of naval service, he had participated in too many war-gaming exercises to count. There was only one wartime scenario where the first action was to embark the commander of the US Pacific Fleet onto USS *Blue Ridge*.

"I've got Pac Fleet on the other line, Chip," Bumpers said. "As soon as I know something, you'll know."

"Aye, sir," Sharratt responded automatically. But he already knew. It was so goddamn obvious that he should have seen it months ago, but he hadn't.

He stood, drew in a deep breath, and walked back into Battle Watch. The activity in the room ceased.

"Watch Officer," Sharratt said, "secure from general quarters and recover all aircraft. There's no war today, people."

Sharratt caught Sorenson's eye and motioned him closer.

"Jerry, I want you to scrounge up every bit of recent intel on the PLA Navy and set up a briefing for my staff in one hour."

58

USS *Idaho*
Sea of Okhotsk

Janet stood at attention in her commanding officer's stateroom aboard the USS *Idaho*.

Captain Lannier sat at his fold-down desk, his armchair half-turned to face Janet. He held a tablet in his hand, and he scowled at the lighted screen. His jawline was a ridge of solid muscle, and when he turned his gaze on her, she felt the heat of his anger.

With exaggerated care, he laid the tablet down on the desk surface and turned his chair to face her.

"At ease, Lieutenant," he said.

Janet relaxed the tiniest bit, allowing her gaze to cut to the tablet. The screen contained a terse radio message, flash traffic. She knew what the message said because she had brought it back to the *Idaho*.

When he finally spoke, Lannier's voice was as tight as a wound spring.

"From the beginning, explain exactly what happened, Lieutenant Everett. From the moment you left the *Idaho* until right now."

Janet told the story in as much detail as she could recall. He watched her closely, lips pressed together, and she felt the intensity of his glare like a spotlight.

Janet paused and took a deep breath.

"While we were monitoring the cable tap, we received emergent intel. Time-critical intelligence that might have impacted the cyberattack—"

"Stop," Lannier said. "What was this emergent intel?"

"We received an unencrypted voice communication between the president of the Russian Federation and an admiral in Petropavlovsk, sir," she said. "The admiral claimed the attack on the *Enterprise* strike force was not originated by the Russians."

"And you believed this intel?"

"That's not my call, sir," Janet replied. "It was new information. I knew... no, I suspected there were concerns about the quality of the intel on the Russians. This was new information."

"You suspected how?" Lannier pressed.

"I—I noticed some details in Don Riley's emails that made me believe he had concerns about the Russian involvement." Janet realized even as the words left her lips that they sounded incredibly lame.

"What details?"

"It's hard to explain, sir," Janet said. "I know Don well, and his email did not suggest to me that he was convinced about our course of action."

Lannier's eyes pinned her in place.

"Continue," he said.

"We were within the window of the cyberattack initiation. There was no way the *Manta* could make it to the *Idaho* and back, so I took it upon myself to make contact with Washington and relay this emergent intel to the Emerging Threats Group—"

"Stop," Lannier said quietly. "You were aware of our orders regarding satellite communications?"

"Yes, sir."

"And you decided to break those rules?"

Janet came to attention again and stared at a spot on the faux wood paneling covering the far wall. "Yes, sir. I sent the *Orca* to periscope depth and established a satellite link. I relayed the information from the *Manta* using the laser comms. I kept the *Orca* at PD for thirty minutes and received a response."

Lannier picked up the tablet and read out loud:

"Operation Red Sunset canceled. Return to *Idaho*. Inform CO make best possible speed to Yokosuka. Maintain radio silence. Weapons use authorized for self-defense only."

Lannier replaced the tablet on his desk.

"Let's review, Lieutenant." Lannier's voice was brittle with barely suppressed rage. "Your ship and over one hundred of your crewmates are in enemy waters on the eve of an attack. You broke radio silence to send a message to Washington, DC, because you had a feeling about an email from your last boss. Those actions put the lives of your entire crew and about five billion dollars of United States government hardware at grave risk. Who in the name of Christ do you think you are, Lieutenant? Who put you in command, Everett?"

"No one, sir."

"Goddamn right! No one!" He picked up the tablet and hurled it against the wall. "Now I'm left with more questions than answers from this cryptic bullshit message, but I can't do anything about it. Do you know why, Lieutenant?"

Janet swallowed. "Because you follow orders, sir."

"Exactly!" Lannier shouted, launching his body out of his chair. "I follow orders because I realize that I'm part of a much bigger plan with a lot of moving parts and a lot of people depending on me to do my fucking job when I'm fucking told to do it!"

Janet said nothing. She found the spot on the far wall and let her gaze bore into it. He was right, she knew. But he was also wrong. He hadn't heard the pleading in the Russian admiral's tone as he spoke to his president.

Or had she imagined that? Had she just been looking for a reason to contact Don and get him to reconsider the cyberattack?

"Sir, I can play you the voice communication—"

"It doesn't matter, Everett," Lanier snapped. "I have new orders, and I intend to follow them to the letter. In a week, we'll be out of this Russian bathtub, and we'll see what the hell is going on. I hope this was worth it, Lieutenant."

Janet wanted the floor to open up. Her career flashed before her eyes. "I understand, sir."

Lannier shook his head. When he spoke again, his voice was calm and measured, but also sad.

"No, Lieutenant," Lannier said. "I don't think you do understand. You are one of the finest junior officers I've ever served with. You're smart, good shiphandling instincts, good with your people, but when you think you're right..." His voice trailed off. "When you think you're right, you lose all sense of perspective. Your decision out there might have gotten all of us killed. And you never even considered that."

Captain Lannier sat down heavily in his armchair. "You are relieved of duty until further notice."

59

The Kremlin
Moscow, Russia

Less than ten minutes into his phone call with the president of the United States, Russian President Luchnik wished he had insisted on a secure videoconference call. He had never met Serrano in person, and he longed to try to read the other man's body language.

But time had not been on his side. Just as all indications pointed to an imminent American attack, a flash message had come across the dedicated computer network link between Washington and Moscow requesting a personal phone call between the leaders of the two countries.

Personal might be stretching the point. Between translators, cabinets of both men, and assorted staff, there were at least thirty people listening to what was being said and parsing every syllable.

"Mr. President," Serrano said. "Vitaly. I think we need to do everything we can to de-escalate this situation."

Luchnik frowned at the phone. Opposite him, Federov arched an eyebrow at the use of his president's given name. Was that a pleading note in Serrano's voice or just a distortion on the phone line?

Luchnik took a beat before responding. Although he spoke English fluently, he liked to go through a translator. It gave him time to think about his answers.

"Of course, Mr. President—Rick," Luchnik replied. Federov looked away in disgust. "I believe there has been a misunderstanding between us."

His mind raced. Why were the Americans coming to him now, at the last possible moment? The reports were flowing in from the Pacific theater that the *Enterprise* carrier strike force had aborted a massive attack. Why?

Luchnik put the phone on mute.

"Do you have any reports from your people?" he asked.

Federov looked up from his mobile phone and shook his head.

Luchnik had instructed his FSB head to put full surveillance teams on his entire cabinet and report any suspicious activity. If the traitor was among them, an American attack would flush them out.

Serrano was talking again.

"I'm glad you feel that way, Vitaly. I propose we begin a phased drawdown of forces along the borders. Each of us should make a public announcement to lower the state of readiness and begin a slow withdrawal over the course of the next week or so. How does that sound?"

Luchnik half listened. If there was no suspicious activity among his ministers, then that meant the threat was not an internal one. He eyed Federov. Or the traitor was sitting in the room with him.

The translator had finished, and Luchnik responded in Russian.

"I agree, Mr. President. Might I suggest you begin by moving your carrier strike force in the North Pacific away from the coast. Let's say, two hundred kilometers. As a gesture of good will."

There was a long pause, and Luchnik could hear whispering in the background. He smiled grimly. His technical people might be able to amplify that and attribute it to someone in the room with the American president. It would be good to know who was advising his enemy.

"Agreed," Serrano said. "As long as the Russian Federation makes a similar move along the border with Ukraine. Move one division two hundred miles inland."

Luchnik took his time responding.

"That is possible," he said after a full thirty seconds had passed.

"I believe there's been a great misunderstanding, Vitaly," Serrano continued. There it was again. The first name usage and the seeming apology.

This time Luchnik responded immediately.

"Misunderstanding?" he said. "That is the second time you have used that word, Rick. You have accused us of many horrible acts to which we have maintained our innocence. It seems you finally believe us."

A long silence. More whispering.

"I think it best if we focus on a process of de-escalation for now," Serrano said. "There will be time in the future to discuss other matters, Mr. President."

"Of course," Luchnik said with a smile. "The future."

His eyes strayed to the map on the wall of his office. He traced the borders of his country with loving detail.

"Thank you for your cooperation, Vitaly," Serrano said.

"Goodbye, Mr. President," Luchnik said. Then he hung up the phone.

White House Situation Room
Washington, DC

Don Riley watched President Serrano hang up the phone. The man blew out a long sigh and sagged back into his chair. He looked drained.

"That could have gone better," he said to the room.

"He's as confused as we are, sir," CIA Director Blank said. "If Riley's theory is correct, until you picked up the phone and called him, Luchnik thought he had a coup on his hands."

"I fear that we've just emboldened him," Serrano said.

"That might be true, Mr. President," General Nikolaides said, "but right now we've got to extract ourselves from one world crisis before we jump into the next one. This situation with Russia is still extremely volatile. One nervous submarine captain pops off a spare torpedo, and we've got ourselves a shooting war nobody wants."

"Exactly, sir," Defense Secretary Howard interjected. "We need to defuse the Russian front as a first priority. I've already instructed the Pacific

Fleet Commander to embark USS *Blue Ridge* just in case we see any sign of aggression from the Chinese military. I recommend we order the USS *Lincoln* from the Persian Gulf to the South China Sea. Maybe that will be enough of a deterrent to make the Chinese think twice about Taiwan."

Serrano straightened up in his seat. "Good." He looked at the chairman. "General, you focus on extracting us from the Russia mess. Defense will handle dealing with the PLA."

"Yes, sir," Nikolaides and Howard said in unison.

"Mr. President," National Security Advisor Flores said, "if we're right about Taiwan, we're going to need to take the fight to them in unconventional ways. The Chinese have been two steps ahead of us the whole time. It's time we changed up our playbook."

Serrano chewed his lip. "You're talking about the pirate thing?"

Flores nodded. "Privateers, sir. There's a difference."

Serrano's eyes roved over the room and found Don. "Put Riley in charge of it. We need to make sure we have an adult in the room. I don't trust those guys as far as I can throw them."

60

Buenos Aires

Marcus Quinn woke to the sound of distant surf. The tall windows of the bedroom were open, and a gentle morning breeze stirred the floor-length curtains. The air hung heavy with moisture and smelled of salt from the nearby Atlantic Ocean.

Next to him, Isabel Montez stirred. She burrowed deeper under the covers, her dark hair spilling across her face. Marcus resisted the urge to brush her hair back so he could see her.

He had asked her to come to him. She had done so without even a moment's hesitation.

That was enough.

Marcus slipped out of bed and padded into the large room on the ocean side of the villa. The space had a parquet floor of dark hardwood and French doors that opened onto a patio, making Marcus believe it had once been a dance studio. When he'd rented the villa ten days ago, the room had been crowded with overstuffed armchairs, sofas, and a large flat-screen TV.

On his first morning in the new house, Marcus removed all the furniture, converting the space back to its original function.

He'd spent every morning here since. It was a place for him to heal his body, sharpen his practice, and be alone with his thoughts.

He opened the French doors, feeling his flesh prickle as the morning breeze touched his bare skin. Outside, the horizon showed as a razor-sharp line of pale pink.

The villa was a good place to hide for now. The owner had been more than happy to dispense with a lease agreement and include a secondhand Toyota Corolla for a thick wad of American dollars.

Marcus sat on the floor, cross-legged, and closed his eyes. His thoughts immediately went to Isabel.

She was here. She was his. He could scarcely believe the fortunate turn his life had taken. With her by his side, anything seemed possible now.

It had not been easy, to be sure, but she had trusted him. Marcus gave her detailed travel instructions, and she followed them to the letter.

Flight from New York to Miami, a new ticket from Miami to Panama. In Panama, she stayed for two days before flying to Rio. In Rio, Marcus contacted her on a burner phone with new instructions.

Leave all of her electronics behind. Take a regional flight from the secondary airport in Rio to the secondary airport in Buenos Aires. Take a cab to the San Telmo district. He gave her a list of three shops to visit and exact times to be there.

Marcus followed her from the time she arrived in Buenos Aires, checking for any sign of surveillance. She was clean; his plan had worked.

In the third shop, he'd paid the proprietor to give her a sealed envelope.

Marcus met Isabel in the Plaza de Mayo, the public park in front of the Casa Rosada. The three-story presidential mansion was constructed in a colonial style and painted a pink color, hence the famous name, The Pink Palace.

Marcus watched her approach, pulling a roller bag, her face flushed in the Argentine summer heat. She wore jeans and a T-shirt. In one of the shops, she had bought a floppy hat and sunglasses. Isabel stopped in the center of the plaza and turned in a slow circle, her eyes searching the crowd for him.

Marcus stood up from the park bench where he'd been sitting, knowing the movement would catch her eye. Her jaw dropped when she spotted him, and he heard her laugh above the noise of the people.

"Ian!" she called out.

Marcus met her halfway, and she threw herself in his arms. Her hungry mouth found his, and she kissed him between laughs.

"Ian...I've been so worried."

"It's Marcus now, Isabel," he replied. "You'll have to get used to that."

"I don't care what you call yourself. I'm with you. That's all that matters."

"I'll explain everything," he said. "I promise."

Marcus had his arms around her, and he felt her body go still. He felt the thud of her heart under his right palm, the heat of her skin through the thin material of her shirt.

Her hand brushed his cheek. "You don't have to tell me anything. I don't need to know."

"I have to tell you," Marcus replied.

The sun was setting by the time they returned to the villa together. Marcus fixed dinner and opened a bottle of Malbec while Isabel showered and changed clothes. Just as Marcus was putting food on the table, she returned wearing a light linen dress. Her damp hair was twisted into a rough knot, held in place by a jade hairpin.

Their conversation limped through dinner. Neither ate much, but both drank the wine. Finally, Marcus stood, opened a second bottle of wine, and held out his hand to Isabel.

"Come with me," he said.

On the patio, he settled Isabel on the sofa with a blanket and lit a fire. He sat on the other end of the sofa, facing her.

Isabel tilted her head back. The stars looked like glittering dust in the sky.

"It's beautiful here," she said.

The fire popped. The surf shushed in the distance.

"I need to tell you who I am," Marcus said. "Who I really am."

The shimmering fire glinted in her dark eyes. Her lip trembled.

"You don't have to tell me," she said.

"Yes, I do."

Marcus told her. Everything.

The second wine bottle emptied, and still he talked. The moon rose and traveled across the night sky, and still he talked.

Isabel's gaze never left his face, no matter how horrifying the subject.

When he had finally emptied his life before the woman he loved, the fire had burned out and the moon had set. Isabel stood up, took his hand, and led him to bed.

Marcus dragged in a deep breath of morning air. He felt unburdened, light enough to rise above the hardwood floor.

Isabel had listened to his life story and accepted him for the man that he was. He was now ready to start a new life with this amazing woman.

That was love, Marcus decided. Real love. Something he'd never felt before. Never thought possible.

He got to his feet to begin his morning meditation. His gaze lost focus. His breathing evened out, centering his mind. His body flowed into the first form.

A lifetime of the same movements was encoded in his muscles. His body flowed from form to form, without hesitation or thought. The monks had taught a boy the movements, the Minister had weaponized those same movements in the man.

A floorboard squeaked behind him, and Marcus paused.

Isabel stood in the doorway. She smiled and stretched.

"Good morning." She twisted her long hair into a knot and stabbed it in place with the jade hairpin. "Is this a private session, or can anyone join in?"

Her fingers traced the healing wound on his side. Marcus shivered under her touch. He kissed her cheek.

"Join me," he said.

They started slowly, finding each other's rhythm in the movement. She was close enough that Marcus could sense her body next to his bare skin. Her breath painted his cheek. He felt their bodies flow together.

The words the Minister had taught him came back to him unbidden.

My mind is my sword.

His right knee lifted, his torso twisted. His left arm swept out, fingers extended.

My body is my shield.

Isabel's lithe body was like a warm shadow. She matched his movements like a mirror: left foot extension, pivot your bodyweight, kick, and land.

My existence is not my own.

Their breath mingled. He felt each beat of her heart match his. Every muscle in his body sang in harmony with hers as they entered the third form together.

I am a weapon of the State.

He sensed her body stiffen, shift out of harmony. Something was wrong.

Isabel's eyes were like chips of dark steel. Her left hand plucked the jade hairpin from her hair, and she stabbed with the speed of a deadly serpent.

Marcus reacted. He shifted his torso backward, sensing the razor-sharp tip of the weapon aimed at his Adam's apple.

He stopped the blade with his open palm. The needle punctured his hand. He closed his fist over her clenched fingers and locked her wrist. His leg swept at her feet, and he drove her to the ground.

Marcus straddled her writhing body. When her free hand scratched at his eyes, he pinned both her arms to the floor.

"Why?" she screamed at him. "Why did you have to tell me?"

"He sent you to kill me," Marcus said, his voice dead. "All along you worked for the Minister."

Isabel nodded, tears streaming down the side of her face.

"I told myself I could pretend," she said. "I told myself that you're not a threat to him. That you would disappear...then you told me everything, and I knew the truth. The Minister will never stop hunting you."

Marcus released her arms, but she did not fight him. The jade hairpin extended through the back of his hand like a bloody spike. He opened his palm and jerked the needle free. He felt no pain.

"I did what I had to do," Isabel said. Her voice was dull.

"Yes," Marcus replied. "I know."

With a swift thrust, he drove the tip of the spike into the soft flesh under her jaw and buried the point of the weapon in her brain.

Isabel's body quivered under his thighs as the life drained away from her beautiful face. Marcus got to his feet slowly and stumbled out to the patio.

The sun was fully above the horizon, and a fresh breeze washed the smell of death from Marcus's nostrils. The small fire pit held the ashes from the flame of the previous night, and the rumpled blanket lay on the sofa where Isabel had left it.

Both seemed like artifacts from a lifetime ago.

Marcus headed to the ocean to wash away the blood.

COUNTER STRIKE
Command and Control #2

When China launches a blitz attack on the island of Taiwan, the world order hangs in the balance and the CIA must mobilize all forces to prevent the start of World War III.

The operation by the People's Liberation Army is airtight, with a high-tech battle network that guarantees total occupation within ten days. The United States rallies every available asset on land, sea, and air to launch a desperate counter strike against the occupying forces.

But in order to win, the US is forced to throw out the old playbook. What is required here is speed, audacity, and the application of the most advanced technology in the US arsenal.

As the head of the CIA's Emerging Threats Group, Don Riley has seen his share of crises, but nothing has prepared him for the choices ahead. With millions of civilian lives at risk, the US must neutralize the Chinese threat without triggering World War Three.

Get your copy today at
severnriverbooks.com/series/command-and-control

ABOUT THE AUTHORS

David Bruns

David Bruns earned a Bachelor of Science in Honors English from the United States Naval Academy. (That's not a typo. He's probably the only English major you'll ever meet who took multiple semesters of calculus, physics, chemistry, electrical engineering, naval architecture, and weapons systems just so he could read some Shakespeare. It was totally worth it.) Following six years as a US Navy submarine officer, David spent twenty years in the high-tech private sector. A graduate of the prestigious Clarion West Writers Workshop, he is the author of over twenty novels and dozens of short stories. Today, he co-writes contemporary national security thrillers with retired naval intelligence officer, J.R. Olson.

J.R. Olson

J.R. Olson graduated from Annapolis in May of 1990 with a BS in History. He served as a naval intelligence officer, retiring in March of 2011 at the rank of commander. His assignments during his 21-year career included duty aboard aircraft carriers and large deck amphibious ships, participation in numerous operations around the world, to include Iraq, Somalia, Bosnia, and Afghanistan, and service in the U.S. Navy in strategic-level Human Intelligence (HUMINT) collection operations as a CIA-trained case officer. J.R. earned an MA in National Security and Strategic Studies at the U.S. Naval War College in 2004, and in August of 2018 he completed a Master of Public Affairs degree at the Humphrey School at the University of Minnesota. Today, J.R. often serves as a visiting lecturer, teaching national security courses in Carleton College's Department of Political Science, and hosts his radio show, *National Security This Week*, on KYMN Radio in Northfield, Minnesota.

You can find David Bruns and J.R. Olson at
severnriverbooks.com/series/command-and-control

||| ||| || ||| ||||| || ||||||| ||| ||||| ||| || ||| | ||| |||

Printed in the United States
by Baker & Taylor Publisher Services